PRAISE FOR *OUTSIDE THE WIRE*

"Gary Edgington's counter-terrorism investigative experience, coupled with his hands-on involvement in Iraq as an embedded civilian law enforcement advisor for the U.S. military makes his writing all the more genuine and cutting edge."

—**Gregory D. Lee**, US Army (Ret.) Chief Warrant
Officer 5/CID Special Agent

"It's been 19 years since I manned the AF field hospital at the Victory Base Complex and took incoming at Camp Sather. Before the end of the first chapter, *Outside the Wire* had me back in the fight. Awesome read and deadly accurate!"

—**Stephen Bercsi,** MD, Lieutenant Colonel USAF

"*Outside the Wire* is a great read—a riveting story told as fiction; or is it? Gary uses his own experience as an embedded advisor in Iraq to look at the conflict with the unique perspective of an experienced criminal/counter terrorism investigator and a highly skilled intelligence officer."

—**Wayne Rich,** US Army (Ret.) Chief Warrant Officer 3, Joint
Special Operations Command

"Edgington has mastered the gritty realism of Iraq: the good, the bad, and the ugly."

—**Aaron Michael Grant,** Staff NCO, USMC (Ret.), Iraq war
veteran and award-winning author of *Taking Baghdad:
Victory in Iraq with the US Marines*

"I just finished Gary Edgington's new thriller *Outside the Wire*. Having spent a dozen years in the middle east I noted that Gary's book accurately portrays the bureaucracy, palace intrigue, and local politics that lives in every US Military headquarters in the region. The duplicity, ruthlessness and cruelty of the enemy is also fully exposed. *Outside the Wire* gives you a first-hand look at the horror, violence, heroism, and humanity of that conflict. Read this book and you'll know what the war was like."

—**Denis Flood,** Captain USNR (Ret.)

Outside the Wire: A Novel of Murder, Love, and War

by Gary Edgington

© Copyright 2022 Gary Edgington

ISBN 978-1-64663-925-0

Published by

≤ köehlerbooks™

3705 Shore Drive
Virginia Beach, VA 23455
800-435-4811
www.koehlerbooks.com

OUTSIDE
THE WIRE

GARY EDGINGTON

VIRGINIA BEACH
CAPE CHARLES

DEDICATION

To my wonderful family, my wife, Lisa, our daughter Megan and her husband Eric, our son Ryan and his wife Emily, and my mom Donna. Your constant love, support, and encouragement continues to sustain me. And for our newest addition, Declan, your recent entry into this world has reminded me of the real priorities in life. You all fill me with pride and most especially love.

And, for my father, Corporal Harold L. Edgington, Los Angeles County Harbor Patrol, End of Watch September 30th, 1979.

For my partner and friend, Sergeant Stephen T. Clark, Los Angeles Police Department 1981 to 2002; Special Agent, California Department of Justice, Counter Terrorism Unit 2002-2010. End of Watch January 3rd, 2018.

Lest we forget.

PROLOGUE

C aptain Erin O'Connor, C Company, 722nd Military Intelligence Battalion, reviewed the intelligence report one final time. It was the end of another fourteen-hour day and she was fried. Sending this document would be her last official act as the boss of C Company. In less than twenty-four hours, she'd be on an Air Force C-17 flying back to the States to join her new husband at the US Army's Intelligence Center for Excellence. Known as the "School House," it was located at Fort Huachuca, in the arid desert of southern Arizona. Erin was truly sick of the desert but at least she'd be with her new husband Wayne, a retired Army Special Forces chief warrant officer-4. They never got a real honeymoon before she deployed, so they'd be spending a blissful week on the beach in Cancun before she reported for duty. This put a little smile on her weary face.

Her new posting at Huachuca was officer in charge of the HUMINT (Human Intelligence) training unit. It was a good fit for her. Her instincts and skills had been finely honed during her last two deployments to Iraq. Now it was time to share her hard-won knowledge with School House students.

Erin knew her decision to send this very preliminary intelligence report up her chain of command was going to be second-guessed by scores of critical eyes. Her unit's latest walk-in source from the Baghdad district of Sadr City hadn't been fully vetted or even polygraphed yet. For some reason known only to the stifling Army bureaucracy, polygraphers at Victory Base were now in short supply. Despite all this, Erin's gut told her this source was telling the truth. She'd watched nearly all the interviews on a video monitor and hadn't seen any red flags that made her feel otherwise. In fact, his story made sense given the current political climate back home. More importantly, it dovetailed with other little whispers of something big brewing from local street sources. Erin's people had been able to verify the source's claim that he had close family ties to top leaders of the Iranian-backed terrorist group the Mahdi Army. This critical bit of corroboration verified the source probably did have the access he had claimed. The rest of his story, the scary part, they were still trying to validate.

During his debrief, the source said the Mahdi Army was planning a new terror campaign targeting Baghdad area Coalition Forces at the massive Victory Base, as well as Iraqi government forces and infrastructure. He said the campaign was in the final planning stage and was receiving logistical and operational support from an unknown foreign source. Erin knew this "foreign source" had to be Iran. US intelligence had long ago established that Iran was supplying weapons, training, and funding to the Mahdi Army.

According to the source, the terror campaign was to begin with rocket and mortar attacks targeting Victory Base housing and US air assets scattered throughout the greater Baghdad area. The alarming part was that a key planner was overheard saying the operation would be a multi-pronged attack like the 1968 TET Offensive in Vietnam. The insurgents were hoping these attacks would cause high American, Coalition Force, and Iraqi causalities, leading to a dissolution of the Coalition and an ultimate American withdrawal. This strategy had worked in Vietnam, and in Spain after the devastating Madrid train bombings of 2004. It could work again, Erin concluded. Unfortunately, the source did not know when the campaign was to commence.

Erin knew this largely unverified intelligence report would be just one of thousands inundating the intelligence community daily. It would likely wind up on some analyst's desk for a month or two before anyone took a hard look at it. By then, it could be too late. All that said, it still needed to be sent.

She reviewed the report formatting, classification header, footer, and portion markings. It all looked good. Since her unit was the original source of the information, they had control over its distribution and classification level. This report had been classified as Top Secret/HCS and would be maintained within a Special Access Program code named "Argon-Lancer." Captain O'Connor pressed the send button on her secure terminal and logged off. It was late and she still needed to pack. She was going home.

CHAPTER 1

BUBBLE GUTS

The medical specialist named Jason pulled the IV needle from my arm and handed me a cotton ball.

"Mr. Sutherland. Please hold this on your arm."

"You can call me Rick," I offered.

Jason bandaged the hole in my arm, and I rose from the examining table and put my shirt back on. This trip to the Troop Medical Clinic (the TMC) was only meant to be a one-week follow-up visit to verify the meds I'd been taking were working for a nasty case of "Saddam's Revenge." I was fine, but dehydrated, and the Army physician—a very thorough and dare I say attractive major named Weaver instructed young Jason to plug an IV into me. I'd have preferred an ice-cold Stella, but in Iraq you take what you can get.

"How do you feel, sir?"

"Hydrated."

Jason smiled. "We aim to please, sir."

"Your aim is pretty good, specialist," I said as I rubbed my arm. "Can I go?"

"Yes, sir, we're done, but don't forget to stop at the desk for your meds and weapon."

Reminding a patient to pick up his weapon at the front desk is not something you usually hear at a stateside medical clinic. Over here, it's the way we roll.

On my way out I spied Major Weaver in her tiny office and stuck my head in to say thanks. She was on the phone, but waved me in. A quick look around revealed a framed photo of a handsome Army captain in dress blues, wearing the beige beret of the 75th Ranger Regiment, and alongside was a folded American flag in a triangular glass case. A small engraved brass plate on the frame read, *CPT Justin Findley KIA 23/09/03*, which explained her memorial wrist bracelet. I wear a similar one on my wrist. Then my eyes fell upon something I guarantee you'd never see in Doc Bailey's office. Standing in a corner behind her desk was a T-shaped wooden rack bearing an Army-issue Kevlar helmet, body armor with rifle magazines stuffed in its pouches, and a shoulder holster complete with pistol. Propped up in the corner was the M-4 carbine that no doubt went with the magazines. I had thought that docs were unable to carry long guns, but this one evidently did. I bet she could shoot it too.

Major Weaver ended her conversation, looked up, and smiled warmly.

"Thank you very much, Major. You've got a great staff here."

"Thanks, Mr. Sutherland, I agree. How are you feeling?"

"All good and ready for adventure."

"Hold up there. You were dehydrated. You need to take it easy for a day or two and drink lots of water. Take the Lomotil for a couple more days just to be sure. The other meds I prescribed are for when you get this bug again."

"Bubble guts?"

"Yep. Everyone here comes down with it at least once.

"Will do, Major. Thanks again, and see ya around."

"Probably." Major Weaver smiled.

I stopped by the clerk's desk and grabbed my meds and pistol, then stepped from air-conditioned comfort into an absolute blast furnace. A large temperature gauge mounted on the wall of the clinic showed a sizzling 120 degrees. I strapped on my pistol belt and started walking back. I didn't have wheels, so I had to hoof it, and it didn't take long before sweat was stinging my eyes and streaming down my back. Did I mention I hate this place yet?

The TMC was a good quarter mile from the center of our small oasis, and my abode was farther still. I planned to get back, grab a Coke at the local Subway, and take a well-deserved break.

The trek back to my pad here at Camp Victory Baghdad, Iraq, was a badly fractured and battle-scarred path. One errant step and you'd be flat on your face. Truth is, this whole place was a slip-and-fall lawyer's wet dream.

As I stumbled along, I spotted a dust-covered white Chevy SUV pull over to the curb about seventy meters ahead. The Chevy, nothing special, had a black plastic GI storage box sitting atop the roof rack. White SUVs were as common here as silver Volvo wagons in West Los Angeles. As the driver sat there, I spotted someone in the back seat and inched closer. The uniformed driver had a cell phone to his ear, and was checking me out through his sideview mirror. The passenger was just a shadow.

What stuck in my head was the SUV's plate number, CZ 8008, because my kid Troy got sent to the principal's office when he was ten for punching 8008 into his calculator while sitting in class. Then the little jokester turned it upside down, proudly showing everyone that he'd spelled "boob." Smart kid, but Mrs. Tipton was not amused.

It was probably just a couple of lost soldiers, I reasoned, as I walked past. Victory Base was enormous, and there were no street signs. I'd been lost a time or two myself.

Just as I dismissed 8008 from my mind, I was startled by a very loud and shrill siren. While I'm no stranger to sirens, this one could have had every mutt in LA howling. Stopping dead in my tracks, I tried to remember what this sound meant. Recognizing my confusion, a young soldier in Army PT gear gently lent a hand.

"INCOMING! Get your dumb ass in a shelter!" she yelled as she turned and dashed for a nearby berm.

BOOM! Fifty or sixty meters in front of me, everything exploded in a deadly cloud of flying debris, flame, and choking dust. The shockwave knocked me on my butt. Slowly, I opened my eyes and inhaled a lung full of dirt, smoke, and who knows what. My right ear was ringing—not good. I looked up to see the tell-tale gray smoke of a high explosive detonation, rising from what used to be a housing module.

As I rolled onto my belly and crawled toward a nearby canal ditch, I felt a sharp sting in my left thigh, which must have been from the fall. My savior in PT gear now got up and ran full tilt for a row of buildings.

I knew I had to find shelter, too, but where the hell were they? I looked around, moved forward a few meters, and spotted one thirty meters away. Jumping up, I ran toward it for all I was worth, which wasn't much after the divorce and paying my share of both boy's college tuitions.

I long-jumped over a small canal as I raced for safety, but for the life of me don't know why I didn't use the bridge. When you're scared shitless, you do goofy stuff. I cleared the canal and dove headlong into the shelter, landing face-first into the lap of a squatting Navy Judge Advocate Corps lieutenant junior grade.

The shelters were rectangular concrete cubes open at both ends and on the bottom, and four or five feet high and about the same wide. With little space to move around in, I quickly made friends with the lieutenant as I gathered my composure. She had a welcoming smile and smelled good, which is always a huge plus in Iraq.

BANG! Another incoming round hit the adjoining housing module. They're called CHUs (Containerized Housing Units). The explosion blew the roof off, and very quickly the fire spread to the adjacent units. Crazy! The base hadn't been hit in at least six months. What the hell's going on?

A loud buzz saw-type noise kicked in, like a huge high-speed machine gun. "Base Phalanx gun," said Campbell, the lieutenant junior grade. The Phalanx was an air defense Gatling weapon developed for the Navy, and the Army had apparently grabbed some for base defense. The Army calls them C-RAM (Counter Rocket, Artillery, and Mortar).

Flying skyward was a line of tracers exploding in a plume of dirty gray smoke, and an incoming insurgent mortar round blown to bits.

When I turned to look back to where the white SUV had been, half expecting to see a burning heap, it was gone. Lucky dudes, or something else? It was strange. The driver checking me out? The passenger in the back seat? Probably nothing, but what mischief could they have been up to? I dismissed it, needing to concentrate on staying alive.

It's moments like this that cause you to take pause and ponder life's little choices. Okay, what the hell was I thinking? I had retired a year early from LAPD to accept this civilian contractor gig. Though Uncle Sugar was paying me big bucks to be here and share my law enforcement and counter terrorism expertise with our war fighters, for me it wasn't about the money. It was about finding bad guys and keeping our kids safe. My job over here was to identify bomb makers and terrorist cells and sic the Special Operations guys on them before they could plant their deadly IEDs (Improvised Explosive Devices). The Army calls this "getting left of the boom." Back home we called it "proactive policing." Same idea, different crooks.

Catching bad guys is what I do. It's fun and I'm pretty good at it. I'd worked in LAPD's Counter-Terrorism Section for years, so I knew a little bit about the local crooks and their playthings. But that was stateside, and this was Iraq.

I glanced at the unloaded M9 Beretta, 9mm pistol, strapped to my right thigh. Nobody on base, except for the MPs, could have a loaded weapon. Perhaps some Pentagon genius decided military members couldn't be trusted with loaded firearms. Call me old-fashioned, but in a place where you can get shot, you need to carry a loaded gun.

That empty pistol symbolized how truly screwed up things were in Iraq, and the war had turned into another American police action. No big set-piece armored division vs. armored division battles now. No massed infantry assaults. Just nasty, pinprick engagements that killed and maimed one or two of our young soldiers at a time. The empty guns, scary rules of engagement, and other nonsense were all part of the same nasty little package.

Suddenly, the roar of approaching Victory Base fire engines brought me back to reality. I watched as a pair of determined GIs tried to penetrate the wreckage of the CHU, but the flames were too intense. When the all-clear announcement sounded, we crawled out of our shelter. Within minutes, the hose jockeys had the flames under control and MPs were doing their bit.

Lieutenant Junior Grade Campbell and I ran over to offer help as firemen removed a body from the CHU wreckage. He was dressed in civies and looked middle-aged, but he was too blackened from the fire to tell much more. He was laid on a rescue blanket so medics could go to work, but it was pointless. I've seen too many bodies.

As I stood watching, I began to feel lightheaded. Then I felt something dripping down my left thigh. It had to be sweat. My T-shirt was soaked through, and my mouth was dry. Then I noticed blood spreading along my left leg. The MP alongside me looked me over and, seeing the blood, he grabbed my arm just before I hit the dirt.

CHAPTER 2

TMC

could just make out a specter hovering over me. Who was it? Where was I? When I opened my eyes wide and blinked, I saw my old friend Jason.

"Where am I?" Feeling around, I realized that I was naked and lying on a bed covered only by a sheet.

"Don't worry, Mr. Sutherland. You're back with us at the TMC. Major Weaver will be with you in a minute."

Round two. My surroundings were a standard issue, if not basic—emergency room, complete with big overhead lights and cabinets full of medical stuff.

Major Weaver walked in carrying a chart. "Back again so soon? How do you feel?"

"Fine, Major," I lied. I wanted to get the hell out of there.

"I'll have Specialist Baker start another IV, then we'll take care of your leg." She put on a pair of latex gloves and lifted the sheet to examine my leg. "You'll live," she announced. Her beautiful, radiant smile was truly something to behold.

"How's your stomach now? You vomited in the ambulance."

"It's okay. No bubbles."

"Good, I'll be back. Specialist Baker will get you prepped." Baker patted my shoulder and then took off behind her.

"I need a couple of things," he said hurriedly, clearly taking note of my curiosity about his quick departure, but I was barely listening. My eyes followed the major until she was out of sight. She was one pretty doc, maybe late thirties or early forties and seemingly very fit. A brunette with her hair tied back in a ponytail with sparkling green eyes that seemed to peer right through me. Her ACU pants, Christian Louboutin desert boots, and tan army regulation T-shirt let me to appreciate her as a human being as well as a healer. I liked what I saw. Even in my weakened condition, I could still look. I also was right about the memorial bracelet. It was for the young Ranger captain in the picture.

The bubble guts had begun right after my trip outside the wire to a small hamlet near Baghdad called Iskandariyah. There, I met with an Iraqi intelligence officer who was one creepy dude. He offered chai tea, a customary refreshment brought to me on a silver tray by an orderly. Though not a huge tea drinker, it looked and tasted okay. I remember thinking the glass was kinda grimy, but what the hell, it was hot water, so how bad could it be? How many have lived to regret those simple words?

The major and I made small talk through an interpreter about what he'd done in Saddam's army, how many people he'd tortured, and what electrical current he preferred. I'm a direct-current man myself. It's hard to go wrong with a good old twelve-volt car battery, alligator clips, and a bucket of saltwater. But I hasten to add I've never tortured anybody, at least physically.

It wasn't until a few hours after returning to Victory that it hit me, when my guts started to rumble, and I felt a huge urge to fart. A wise man once said an old guy should never trust a fart nor waste a boner. I agree, especially when your guts are churning. I followed that sage advice and quickstepped down the fifty-meter gravel path to the men's latrine. Soon thereafter, I was doing regular fifty-meter dashes from my CHU every half hour. People always said I was full of shit.

As I lay prone in that miserable hovel and prayed for sleep or death to end my agony, my razor-sharp detective instincts kicked in. It had to be the tea. The microbes on the rim of that soiled tea glass that I'd drank from just hours before were now doing the Sadr City two-step in my gut. The "revenge" caused me to blow from both ends with shocking regularity for the next forty-eight hours before slowing down.

Specialist Baker returned with an IV set-up and got to work searching for a victim—oh sorry, I mean vein. He scanned my arms and looked at the site of the previous IV, before announcing he'd try a new one. I nodded.

"So, what brings you to Iraq?" said Baker, breaking the silence.

"Heat, dust, dysentery."

Afraid to annoy him, I got serious. "Actually, I'm a retired LAPD lieutenant and work in the counter-IED shop." Improvised explosive devices are the scourge of this war and a very high priority for the coalition forces.

"You're a contractor?"

What else could I be, a tourist? "Yep, just a tired old double-dipping whore."

"Who do you work for?"

"Applied Logistics."

"Never heard of 'em."

"Neither had I until I saw their ad. They were looking for cops with counter-terrorism experience to work counter-IED. I applied and bang, here I am."

Baker grinned. "*Bang* is right. I'm thinking of getting into law enforcement myself. I tried the state police, but they said I lacked maturity and had too many speeding tickets, so I enlisted the next day."

"Where you from?" I wanted him off the cop thing in case he wanted revenge for all his speeding tickets.

"Greenville, South Carolina," he replied, as he tied a rubber cuff around my arm while still probing for a vein. "Sir, please make a fist."

I complied.

"Now open and close it a few times." His intent gaze told me he'd found the spot, and I braced myself as he plunged in the needle. Then, he wiggled the damn thing around like a blind man's cane in search of the curb.

"Sorry, sir, thought I had one. You have small veins. Probably from dehydration."

"But I've got a big heart," I said.

He switched to another spot in the same arm and stuck me again, which *really* smarted. Then, nothing. Perhaps payback for the speeding tickets.

"Sir, I hate to say this, but I have to go back to the same spot I used this morning."

"Okay, Specialist. Do your worst." I gritted my teeth.

Finally, success! "Okay, sir, I'm done for now."

I had to know. "Specialist, exactly how many tickets did you get back home?"

"Enough." He grinned.

The IV must have included a little cocktail to ease my suffering as I was soon very relaxed. A nice safe place, but not worth catching a piece of frag for.

The good major walked back in, this time wearing a surgical smock. She pulled up the sheet and checked out my wound. Then she said something in doc lingo to Baker and another soldier, whom I assumed to be either a nurse or a doctor. They began sticking needles all around the wound, painful at first until it went numb and I drifted off to sleep.

Before long, I was joined by the lovely and talented actress, Jessica Biel, who's got a thing for retired middle-aged cops. Now that I'm a wounded war veteran—*well, sort of*—she may never leave me alone. Just as things were getting interesting, I felt a gentle pressure on my shoulder.

"We're all done, Mr. Sutherland." Reluctantly, I returned to reality and heard a girlish giggle, undoubtedly from the good major.

"Mr. Sutherland, time to wake up."

My eyes popped open to a very amused major doctor.

"You said 'Jessica' a couple of times. Is Jessica your wife?"

"Ahh . . . just a friend. Was I out long?"

"Couple of hours. You've been such a loyal patient today, so I thought it might be a good idea to let you sleep for a while. We moved you to a bed in the ward, but because of the open wound and the possibility of infection, we'll be evacuating you to a hospital in Germany."

Crap! I'd heard about this order from Central Command, aka CENTCOM, through a friend who had recently been in a wreck on base and got some nasty cuts. By CENTCOM decree, that same night he was put on the first available airlift to Landstuhl Regional Medical Center in Germany. You'd think leaving our little garden spot for the land of fräuleins and beer would be a good thing. Not so fast!

This was a US Army show, and these guys were experts at turning the simplest thing into a mind-numbing ordeal. In fact, I had it on good authority that there is an Army Directorate of Boredom and Discomfort at the Pentagon. Last year they got a productivity award from the Secretary of Defense. I swear it's true.

My friend informed me that the trip to Germany was awful; he waited and waited and was bored out of his skull. Miserable flight. They kept him on base, patched him up, and had him back to Victory in ten days. No surprise. I would have loved to get out of this shithole for a couple of days, but not that way.

"Sure, I understand, Major. By the way, I'd like to introduce myself. I'm Rick Sutherland, retired dragon slayer, and protector of women, children, and small dogs everywhere."

She took the hand I held out and smiled. Perhaps there was hope.

"Dragon slayer, huh? I thought you were an old LAPD retread. I'm Major Weaver, Nancy Weaver."

"Glad to meet you, Major."

"Is there anything I can do for you?"

She was out of that unflattering surgical gown and my mind raced with possibilities. I got a good look at the girls, and she caught my glance. She knew. Women always know. They're smarter than men, but we can write our names in the snow.

"Yes. Thank you, Major. Do you think someone could get my cell phone? I need to call my office to let 'em know what's up."

She handed me a bag from my bedside table. "Here's your stuff, including flat badge and ID, and your weapon is with the MPs."

"Well, Major, thank you again." *Interesting,* I thought, *that she knows the slang for the small badge cops carried in their wallet.*

"You're welcome, Mr. Sutherland."

"Call me Rick."

"Okay, Call Me Rick, you're welcome. By the way, I like *big* dogs."

"So do I," I fired back.

A smartass. I like that.

I was lying about calling the office. They could wait. I needed to call Baby Bro Mikey and have him get my name off the evacuation list. Mikey had a little juice around this place, and I learned a long time ago you can't be afraid to pull strings. Mikey would help. He'd better. I had pictures.

I powered up the Nokia phone I'd bought at a haji shop next to Camp Liberty's Post Exchange, the largest PX on Victory Base. Camp Liberty is one of the interconnected US Army controlled camps that make up the Victory Base Complex. Also, part of VBC was Baghdad International Airport, locally known as BIAP, Sather Air Force Base, Camp Striker, Camp Slayer, and the Al Faw Palace, which was the headquarters for Multi National Force–Iraq, also known as MNF-I. There were a couple of other camps within the confines of the Victory Base Complex, but I won't bore you with them here.

Liberty PX, a large prefab building like a Costco but smaller, had the best selection of frozen steaks, clothing, computers, TVs—everything for the modern warrior. Next to it were a cluster of smaller shops where you could buy your next Harley or F-150 at a reduced price. There was also a large bazaar, where you could buy anything from a hookah to a belly dancer outfit. It's where I got mine.

I punched in Mikey's number and waited while his magnificence was summoned. Generals don't usually get summoned unless it's a bigger name on the other line, or you're his big brother calling, and you have pictures.

"Rick, what's up? I've got a meeting at the Palace."

Al Faw Palace, he meant. The Palace was only a mile or so from his office, so I wasn't worried. Besides, he traveled in a shiny, black armored suburban with red and blue lights and siren.

"Mikey, the IDF attack that happened a few hours ago?" IDF is Army speak for Indirect Fire—mortars, rockets, and such.

"Yeah, I heard one KIA civilian and one WIA soldier." He sounded a bit puzzled.

The *killed in action* was the guy they pulled from the CHU. The *wounded in action* was me.

"Mikey, I'm the WIA. I'm in the Victory TMC. The doc dug a small piece of frag out of my left leg. It wasn't deep, just a couple of stitches. I'm fine now. But I need you to pull some strings and get me off the evac list. They want to ship me to Germany."

"Rick, that evacuation order is from CENTCOM. It can't be ignored."

"C'mon, you got juice around here. Make it happen."

"It's not that easy."

"Bullshit, Mikey. I got faith in you. Besides, I still have pictures of you in the Cher costume from Halloween. I could send you a sample if you'd like."

I knew that would strike a nerve. Sometimes for a cop it's all a matter of applying the proper amount of persuasion. Mikey's my kid brother and I love him, but like most brass, police chiefs, and presidents, he's full of crap.

"I'll make a few calls. Just stand by and say nothing about talking to me. Keep your phone on. I'll call you in a bit."

The line clicked off. *Great, Mikey's on the job.* I closed my eyes and took a little nap.

A couple hours later, my dozing was disturbed by my new favorite major doctor, who stormed in looking a wee bit pissed. I could probably guess why.

"Mr. Sutherland, do you happen to know anyone at 3rd Infantry Division Headquarters?"

"I might."

At that precise moment, my cell started buzzing. I glanced and saw it was an 805 number. It had to be my son Troy at UC Santa Barbara. That kid had great timing. I looked at my watch. It was morning there.

I innocently held up a single finger and mouthed *sorry* as I answered the call. The obviously unhappy Major Weaver stopped, did an immediate about-face, and disappeared around a corner.

"Troy, how are you, my boy?" I said in a lighthearted tone, not wishing to betray my current circumstances.

"Dad, it's more like, how are *you?*" he asked, dead serious.

"I'm fine. I miss you guys, but otherwise good to go."

"Uncle Mikey said you'd gotten hurt in an attack on the base."

"He did?" *That's not good. Mikey spilled the beans.*

Then my other son Jake piped in. They were double teaming me. "Dad don't be pissed at him. He wanted to tell us before we heard it on the news. He said you were okay."

"Jake, how are you?"

"We're worried about you. So is Mom. She suggested we call."

"Tell your mom I'm fine and I'll email her as soon as I can. Honest guys, it's nothing. Just a small cut on my thigh. No big deal."

I looked up just in time to see the toe of a GI desert boot in the hall just outside my ward. Someone was standing outside my door. Bet I could guess who it was.

"Guys, I've got a two-week leave coming in about a month. Why don't we meet up somewhere in Europe? Your choice. Put your heads together and come up with a plan and I'll make it happen."

"That sounds great, Dad," Jake responded. "But you've already done enough. You need to come home."

"Look guys, I promise you I'm not taking any risks. What happened was a complete fluke. Wrong place, wrong time. You have a better chance of getting hurt on the 405 than you do in this place."

"Yeah, but you're not on the 405, you're in Iraq. There's a war there."

Troy had me on that one. "Yes, there is a war here. But it's not my job to fight it. I'm an analyst. What I do is important, but it's not dangerous."

There was silence for about thirty seconds. They were worried, and what I said was *mostly* true.

"Okay, Dad," Troy said. "But you've got to promise us that you're not going to take any stupid risks. We need you around."

"I promise I won't." We said our goodbyes. I set the phone down and I braced myself for an ass chew'n. I didn't have long to wait.

After a minute or two, in walked Major Weaver, still wearing her war paint.

"Everything okay?" she asked solicitously.

"Yes, thanks. My boys heard about my little scratch and were checking up on me."

"Well *Call Me Rick*, as I started to say, you won't be evacuated. We've been asked to treat you here. So, you'll be staying with us for a few days. This means we'll have to closely monitor your white blood cell count and temperature to be sure you don't have an infection."

Almost on cue, speedy Specialist Baker walked in with a phlebotomy tray.

The major went on. "The specialist will be drawing a blood sample every two hours. As I said, we want to make sure there's no infection in that open wound of yours. Enjoy!"

With that, she gave the specialist the go-ahead-and-have-fun nod. He didn't disappoint. This time he found a new vein, in my friggin' hand. Man, that hurt!

The ward I was on must have been designed by the pogues at Boredom and Discomfort. It was a long, rectangular space with at least ten beds, none of which were occupied. No TV or DVD player, just a big empty room. Oh, and did I mention it was dark? Three small windows and almost no sunlight. I've seen more cheerful cells in the Tower of London.

Bored, I dozed off for what must have been two hours when I felt a gentle nudge on my shoulder. Yep, you guessed it, Count Baker was standing by to draw more blood.

"Mr. Sutherland, it's time."

"Specialist, please call me Rick." I offered my unpunctured hand.

"Jason." We shook and made small talk while he worked—life back in Greenville, how the Army was treating him. It was my usual pre-interrogation menu.

Twenty questions were over, and it was time for business now. I started with a question I already knew the answer to.

"Jason, what happened to the guy who didn't make it?

"Frag and blast effects. That was the first IDF attack we've had since I deployed."

"Poor guy was probably sitting in his hooch watching a movie or grabbing a little mid-morning nap and BAM, lights out. Jason, this place sucks."

"Roger that, sir."

Now that we were old buds, I decided to spring my trap.

"Say, Jason, did you happen to see the piece of frag they dug out of my leg? I work IEDs, and I might be able to figure out what it was if I can get a look at it."

Okay, that was bullshit. Not complete, but close. I might not be able to tell anything by looking at it, but a souvenir to take home would be nice.

"Major Weaver bagged it to be sent over to the JEFF Lab." The Joint Expeditionary Forensic Facility is the local version of CSI.

"Has anyone told the MPs about the frag you dug out of me?"

"I called the duty NCO, but he didn't seem too interested." *No surprise there.* "Do you want it?"

"I'd be grateful, Jason. Might help me find bad guys and pick up chicks."

"I'll take care of it, but I need a favor in return."

"Sure, name it."

"I need to pick your brain about how to get a cop job when I get out. Maybe some pointers, help me with interviews?"

I flashed a big grin. "Happy to help any way I can." I was starting to like this young Southern boy, even though he sucked as a phlebotomist.

Soon, his business was done. I drifted off to Never-Never Land again. When I woke a few hours later, I spotted a small plastic container on the nightstand by my bed. I did feel a pang of guilt; after all, I didn't want to get young Jason in trouble. I could see that it held a small dark object, so I popped off the lid, and there it was, a nasty-looking, jagged, quarter-sized piece of metal about an eighth of an inch thick.

This was evidence, like anything recovered from a crime scene or a victim's body. Snagging it was a no-no that could get both mine and Jason's asses in a sling. Back home, I'd never have considered such a thing, but over here it was a bit different.

I closed the lid on the vial and hauled my drugged ass out of bed. My left leg hurt a little, but I was able to hobble over to my ACU blouse and slide the vial in an upper arm pocket.

No sooner had I sat back down when in walked my local boss, George Armstrong, in-country manager with Applied Logistics. George managed five other guys embedded with Army intelligence and counter-IED units in Iraq. Why a company called Applied Logistics employed ex-cops to advise the Army on bombs and terrorists escaped me. Didn't they already have that stuff down?

George was a retired Army Military Intelligence colonel. He more or less understood us law enforcement types. Had a brother who was a cop back in Hogwallow, Arkansas, or someplace. He let me do my job in the counter-IED shop and stayed out of my hair. As long as the paychecks cleared and the boss was cool, what more could I want? Well, actually a whole lot more.

George walked over and clasped my hand warmly. "Good to see you, Rick. How are you feeling? How's the leg? I came over as soon as you could have visitors."

"I'm fine. It's really not bad, just a little sore. They're taking good care of me."

George reached into his pocket and handed me a sealed envelope. "Somebody left this for you. One of the guys said it might be from an interpreter." I glanced at the envelope. *To Mr. Suderland important.* The script looked like the author was having the DTs and he misspelled my name. "Thanks, George, I'll have a look."

"No problem, brother. I'm just glad you're in one piece." This was the first time he'd ever called me brother. Guess he liked me.

Then George said, "CEXC and EOD are working to ID rounds that hit us yesterday." CEXC, pronounced "sexy," by the way, was another one of those mystifying acronyms I've had to learn. CEXC stands for Combined Explosives Exploitation Cell. No, I'm not making that up.

Then, I recalled the mysterious white SUV.

"George, just before the first-round hit, I saw something kinda weird." I described the SUV and what I saw. From his expression, I was sure he wasn't quite getting it. Not a surprise. He was never a cop. He didn't get the whole "everybody's a suspect" mentality cops are sadly afflicted with.

"Is there a way to track a vehicle by the plate or stenciled ID number? The plate was CZ 8008."

"That depends."

"Depends on what?" *How difficult could this be?*

"Depends on who issued the number, and if their records are up to date, but I'll check on it. I'm gonna head out now and let you get some rest. Take it easy and get healed up. Here's a couple of magazines to help pass the time." He handed me a *Sports Illustrated*, not the Swimsuit Edition, and *Condé Nast Traveler*. George was one of the good guys.

I took up the envelope George had given me and carefully opened it. It had a single page inside.

Mister Suderland, it began. Common mistake.

My name is Mohammed. Gee, that sure narrowed it down.

I am told I can trust you. That you are an honest man. I met you a few months ago. I was an interpreter with the Americans. I have some information that could save many American lives. I want you to have it. It is very dangerous for me to tell anyone but you. There are people here that will kill me if they know. Please call me soon. 6442311.

Who the hell was Mohammed? The only recent trip I'd taken had been to Iskandariyah and Yusufiyah on an IED strike follow-up. I couldn't recall specifically meeting with an interpreter on that trip.

Those two hamlets, along with Mahmoudiyah and Latifiyah, were known as the Sunni "Triangle of Death." The "Triangle," as I've heard a few call it, was about twenty miles southwest of Baghdad. About a million people called it home, mostly Sunni Muslims, with pockets of pissed off Shias just to keep it fun. I'd been to all four towns, and none was my favorite.

Looking for a Mohammed out here was almost as bad as looking for a Joey and Tony in Manhattan. Good luck.

Why had this guy singled me out to share this information? Based on the line, "There are people here . . ." it was reasonable to assume these "people" were somewhere on Victory Base. But who and where? This letter was what you would call a plot complication. Should I turn this over to the MPs or should I run with it for a while and see where it takes me? Could be fun, get the investigative juices flowing. What's a retired detective to do?

Just as I was putting the letter away, in marched Major Doctor Weaver. Didn't this chick ever go home? I couldn't help thinking she needed to get laid. But then, didn't we all?

Her expression told me I was screwed, so I kept my mouth shut. Sometimes I'm very good at that, and sometimes not so much. I gave the major my most casual "Hi."

All I got back was barely a grin. She had to know. Should I fess up? Nah.

Without a word, she opened my medical chart and did that doctor thing where they pretend to study all the notes about your temperature and pee-pee color. Then she looked at me and sighed.

"Unfortunately for the rest of us, Mr. Sutherland, it looks like you'll live."

Now, that wasn't very nice. There were people back home who cared about me and wanted me to come back. I was also pretty sure Mikey still liked me, even though I kept reminding him of those Cher pictures.

"How were you going to get your little souvenir home?" Her every syllable dripped cobra venom.

I made like a statue and played dumb.

"Mr. Sutherland—"

"Call me Rick, remember? Mr. Sutherland was my old man."

"Oh, Rick, I'm not likely to forget you. That bullshit call to your brother was bad enough, but this little stunt with the frag can get us all in trouble."

Wow, she was hot when she was mad.

"Major Weaver, I apologize. I'm just a dumb civilian trying to get by in your world. You're right, I shouldn't have called my kid brother, the major general. I should have just rolled with the procedures you guys have in place."

Her eyes softened ever so slightly.

"Major, I've been a cop my whole life. I catch bad guys. It's in my DNA." The DNA thing was laying it on a bit thick, but maybe she'd relate to a scientific reference. "A guy got killed and I got wounded. I take stuff like that personally. I want the bastards who did it. That's why I didn't want to go to Germany. I wanted to have a look at that frag and try to identify the insurgents myself. Maybe I could do some good around here."

"Mr. Sutherland . . . oh, excuse me *Call Me Rick*. Don't try to bullshit me. My dad's a cop. So's my brother. I've heard that just-want-to-catch-bad-guys crap before. I'll let this slide, but not for your sake. Baker's up for promotion, and I don't want to screw up his chances. But if you so much as blink at one of my staff, I'll introduce you to some of the most unpleasant, but medically necessary tests I can devise. You read me?"

She wasn't quite so hot now. I gulped, imagining what orifices might be violated during these medically necessary tests. Collecting my thoughts, I made ready to gently return fire.

"Sorry, Major, you got me." I gave her my most apologetic, "Ah, gee, Sarge" look. What the hell, it had worked before. "I guess I was laying it on a bit thick. Sorry."

As if by magic, her pissed off pit-bull face softened.

"I know I crossed the line. It won't happen again." *At least next time, I won't get caught.* "Major, I'm actually a pretty good guy who sometimes cuts a few corners. I meant no harm."

Major Nancy Weaver turned and walked off.

"Can't win 'em all," I muttered and had settled down when in marched a staff officer. He took one look at me and announced, "In here, General." Major General Michael Sutherland, Commanding General 3rd Infantry Division, known as "The Rock of the Marne," walked over to my bed just as I had stretched out.

"The doc says she just spoke with you. She didn't look happy."

I sat up, grinning. "You should be a detective."

"Hey, asshole, I came over as soon as I could. The staff said no visitors for a couple of hours. Said you needed some sleep."

I smiled again, and we gave each other a bear hug. I glanced around, then whispered, "Thanks for making the call."

"No sweat. I understand."

Mikey and I talked for a while, and I showed him my wound. He called me a big baby, the usual brotherly love stuff. But when I asked him about the guy who got killed, he stopped.

"Mike, is something wrong?"

"Yeah, I knew him. He worked for me during some meetings a couple of months ago. Seemed like a decent family man. Only wanted to help his country and end this damn war."

"Do you remember his name?"

Mikey shook his head.

Mike's staff officer, a fit looking colonel carrying a small black computer bag, cleared his throat.

"Sir, you have a secure telecon at the Palace in twenty."

"Thanks, Bob," Mike said. "Okay, Rick, I've gotta go. The meeting is with the Sec. Def., CG, and CENTCOM. Big juju. Base security, upcoming visits. The usual."

Those were some big names. The Commanding General and CENTCOM were probably routine, but the Secretary of Defense was big juju. *Was something brewing?*

"Bro, thanks for helping me out."

He grabbed my hand for a squeeze, nearly crushing it. What are they feeding him? Can't be the same crap they feed the rest of us.

"Take care, Rick. I'll call you later."

My room was beginning to feel like a downtown Greyhound Station. I needed some peace to think and rest. Besides, I was getting hungry. Really hungry. In fact, here's a quick note for the uninitiated. Rule number one for law enforcement is "a good cop never goes hungry." There's a second and a third rule, but I won't bore you with those yet.

My stomach was growling, and for once it didn't feel like bubble guts. I considered my limited dining choices and looked at my watch. No room service in the TMC, and the nearest dining facility, the DFAC, named the

Coalition Café, was closed. The CC, as it's known locally, was managed by a guy from New Orleans who called himself Big Daddy. He presided over the hot wings bar, shouting out he had fifty-seven kinds of wings. He didn't have fifty-seven, but he had a bunch. You could tell he cared about the soldiers he served and wanted to bring a little touch of the Big Easy to their daily routine. He was a very cool dude.

Just as I lay there pondering sustenance, Major Weaver walked in and gave me a perfunctory smile.

"Major, I'm starved. Can I bum a ride to Subway?"

She checked her watch, then said, "I'll haul your sorry ass. I need some air anyway." Then she looked again at my lovely GI hospital gown exposing my bony, nearly translucent legs. "What d'you plan to do for pants? Yours are all cut up."

"Wonderful. Don't suppose you have any extras lying around?"

She shook her head, like I was still on her shit list, but I had a feeling otherwise. "Where's your CHU? We can stop there and pick up a pair."

I liked the way this woman thought. Now, if I only had a little scotch or tequila, we could get to know each other better.

Specialist Baker handed me a crutch and a pair of gray sweatpants. They were a little fragrant, but beggars couldn't be choosers. When I emerged, she was waiting in a faded black Ford Expedition, engine running and AC on full speed.

She glanced my way. "You like pizza?"

That shocked me. "Pizza? I thought I was supposed to be on a sawdust and grass diet."

She shook her head. "You're ornery enough to handle it."

"Okay, but Pizza Hut always has a line a mile long."

"Yeah, but we're not going there. Ever been to Northside Pizza over on Liberty?"

I'd heard rumors of a pizza joint on Liberty.

CHAPTER 3

THE BAGHDAD DIET

Major Weaver took a couple minutes to pilot the worn SUV to my neighborhood. Neither of us had much to say, though I wondered what was on her mind. Either she couldn't wait to get me naked (least likely scenario), or she was just being polite and was ready to drop me like a bad check once we had our meal.

CHUs are pretty small. Just two single beds with equally small wardrobes and nightstands. Mine was a mess. Both beds were unmade, and clothes strewn everywhere, but it was all subterfuge. I had no roommate. Bob Wright from Tulsa went home two months ago without informing the base office, which permitted me a rare bit of privacy.

"Disgusting," uttered Major Weaver, critically surveying the scene.

I grabbed a set of ACUs from the wardrobe. "Former roommate's back in Tulsa. He did me a solid and never told the office he was leaving."

"I see," she said, folding her arms. "Another little scam."

"Just trying to get by in a war zone." The major nodded then she stood for a moment, seemingly lost in thought.

"I haven't had to treat many combat wounds. Since the surge, we see nothing but cases of the flu, coughing, low-grade fevers, the usual crap. That guy they brought in with you was bad. Lacerated abdomen, peritoneum blown open, intestines shredded. Must have taken most of the blast." Her voice trailed off, a sign that losing him had hit her. She had a heart. I wasn't surprised.

"Who was he?" I asked.

"An interpreter."

We both knew this crappy war would be impossible without the brave interpreters. In Iraq, *trusted* interpreters were tremendously valuable.

"Damn shame," I offered. "Look, I've gotta change, so give me a minute."

"Got it." She opened the door and walked out, lost in thought.

I caught a glimpse of my wound in the mirror. Not as bad as it could have been. I was damn lucky. A little higher and to the right and I would have lost the jewels. Most of the flab around my waist was now gone. I'd lost fifteen or twenty pounds since coming to Iraq, thanks to daily trips to the gym and a weight-loss regime called the "Baghdad Diet." Who needs $1,500-a-day ashrams, Pilates, and water distilled from the tears of Fijian angels when you can drink reclaimed pond water from Camp Liberty swamps, bask in stifling heat, enjoy chow prepared by talentless kitchen drones, and get tons of exercise? Then, of course, there's the shits. All this plus travel, excitement, and they pay you to boot!

Getting my ACU pants over the dressing was a bitch. I laced up my spare boots and emerged from the CHU ready for anything. But something was missing. *Holy shit! My pistol!*

Noting my frantic self-pat down as I emerged from my CHU, Major Weaver shook her head, smiling knowingly.

"MPs have your gun. Remember, I told you that before?"

"Oh, yeah. Must be the pain meds."

"Or your advanced age. Don't worry, I'll protect you." When she patted her M9 pistol that she carried in a shoulder rig, I saw that its magazine well was as empty as the minds which decreed that empty weapons rule. Empty guns in holsters and empty staplers on desks are equally worthless.

When we climbed back in her SUV for the ride to Northside Pizza, I broke the silence in the hope of finding common ground.

"Your dad and brother are cops? I'm a retired cop, and my little brother is in the Army. How's that for a coincidence?"

"Did anyone ever tell you that you're funny? Is that why you insist on saying such dumb shit? Dad's a retired sergeant with Richmond PD, and my brother Rick's with the Virginia State Police."

Hmm. More common ground.

"Your brother's named Rick? Another coincidence. I'm Rick, too."

She finally laughed. *Victory!*

"What did you do in LA besides annoy the shit out of people?"

"I retired as a lieutenant II last year, after twenty-nine years with LAPD. I worked Narcotics, did some time in IA and Homicide, but most recently worked counter-terrorism on the FBI Joint Terrorism Task Force."

"Is the terrorism thing what led you to Iraq?"

"Mostly, and two sons in college."

"Just the two boys?"

"Yep, Troy's at UC Santa Barbara studying computer science and IPAs. Jake's a biology major at Oregon State and wants to be a doctor. Another coincidence, and in the spirit of full disclosure, I once got a speeding ticket from the Virginia State Police."

"Bet you deserved it."

"I was doing ninety on I-95, trying to get back to Quantico for a class at the FBI Academy. Trooper Orville Buckley did the honors, and I invited him to LA to return the favor."

"You cops always expect to get out of tickets. It's bullshit. You need to get dinged like the rest of us."

"Just simple professional courtesy. Doctors and lawyers, they do it all the time, so why not the cops?" I got her attention, and continued. "As a young boot officer, I was taught to take care of fellow cops, firemen, docs, and nurses, 'cause one day, if I'm getting my ass kicked on the side of the road or bleeding out in the OR, they're the only ones I can count on."

"That's the same excuse Dad gave. I guess there's a tortured logic to it."

"Tell me you didn't leave a stethoscope where a cop would instantly spot it when you got stopped." That elicited a wicked smile.

Northside Pizza occupied a small prefab building and Conex-sized trailer in a lonely corner of Camp Liberty, easy to miss behind a haji shop that sold pirated DVDs. We ordered a large pizza, half sausage, half veggie. They were out of pepperoni. *WTF?* You'd think there was a war going on. She was still feeling conversational, so we kept on talking as we ate.

"I went to UVA undergrad, then got a scholarship through the Army for medical school. Had a four-year commitment when I graduated, but it agreed with me, so I stayed on. I'm now coming up on nine years. What about you? What's your story?"

"I'm a Pisces, blue is my favorite color, and I enjoy pulling the wings off moths."

"Cut the crap. What's your story? No bullshit."

"Okay, you know how and why I'm here. I'm divorced."

"Only once?"

"Yes, only once. We were together nearly twenty-one years, or about three hundred in dog years. Charlotte's a lawyer. We met in court while I was still a street copper, and she was the public defender on a case in which I was the arresting officer."

"Attractive?"

"Yes, still is. Like you, she didn't warm to my quick wit and soap-star good looks. In fact, she tried to nail me under cross-examination, but it backfired, and she lost the case."

"What happened next?"

"Nothing. I didn't see her again for a couple months, then ran into her on the courthouse elevator. I asked her if she remembered me, and she said no. So, I reminded her, and she shocked me by asking if she could buy me a cup of coffee. I accepted, and that night was our first date."

"The rest is history, right?"

"Something like that. What about you, Major Weaver? You know all my secrets."

"I've never been married. Engaged once. Justin was a captain in the Ranger regiment. He was killed in 2003. Ambushed in the Hindu Kush."

"I'm sorry." She checked her watch and said she had to get back.

"Me too. Jason needs to bleed me again."

"Nah, you've had enough. I'm going to discharge you in the morning."

"Can we stop by the MP's office to reclaim my pistol?"

"No problem."

On the ride back, it was quiet. Nancy was probably as deep in thought as me.

My marriage to Charlotte, like our courtship, was a whirlwind. I popped the question after two months, but in hindsight realize that we should have waited and gotten to know each other better. Still, we produced two fine young men, so we must have done something right.

Truth is, nobody was solely to blame for our divorce. We both screwed up. Char and I waited until both boys were off to college before filing for divorce. Though tough at first, we all got through it. As divorces go, it was simple—no acrimony, no fighting over assets, just a simple parting of the ways.

When Nancy announced, "Okay, we're here," I was jolted back to reality.

"Thanks. This shouldn't take long."

She parked the big SUV and hopped out. "I'll be in the PX," she said, and walked over to the entrance while I strode into the MP Shop. The 633rd Military Police Battalion was a reserve unit based out of Fort Carson, Colorado. I identified myself to the duty NCO as the poor schmuck who got hurt in the recent mortar attack.

Sergeant Hadley looked up, surprised. "So, how're you doing? Didn't they dig some frag out of your leg?"

Hmm. There was more to this question than just a friendly inquiry. How much did he know?

"I'm fine, Sarge. Just a little cut." I needed to deflect this line of inquiry, and when I recognized an officer walk past who looked familiar, my brain raced to recall who it was while pretending to pay attention to the inquisitive sergeant.

"Harry!" I blurted, attempting to get his attention so I could shuck this NCO with his irritating questions. The officer stopped, and sure enough, it was Harry. Lieutenant Colonel Harry Arnold, US Army Reserve, in civilian life, Captain Arnold of the Jefferson County Sheriff's Department. I'd first met him at Quantico during an FBI National Academy session. LAPD usually doesn't send lowly detective lieutenants like me to the NA, but I somehow got selected. The two of us spent a few nights swapping lies in the Academy's pub, more commonly known as "The Boardroom."

"Harry, it's Rick Sutherland!"

Lt. Colonel Arnold seemed annoyed until he saw my grin. "Rick! What the hell are you doing here, and why are you wearing that?"

Another NCO ushered me through the waiting room and into the sanctum sanctorum. I walked past a major, whose name tape read Copeland. He was on the phone describing what "cowardly, untrustworthy dipshits" the IPs were. Of course, he was referring to those stalwart defenders of peace and justice, the Iraqi Police. I chuckled when he called their local commander "The Supreme Douche Nozzle." Hell, if anything, he was being kind. I'd had some dealings with the Nozzle myself, and Copeland obviously heard my chuckle and nodded as I limped by. I didn't know him, but liked his style.

Harry rushed in to grip my hand, nearly crushing it.

"Christ, Harry, I've walked past this place a million times and had no idea you were here."

"Just arrived," he whispered. "The old CO got sent home. Kind of a mess. Coffee?"

"Sure."

We sat in his office, and he inquired about my crutch. "Fall off a curb?"

"Wounded in action, not that you Army types will ever recognize the sacrifices we civilians make."

He looked puzzled, so I helped him out. "I was hit in that mortar attack yesterday."

"*You* got hit? How are you still here? Shouldn't you be in Germany with a nurse under each arm?"

"I told you my baby bro is a general, but you didn't believe me." *Better downplay this,* I reminded myself. This guy was a bud, but this was also

Army shit, and I didn't want to stir it up. "Besides, it was nothing. Really just a scratch. Couple of stitches and good as new."

Harry had heard enough bullshit in his career to know its pungent odor, giving me the "yeah, right" smile and letting it go.

"That reminds me," I said. "My ride's probably waiting for me."

"Hold on a sec. What brings you to Iraq? I know it's not the scenery."

"I retired from the city and took a contractor gig in the counter-IED shop."

"I figured you'd land some cushy studio security job," he smiled. "As you can see, I'm still moving in. What can I do for you?"

"I came to get my piece. Your guys took custody of it when I got hit."

"Okay, let me check." When he left the room, I snooped around. Usual crap on his desk—forms and such. Then my eyes fell on a US Government Classified folder with an orange stripe bearing the code words *Argon-Lancer.*

Harry returned with my gun belt complete with M9 paperweight, and I pointed at the folder on his desk.

"Who comes up with these code names?"

"A computer somewhere. But this mess should be called 'Steaming Turd.'" He looked at my security badge, which indicated I had a Top Secret/SCI security clearance and knew the secret handshake.

"Rick, this thing is a nightmare. It torched my predecessor and could burn me too."

"It's a Military Intelligence shit show. The 722nd MI had a walk-in source." Harry stopped himself and opened the file. I could see a picture of an Arab male about forty years old, but he waved his hand in disgust.

"He got whacked before they got finished with the debrief. His story was never fully vetted. But if it's true, it would be huge."

"I'm surprised I didn't hear about the murder."

"They do HUMINT collection and put a very tight lid on the information." HUMINT stands for human sourced intelligence.

Now I was really curious, but let it go. I didn't want to press for details. Not yet.

"Harry, I gotta head out. Let me know if there's anything I can do to help." As I headed for the door, Major Copeland opened it.

Harry stood. "Hold up a sec, Rick. Let me introduce you to a fellow Left Coaster. Ben, didn't you live in LA?"

"Sure did. Also went to UCLA, but that wasn't my fault." Major Copeland stuck out his hand. "Ben Copeland. Mobile Training Teams, sort of."

Mobile Training Teams, also called MTT, are Army teams that run around the country training our valiant brothers in arms, the Iraqi Army (IA) and the Iraqi Police (IP).

I shook his hand. "Rick Sutherland, overpaid civilian," which provoked a chuckle.

"Rick's retired LAPD," Harry said. "Worked the Joint Terrorism Task Force. We met at the FBI Academy. He's over at the counter-IED intelligence group."

"Looks like you've been around the block," said Copeland, nodding toward my right leg and crutch. "What happened?"

"Slightly wounded in the IDF attack."

Copeland frowned. "Yeah, been a while since they've hit us here. Good to meet you, Rick. Keep your head down. Gotta go meet with IP leadership."

"Ah," I said, "his Grand Nozzleship?"

"The very same." With that, he smiled and left the room.

"Seems like an okay guy," I said to Harry.

"Ben's good people. Really gets it. Been a huge help to me. Fluent in Arabic and Farsi. His dad was with the State Department and he's lived all over. Has a handpicked team, all fluent in Arabic and Farsi, all with specialized cultural training. They work with the IAs and do some training, but also collect on them and the IPs. He doesn't report to me. He falls under the CG for this AOR." AOR is area of responsibility. Yes, I know; why don't they just speak English? But what's worse is, I'm told the Navy acronyms are even more incomprehensible.

Collecting intelligence on the Iraqi Army and police made sense.

Mobile Training Teams would be perfect for that role. Too many bad guys were running around in Iraqi Army and police uniforms.

"Hey, man, it's great to see you again. Let's have chow sometime," Harry said as he passed me his card and shook my hand.

Outside, I spotted my favorite doc, Major Nancy Weaver, standing alongside her SUV and speaking with Copeland. They seemed to be winding it up when I reached them.

"Another satisfied customer?"

Major Copeland smiled and nodded. *Had these two played doctor?*

"One of the major's guys came in with diarrhea a month ago, just like you." I groaned. "Did he need as many blood tests as me?"

"No," she popped back, "you were a special case. Major Copeland, tell your soldier if it starts up again to come back and see me. We'll try something different."

"I will, thanks," he said, turning to me with his sage advice. "Take care, Rick, and keep your head down."

"Thanks, Major. I will."

Thank God Nancy's car had good AC. We pulled out of the parking lot just as George was pulling in. He saw us both and waved. I waved back, and we were back at the TMC a few minutes later.

"I'm gonna give you something to help you sleep tonight. We'll check you in the morning, and if you're clear, I'll throw your ass out."

"Gently, I hope."

"Maybe," she said, looking up with that now familiar wicked, tantalizing grin.

CHAPTER 4

LES LIAISONS DANGEREUSES

Whatever she prescribed, it knocked me out. I didn't wake 'til nearly noon the next day. In fact, they had to wake me to draw blood. About thirty minutes later, Major Herself walked in. "Nothing's changed. You'll still live," she said in mock disgust.

"Gee, thanks, Doc, you're the best."

"I want you to take a day or two off. I told your boss. Shockingly, he has no wish to see you either."

"I'll catch up on my *Sopranos* DVDs. Can I bum a ride?"

"Sure, let me get the keys."

As I got dressed, I overheard a familiar voice introduce himself to Major Weaver.

"Major, I'm Sergeant Hadley, 633rd MPs. You had a civilian patient named Sutherland? I'm here to collect a piece of frag you dug out of him."

There was a pause. "Sergeant, he's been discharged." Technically, that was true.

"That frag is evidence; we need to get it to the lab."

"Yes, the frag. It was so small, one of my med techs just let him keep it. I've dealt with the tech."

"Yes, ma'am. But I'm gonna need to speak with Sutherland."

My larcenous heart was pounding away. *Will I get caught?* Did I give a shit? Well, kinda.

"I've ordered him to stay in his CHU and get some rest. Can this wait 'till tomorrow?"

"Yes, ma'am, I suppose so."

"Very well, then. Thank you, Sergeant." That last bit was Army speak for "you may run along now, peasant." Damn, she was good. Sergeant Hadley gave his obeisance, turned, and left. I chuckled softly to myself. I'd been bitching for months about how bad the Army guys were at collecting evidence. I guess they listened to me. Hoisted by my own petard once again.

Nancy dropped me off near my CHU at Château L' Brickyard. She busted my chops over the purloined frag again, but this time it was with a hint of a smile.

"What are you doing tonight?"

"Me?"

"Yes, you. I asked what you're doing tonight?"

"Not much besides chow and crochet class."

"Care to join me for dinner?"

"Well, I suppose so. Is this a date, Major?"

"What do you think, Call me Rick?"

"Remember, I don't have wheels."

"Okay, deadbeat, I'll pick you up here at 1830. We'll go to Sather; the Air Force has better chow."

"Yes, ma'am. See you then."

I hobbled back to my hooch with just a bit of a bounce and collapsed on the bed. I was fried. This getting wounded stuff was very taxing.

I awoke an hour later to the noise of some guys playing grab-ass outside. I looked at my watch; time to get up. I checked my email. I had a couple of old messages from the boys. It was good we'd had a chance to talk. Hopefully, they felt a little better about me being over here.

There was also a nice email from Charlotte. She was always a thoughtful person and a great mom. She never missed a game or school event. I, on the other hand, was probably a little too busy playing cops and robbers. For a divorced type-A lawyer and smart-assed cop, we got along very well. Fact is, we'd probably still be married if we'd listened more and spoken less.

I decided to take a shower and get cleaned up. I grabbed my kit and headed seventy meters from my hooch to the shower facilities. It was late afternoon, and I had the place to myself.

As I toweled off, I started thinking about the interpreter killed in the mortar attack, wondering if our paths had ever crossed. I needed to know more about him. I usually picked up an interpreter any time I went outside the wire on one of my fact-finding trips, and thus far, I'd worked with half a dozen. But this guy did not ring any bells. I needed to do a little more digging. Then there was the MI source that had just gotten whacked. Coincidence? Probably not.

I still had time before my rendezvous with Nancy, so I headed over to the office to snoop around and see what I could pick up. Heads jerked in surprise as I limped in. You'd have thought I was a ghost.

George was on a special secure phone called a STU with somebody important. You could always tell, because George's vocabulary grew exponentially. He waved me in and rolled his eyes. I plopped down and scanned the room. Nothing new. No files with my name on them. Always a good sign. He said "bye" and was off the phone.

"How's the leg? I thought you were supposed to be in bed?"

"I'm alright. Doc says I'll live. Anything from CEXC on the mortar rounds?"

"Nothing yet."

"You got the victim's name?"

"No, not yet, but it's not in your lane," George responded.

There was that lane crap again. This lane stuff was an Army idea having to do with staying focused on your mission and not drifting over into someone else's mission lane. This idea worked for some, but it was extremely frustrating to a high-speed, medium-drag guy like me with more questions than patience. This nonsense would hinder my own little investigation, but what the hell, I always enjoy a challenge.

"Okay, George, so it's not in *your* lane. But you're not in the Army now, so do you really have a lane?"

"Old habits."

I shook my head. This was a complete waste of time. George might have his finger on the pulse, but the patient was dead.

"By the way, can you do me a favor? When you get the lab reports, can you cc me?"

"Not in your lane."

"I'm a cop, George. I can pick any fucking lane I want."

He shook his head. "You're a saggy-ass LAPD retread. Not a cop."

"Sure, George, whatever."

"How's the big boss?"

"Just got off the phone with him. He was worried about you. Sends you his best."

"My best to him too. Thanks, George, I gotta head back."

With that, I got up and beat a hasty retreat back to my CHU.

Nancy showed up right on time, which was a good thing, as it was still hot as the bowels of hell.

"Hey, old man, you need a ride?"

Old man? That really hurt. "No, I'm waiting for my proctologist."

"Well, hop in. I have gloves and K-Y."

She probably did, too. She smelled good. Since everywhere I'd been in this dusty little hellhole smelled like shit, getting in a car with a freshly showered and perfumed lady doc was a very nice change, even if she was in uniform.

On our way to Sather Air Force Base, which is located at the Baghdad Airport, we passed through another Army installation called Camp Slayer, a weird place, sort of Epcot meets *Lawrence of Arabia* on acid. Weird architecture and man-made lakes. The land had once belonged to some tribe, the Hekawis, or something. That is until Saddam decided he needed it more for his Abu Ghraib Palace complex than the Hekawis did. A few dead guys later, the tribe agreed with him. Funny how that worked.

One of Saddam's more ornate buildings was a palace-cum-house of horrors called the Perfume Palace. There was also a huge complex in the middle of one of the lakes that the Baath Party leadership used as a recreation center. These scumbags would kidnap unsuspecting women off Baghdad streets, bring them back, rape them, and who knows what else. They'd dump the bodies in the lake and let the fish do the rest. There were some freakish looking fish in that lake.

Other tourist musts were the unfinished *Victory* over America Palace and nearby Flintstones Village, both rich in the bizarre irony only a place like Iraq could deliver. A French construction company was building the Victory over America Palace until work stopped in 2003, just before the balloon went up. They got out of there so fast, they left a huge tower crane and tractor-trailer rig that was still parked inside the palace. Across from the palace was Flintstones Village. A bizarre sort-of playland thrown together for Saddam's grandkids. Supposedly, he had it built out of guilt for having their daddy whacked. What a guy.

We arrived at the Sather chow hall and got in line. I selected low-fat, low-sodium, zero-cholesterol, breaded veal cutlets, and she chose baked fish. *Quelle surprise.*

We found a quiet corner of the dining room and sat down. She eyed my plate critically, no doubt calculating the saturated fat and sodium levels.

"Going heart healthy, I see."

"Yeah, I'm like a culinary crash-test dummy."

She regarded her plate dubiously. "We might all be."

The sun shining through a large glass door backlit her dark hair perfectly. She looked over at me with her eyes twinkling. I braced for another *zinger.*

"So, how does a tired old fart like you wind up in Iraq?"

To my hopeful ears it almost sounded like, "Of all the gin joints in all the towns in all the world . . ."

"I'm with *Rolling Stone* doing an undercover story on the Iraqi disco scene."

"Disco is dead."

"Like I said before, two kids in college," I replied.

She frowned. "There's a lot easier ways to make money than deploying to a war zone."

"You asked why I'm here. The payday for a year over here will just about take care of my half of both tuitions."

She had still more questions about my family. "Still talk with the ex?"

"Yes, mostly about the boys. She emailed me after I got hurt."

Major Weaver nodded, then asked, "She still in LA?"

"Charlotte has a very nice little shack off Montana in Santa Monica," prompting yet another nod.

She finished dinner before me. I always thought cops were fast eaters. I'd wolfed down many a Super King Fat on the hood of my black-and-white between radio calls. Must be the same for docs. I was curious why she stayed in the Army.

"Why aren't you back home in Fairfax with a waiting room of rich patients and a Benz in the driveway?"

"The Army sent me to med school. Now it's payback time. But I like it. It's tough to be away from home, but I feel like I'm part of something here. Not just flu shots and aspirin. 9/11 really changed things for me. Losing Justin in Afghanistan. Seeing those people jump from the towers. Guess I just want to hit back."

"Lost a friend with NYPD. Ran into Tower One and never came out. I get it."

"We lost a lot of good people that day," she said. "That's why I'm here."

"I have to admit, that's a very big part of why I'm here as well," I responded. "Unless you've worked on the inside, you don't really understand the threat that those guys pose. Our enemies are smart, well-funded and have lots of patience. That's why I'm here. No more 9/11's."

It was time to lighten things up. "You go for some ice cream?"

"Pralines for me."

I got up and hobbled over to the ice cream bar, wishing with every step I could get more than just ice cream. Sometimes you just need a cocktail or even a cold beer. I'm a small batch bourbon man myself, but I'd have settled for a big-batch one at that moment.

We headed out to her car when she surprised me with another question. "You like cigars?"

"Got some back in my hooch," I replied.

She reached into her cargo pocket and pulled out a tan leather cigar case and lighter. "I know a quiet spot on Slayer where we can smoke in peace. How's that sound?"

"Let's roll." As we drove onto Slayer, I said, "How long you been into cigars?"

"Habit I picked up in med school. I usually burn one a week, sort of a treat to myself."

"When I was a kid, I had a doctor who chain-smoked in the exam room. Things are a little different now."

She chuckled. "Yeah, smoking will kill you, no doubt about it, but it can also be a comfort. Occasionally, it's okay."

She parked the black Expedition in a deserted area near Flintstones Village. We both got out without saying a word and walked up a narrow path to the upper floor entrance. It was dark. I pulled out a small red LED light as we entered.

I heard a foot crunch on gravel behind us. I turned toward the sound and caught a glimpse of a shadow passing under a nearby light. "Somebody's here," I whispered.

She stopped and turned around, looking in the same direction. "Relax, *Call Me Rick*, I'll protect you."

"Just maintaining situational awareness."

"They're just here cause it's quiet. Like us."

She took my arm and together we walked a little farther into the labyrinth. We stopped at a spot that overlooked the man-made lake and the unfinished Palace of Blah Blah Blah. She stopped and looked out over the lake.

Without a word, she pulled out a sizable pocketknife, an Emerson or Coldsteel, and trimmed both cigars so deftly it would have made a mohel blush with pride. She'd seen my eyes widen as she flicked open the four-inch blade.

"For castrations and circumcisions," she said.

"I've already been trimmed."

"I know."

"You know a lot."

"I'm your doctor."

Our eyes met. Now was the time. When I leaned over and kissed her gently on the mouth, she responded and clutched my hand. I dropped my cigar. My hands began to wander from her waist up her back and around to her breasts. I felt her tense slightly, then respond more intensely. She pressed her hips against me and giggled.

"Somebody's awake."

"It's been a while."

"For me, too."

Ordinarily, I would have charged forward in no time, but something was different here. Oh, we were horny, all right, but there was a real connection percolating. I could see myself with this woman for more than a couple of booty calls, and I kind of hoped she saw me the same way. That sounds like a line from a Lifetime movie, delivered by the handsome guy who's actually the ax murderer, but hell, that's how I felt.

I was about to offer to slow down when she whispered, "I have a blanket." Lord knows, I've christened many a back seat, then of course, there was the legendary LAPD Academy "Rock Garden," but something about being in Iraq with MPs patrolling around threw cold water on the whole thing.

"My hooch is empty. No roommate."

"Oh, that's right. Let's go to your place."

"You're the driver."

Suddenly, I heard more footfalls. I froze for a second and just listened. They were close. Nancy was moving so fast she must not have heard it. I did a quick 360-degree scan as I got in the Expedition. Nothing. I buckled up and looked back toward the village, just in time to see two dark figures emerge from one of the small outbuildings. The hair on the back my neck stood up. Nancy didn't see them. I reached down with my right hand and popped the retention strap on my holster. Unbeknownst to Her Doctorship, I covertly slipped a loaded magazine into my pistol. It clicked into place. Nancy glanced at me.

"What are you doing?"

"Nothing."

She looked at my right hand. "Bullshit, you just loaded your pistol."

"I just saw two dudes that didn't look right. Let's get the fuck outta here."

Without demur, she fired up the beast and punched it, throwing up a huge cloud of dust. I watched as two males crouched, disappearing in the darkness. I could see one of them had a big rifle. A very big rifle.

We got back to Victory in record time. I could barely get the key in the lock when we got to my room. Need I say more?

CHAPTER 5

CLUELESS

I had a bounce in my hobble as I headed for chow the next morning. I spied George by himself in a corner at the oasis DFAC, so I joined him.

"Did you hear about the two bad guys that got capped over on Slayer?"

I nearly spit out my oatmeal.

"No."

"MPs engaged two guys dressed in ACUs near that unfinished palace of whatever. Both are dead. Looked like a sniper and observer team. Had a long gun, night vision, the whole thing. They're reviewing ISR video to see if anyone else was involved." ISR stands for Intelligence, Surveillance, Reconnaissance, and refers to the ubiquitous surveillance drones hovering overhead.

It had to be the two guys I saw skulking around the village. *Shit!* Nancy's Expedition could be on that surveillance video. Not good. I'd get sent home, but it would be a career ender for her. I couldn't tell George we were there. All I could do was pray that the ISR drone hovering overhead was otherwise occupied last night.

However, I was right about what I saw. There was also another nagging question: what, or more importantly, *who*, were they after?

"I've asked for the reports. Should be a couple of days or so," George offered.

"I'd like to have a look at them," I replied, trying to sound as casual as possible.

"By the way, what did that letter say?"

"What letter?" I replied. I was still thinking about the sniper team we'd run into.

"The letter I gave you at the clinic."

Oh, that letter. It was too soon to let him in on it. The letter was interesting, and if credible, its implications could be very serious. George would want to turn the letter over to the MPs or CID without letting me run with it for a while. It was now time for me "to break contact," so I decided to do what all real heroes do in a serious dilemma—feign illness and run away. With all the dramatic flair I could muster, I grabbed my bandaged leg and winced.

"You okay, buddy?"

Sometimes I really hated myself, but I had to do what I had to do.

"This bitch is really starting to hurt again. I should probably pop a Vicodin."

He got up. "C'mon, I'll take you back to your hooch."

I nodded, still wincing. He grabbed his keys and off we went. The five-minute ride to my hooch was quiet. I knew something was on his mind, and finally as we pulled up in front, out it came.

"Look, Rick, let me speak as a friend, not a boss."

He sounded like my dad saying, "This is going to hurt me as much as it hurts you." Yeah, right. I was all ears.

"Rick, you were never in the Army, and I understand that, and I'm sure this is all a little weird and dysfunctional to you. But there is a method to the madness." He sighed, then went on. "Some MP sergeant came over yesterday looking for you. Something about frag they dug out of you." George studied my face as I listened. "Said it was evidence, and they need it. I thought you might know about it."

Persistent bastards. This wasn't good, but it was better than a lecture on abstinence in a war zone. Time to be honest. Kind of.

"Yes, I've got it. I'm a counter-IED guy, and investigating this shit is square in my lane."

"But what can you do with frag?" George asked.

"I'm going to have a friend at the lab have a look and then send it on to CEXC. George, it's not following the rules, but I want to find these guys. To CID, it's just another indirect fire attack. To me, it's personal."

Deep down, George probably knew I was blowing smoke up his bloomers. But he also knew I was right about the MPs and CID. *This was personal.*

"Don't worry about it. I'll cover as long as I can. Just take care of your leg. If you need anything at all, give me a call." George was a good dude.

I shook his hand and bailed out of the Suburban so fast I did hurt my leg as I hit the ground. I wasn't entirely faking. I walked around the corner out of his sight and stopped. I wasn't going back to my place yet. I needed to think.

Instead, I went to the bus stop and plopped down on the bench to wait for a ride to Camp Liberty. Across from me was a wrecked guard tower left over from the previous owners. Its last occupant had clearly had a rough day dodging Yankee bullets—probably shitting his pants, judging by its shot-up exterior. Hell, I would be too.

I've had a couple of caps popped in my direction, and one that connected. The first time was sort of surreal. I didn't believe it was happening until I heard the impact of the .30-caliber round inches above my head. The second time, well, that was *real*. Bullets are great little wake-up calls if you survive long enough to hang up the phone.

My quiet musings were interrupted by the familiar and very loud sound of a vehicle siren. I looked up to see a convoy headed toward me. The lead vehicle was an Iraqi Army pickup truck with two IA soldiers up front and a third in back aiming a Soviet-style DShK heavy machine gun my way. The thing was pointed directly at me. I could see live rounds in the belt, ready for business. I'd started to hobble out of the line of fire when the gunner trained his gun away from me. Then the bearded dipshit gave me a little wave and smile. *Oh, okay. That makes it all better.*

An armored reconnaissance vehicle passed by next, the driver sounded a siren again, I have no idea why. No other vehicles were around, and I was the only poor slob in the area. Then I spotted the red and blue lights mounted front and rear just like what cops had back home. Lights and sirens in a war zone, smiling Iraqis pointing heavy machine guns at me. I had to be in another dimension, or the Oasis-bottled water I was drinking was laced with LSD. I needed a new job.

When the bus arrived, I got on in record time. To my relief, the short ride to the Liberty PX was uneventful. I got off and walked over to the Cinnabon to grab a gooey pastry and coffee—thinking man's food. I watched the heavily armed boys and girls as I ate. Most Americans back home just didn't get it. These kids were amazing. They endured unbelievable hardships, humping hundreds of pounds of crap through blazing heat and blinding dust without complaint. Kept themselves in amazing shape, then ruined it by eating this shit. The irony of life.

To preserve any latent prints on the letter or the envelope, I had put them in a ziplock baggie. I pulled the baggie from my cargo pocket for another look. There were no obvious clues or marks on either the envelope or the paper. My friend at the JEFF Lab, Ryan Lee, a retired LAPD criminalist I'd known from our patrol days in West LA Division, could do the latent prints exam. He was smart guy with a good heart, but a little more by-the-book than I care for—but so are most people.

My cell phone started buzzing.

"Rick, it's me," Nancy said.

"Who is this?" I replied innocently.

"Cut the shit. I just got a strange call. The guy who got killed the other day in the mortar attack."

"Yeah."

"He was already dead."

"Dead in his hooch before the attack?" I asked.

"It's not confirmed, but it looks like it. Balad did a preliminary examination of the body and took some temperatures. They put the time of death a few hours before the attack." She had my attention now.

"When they brought him in, I had a feeling something didn't look quite right. I thought I saw a little lividity in his thighs and calves, but the blast damage and burn marks made it hard to tell. We took some pictures of the body for our records, and I just reviewed them. No doubt about it. Early hypostasis."

"Is that doctor talk for lividity?"

"Yeah. I also thought I saw slight bruising around the trachea, but again, it was very hard to tell."

"Strangulation?"

"Maybe, but a pathologist should see it."

This was interesting.

"You worked homicide, didn't you?"

"In another dimension."

"Well, this guy was dead before the attack. Which means this could have been a murder, not some random IDF victim."

"What was his name?"

"Mohammed Jbar Salim."

Son of a bitch! It had to be the same guy who sent me the "Mister Suderland" letter. The bastards got him before he spilled. Most Army dudes might dismiss it as all a coincidence. Not a chance. It had to be the same Mohammed, I'd bet the hookah on it. In my business, you quickly learn coincidences are for movies and politicians, not the real world.

A good ol' whodunit double murder investigation was just the kind of diversion I needed. Well, I already had a diversion. But another one couldn't hurt.

I quickly began organizing what I knew. It wasn't much, but I had a feeling more would follow. *A guy sitting on some hot info got whacked in his hooch, then his place caught a mortar round, maybe two for good measure. But why bother? Unless the IDF attack was meant to hide the murder. Just like we saw in arson homicide. Fire, or in this case, high explosive, masks the murder and destroys the evidence. Two for one.*

"Rick, you still there?"

"Yeah, I'm here. Sorry, I was absorbing what you said."

"I can hear you breathing. You need more cardio. Can you meet me over at Green Beans at say 2100?"

"Sure. Why so late?"

"I have a staff meeting. What d'you think about the murder possibility?"

"It's possible, but we need to see the autopsy report."

Now was not the time to tell her about my "Mister Suderland" letter from Mohammed, or that there was another dead informant. I really liked her and could probably trust her, but sure as fat boys like cookies, "probably" is a word that'll get you in trouble. Regardless of her encouraging me to investigate the thing, she was, after all, Army. If I overstepped my bounds, she might go Army on me and blow the whistle. Then before you know it, CID would be tearing around with their hair on fire rounding up the usual suspects and spoiling all my fun. I wanted to run with this for a few days. *Who knows, maybe it'll make a good book.*

"I'll see you later at the Beans."

Green Beans was the local Starbucks clone. The military had come a long way from a cup of instant coffee, heated over a burning chunk of C-4. I was thinking if a guy could only get a real beer every so often, this place might be tolerable. Ah, probably not.

I got out my note pad and started making a to-do list. Really, I'm not that organized, and if you saw my desk you'd agree, but I needed to start thinking about how to unravel this one and not get my tit in a wringer.

For starters, I needed to track down the cellphone number mentioned in the letter. But this wasn't like the States where you could write up a search warrant or administrative subpoena, serve it on the cell carrier, and get the information quickly. This was Iraq, where nothing was easy except getting killed. The only way I'd get lucky on the number was if it came up in some intelligence database, and if so, that could be very good or very bad. I'd have to be careful. All the databases I used tracked who made the inquiry and let other folks know you were checking it out. If the number was hot, bells and whistles could start sounding between Victory and Langley. Not so good for Rick.

I also needed to see a picture of the dead guy, Mohammed Jbar Salim. Our paths might have crossed. I needed to know everything I could about him. Victimology as we call it. This would probably also mean a road trip. George might shit a brick, because of my little scratch, but he'd relent in the end.

I'd need the ops officer to book a flight for me. Captain Hodges would do it, but it would cost me. A reservist who'd begun his career as an enlisted guy, Hodges knew how to cut corners and play the system. He also had a serious weakness for cigars. The guy smoked an El-Cheapo PX Special every day. I'd tried one once; tasted like camel shit rolled in *The Baghdad Times*. Luckily, my sons were keeping me well stocked with Macanudos. I had an extra box I could sacrifice for the cause.

I got up and was headed for the bus stop when someone shouted behind me.

"Rick!" I turned to see where it was coming from. All I saw was masses of boys and girls in green digits moving in and out of the Liberty PX. I kept walking.

"Rick, you gonna make me chase you?"

I turned again to see good old Harry Arnold jogging up. "Need a ride?"

"I was gonna take the bus back to Victory."

"I'm heading back too."

"Great!" I made it as sincere as I could. Harry was a friend, but if he got wind I was doing a Columbo impression on his base, he'd shit bricks.

We walked over to his SUV and got in. Harry didn't say much, aside from the usual chit-chat, which wasn't the Harry I remembered. Something was definitely on his mind.

I decided to prime the pump.

"How many combat deployments have you had?"

"Desert Storm and twice for round two."

"I'd say you did your part."

"Yep, but I've been lucky. Some of these kids have had it pretty tough, but they keep coming back for more."

"Your unit settled in?" I asked innocently.

"They're fine. It's the other bullshit I have to deal with."

"The dead informant?"

"That's the one."

"Anything I can help with?" said the spider.

Harry thought for a minute before answering. "Okay, here's the deal. MI had a walk-in source that got whacked."

"Right." *He'd already told me this.*

"The CO of the previous MP unit really stepped on his dick."

"What'd he do, if I may ask?"

"Soldiers from his unit were supposed to babysit MI's source. But the assigned guys were the unit fuckups. They got lazy and let the source wander off. Suspect or suspects unknown, popped the source with a single rifle shot."

"Where was he killed?"

"Eagle Lake."

"Harry, the perimeter walls at Eagle Lake are too tall for a bad guy to get the high ground for a shot."

"I know. It had to be someone inside the wire that popped him."

"Do you know what was used?"

"Nope. Through and through. No recovered slugs. Had to be a rifle. The whole top of his head was taken off."

"Are his guards still around?"

"They got sent home after a serious grilling by everybody from their CO to CID. They're fucked. Their unit RIP'd about thirty days ago." Relief in Place, he meant.

"And then I walked right into this shitstorm. That IDF attack the other day really ramped up the pressure."

"How's that?"

"Someone—DIA, CIA, who the hell knows—just picked up some new SIGINT that one or several of the local nationals working on base were helping the insurgents, supplying targeting data for future IDF attacks." By the way, SIGINT stands for signals intelligence. It's basically eavesdropping on phone calls and radio traffic.

"Having bad guys inside the wire can't be a huge surprise to anyone, especially after last night's little dust up," I said.

"You heard about that?"

"My boss filled me in over oatmeal. There must be some likely candidates around here you can haul in and sweat."

"Not that easy. There are dozens, if not hundreds, working on this base. I can't grab 'em all."

"CID's got the handle on this, right?"

"Yeah, but I'm thinking it might not be their first team. A couple of regular Army enlisted types," Harry said. "I wished it was a couple of pissed off reservist cops with bad attitudes and zero patience just like you. But instead, I think we're stuck with the Apple Dumpling Gang."

As we crossed a canal separating Liberty from Victory, I spied the JEFF Lab on the left. I had business there, and CEXC was also nearby.

"Harry, can you drop me off at the JEFF Lab? I've got to pick up some paperwork."

"Sure, let me find a nice soft spot to push you out."

"Funny, but not nice." Harry pulled up in front of the lab.

Just as I popped the door handle, Harry turned to me. "Rick, I'm gonna need that frag soon. No bullshit phone calls, no excuses."

"You got it." Harry wasn't playing.

The side entrance took me by the CID office, so I peeked. Sure enough, two baby-faced NCOs were in the corner, one doing pushups while the other counted them off. That had to be the two Harry was describing. Not a good sign. I have it on good authority Columbo couldn't do a single pushup.

We were in trouble. More people were getting whacked than in an Agatha Christie novel, and these two goofs were having a push up competition. Let's start with why were they in the office? Big cases are not solved sitting at a desk. You have to get out there. Talk to people, task informants, look at evidence. Okay, maybe I was being a little judgmental. But probably not.

I turned back to the hallway in time to see Ryan Lee scoot by like a scalded cat. He saw me, but didn't even nod, aware that it was favor time again. I limped toward the desk, playing it for all it was worth. He still acted like he didn't see me.

I played the sympathy card again, wincing mightily as I shifted my weight. You have to go with what works.

Ryan jumped up in sudden empathy. "You okay, man? Let me get you a chair, partner." If I'd known how well this worked, I'd have gotten shot right before the LAPD captain's exam. I'd still be in LA instead of this dump.

"It's okay," I said. "I'm fine."

"Bullshit." He pulled a chair over. "Have a seat."

So, with a heavy sigh, I plopped down. My leg actually did hurt a bit.

Ryan pushed aside some sealed evidence bags holding what looked like chunks of scrap metal, blast frag, wiring, and circuit board, the usual crap they pick up around here.

He motioned to a bag. "This is what they recovered in the IDF attack. Looks like it came from a PLA Type 67 82mm mortar round."

"A gift from our creditors," I replied. We were picking up Chinese made, People's Liberation Army (PLA) ordinance all over Iraq, from 60mm mortars to 122mm rockets. The Chinese were gleefully selling tons of their murderous crap to the Iranians, who, in turn, smuggled it across the border to be used to kill our kids.

I reached in my pocket and pulled out the plastic bag holding Mohammed's letter and the plastic vial holding the frag. "Ryan, can you take a look at these?"

"Did you handle the letter?"

"Yeah. I had no clue what it was until I read it. Maybe you can still pull some prints?"

"Maybe." He seemed a little put out that I'd contaminated evidence. As I said, Ryan was a little tight-assed.

"You gonna book it in?" He put on his own gloves before taking it out of the bag.

"Ah, I hadn't planned on it."

Already examining the letter under a huge lighted magnifying glass, he looked up. "What d'you mean?"

"Well—" I hesitated. "I'm kind of looking at this on my own right now."

"What the fuck, Rick. You want to get me fired?"

"No, of course not. You and I go back a long way. I just need to keep this off the radar for a couple of days until I get it figured out." Ryan was a bit excited.

"Okay, say I lift some prints, then what? What if I match them to some Al Qaeda asshole? What do I say when someone asks where it came from?"

"I'm asking a huge favor, but I really need to sort this out first. I think the victim in the IDF attack sent me this letter, but I need to be sure. You pull his prints off it and—"

Then he looked at the frag. "What's this about?"

"They dug that out of me."

"You in trouble?"

"No." *Not yet, anyway.* "But I think I'm onto something big. I don't know yet just what, but I need time to flesh it out before I hand it over to CID."

Almost on cue, the Apple Dumpling team walked in, yapping about who they thought would make the *American Idol* finals. Wyatt Earp would be spinning in his urn. Ryan looked at me, and I looked at him. He knew. Sometimes it takes a cop.

"Okay, but you owe me."

I looked him in the eye and shook his hand. "Thanks, partner."

CHAPTER 6

SHOTS FIRED. OFFICER DOWN

I was walking back toward my CHU when my cell started buzzing again. *What now? Don't these people know I was wounded and needed my rest?*

"Yes, I answered firmly."

"Oh, sorry sir, it's Jason, uh, Specialist Baker. I just got off and was wondering if I could meet with you for a few minutes. Talk about police jobs."

Damn, I was pooped, but I couldn't put this kid off. He'd done me a solid.

"Sure, Jason, I'm near the Coalition Café. Meet me outside. We'll find a place to talk."

"Thank you, sir, I'll be there in five."

I found a picnic table under an awning. Jason arrived moments later.

"So, you want to know about being a cop?"

"Yes, sir. How to prepare, what's it really like."

I gave him my standard speech about preparation, what oral boards are looking for, and red flags to avoid. I advised him to pick an agency that had a robust investigative component, in the likely event he'd get tired of chasing taillights and want a real job. Then I told him a story.

"Jason, my dad was with LAPD before me. He pinned my badge on when I graduated the academy. It was a very big deal for him and me too. He worked headquarters Bunco Forgery. Basically, paper crimes. He was a supervising detective, a D-III. I was riding with my training officer Clarence 'Crusher' Jones. He was very big and wasn't afraid to take care of business when needed. We got a message to call the watch commander. Jones made the call. He returned after a few minutes. His voice broke as he spoke. 'Rick, your dad's been hurt. He's at UCLA.' At first, it didn't register. My dad didn't work a shoot 'em up squad. I was confused. Unbelieving. I asked if he had a heart attack? Was he okay? Jones said he didn't know. But he did."

I looked at Jason as I spoke those last words, his eyes and expression unflinching.

"We rolled from Newton to UCLA code three. I rushed into the ER and Dad's partner Tom Fallon was standing there, tears in his eyes. I froze, not wanting to believe. Not my dad. He was bulletproof."

I prepared myself, as if that's even possible. Tom said, 'I'm sorry Rick, your dad's gone.' Then he told me what happened. They stopped at a liquor store on Wilshire for a couple of Cokes for the ride back. Dad got out and went inside. He walked straight into a robbery in progress. Both suspects shot him, then ran out the front door. They ran straight into Tom, who dropped 'em both on the sidewalk. I later learned that Dad shot one of the assholes just before he died. Thank God both crooks were dead. I don't think I could have stood an LA murder trial."

"I'm telling you all this, because I want you to know that in police work, unlike most other professions, things can go to shit in a big hurry. Usually when you least expect it. You never know what's around the corner. Could be a kid who wants to give you a hug. Or an ex-con who's not going back to prison. God forbid you get in a shooting. It's a living hell, trust me, and it's the absolute last thing you ever want to do. Except, of course, getting shot yourself. The press and the lawyers are relentless. Then there's the brass. It's a reality of this business, and you need to know that before you start."

"Sir, with all you've been through already, why are you here?"

"After Dad's funeral, one of his old partners from patrol gave me a bear hug. Then he said, 'Rick, your dad used to say we're the only thing between the thugs and John Q. It's up to us to get 'em off the street. Rick, now it's up to you.'"

"I've never forgotten those words, and I guess it's why I'm here and not home learning to play golf."

"Yes, sir," Jason replied. "Thank you for speaking with me. Also, thank you, sir, for being here." We shook hands and Jason walked off.

CHAPTER 7

SHOTGUN WEDDING

finally made it back to my pad and stretched out for a nap. I was fried and was snoring in seconds.

So, there I was—me and Heidi Klum. Seal was on tour again and Heidi had slipped into something more comfortable, but just as things were getting interesting, I was brought back to reality by the sound of someone pounding on my door. The place seemed to rock with every blow as I pushed Heidi out of bed and jumped up. Shit, it was dark outside. Something told me I'd screwed up. I peeked out the window only to see Nancy staring back, none too pleased, again.

"You, okay?"

I fumbled with the door lock. It was dark. Nancy yanked open the door and flipped on the light, as my eyes slowly adjusted.

"Shit. Sorry. Guess I overslept. Sorry, really."

She gave me a hard look, then softened, switching into doctor mode. She felt my forehead and gave me the once over. Satisfied that I'd live, she smiled.

"Guess I was tired."

"You've been pushing yourself too much."

"Probably should save my strength and take more vitamins."

She grinned. "You're right," as she wrapped her arms tightly around me. "I took an oath to do no harm."

In that moment, I got my second wind. She smelled nice, better than me. Inhaling deeply, I held her close. "How'd you know I was here?"

"You snore worse than anyone I've ever heard. The window was vibrating."

"Maybe I need a doctor."

She kissed me deeply as I pressed her against the door, unzipped her blouse, and pushed it off her shoulders.

"Victoria's Secret?"

"Lands' End. Shut up."

Gentlemen, it's true what they say about doctors. Hell, after she was done with me, I'd have copped to kidnapping the Lindbergh baby and being on the grassy knoll.

We lay there for some time, our legs and arms intertwined. I'd pushed the room's crappy single beds together, but Four Seasons it was not.

I'd barely known this woman a week, and as I suspected, something more than multiple orgasms was developing between us.

As she drifted off, I lay still, watching her chest rise and fall with every breath. The outside lights provided just enough contrast to make out the lines of her face. God, she was beautiful, and so was the rest of her.

I awakened before Nancy. The sun had yet to rise, but we couldn't afford an embarrassing morning-after moment as we greeted the new dawn. As I leaned over to plant a gentle kiss on her forehead, her eyes opened, her mouth widened into a satisfied grin, and then she raised her arm to look at her watch.

"Shit. I gotta go."

When I leaned over to kiss her again, her mouth and body surrendered instantly.

Reluctantly, we threw on our clothes and stepped outside with me leading the way. After quickly surveying the walkway for prying eyes, I gave her a nod and she walked alongside me on the deserted path to the common area where only a few early risers were smoking and clowning around nearby a concrete shelter.

Just then a shrill incoming alarm split the air, and Nancy looked alarmingly at me seconds before we dove into a rapidly filling shelter. A second later came a whistling sound, and I curled up tight bracing for the impact. The blast was deafening. Even when surrounded by five or six inches of concrete and steel, I could feel the shock wave.

In the shelter with us was a senior-looking NCO, mumbling, "Fucking 122s." The rocket, likely of Chinese origin, had impacted the area near my CHU and was too close for comfort.

The CHUs were flimsy, modular trailer-like buildings lined up in double rows back-to-back. The whole area was surrounded by a T-wall, "Texas Barrier," which resemble highway dividers on steroids—ten or twelve feet of steel-reinforced concrete intended to shield buildings from incoming ground-based nasties and frag.

Another rocket struck close by the shower and latrine buildings. Overhead came a deafening explosion. The air defense system had bagged one before impact, giving us points on the board. Frantic yelling was heard from the hooches—the living quarters, on the other side of the wall, which was confirmation that some of the sleeping soldiers had survived the blast.

I straightened up in time to see Nancy jump out and dash toward the screams. Shit, I didn't want to follow, knowing all too well that another round could impact momentarily, and getting vaporized wasn't part of my retirement plan. As I pulled myself out and hobbled after her, Nancy was running down a breezeway separating the hooches from the T-walls, which were disappearing into a cloud of dust and smoke. Rounding the corner just seconds behind her, I stood in horror.

One hooch had been shattered, its roof and walls of adjacent CHUs were gone, and all that remained was fully engulfed in flames. The smoke was thick and black, and I could barely breathe. Nobody could have survived.

"Rick!" Nancy screamed, emerging from a smoke-filled doorway while carrying the blood-soaked body of a young female soldier. I cradled the girl's legs and waist as Nancy held her head and upper torso.

"I've got her," I said.

"Put pressure on the wound," Nancy ordered.

A sudden stream of blood was pulsing from the back of the young soldier's left thigh, and I squeezed down hard to force the gaping wound to close before we hustled her off to safety. A casualty assembly point was being set up near a large diesel generator, and we lay her down on the gravel just as someone shoved a web belt into Nancy's hands for her to use as a tourniquet. She checked the girl's vitals.

"She's still with us, Rick. Stay with her, I'm going back."

A sudden blast of flame and smoke erupted two hundred feet overhead. The CRAM gun had intercepted another incoming rocket. As I blinked away the effects of the flash, I saw Nancy sprawled on the ground face down. A baby-faced kid squatting next to me was carrying a first-aid bag. I looked the boy in the eye. "You got this?" He nodded.

"Keep her legs up," I shouted to the soldier while dashing to Nancy's side. She raised her head.

"Don't move!" I instructed her. "It's okay, I'm here."

Ignoring me, she pushed herself up and rested on her knees. "Knocked the wind out of me. I'll live."

I insisted she stay and catch her breath, but she wouldn't hear of it. The next thing I knew, she had jumped up and was gone.

Firetrucks arrived, and as I glanced back at the wounded girl and rushed to her side as two more soldiers ran up.

"We've got her covered!" said the medic, applying a dressing to the bleeding leg wound while his partner readied the IV.

Passing another knot of soldiers, I headed back to the inferno to search for Nancy. Casualties lay everywhere. One body was missing its upper torso, and then I saw Nancy who was working to get a badly mangled victim out of a wrecked hooch. I ran up and helped her carry another young female soldier to the collection point before I noticed the girl's scorched face. She was moaning. Setting her down on the waiting stretcher, Nancy went to work to save the girl's life.

Stepping back to watch, I saw blood dripping out of Nancy's right arm and onto the patient's chest and instinctively grabbed a combat dressing from an open-aid bag and placed it over her wound.

Her eyes never left her patient.

Soon, the place was swarming with medics and MPs, as the base fire department and soldiers made short work of the fires. Every hooch had a fire extinguisher, and by the time the trucks arrived many of the blazes had already been dowsed. A doctor I recognized squatted next to Nancy to examine her arm.

"Nice work," he said to me.

"Eagle Scout," I lied. Brother Mikey was the Eagle Scout in the family.

With nothing more left to do, since Nancy was busy and didn't need me hovering over her, I left and went straight to my office. I needed to check and see if the latest intel offered any clues as to the asshole responsible for the carnage. The place was deserted, and everything hit me. My blood-smeared hands started to shake, and my heart felt like it would leap from my chest. I remembered to inhale deeply and hold it for a moment, then exhaled and felt the stress begin to leave my body. Christ, I hated this fucking place. Nothing could have been prepared me for what I'd just seen. When I closed my eyes, I was haunted by that poor girl's burnt and battered face. Someone's daughter, girlfriend, wife, or maybe even somebody's mother. The sorrow and horror gave way to rage, and I wanted these fuckers. Time to hitch up my big-boy panties and get back in the game. Time to hunt.

It took about an hour of sifting through the bullshit before I came across some intel that showed promise. According to a recent cell signal intercept, a couple of guys had been overheard blabbing on their cell phones about a big wedding. One schmuck said he'd seen the wedding location and it was perfect. "Many people will be there." The intercept was local. The report didn't list the guys by name, just that they were both identified as Mahdi Army.

The Mahdi Army were a happy little group of Shia malcontents led by that party animal, Muqtada al-Sadr. During the eight-year war, they were recruited by the Iranians to combat Saddam, but ever since the change in management, they'd been operating from Basra in the south to the Baghdad suburb of Sadr City. I had read somewhere that they had about 60,000 members, depending on prevailing attitudes and the day of the week. Hezbollah, also a Shia group supported and directed by Iran, claimed to be a political and social welfare organization. However, until 9/11, they had killed more Americans than any other terrorist organization. The list of atrocities perpetrated by these terrorists was endless.

Terrorists use common words or phrases to disguise what they're really talking about, and one such word was "wedding," which had been associated with a planned attack. I needed to discover who they were and would need classified systems of information that would supply the details. These systems were kept in a secure area of our office, referred to as an SCIF—Sensitive Compartmented Information Facility. It is the repository of all the juicy secrets and is called the "High Side."

With full access to the systems, I still couldn't get into the SCIF after normal business hours and should have waited until it was opened by the facility security officer—the FSO. But, as my dear ol' mom used to say, "should" is a word for cowards. She was never one for waiting. Sometimes she broke a few glasses, but she always got things done. Mikey going to West Point was a classic example. She never rested until he got his appointment. You need something done, put a mom on it. Charlotte was the exact same.

I scanned the room. Clear. A long-retired Air Force senior NCO named Bill Yardley was our Facility Security Officer. The FSO was that humorless guy or gal responsible for securing the office's classified material and ensuring that only those with the secret handshake had access. He was also the guy who sent me nasty weekly notes when I left classified material on my desk. He did little after-hours desk inspections, and I kept him busy.

Bill, the guy who opens the SCIF each morning and shuts it down at night, was a little anal and somewhat forgetful. He especially had trouble with remembering the combination to the digital lock on the SCIF door. More than once, I'd seen him stare at that lock, wishing the buttons would push themselves. I'd seen him, many times, use a cheat sheet with all the lock codes and passwords. It had to be hidden somewhere in his work area, and now it was up to me to find it.

As a former law enforcement officer sworn to uphold the Constitution, protect the weak, and not tell lies, I'm embarrassed to admit that this was not my first stab at forced entry. That inaugural offense was in eleventh grade and involved a letter opener and the top drawer of a physics teacher's desk.

I didn't think this mission would require much brute force, just a little imagination and a wild-ass guess. Something I'm good at. After this morning's horrors, I needed a win.

I searched Bill's cubicle, methodically scanning every inch. If I was a cheat sheet, where would I be hiding? Under the blotter was too easy, but I gave it a shot anyway. The blotter was clean.

Then I spied it. *It* was named *Phyllis,* the love of Bill's life. He called her every day without fail. She was one scary looking woman, a latter-day Medusa but with big hair instead of vipers. Hiding the cheat sheet in that picture frame would be like keeping valuables in a rattlesnake's cage. Only the foolhardiest or blind would dare attempt entry.

I slid open the backing, and there it was. After copying down the combo, I replaced everything exactly as I'd found it. Then I went to work on the SCIF door lock, punching in the code and the lock clicked open.

I fired up a JWICS (Joint Worldwide Intelligence Communication System) terminal, a classified multi-agency intelligence sharing system, and entered my user ID and password. Using the correct date and time sequence code, I quickly was able to retrieve the original intelligence report on the cell call intercept, which also made for some interesting reading.

According to the report, the actual intercept was a week old to the day. Based on cell-site triangulation, the call was placed in a lovely little burg called "Yusufiyah." The number dialed was in or near some neighborhood named Al'Kharjia. Never heard of the place, though I'd been to Yusufiyah several times and was somewhat familiar with the local situation. The town was under Sunni control, but Shia elements also caused many a sleepless night for the local US Army commander and the Iraqi Army. A couple of quick open-source searches later and I'd learned that Al'Kharjia was a hood on the other side of the wall from the Eagle Lake area of VBC. Now that was interesting. Eagle Lake was near where the "walk-in" source got popped.

The Mahdi Army had a group of happy souls based in the area and could always be counted on to bring mirth and good cheer wherever they went. Usually, the mirth consisted of a buried 155mm artillery shell just waiting for some hapless American or Iraqi Army convoy to pass by. I made a few cryptic notes from the report, closed it. I needed to be careful since even my notes could be classified.

As I put my notebook away, I remembered the telephone number on the letter I'd opened the other day. I still needed to run that number to see if there was any reporting on it, but I had to be careful with this as well. If the number had been flagged by the Agency, or say DIA (Defense Intelligence Agency), I might have some serious explaining to do with a few humorless dudes across a table from me. It was risky, but so was taking a retirement job in Iraq. I threw caution to the wind and forged ahead.

I logged into another system and entered the number. Bingo. It came up in yet another intercept between known Mahdi Army associates based in the Yusufiyah area. One mope was named Ali Ahmed Al-Shahidi, the other was Khalid Al-Rashidi. A field trip was now definitely in order. I did some more searching and found some entries on Khalid Abu-Ali Al-Rashidi. Khalid was associated with insurgents responsible for two IED attacks targeting a local Sunni insurgent leader. Khalid had a small restaurant/haji shop in Yusufiyah, a wife, and three boys. There was also a report from the Los Angeles FBI Joint Terrorism Task Force that a guy named Khalid Al-Rashidi had met with a local guy possibly associated with Iranian intelligence, MOIS. The other guy, Al-Shahidi, was a zero.

I logged off the computer and shut off the lights, and in yet another case of impeccable timing, I closed the SCIF door just as George walked in. Thankfully, he was never early. Immediately, I shifted to my "I do this all the time look," which he wasn't buying.

"Rick, did Bill open up?"

"Ahh, not exactly."

"What were you doing?"

"Working, boss. But if I tell you—"

"Yeah, I know, but how'd you get in?"

"Phyllis."

"Bill's wife?"

"The very same."

He moved to where I was standing and saw the smiling Medusa on Bill's desk. "Was the code in that frame?"

"Yep."

"I warned him about that."

"So did I." I was trying to be helpful.

George grinned for a microsecond, then sobered up.

"I thought we talked about you cutting corners the other day."

"Yes, Dad, you got me there. I screwed up. But I was doing the Lord's work."

"Okay, so what did you learn? Anything related to this morning?"

Think fast, I had to give him something, but I didn't want to lay it all out yet.

"I found an intercept from a week ago. The bad guys were talking about a wedding, which I'd bet your paycheck was this morning's attack."

"How d'you know?"

"Timing. The words. It all fits." I explained the wedding day reference and room for lots of guests, and he got it.

"Who made the calls?"

"Some Mahdi Army dude to some asshole in Yusufiyah."

"Does the asshole in Yusufiyah have a name?"

"Khalid Omar Abu-Ali Al-Rashidi."

"You probably want to go there, right?"

"Please, Daddy, may I?"

He shook his head. "You're a real prick sometimes."

"My best quality."

"How's your leg?"

"I took it easy yesterday. It's fine now."

"I know you're probably lying, but after this morning . . . yeah, you can go, but proceed with caution. Do some of your famous detective magic." Then, he pulled out a small notebook from his front pocket and leafed through it. "I know the intelligence officer there, Chris Shore. Very sharp. The new CO is Captain Larry Clark. I think he may even be a cop back in the world. Another broken toy, just like you."

"Funny." He knew me too well. He saw the look I was trying desperately to hide.

"Don't worry, Rick, us amateurs won't fuck this up for you. Just be careful and stay off the radar and take care of that leg."

"Can I borrow your M4?"

His expression soured as he considered my request, and then reached behind his desk and handed it over along with his magazine carrier.

"Five loaded mags. Don't shoot anybody with it, or we'll all be in the shit."

"I'll be good. I promise."

"Fuck you. Talk to the ops officer and have him set up a flight. And Rick, no more SCIF bullshit. If it's closed, you wait. Clear?"

"Roger that, boss." I stopped and turned to George. "What I saw this morning. The kids. The blood. We gotta do something."

"I know," George replied. "We gotta stop these attacks. Whatever it takes."

It had been an hour and a half since I left Nancy, so I headed back to my housing area to secure the M4 carbine in my CHU. The fire department and MPs were still on scene, as were a ton of Army types. As you'd expect, the place was a mess.

My cell started buzzing. It was General Mikey.

"Rick, you okay?"

"Yeah, I'm fine, but they hit the housing area where I stay. It was bad. We lost some kids."

"I know," Mikey replied, his voice filled with barely controlled rage.

"It was some damn good shooting. Direct hits on a couple of hooches and a latrine," I observed. "They knew what they were doing."

"You're fine, right?"

"Yeah, Mike, I'm fine."

"Rick, where are you now? We need to talk."

I looked around for a landmark. I was next to the Victory PX. What does he want? Sounded like I was being called to the principal's office.

"By the Victory PX."

"I'm sending a car over. Black Suburban."

"I'll be in the red chiffon."

"Do you ever stop?"

"No."

"He's leaving now," baby bro replied tersely, and then, *click*.

I figured he must have gotten wind of something, but what? Nancy? My sleuthing? What's the worst that can happen? They send me home?

As I stood in the parking lot waiting for my chariot to arrive, I did what all cops do. I started taking in the sights and looking for bad guys. I scanned the half-tent, half-building that housed the PX. I studied the ever-vigilant private security guys guarding the front door. They were all from Uganda and were generally wonderful folks. They always had a smile and loved it when you called them by name. The rack of brand-new bikes outside the back door were covered in dust and crap, a clear indication they'd been in the elements for about two to three hours. It doesn't take long for the local fairy dust to accumulate.

My gaze shifted to the local jewelry store next door. The guys who ran the store were not the usual rug merchants full of compliments and phony grins, but I couldn't recall any of those jokers smiling. Overall, I rated them a pretty humorless bunch. Mainly they sold cheap wedding ring sets and gangsta bling, what we used to call a "Mr. T starter kit." Today, kids would look at you like you were part of a Klingon delegation if you used that phrase.

I saw one of the happy bling merchants step outside with the classic felony look to make sure the coast was clear. The guy was the younger of the three dudes that ran the place, tall and thin, about twenty-eight to thirty-years old, and wore a white kufi skull cap. It's hard to describe, but after thirty years of chasing turds you can recognize a floater pretty quickly. I casually glanced in his direction and then slowly turned away, positioning myself to see his reflection in the window of a nearby parked car. It was probably nothing, but what the hell.

I watched as the kid went back in. Looking at the reflection, I could see through the open front door that he was talking to that guy whom I always pegged as the Head Motherfucker in Charge. Mr. HMFIC had a full gray beard and was wearing a matching white thawab and kufi as he stood behind the jewelry counter, checking his watch every few seconds. He looked pretty amped. I watched as he really lit the kid up, screaming and flailing his arms in the air. After another minute or two, Mr. HMFIC moved out of my view toward the back of the store. I looked at my watch and noted the time: 1030 hours. My stomach rumbled.

The kid closed the front door, ruining my view into the store. Suspecting that my presence may have spooked them a bit, I moved to a different spot across the street near a canal that was further away but less likely that I'd be spotted.

I glanced up to see a pair of Blackhawk helicopters land over near the palace, and riding shotgun overhead was a pair of Apache attack helicopters. Then I spun around and saw the back of an Army uniform enter the shop. Probably some love-sick GI about to blow his pay on his girl back home who's already banging the neighbor guy.

Holy shit! That white Chevy SUV with the storage container on the roof was now parked next to the shop. Though I couldn't see the plate to confirm, it had to be the same one. My phone started buzzing. Shit.

"Rick."

"Hey, it's me." No mistaking that voice.

"Hey me, how are you? I've been worried."

"It was horrible. I've never seen anything that bad before. We lost the girl you helped me with."

"I'm sorry."

"Where'd you go?"

"I went to my office and did a little research."

"We've got to find these fuckers."

"I'm on it."

"How?" she asked.

Okay, stud, now you've done it. You've opened your trap.

"I've been working on some things since the first attack."

"Like what?"

"Like we can't talk on a cell about it."

"Where are you?"

"Across from the PX."

"I need to see you." *Click.*

Great. She'll show up about the same time the war wagon arrives. Glancing back at the store, I saw the closed sign in the window and could just make out the GI still inside. I could see HMFIC and the GI talking. The GI handed something to HMFIC. I wished I had my little point-and-shoot camera. I used to carry it all the time, then FSO Bill Yardley got all stressed about it. Cameras were *verboten* in a secure facility.

A shiny black SUV war wagon pulled directly into my line of vision just as things were getting interesting. It reminded me of doing surveillance with untrained detectives, or even some Feds. To be fair, effective surveillance requires a great deal of specialized training and vehicles. Your average local detectives and street agents simply don't get the opportunity or much training.

I moved to reestablish my eye on the shop, but no luck. The Suburban driver waved me over. It was Command Sergeant Major Royce O. Galloway. This guy was a living legend in the Army. Nobody, but nobody, messed with CSM Galloway. He'd seen combat at the end of Vietnam, then Grenada, Desert Storm, and other places that no one talks about. He started in the infantry, then moved to the 75th Ranger Regiment, then to an Army Special Mission Unit that nobody talks about. Now he worked for General Mikey at 3rd Infantry Division.

When I climbed into the passenger seat, Nancy pulled up. We made eye contact. I tried to covertly wave her off. No go. I looked back over at the shop. The SUV was still there, but I could no longer see the GI.

"Sergeant Major, I gotta jump out for a second." *He's not gonna like this*, I thought. Command sergeant majors wait for no man, but I got out and walked over to her.

"You hung up before I could tell you. I've got a meeting at 3rd ID."

"Oh. Sorry." She looked at the CSM whose attention was apparently elsewhere.

Then she whispered, "Can I see you tonight?"

"Sure."

"I need to talk with you. I blew it today and a kid died."

Reflexively, I started to reach out to her, then stopped dead in my tracks and glanced at the CSM. His eyes were fixed on us.

"I'll call you later."

When I got back into the car the white SUV was gone. So was the GI.

CHAPTER 8

BAD BOYS

I t was a quiet ride to HQ 3rd ID. That was just as well for me. Lately, the more I talked, the worse it got. Silence was golden. We pulled up in front and stopped. CSM Royce O. Galloway looked at me in the rearview mirror. "Be careful."

"What do you mean?" I responded lamely.

He chuckled briefly and said, "Tell them I went to chow." Then he drove off.

I clipped on my badge and signed in at the front desk. I walked up the stairs to the Ivory Tower and was immediately greeted by Mike's chief of staff, Colonel Bob Torchirelli. He was a short Italian-American dude who grew up a block over from Mulberry Street in Little Italy. I'd been there once myself and found the food disappointing except for a famous cannoli shop that had a line going out into the street.

From the looks of him, I doubted Colonel Torchirelli ever ate cannolis. The guy was about five-seven and looked like a steel *I* beam with a uniform stretched over it. No one I know could give an ass chewin' like Bob, except for one. That, of course, would be baby bro.

"Hey, Rick, good to see you."

I winced as he crushed my hand. He had the grip strength of a dozen pit bulls. I recovered my composure and said, "Hi." He politely asked about the leg, but really didn't give a shit. Neither did I.

"The General will see you shortly."

I almost said, "Who you callin' Shortly?" but thought better of it. Sometimes I'm capable of discretion. I know, it's amazing.

The door of Mike's presence chamber flew open as a clearly savaged Lt. Colonel Harry Arnold skulked out. Harry gave me the "I'm too old for this shit" look as he passed by. That can't be good.

"Rick, get your sorry ass in here."

I walked into a brotherly bear hug that nearly crushed what was left of my sagging frame.

The door closed behind me with a thud. *No escape.*

As you might guess, Mike's office was pretty cool. The usual soldier crap on the walls—plaques, flags, and swords. I took a seat in a very comfy overstuffed leather sofa. He took the chair opposite. On the wall across the room was a photo of our dad in his LAPD uniform flanked by Mikey and me in our little cowboy outfits. Next to it was a photo of us in our respective uniforms standing behind Mom as she received the flag at Dad's funeral.

"How's the leg? Don't you have a crutch or something?"

"Don't need it. The leg's fine."

"Coffee?"

"Sure, black."

"I heard from the boys. They said they spoke with you."

Mikey handed me a steaming mug full of mud and sat back down. "Mom sent me an email. She thinks you should come home. She was never crazy about both of us being over here. But now with your injury—"

"Mom needs to relax. How the fuck did she find out? Did you call her?"

"I told her. She watches the news. Better to hear it from me than CNN. Don't worry, I told her you were fine. Just a cut."

"Mom watches Fox. I was going to call her myself. Now she's all amped up."

Mike ignored my last comment. "Rick, I think she's right. You've got kids at home. You're a retired cop, not a soldier. After what happened to Dad, if Mom lost one of us, it would kill her." I started to respond, but he held up his hand to stop me.

"Rick, you've been lucky twice. There may not be a third time."

"Twice? What do you mean twice?"

"This morning."

"Oh, yeah," I said. But I hadn't even thought about it that way. Don't ask me why. My mind now flashed to the fresh images of burned and shredded young people.

"Rick, I'm going to set up a new gig for you with Joint IED Defeat back home. You've done great work here, but there's nothing more for you."

"You done?" I replied tersely.

"Yes." Mikey stiffened in his chair. This was gonna get ugly.

"Okay then." I wanted to rip him a new one, but instead took a more evolved approach. "Mike, I understand your concern. You're right. This war shit is your world. But I'm not exactly new to getting shot at either. Not to mention at least five on-duty crashes that I can remember. Thanks for your concern, but I'm not going anywhere."

Mikey's expression hardened.

"As for Mom, she's a pain in the ass, and you know it. She's got more opinions than a room full of lawyers. Most of them are wrong and the rest are dumb."

Mike checked a grin. He knew I was right.

"You've got some big problems around here. Dead informant, two IDF attacks, wandering snipers. I've been watching your sleuths at work, and in my professional opinion, you're well and truly fucked. Christ, they'd step over Charlie Manson to pick up a broken AK-47 or pop a couple of GIs for screwing. The rules have changed, and you guys can't blow shit up anymore. You have to play cops n' robbers now and make nice-nice with locals. That's why you need guys like me. I'm no soldier, but I sure as shit know how to catch bad guys."

Mike sat stone-faced. I knew I'd have him with the dead informant comment. *But he'll shit if he knows there are two dead informants.*

It was a bit unnerving. Generals usually don't respond well to lectures by dipshit civilians. But to his credit, bro kept his cool and didn't toss me out the window.

Mikey held up his hand. "I've already started the process to rotate you home. That's it, you're done."

I got up without another word. *We'll see about that, baby bro.*

I hitched a ride back to my office. George was waiting for me. I was not going to tell him the truth about my meeting with Mikey.

"How's the general?"

"How'd you know I saw him?"

"They called looking for you."

"To answer your question, the general is generally good, but full of shit as usual."

"I suppose you helped him out." George smiled.

"That's me."

"Your buddy at the JEFF Lab was looking for you. Seemed kind of excited."

"I'll call him."

"You're booked on the Iron Express flight day after tomorrow at 0630. I've arranged a ride to the pad for you. Your return is open."

"Thanks, boss. Now if you'll excuse me, I've got some work to do."

I needed to pull a rabbit out of my ass if I was to change Mikey's mind. I walked into the SCIF and sat. I needed to get some background on my victim/pen-pal Mohammed.

I did some typical inquiries in JWICS and got zip. This guy was a black hole. Then I hit something. According to a certain agency's reporting, Mohammed was the cousin of Ali Bin Omar Mosedeh, a Mahdi Army honcho based in the Triangle of Death. Mosedeh escaped to Iran during the eight-year Iran-Iraq war and was recruited into the Pasdaran, also known as the Islamic Revolutionary Guard Corps (IRGC). Their proper name is the Guardians of the Islamic Revolution.

The IRGC controls the religious police known as the Basij, the missile forces, ground forces, smuggling, and border control. The infamous Quds Force was a Special Operations unit that is part of the IRGC. The Quds Force—part spy, part commando, and all asshole. Their specialty was blowing up embassies, marketplaces, schools, and other places where the naive and unsuspecting congregated like lambs awaiting slaughter.

Mohammed's relationship to Mosedeh could have given him access to some juicy intel on Mahdi Army Operations. Who knows what Mosedeh may have shared with him? It was all starting to make sense. Mohammed probably got whacked because he was suspected of being a snitch and maybe was even involved. Mosedeh could also be face down in a ditch.

My honey-do list was getting longer by the minute. Besides going to Yusufiyah to talk to this Khalid guy, I needed to sniff around for intel on my victim, Mohammed. I logged out of JWICS and went back to my desk. I plopped down, and someone yelled that my phone had rung a couple of times. That was unusual; I never get calls at my desk, at least I think I don't, and there's a reason for that . . .

You see, the Army didn't believe in voicemail, so you could call me until your finger fell off, and if no one was there to answer, you'd be wasting your time. I once mentioned this to George and he replied, "In the Army E-3s and E-4s are answering machines." Okay, I guess if it works for them. That's why I rarely bothered to hand out my desk number. Ryan Lee was one of the chosen few who had it.

I called Ryan at the JEFF Lab. He answered halfway through the first ring. Guess he was waiting for me.

"Ryan, it's me."

"What took you? I called an hour ago."

"Army BS."

"We need to talk," Ryan replied tersely.

"Okay, let's."

"Not on this line. Meet me outside the Oasis DFAC in ten."

"It will take me more—"

Shit, he hung up on me. There was no way I could get over there in ten minutes. I limped over to George's office. He was gone. I grabbed his keys and left him a sticky note. He loved it when I did that.

I jumped into George's standard issue dusty white Ford Ranger and took off. Just as I was crossing over a small bridge spanning a canal, my cell buzzed.

"Hello," I said tersely.

"Well, screw you too."

Oops. It was Nancy. She sounded fried and a bit pissed off. Note to self: *Never sleep with a pissed-off doctor.* Size could end up being the least of your problems.

"Sorry," I offered.

"Okay. I really need to talk to you."

"I'm on my way to a meeting. Shouldn't take long."

I didn't want to tell her I was going to meet with the JEFF Lab probably about the piece of frag she dug out of me. That could stir up other shit I didn't need.

We agreed to meet in an hour at Green Beans.

I arrived at the Oasis in eight minutes. Just as I got out, my phone went off again.

"Rick, where is my car?"

"Sorry, boss, I had to run over to the lab."

"I've got a meeting at the Provost Marshal's Office at 1600. I'll need it back before then." The time on my phone read 1430.

"No problem."

I really need wheels of my own. I'm a very busy guy.

I spied Ryan. Puffing away. There were three burned cigs at his feet. Someone was a little stressed.

"Hey, what's up?"

"What's up? What's up? That piece of frag. That's what's up."

"Okay. Tell me."

"First off. The frag looks US. Probably 120mm mortar."

"How do you know?" Stupid question. He's the science guy. Of course, he knows.

"The dimensions fit the 120's profile. We also found some other pieces that also fit. Oh, by the way, my boss knows."

Well, that's not good. I tried to keep my cool James Bond-like demeanor, but inside I was screaming. If he fessed up to his boss, an even tighter-assed prick than my office's FSO, we were truly screwed. No kisses or foreplay. Just a simple bend over and grab 'em, San Quentin style.

"How'd he find out?"

"Saw me doing some research and started asking questions. I've put him off. Got maybe twenty-four hours while I do the report."

A day wasn't much. But I really had more than that. It could take weeks for the Army to really start sniffing around. As soon as word got out, the Army would go into defense mode and order some investigation. That would be worth a couple of days while they figured out who was going to get the handle. Then they had to staff it and have meetings to plan meetings. Then there were the endless PowerPoints. You get the picture? Besides, no one would be apt to make any snap decisions when the *e-word* was in play. A premature decision that could cause more *embarrassment* to the Army would be a career ender. Nothing to panic about yet.

"Okay, we've got time," I said in my most reassuring voice.

Then he dropped the real bomb.

"Fuck time! We've got bigger problems than that." Ryan paused. "Based on your piece of frag, plus others we got, the mortar rounds were probably laser guided."

Okay, I wasn't exactly sure of all the ramifications of that last tidbit, but I was sure it wasn't good. Besides the obvious risk to Ryan and yours truly, this latest revelation could be a showstopper. Laser guided meant that there had to be someone on base with a laser-designator unit. This device projected a laser beam at the intended target, which the incoming mortar round would home in on. As long as the target was "painted" with a laser beam you couldn't miss.

Since Gulf War Round One, everyone, including Saddam, had gotten a lesson on how lethal these things could be, meaning that the insurgents had access to some state-of-the-art stuff. The Army didn't just have these things lying around everywhere. So, what was the source?

Ryan said, "The round was probably an M-395 precision-guided mortar round. There are only a few in country."

"How do we know this isn't some knock off made in Shanghai?"

"We don't yet. I've been looking at some of the other frag from the scene. It was all Chinese 81mm stuff."

"So, they used two types of mortars. Why?"

"Maybe to make it look more like a conventional mortar attack and cover the real purpose."

"This means my guy in the hooch was probably murdered. Otherwise, why bother to use two different types of rounds?"

Ryan looked up at me a little more wild-eyed than before.

"Murdered?"

I couldn't hold out on him now. I explained my theory that he was murdered before the mortar attack.

"Rick, why are you running with this? We need to run this up the chain."

"Slow down, we still have time. Besides, if anyone falls, it will be me."

I stroked Ryan's stressed out feathers a little more, and soon he crawled back from the ledge.

"Okay, I'll drag my feet on this a bit more. I also need to do a metallurgy test to confirm it's ours," Ryan offered.

My gut told me it wasn't gonna be ours. Then it hit me. *Laser guided? Shit.* The two dudes in the white SUV. Could they have had some kind of laser designator? Did they guide the round into Mohammed's hooch? What about this morning?

CHAPTER 9

RED LEG

still had time before George needed his car, so I drove over to Green Beans. Nancy was already there, her red eyes fixed on a cup of herbal tea. She forced a smile.

"You want anything?" I asked.

"I'm good," she said.

I walked up to the counter and ordered a latte.

Drink in hand I joined Nancy. I could see tiny drops of blood on the tops of her desert boots. She looked exhausted.

"I lost that girl." Her voice cracked. "The first one this morning."

"Damn. I'm sorry. But you can't blame yourself. You did everything you could."

"Rick, I screwed up. She was in surgery when I got there. The other docs were busy, so I scrubbed and took over the case. I fucked up, and now she's gone."

I'd known Nancy both professionally and personally for several days now, and I knew there was more to this story. The room was empty except for the MPs and bunch of Aussies swapping lies in the far corner. The

Indonesians working the espresso machines wouldn't notice or care, so I put my hand on hers.

"You didn't fuck up. If anyone could have saved her, it was you. No doubt in my mind."

She shook her head and moved her hand away.

"Not here," she whispered.

What can you say at a time like this? I wisely decided to let her vent.

"I ordered some pain meds for her and she went into cardiac arrest. I should have checked."

"Was she conscious? How could you know?"

"She was in-and-out. Third degree burns all over her chest and legs, lacerations from frag and glass, blood loss. She was screaming. I gave the order. She started to calm down. Then she arrested."

Tears streamed. I needed to change the subject and get her mind off this. Maybe she fucked up, maybe she didn't. I'm no doctor, but I did know torturing herself over it would do no good.

"Come on, let's get out of here. I need to talk to you."

We walked over to my ride. Well, George's ride.

"Look Dad let me borrow the car."

She got in without a word. I kept my trap shut until we pulled over to a somewhat shady spot on the road to Eagle Lake.

"By the way, you were right. That guy who died in his hooch the other day, Mohammed. He was murdered. I've been doing some sniffing around. I also think there is someone on this base who is helping with these mortar attacks, and Mohammed knew who it was."

I had her full attention.

"I can't prove it yet, but it's looking good. I'm going to Yusufiyah day after tomorrow to talk to a guy."

"I'll come with you. I've got to go there to do an inspection of their med shop."

Great, now she wants to come along and play detective with me.

"Sure, that would be great. But can you get a seat on the bird?"

"What are you on?"

"Iron Express 0630."

"At the Victory Pad?"

"Yep."

"Okay, I'll see you then. Sorry, I'm not feeling very social right now. I'll call you later."

I drove her to her hooch in the Red Leg housing area. I pulled into a turn out and stopped. Nancy turned away from me and wiped a tear. She was hurting bad. Time for more distractions.

"Can I ask you a question?"

"Sure what?

"This is probably the wrong time, but why are you with me? I'm just a broken-down old cop with a piss-poor attitude and ready wit. You, on the other hand, are a beautiful, talented Army officer who, by the way, is also a hell of a doctor."

"Thank you, but I'm not such a great doctor."

"No, I believe you are. I saw you in action. It was awe-inspiring." It truly was. She should get a medal for the courage she showed.

Nancy smiled sweetly and squeezed my hand.

"I guess you remind me of my dad and brother." She sighed before continuing. "Mom died of breast cancer when I was seven. Dad was a sergeant running a narcotics team. Despite the demands of his job, he was always there for us. He was really *mister sergeant mom*." She paused. "I overheard you talking to your boys the other day. Your tone, your words. It was as if I was hearing my father speak to us. You have many of his qualities, including the lame jokes."

Mission accomplished. Now for a final distraction. A completely unrelated stupid civilian question.

"Okay, Major Weaver, one final question. What is a Red Leg?"

"Artillery."

"Artillery?"

"Red is for artillery, yellow is cavalry, and light blue is infantry. Each branch has its own color. Artillery guys used to have a red strip running down the seam of their uniform pants. Hence Red Legs."

"So, it's an Army tradition thing."

"Yep, that's it." Then she gave me that "How can you be so stupid?" look all men cherish.

My route back to the office took me past the PX jewelry store. I slowed as I drove past. Nada. I did a lap around the block. Still nothing, but I had a feeling and needed to call George. *I'm gonna need his car for a while longer.*

"Armstrong."

"George, I need your truck for a couple more hours. I think I'm onto something."

"What ya got?"

"I can't say on the phone, but I think I'm getting close to unraveling this thing. I've got to watch a place for a bit. See if my hunch is right."

"Shit, this is going to screw me up. Okay. Just be careful and keep me informed. By the way, General Sutherland's office called while I was out. Any idea what it was about?"

"Yes, I do. Stall him."

CHAPTER 10

WRONG TURNS

I drove back to the PX area and parked across the street next to some vehicles belonging to 273rd Engineers. From this spot, I held the jewelry shop and the PX parking lot. No binoculars or a camera, but I'd make do. I was going to give it a couple of hours.

After three, I was bored out of my mind and soaked with sweat even with the AC running full blast. Time to leave. I put the little truck into reverse. My phone started buzzing.

"Yeah."

"It's George. Some light bird named Arnold just left looking for you. It's about that frag again."

"Yeah, I know. George, I need a—" At that exact moment, I saw a white SUV drive by. It looked right.

"George, something's happening, I gotta go."

"Rick what's going—" I tossed the cell on the seat next to me, shifted into drive, and sped through the lot looking for a way out. The SUV was heading southwest toward the Coalition Café. I cut through a breezeway between buildings, only to be greeted by several parked Husky mine clearing vehicles. I threw the truck in reverse and punched it, kicking up a huge cloud of dust. I got on an access road, pressed the gas and after a few moments, I found a driveway and pulled onto the street, accelerating as I blew past my BFFs at the 633rd MPs.

My quarry was gone. I played a hunch that took me past the Coalition Café. I was right. The SUV, now empty, was parked in the transient tent area. I parked about 100 meters away and sat. I didn't have long to wait. Two guys dressed in ACUs jumped in the SUV and took off.

I pulled in behind them. It was the right car, "8008." I had to watch my speed in this area. The MPs worked radar and would like nothing more than to add my scalp to their collection. I'd been stopped twice.

I followed the SUV around the Baghdad Airport ring road, through a couple of security check points, over to a housing area on Camp Stryker. They parked and disappeared on foot behind a row of T-walls. I settled in. Ten minutes later, they were on the move again. Straight to the Stryker chow hall. I parked about fifty yards away. It was nearly dark. I checked my watch; Mickey said it was 1800hrs. I needed a better look at these two mopes.

They entered the DFAC together. I waited about five minutes and then walked in, grabbing a tray as I scanned the room. One had his food and was getting a soda, the other had his back to me in the hot chow line. I got in line and watched. Soda boy kinda looked like the guy I'd seen in the jewelry shop. The other guy glanced in my direction, giving me a chill. It was the same guy who eye-fucked me in his driver's side mirror the day of the first attack. This was big juju.

I grabbed some fried shrimp and fries and went over to a tall refrigerator with glass doors. I used the reflection in the doors to get a better look at them. No doubt about it, it was the same guy who eyeballed me that day. Soda boy was absolutely the dude I'd seen in the shop, and I was pretty confident the guy who had been in the back seat. He probably ran the laser designator while the other guy drove. A regular Frick and Frack team.

I picked a crowded table across the room that gave me a good angle. My phone went off. It was George. I was doing the Lord's work, so I let it go. I ate slowly as I watched. My phone buzzed again: *George. Shit!* I had to get it this time.

"Hey, what's up?"

"What's up with you?"

"I'm at the Stryker DFAC."

"General Sutherland's office called again."

"Why?"

"Didn't say, but some colonel named Torchirelli didn't sound happy. Said he needed you to call back ASAP."

"Fuck him, I'm busy."

"Fuck him? No, Red Rider, fuck you. Your doing-it-your-way bullshit stops now! I don't give a shit if you're watching Bin Laden build a bomb. Get your ass back—"

Right on cue Frick and Frack got up and headed for the exit.

"George, they're moving again. I'm gonna call you as soon as I can. Out."

"Goddammit, Rick! No."

I slowly headed for the exit. I hated being rude to George. Mikey knew me and probably expected it. I didn't care what Torchirelli thought.

I stepped outside into darkness. The light above the door was out and Frick and Frack were gone. Following two crooks with one retired lieutenant of defectives really sucked. Back home, we'd have at least one, possibly two full surveillance teams and a bird in the air to do it right. Following a pair of crooks with one old guy at night was nearly impossible and damn dangerous.

I walked down a breezeway only to run smack dab into Frack, or was it Frick? He bumped into me and moved past with a mumbled, "Sorry." *That ain't good.*

He was obviously checking their tail and I just got burned. I moved on by replying, "No worries, man," as casually as I could. My semi-arrhythmic heart was now nearly pounding out of my hairless chest.

The truck's dome light illuminated my face as I got in, so I pulled the bulb. Then the damn phone started vibrating again. I turned it off and tossed it on the seat.

I waited a minute before I pulled out of the parking lot, keeping an eye on the white SUV as I drove. I could see only one occupant. I made a left onto the main drag, drove about two hundred meters, blacked out, and pulled into a lot facing the street. From my position, I held both DFAC's driveways. I pulled out a magazine and loaded my pistol, chambering a live round. I flipped the safety up into the ready-to-party position and slid it under my right thigh. I didn't expect trouble, but in the words of a beloved old sergeant of mine, call sign "SAM-12," "If you're always prepared, you never have to get ready."

I sat there for about thirty minutes before the SUV started moving again. They pulled out onto the street and backtracked toward the Stryker housing area. The passenger got out, disappearing behind a T-wall. The SUV then took off at a pretty good clip. I was now faced with a choice: do I follow the passenger on foot and risk another face-to-face meeting? Or should I follow the SUV? I chose the latter.

I could just make out his taillights about two hundred meters in front of me. He was stopped at an internal checkpoint and showed his ID card. I made a mental note to have the records pulled for this checkpoint and the mess hall. I had three Humvees and a MRAP, Mine Resistant Ambush Protected, vehicle for cover, which, by the way, is a whole lot of cover. With all this iron in front of me, it made it hard to keep an eye on the crook. The SUV pulled forward and made a sudden right. The little convoy of Humvees I was following did the same. I relaxed for a second, feeling like this may work.

We continued for about a mile and then stopped at another checkpoint. I pulled a little to the left, giving me the slightest glimpse of my crook. He pulled forward and now out of my view. Then the convoy in front of me was waved through and I regained a visual, just barely. He negotiated a set of staggered concrete barriers and then pulled onto a four-lane divided highway, with a wide sandy median and tall sound barrier walls on both sides of the road.

I slowly pulled out onto the highway, giving him a chance to build some distance. I was so focused on the crook that it took me a few seconds to realize I'd never been on this road before. Not surprising given the size of Victory Base Complex.

I could still make out the crook car a couple of car lengths ahead of the convoy as we motored along. Then, for some reason, the convoy pulled over to the right and stopped. My cover was now gone. I drove past glancing at the driver of the lead vehicle. He and his top gunner gave me a very funny look. *Okay.*

The white SUV accelerated to what looked like seventy miles per hour, way faster than I'd ever seen anyone drive on base. I glanced over at the high walls on my right. I could make out the tops of what looked like Iraqi apartment buildings. Then I passed a mosque on my left.

My gut tightened and my asshole slammed shut as I realized I'd just driven off the base and was now on the infamous "Baghdad Airport Road," also known as Route Irish. My pucker factor was now redlined.

Being a civilian outside the wire in an unarmored pickup truck with nothing more than a 9mm pistol and a middle finger could also get you killed pretty quickly. Or if you're really not lucky, you could get kidnapped, tortured, star in your very own propaganda video, and then killed.

As far as I could tell, we were the only two vehicles on the road. A streak of green tracers arched skyward from just on the other side of the wall. *Probably just happy fire at some wedding or birthday celebration,* I assured myself. The natives were restless, and I was up Ali's creek with a tennis racket for a paddle. This might be exactly the kind of thing General Mikey had been lecturing me about. I was completely alone following a no-shit bad guy onto his own very deadly turf.

The SUV's brake lights came on as he made a sudden left crossing over Airport Road and into what looked like a Baghdad neighborhood. I checked out my rearview and could see the convoy moving slowly back in the distance. Maybe I could get help from them. But, more likely, they would only be there to recover my bullet-riddled body.

I did a slow drive by where the crook had turned and saw him stopped, standing by his car. He turned around and looked right at me as I drove past. Then he jumped back in his vehicle and took off.

I'd seen enough. Time to get out of dodge. I looked for a place to turn around. There was none. I could see an overpass in the distance.

Beyond it loomed deepest, darkest, and meanest Baghdad. It was a point of no return. I looked in my rearview again. No convoy. They must have stopped again. *Shit!*

I slowed and looked at the center median. I had to cross it. It was my only way back. I dropped the manual transmission into first gear and made a hard left, headed for the sand. I could feel my front wheels bog down as the little Ford struggled for control and traction. I pressed the throttle and tried to power across. The front wheels bit into the sand and made a hard left as the ass end started to spin round. I fought hard to straighten the wheels. Then I spied a set of headlights approaching fast. It was the SUV. I saw a muzzle flash from the driver's side. Instantly, a puff of sand kicked up on my left.

I backed off the gas slightly, then punched it again, hoping this would free me. Nothing. Then I heard a metal ping on the tailgate. He was getting the range. It wouldn't be long now.

I muscled the wheel to the right and prayed. The Almighty must have looked up from his beer because the front wheels straightened out and the rear wheels finally got full traction. I glanced in the mirror only to see more flashes from the SUV. Two more pings sounded behind me. Then another. I felt a thump in the car seat. The glovebox door popped open. There was now a fresh hole in the seat about two feet to my right and a matching one in the glove box door. The papers inside the box were smoldering from the tracer's impact. I ducked, as if that would have done me any good. He was zeroing in for the kill.

The front end of the Ranger lurched upward as the little pickup jumped the curb and got back on pavement. I shifted out of first and into third as I gained speed. I was now heading back toward VBC.

I could still see the SUV. He was closing fast, but for some reason had stopped shooting. This was going to terminal in a hurry. I felt for my pistol and verified that the safety was still off. Then I looked up and saw the little convoy had merged over to the left lane, opposite me. I was suddenly blinded by a spotlight from the lead vehicle. I accelerated and pulled to the right, continuing back toward VBC. A second light from the vehicle's top turret lit up the white SUV. I watched as it slammed on its brakes and made a U-turn. I had to concentrate on finding an off-ramp that would lead me back to the base. I stole a glance in the mirror, just in time to see the SUV make a left back into a Baghdad neighborhood. *Whew. Damn, that was way too close.*

I slowed and heard a loudspeaker as my car was once again bathed in white light. I was being ordered to pull over in both English and Arabic. Since I had at least one .50 caliber machinegun, plus numerous other nasties pointed at me, I promptly complied.

The vehicles lined up in echelon, with guns and spotlights trained on me. I jumped out, hands raised in the air, with my back to them. I wanted them to see that I posed no threat. I stood there, heart pounding. They ordered me to walk backwards toward them.

"Stop. Now get on your knees facing away from us." I complied instantly. *I know how this is done.*

"Is anyone else in the truck? Is there a weapon in the truck?"

"Yes and no." Then I clarified. "No one else is in the truck. My pistol is on the front seat."

Four soldiers approached my truck and gave it the all-clear. One recovered my pistol and emptied it. They got me up and the patrol leader, a second lieutenant named Walker, approached. I showed them my CAC card and LAPD retired badge and ID.

"What the fuck, sir?" Lieutenant Walker pointedly asked.

"I made a wrong turn," I answered sheepishly. It was then I recalled the immortal words of Daniel Boone: "I've never been lost, but I've been confused for a month or two."

CHAPTER 11

EOD

Even though I didn't get back to my CHU till 0200, I was in the office early the next morning standing tall when George arrived. He glared at me. Poured himself a coffee and motioned me into his office closing the door behind me.

"Timing is everything, boss."

I recounted what had happened the night before and the other bits I'd uncovered. I also touched on the new ventilation holes in his ride. He was a bit freaked about that, but overall, surprisingly calm. I saw there was a folder with classified markings on his desk.

"This is for you. Read it and bring it back."

"Hot stuff?"

"Seems to mesh with your little fairy tale."

"Once again, sorry about last night," I offered.

"Forget it. As painful as it is for me to say this, you're clearly onto something. You're right that we need more before we kick this up to CID. I'll work on getting the SUV driver's name this morning."

"I think you should hold off on that," I interrupted. "They must have a source on the inside. If they get wind we're asking questions, they might bolt. Hell, they may have already. But my gut tells me no. Whatever is going on, I think it's too big to abandon."

"Based on this, I think you're right." George pushed the folder over to me.

"I'll be back. I've also got to smooth out some feathers with the MPs from your little adventure. But don't worry, I won't spill the beans."

The folder was marked *Top Secret//SI///HCS* and bore the two-word code phrase *Argon-Lancer*. The same code phrase on the report Harry Arnold had. I opened it and saw a photocopy of an Intelligence Information Report. I read the first paragraph and was bored in record time. I guess George meant well. Then I got to the body of the document and stopped dead in my tracks.

It was a detailed report on the same Military Intelligence (MI) source who was murdered in Eagle Lake. He was a Shia from Sadr City; a hot bed of the Shia insurgency, Sadr City was like an oozing carbuncle on Baghdad's ass.

This source said there was a guy on Victory Base who had been supplying targeting data to the bad guys. The source said he was an older man with a full gray beard and was working with an unknown US service member. There was no further description. The report ended. This info fit perfectly with what I'd seen and learned thus far.

I placed the folder back on George's desk and locked the door behind me. Lots to think about and do before tomorrow's trip. But first things first. My belly was growling, so I walked over the Coalition Café for breakfast. Remember rule number one of police work? Take notes, there might be a test.

I got in line behind some 63rd Explosive Ordnance Disposal guys. EOD guys defuse IEDs and blow shit up. Fun stuff if you're a stupid, pimple-faced fourteen-year-old boy playing with firecrackers in the backyard. Deadly serious when you happen to be in Iraq. I'd had the pleasure of working with a couple of 63rd guys a few months back. Really smart pros.

EOD soldiers ply their trade with unmatched skill and nerves of steel. These same EOD guys probably worked the recent IDF attacks, collecting evidence and rendering safe any unexploded rounds found in the debris.

I'm a friendly sort, so I tried to strike up a conversation with them. I waited for an opening, but it never seemed to appear. I couldn't ask them about the weather or chow hall menu without sounding like a complete asshole, so I waited for a lull to strike. One of the guys, a sergeant first class whose nametape read Nelson, turned to look in my direction. He nodded. I struck like a black mamba.

"Hey, is Hudson still around?"

SFC Nelson laughed.

"You know Hudson?"

"We worked an IED strike together. Phil Harper was with him," I replied.

"Harper rotated back, but Hudson is over on Liberty."

"Did you guys work the attack?"

"Yeah, we were there." I could hear the anger in his voice.

"My hooch is over there. I got a few kids out—"

The chow hall doors opened, and we all went inside. The two EOD guys walked over to the hot line. I grabbed some bacon and coffee and sat down in a quiet room off the main dining hall.

To my surprise, the EOD guys joined me.

"You're Rick, the LAPD guy, right?" Nelson asked. "Hudson told us about you. Said you are okay . . . for a civilian."

"I'm honored," I replied.

"Don't be. Hudson's a bad judge of character. Three ex-wives."

"Poor bastard."

A few minutes into trading war stories about Hudson, catching crooks and blowing shit up, I sensed an opening. These guys knew what was used in the attacks and no doubt wanted a little payback. Maybe I could be their instrument. I looked around. The coast was clear. I went for it.

"Did you guys recover anything interesting?"

Nelson stopped and looked up. He put his coffee down and glanced around.

"You're a six-badge, right?"

I pulled my badge out from my ACU blouse. He wanted to make sure I had the secret handshake.

"Okay, this is close hold, but since it's your job to hunt these fuckers." It had only been my job lately, but I didn't bother to correct him.

"We recovered one round that was a dud. It's a knockoff of one of ours." He leaned over to whisper. "A laser guided 120mm mortar."

"Chinese?" I asked innocently.

"Looks like it, but it might be Iranian made to look ChiCom."

One of the other EOD guys chimed in. "I'd like a couple of minutes with the prick who gave them that technology."

"CID and MPs are clueless. They have no idea what to do. They haven't even asked to see it yet. You want to look at the round we found? It's at our shop," offered Nelson.

"That'd be great."

"Tomorrow morning after chow?"

"I'm heading down to Yusufiyah tomorrow morning. Could I see it today?" I'm a pushy bastard sometimes.

Nelson thought for a second. "Sure, no problem. You can ride with us. But you'll have to take the bus back."

For the next couple of minutes, we shared more stories. Theirs were scarier.

We arrived at their compound. Typical nondescript Saddam-era buildings painted the standard issue dirt-colored tan. We walked in, and my jaw dropped. The place was chock-full of battlefield trophies and mementos—155mm artillery shells that had been used for roadside IEDs, copper plates from EFPs (Explosively Formed Penetrator), plaster rocks made to disguise a bomb, all kinds of machine guns, mortars, and rockets. My favorite was the picture of a dead donkey lying beside the road. Poor mister donkey's insides had been replaced by a live 155mm round wired to a remote detonator. The bad guys were very creative. They use dogs, donkeys, and sometimes people.

They showed me the defused mortar round, which was lying on a workbench surrounded by several desk lamps.

"I was taking photos for our reports. It has the usual Chinese markings. In fact, I think it's too well-marked."

I looked at Nelson a little puzzled.

"I don't know how they actually mark one of these rounds, but I'm betting since it's so hot shit new and top secret, they play all sorts of games."

SFC Nelson made sense. You would think if these were being covertly supplied, they wouldn't be so clearly marked. Hell, we do the same thing when we do sneaky stuff. Why wouldn't the Chinese or the Iranians?

The round was in remarkably good shape.

SFC Nelson explained that it had come straight through the sheet metal roof of a hooch and landed nose first in a bed. Heat from the rocket motor caused a fire, but the warhead was a dud.

I looked at the nose. You could see remnants of the guidance sensor that would have homed in on a laser beam.

I'd seen enough. I thanked them, shook hands, and headed out. On the bus ride back, I made some rudimentary notes. We were getting closer to the confirmation we would need. This case was moving very fast.

CHAPTER 12

VIOLATED

The ride was mercifully short, and I was back in my hooch in no time. I needed to prep for tomorrow's field trip, so I got out my daypack, CamelBak, and IBA body armor. That shit was made of Kevlar just like a regular police vest, except it had pockets on the front, back, and sides for ceramic pieces called SAPI plates meant to stop a rifle round. With all the plates installed, the groin protector, and the collar, the damn thing weighed about thirty-five pounds. I only used the front and back plates. I know it was kinda stupid, but I was just an advisor, not a combat soldier.

I kept the armor on top of the wardrobe. As I hauled it down, one of the side plates slid off the edge. Ten pounds of SAPI plate crashed square onto the toe with the ingrown nail. I shouted curses and screamed just like my old man would have done. I got all my best swear word combinations from him. One of the guys across from me knocked on the door to make sure I was okay. I opened it still cursing like a Navy chief.

"Dropped the mother-fuckin' SAPI plate on my foot," I blasted before I recognized the concerned expression of Chaplain Major Gus Pickett.

"I've done it too. You okay?"

"I'm fine. Goddamn thing hurts. Ahh, sorry, chaplain."

"No worries, He understands. You know, it's a sign."

"What do you mean?"

Almighty to the rescue again?

"Rick, it's a sign from you know who." He glanced upwards. "Put it back in your vest."

I smiled sheepishly. "Okay, I will. Sorry about the cursing, Chaplain."

"Nothing I haven't heard a million fucking times before."

He grinned and walked away. I closed the door and gently tugged my boot off.

The toe was bleeding a little, but not broken. I needed to soak it, so I put on my PT gear and headed for the shower. The showers/latrines on Victory were always a treat. Especially for middle-aged, pasty, old farts like me. Talk about feeling out of place. In the mornings, the showers were full of fit young warriors. I stuck out like a pulled pork sandwich in a Baghdad bazaar.

Once I found a fresh turd in a shower stall. I was told this was part of a weird "Mad Shitter" joke peculiar to the Army. I was also told that the Indonesian maintenance workers at Victory will sometimes take a dump in unusual places to show their love for the infidel Americans. Whatever it was, it was disgusting, but well in keeping with the overall patina of Iraq.

The place was deserted when I walked in. I found an empty stall and closed the curtain. I'm not modest, just intimidated. I sat on a little bench built into the stall and let the water run on my foot for a while. It seemed to help. Then I plugged the shower drain with a plastic stopper I had and filled the basin with warm water. I turned the water off when it was about three quarters full and let my foot just soak. It felt wonderful.

Suddenly, the latrine door opened then slammed shut. Someone was a bit pissed. We've already established that I tend to be a tad nosy, so I made like the proverbial fly and just listened.

I couldn't tell what he was saying. It was sort of muffled gibberish, like what came out of my ex after she'd drained martini number four. Then I heard the loud click of the latch on the door being locked. *Okay, I get it. He thinks he's alone.* Some guys like a bit more privacy. It could happen.

Now, I'll freely admit I have a few fantasies, but none involve an Army latrine and a mumbling dude with anger-management issues. Fearing the worst, I steeled myself and prepared to defend my maidenhead. The guy moved to a stall about five down from me. I could hear him stripping off his clothes. He turned the shower on, and I decided now was the time to sneak a peek at my mystery date. I carefully removed my right eye from its socket and snuck it out around the curtain. Nothing special. Just a garden variety white boy. He suddenly stopped as if listening for something. I retracted my eye and waited. He soon resumed his shower prep, completely clueless as to my presence. I was still pretty good at stealth.

The guy's a bit odd but probably harmless, I thought. He started his shower, so I decided it was time to take a peek. I could see his daypack was wide open and sitting on the bench outside his stall.

He had the usual showering crap. Towel, razor, soap dish. I could also see what looked like rosary beads, which was not that unusual. Some guys get religion in a war zone. After the latest attacks, I completely got it.

I decided to give him a little surprise when he emerged from his shower. I toweled off my foot off and slipped on my flip-flops. He still didn't know I was there. Then I heard him mumbling again. Sounded like a mix of a Slavic language and maybe Arabic. But what the hell do I know? I never got better than a *C* in French.

He turned off the water and pushed back the curtain. I gave him a couple of seconds and made my move. I threw open the curtain and casually stepped out. I swear he jumped three feet straight up. Then he did something odd. He covered up like a surprised schoolgirl. Guys don't do that with other guys, just like we don't take the urinal next to a guy when one three down is vacant.

I smiled and, clumsy me, I bumped into his daypack, knocking it off the bench.

"Oh, man, I'm so sorry. Let me help you," I offered solicitously.

I bent and took a good look. I saw the string of beads. *Good Catholic boy,* I thought. I picked up a small towel and out flopped an Arabic-English guide.

"That's okay," he replied in thickly accented English.

"Sorry, man, my mistake. Let me help you."

"I have it," he replied, clearly irritated.

"Okay. Sorry, man."

I grabbed the beads, which had fallen to the floor and handed them to him. I noted something rather critical was missing. Even a heathen like me who's had one Catholic wife knows there's usually a crucifix attached to a set of rosary beads. But these weren't standard-issue rosary beads. There was just a multi-strand green tassel at the end—no crucifix. Jesus was MIA.

As he took the beads from me, he had that look I've seen countless times before. It was like I just caught him backing out of a 7-Eleven with a bag full of cash in one hand and a Glock in the other. I looked at his gray Army issue PT shirt hoping to spot a name. Nothing. I looked at his pack. Guys usually stencil their names on it somewhere. Then I spotted it. *Khanov. Sounds Russian,* I thought. But what he was mumbling didn't sound completely Russian.

Khanov was a religious dude, probably a Muslim, perhaps Chechen, and dare I say, a bit shy. That all fit. Finally, he was also a bit weird, which in Iraq could actually be a virtue.

It was time for me to say goodbye. I smiled my best, most insincere "fuck you too," picked up my shit, and got the hell out of there. Of course, I had to unlock the door first.

I never forget a face. It's names that I'm not so hot at. I dread those moments when I have to introduce a friend to someone else whose name I should know but cannot recall. Memory was the second thing to go. Tolerance for people who can't remember my name was first.

I stumbled through the gravel to my hooch. Walking on gravel is so much fun when you're wearing flip-flops. Imagine my joy at three in the morning when I was running back and forth to the latrine spewing from both ends.

I got back to my hooch, prepped my daypack, and filled my CamelBak's water bladder. I also threw a couple of extra loaded pistol magazines in pouches on my vest and checked my borrowed M4 carbine and its magazines. I was done.

CHAPTER 13

RING KNOCKERS

decided to head back to the office to check in with George. He wasn't there. But there was a note reminding me to call General Mikey.

"Hi, it's Rick Sutherland for the general."

I was put on hold. There wasn't any of that canned *muzak* for my listening pleasure. Just dead silence.

"Rick."

"Yeah, Mike, what's up?"

"Well, what's up with you?"

"Just chillin' with my homies."

"I heard about last night. Christ, what the fuck were you thinking?"

"Yeah, well, I got lost. It can happen. Besides, you guys don't have street signs around here."

"I'll put in a suggestion to Iraq Trans. So, what were you really doing?"

Do I outright lie? Or manage information? I went with door number two.

"I was following up on an IED cell working in the Triangle." Which was sort of true.

"Okay, that's at least partially bullshit. We both know what you're really after. I also know you're heading out tomorrow. I'm not calling to tell you to pack up your shit and head home. I heard you may be onto something. So, I'm gonna let you run for a while. Just keep me in the loop and try not to create too much collateral damage."

"I'll be nice. I promise." *Let me run for a while? Does he not know me?*

"We both know that's gonna need a miracle," he said. "But here's the bottom line. You've got my full blessing, but don't advertise it. There's gonna be some pissed off people out there if they find out what you're really after. My intel guys are good, but they've got too many rules to follow. You, on the other hand, ate the rule book."

He paused for a moment. We were speaking on an unsecured line, so he had to be careful.

"We need to find these fuckers and grease 'em. You can operate outside your lane and everyone will say 'fucking civilians' and just shake their heads. Doing things your way and pissing people off is one of your many talents. I want you to be my eyes and ears on this. You're not in my AO, but don't worry, I've handled that."

He let all of that sink in. "One more thing. There's a Major Copeland heading out to sniff around a bit. He's got some skilled people with him and maybe they will dig something up. We've also got some SOF guys out there. They will handle the fun stuff when the time comes. But nobody will know about what you're doing unless you tell them. Rick, just do me one favor."

"What's that?"

"Don't get your ass shot off. Mom would never forgive me."

"So, let me get this right, you're not calling to clip my wings and send me home?"

"Rick, I lost a friend the other morning. He was a patriot, a great solider and father. This is personal. Find these shitbirds and get word to Sergeant Major Galloway. He'll handle it from there. That's it. You got anything for me?"

It took me a couple of seconds to respond. "No, Mike, nothing I can tell you over this line. But my boss has it all."

"I know, your boss briefed me. Okay, bro, watch your six."

The SOF guys Mike mentioned were probably guys from one of the many Special Operations Forces elements running around Iraq. These guys were trigger pullers from the SEALs, 75th Ranger Regiment, Army Special Forces, and elite operators from our coalition partners like the British SAS and Polish GROM. They did a lot of the "wet work" around here. For some reason they call breaking stuff and killing bad guys "going kinetic," or "direct action," DA for short. Don't ask me why. Guess it must sound better or something.

So, Mikey wanted me to do what I did best. Catch crooks and piss people off. Okay, I could handle that.

George walked up to my desk. "Did you call the general?"

"Yes, boss. He sure seemed to know a lot."

George winked and tapped his West Point ring on my desk. Funny, I never noticed it before. Mikey never wore his.

"Were you two at the Point?"

"I was a year ahead. We were on the rugby team."

"It's like the Mafia."

"Or like you cops."

"Let's grab a bite. I'll drive."

I filled him in on what EOD had said about the laser-guided 122mm round. I had his full attention. George dropped me off on the street near my CHU and wished me good luck on the next day's trip. I was feeling pretty darn good. I had a full belly, my leg felt good, and I was getting closer to solving this "case."

I was about to insert my room key into the lock when the phone started buzzing. It was Major Herself. It had been nearly a day since we'd spoken.

"Hey, old man, where you been all day?"

"Boring superhero stuff. What about you?"

"I know about what happened last night."

WTF? How the hell did she find out?

"Jason's roommate was on the patrol that stopped you on the Airport Road. They had a pretty good laugh. What were you thinking?"

"I was following that SUV."

"Outside the wire? Are you trying to get hurt?"

"That's how I met you. I was going for a double."

"Alright, asshole, I've got to get home and pack for tomorrow. See ya then."

Whew, that was a close one. Thank God she didn't need a back rub or something.

CHAPTER 14

PASSENGER LOADING ZONE

went into blissful slumber mode pretty quickly. The next thing I knew my alarm was blasting. I looked at the clock face: *4:00 am.* Man, that sucked. It was so early and uncivilized. Only farmers and adulterers got out of the rack at that hour. I pulled on my ACUs. My left big toe was as red as Ted Kennedy's nose. I gingerly laced up my boots, grabbed my shit, and I was ready for adventure.

My leg was still good. I'd changed the dressing before I went to bed and noted the wound was closed and not a bit tender.

I got a ride to the helo pad with a sergeant from the office. It was early for both of us. I checked into the waiting room tent and grabbed a spot on the bench.

Five minutes later, in walked the hottest looking badass this side of the Playboy mansion. Nancy had all her shit; Kevlar helmet, vest, pistol, mags and M4 carbine. She also had a daypack and a medium black duffel bag. My favorite healer was ready to drum up some business, and I was sporting wood.

For a fleeting moment, I wondered how fast I could get that crap off her for a quickie. Then a full-bird colonel and his command sergeant major walked in throwing cold water on that fantasy. He nodded at Major Nancy "Rambo" Weaver and didn't give me a second look. I'm sure he could tell I was yet another overpaid, underworked civilian contractor. *Yep, that's me.*

Nancy pulled off her gear and sat beside me. She smelled good.

"Good morning, Major."

"Morning, Mr. Sutherland."

I offered her a bottle of water and got a wave off. Guess she wasn't thirsty. "Hydrate or die," as they say. The management around here even has little color-coded information cards posted above the urinals. Can't say I have any knowledge of what they have on the female side. Anyway, the pisser is supposed to look at the color of his effluent and compare it to the illustrations on the card. Clear as mountain spring water means all is well and you are good to go. Piss the color of a nice amber ale means you're about to flop over. I was putting out Corona Light this morning, so I guessed I'd make it. I know some would call bullshit on the whole piss card thing, but I swear it's true.

Having my offer to hydrate rebuffed, I was about to fire a typically clever but ill-timed wisecrack when the contractor who served as gate agent—sans smile and typing fingers—called our names and told us to go out to the pad. Nancy stood, grabbed her pack and duffel, and put on her Kevlar. Mine was fashionably hooked to a MOLE loop on my vest.

The MOLE system enables fashion-conscious warriors such as yours truly to attach all manner of bitchin' shit to the outside of our vests. There must be hundreds of these MOLE loops sewn onto the exterior of the vest by some mind-numbed factory worker. On mine I had magazine pouches, my first-aid kit, and strap-cutting tool you're supposed to use if you have to un-ass the chopper in a hurry. The thing had a hooked blade perfect for slicing though seat belts or bra straps. Come to think of it, it might even work on a thong. Was Nancy wearing one? That may require some additional investigation, but that's why I'm a detective.

I don't want you to think I'm a dirty old man. I'm just a guy trying to ensure the survival of the species. There was a time when I wasn't a blazing beacon of libido. In fact, I remember my sergeant in Van Nuys vice telling me that I "couldn't get laid in a women's prison with a fist full of pardons." He was right.

Enough of that.

I threw on my pack and followed Nancy, who respectfully followed the colonel. The good sergeant major quickstepped in front of me, probably to check Nancy out. *Sorry, bub, she's taken.* We got in the rear door of the Blackhawk. I've ridden in four different kinds of police choppers, an MD 500, an old Korean war-vintage Sikorsky, and a Jet Ranger up in Alaska. I've always enjoyed them, but that was all civilian fun and games. Flying in a chopper with machine guns pointed out the side doors was a sobering reminder that this was a war zone and things could turn to shit in a hurry.

After the crew chief got everybody on board, he climbed in back with us and checked that I had fastened the four-point harness correctly. One look and a thumbs-up told me I was good to go. The chief and his gunner took their places beside their machine guns, the pilots applied power, and off we went. Another adventure in camel land was about to begin. I was excited. Then I looked at Nancy. She was gazing out the window looking at BIAP, several hundred feet below. My mind was spinning with self-doubt. *What does she see in me? Why is she traveling with me? What the hell am I doing? I hope my stupidity doesn't get us both killed.* I'd fallen for her.

CHAPTER 15

E-TICKET

A ride in a Blackhawk can be a hoot. I looked out the chopper door at the vast expanse of sand. We had left the relatively green fertile area that borders the Euphrates River and headed southwest out over the vast empty expanse of sand that is Western Iraq. Not much out there except for roads that seem to go nowhere, tank revetments, and the occasional herd of camels cavorting about the desert.

I looked down and saw what looked like an ancient hilltop fort or walled village. I have a thing for history and love to look at dusty old rocks and stuff. Most of the cops I worked with thought I was nuts, but I'd rather read Pressfield or Durant than *Sports Illustrated*. Iraq is an ancient land. It was old when Alexander the Great visited in 331 BC. He died in Iraq eight years later from typhoid fever; but some say he was murdered. *Yet another unsolved homicide.*

After about ten minutes, we started back toward the river. I could feel our bird slow and begin its descent. Before I knew it, we were on a helipad at some FOB (Forward Operating Base) I'd never seen before. I watched as soldiers took overwatch positions in the field surrounding us. To our right, I could see a reed-filled marshy area. Perfect concealment for a sniper or an asshole with an RPG (Rocket Propelled Grenade). A pair of GIs armed with SAW light machine guns covered the marsh. I watched as the colonel and his sergeant major jumped off. I noticed that both had Special Forces, Airborne, and Ranger tabs. The Army guys call the three tabs "Triple Canopy." *Good guys to have on your side.*

There were no new passengers or baggage to load, so we were off in an instant. It was just me and Nancy on board now. We flew at about 300 feet over drab, colorless towns. Everything was tan or brown with an occasional red water tank on the roof just to add a little color. Occasionally, we'd pass a US convoy of Humvees and APCs.

A wise man cautioned me not long after I arrived in-country to fly whenever possible. He was right. You are much safer in the air. No IEDs to worry about. Just the occasional pot shot from an AK-47. But I must admit I still like to occasionally travel with the boys on the ground. You can see more and get a better feel for what's going on. It's like contrasting walking a foot beat with riding in a black and white. Few would disagree that you can really learn what's happening in a neighborhood by walking it.

The Blackhawk suddenly went into a dive, flared, and jinked to the right. I watched as the crew chief pushed in the electronic safety that would allow him to fire his 7.62mm machine gun. Pyrotechnic flares started shooting out of both sides of our bird. They flashed and popped, generating clouds of white smoke. I could feel myself tense up as I watched. Was some stinky little asshole lining us up with his SA-7 SAM? The SA-7, by the way, is a heat seeking, man-portable, anti-aircraft missile.

Getting smacked with either an RPG or SA-7 would not be fun. The riding around playing GI Joe stuff was a dream come true for a guy like me. All was cool as long as the dream didn't turn into a fiery nightmare.

The crew chief looked back at us and then said something into the intercom. A couple of seconds later, the pilot pulled the hawk straight up. I was pressed in my seat like a panini without the pesto. We climbed for a few seconds. Was it to avoid that wayward SA-7 with my name on it? Suddenly, we stopped and hung for a second in mid-air, nose pointed straight up.

I looked at Nancy. She wasn't smiling. The pilots nosed the helo over, and we dove like a rocket. Just before we hit a grove of palm trees, the pilot banked to the right and then to the left. The chief looked back at us. He was grinning. I looked at Nancy. She was now smiling too.

They were fucking with me. Trying to get me to blow chunks, and it was working. I gulped down the remains of this morning's Pop Tart and coffee and held on. If I blew chunks, it was going on the floor. I weakly smiled back at the chief and gave him a thumbs up as I looked for a barf bag. I could feel drops of sweat pouring down my face and sliding down my back.

I was now holding on with every fiber in my body, trying to maintain and not embarrass myself and the team. I could see that Nancy's expression had turned from one of devilish delight to mild concern. *Christ, she ought to be.* I thought all these quacks took an oath to "do no harm." Maybe she missed that day at medical school.

After what seemed like four hours, but was more like four seconds, the helo straightened out and started to climb back up to cruising altitude. Nancy was trying to communicate something to me. You really couldn't talk on a Blackhawk, only pass notes and give lame hand signals. The noise from the rotor blades could ruin your hearing. In fact, you must wear ear plugs or they kick you off.

Nancy passed me a note. "Are you okay?" I gave her a nod. She gave my hand a quick squeeze. I suddenly started feeling much better. It was a miracle. Call the Vatican.

The helo started to descend again, this time in a little more civilized fashion.

Soon, we were flying over the town of Yusufiyah. Nothing remarkable. Just the usual nondescript drab buildings in varying stages of collapse. We landed on the pad. I twisted the button on the four-point harness and grabbed my pack. Nancy was already out and walking away. *Christ, she moves fast.* I hopped off and landed wrong. My leg let me know it was not happy with that move. *Still not a hundred percent.* Nancy, who was now talking to a young sergeant, glanced over at me just as my feet hit the landing pad. She saw me wince a bit. She turned and continued talking to the sergeant.

CHAPTER 16

FORT APACHE

"**M**r. Sutherland, I'm Sergeant Goode. There is an urgent call for you in the TOC."

The TOC is Army speak for Tactical Operations Center, which was the command post for the little outpost we were at.

"It was from headquarters 3rd ID. They want you to call back as soon as you land."

Another phone call? This was getting stupid. I needed breathing room to work, not long-distance mothering. Suddenly, I felt very weak. I was having Scarlett O'Hara-like vapors. It was serious. Maybe I could even die or something.

"Sorry, Sarge, but I'm feeling really bad now. Do you guys have a place where I can drop my shit and lie down for a while?"

Nancy, quick on the uptake, chimed in with her expert medical opinion.

"Sergeant, Mr. Sutherland should probably get some rest. I think he hurt his leg when he hopped off the helo."

I bit my lip to keep from giggling. Man, she could lay it on thick. *This chick is a bigger bullshitter than me.*

Sergeant Goode showed us to our quarters. Typical beat-up trailer housing. In fact, I'd stayed in this particular hooch before. After I made a quick security check for camel spiders and other nasties, I went next door to Nancy's. I gave her door a soft knock. My intentions were purely dishonorable. At that very moment an officer walked up, this time a captain. He was in a hurry too.

"Mr. Sutherland, General Sutherland's office called. He's still waiting for your call."

Busted. I should have just stayed in my hooch.

I walked in silence over to the TOC escorted by the captain. As we walked, I got a look at his name. Clark. I knew a Danny Clark on the job back in LA. George said the CO of this place was a copper back in the States.

Danny Clark retired out of LAPD's Special Investigations Section (SIS) a couple of years ago. SIS was a handpicked, highly trained squad of detectives out of Major Crimes Division. They specialized in following career criminals around and occasionally canceled their tickets when they did really bad things. They used to do a lot more ticket canceling back in the good ol' days. Not so much after the local news hounds started calling them a "death squad." I suppose if you're an ignorant reporter and don't know any better, you could call them a "death squad." But the career violent felons who were crazy enough to shoot it out with SIS needed to be culled from the herd.

If this guy was LAPD, I was going to be in tall cotton on this trip. We walked through the TOC to a small office shoehorned into a corner. I saw an LA Dodgers hat on his desk. That would be a clue.

"Say, Captain, you from LA?"

He grunted in the affirmative. *Guess he doesn't like me too much.*

"Yeah, so am I. Retired from the City last year."

He looked up, obviously surprised. I was getting warm.

"Do you know a Danny Clark? Retired a while back?"

"Uncle Danny? You know him?"

"Did he work SIS?" I asked.

"Sure did." He was smiling. "He's retired now. Lives in Idaho."

"Where I should be. Yep, that's the Danny I worked with. He once showed me pictures of his house up near some last stop before you get to Canada."

"Bonners Ferry," Captain Clark responded.

We exchanged the official LAPD secret handshake like long lost brothers.

"Rick Sutherland," I said.

"Good to meet you Rick, I'm Larry Clark."

"It's good to meet someone from home, even if it's in this God-forsaken place." He smiled. "You work for George, right?"

"Yep. That would be me."

"George sent me a message that you were coming down. But he didn't mention you were retired from the City."

"So, how long you been over here?" I asked.

"In-country about seven months, but only been here for about three weeks or so."

"Where do you work back home?" I asked, trying get more LAPD talk going.

"Commercial burglary out of Van Nuys," he replied.

"I know the place well. I worked vice and narco in Van Nuys years ago. That's how I met your Uncle Danny. Great copper and a hell of a shot. I swear he could draw smiley faces with his .45."

"I think he did a few times," Captain Clark said.

We bullshitted for a couple of minutes about Van Nuys and the department. Who was screwing whom. Who got screwed by whom. It was all gossip and bitching, which are the two things cops do best.

Now that we were BFFs, maybe I could talk him out of that phone call to Mike.

Just as I was about to propose blowing off the call, he said, "Let's make that call."

He dialed the number on a secure telephone and handed me the receiver. It rang twice.

"I'm getting voicemail, they're not home."

Clark glowered at me. I decided to give it a couple more rings.

A staff officer answered. I asked for the general.

"Rick, it's Galloway. Higher at the Palace is asking about you and what you're doing. We think someone is going to ask for you to be recalled. Suggest you get moving before they figure out where you are."

"Roger that. Thanks for the heads up. Anything more?"

"Just try to stay off the radar and be careful. I've been in a few fights with the boys you might run up against. They are nothing to fool with."

"Thanks, Sergeant Major, will do. Out here." I hung up.

"Captain, is Chris Shore, the S-2, around?" The S-2 is an officer who specializes in intelligence. Shore was the intel officer George had told me about. I needed to run some names past him and see about setting up a little visit.

The "Two Shop," as they called it, turned out to be in a little plywood shoebox just off the TOC. I'd sure like to know who supplies the plywood around here. Everywhere you look, it was concrete T-walls, funky Iraqi cinder block walls held together with bubblegum, string and, of course, the ubiquitous plywood.

Anyway, the good captain and I squeezed our way into a tiny office occupied by a young female lieutenant, with very blonde hair tied in a tight ponytail. She was feverishly working at her computer and didn't notice our approach. George had said the S-2 was a guy named Chris Shore, so this couldn't be him.

"Captain, sorry, but I need to talk with the S-2," I whispered, not wanting to disturb her or embarrass myself.

The young and, I might add, very attractive lieutenant turned to me and smiled. "You've got to be the infamous Rick Sutherland George warned me about. I'm Christine Shore, the S-2 around here. Welcome to JSS Yusufiyah"

We shook hands and I immediately noticed a very big rock on her finger and a photo of an even bigger Green Beret officer on her desk. *Must be hubby.*

By way of explanation, a JSS is a Joint Security Station, meaning that it is a facility jointly occupied by US Army (in this case) and Iraqi Army personnel.

"I'm very familiar with the guy you want to talk to. He's well known around here. He's got a small restaurant and a haji shop next door."

"Diversified in a wartime economy. Very wise."

I didn't even get a courtesy chuckle. Lieutenant Shore pulled out a file she'd put together on our guy. I studied the photo stapled to a bio sheet. Khalid Omar Abu-Ali Al-Rashidi was a cross between Steven Tyler and Omar Sharif, with a unibrow thrown in for good measure. He looked to be about 40.

"Lieutenant, what do you have on this guy?"

"He's a local Shia. Lately, he's gotten more juice around here. We think he helped finance a successful IED attack on a couple of Sunnis who ran local Baath Party gangs. I've talked to him a couple of times. Speaks fairly good English. Not sure where he learned it. We have some intel that he went to Shiraz University in Iran, but it's pretty sketchy. He has a wife and three boys. Two of them are military age and haven't been seen in a while. We heard recently that they may be living with extended family in Los Angeles. One or both might be at UCLA."

"Shiraz, like the wine?"

"Yes. Iran used to be the leading wine producer in the Middle East. The best wines came from Shiraz. Shiraz University, from what I've read, is fairly Western-oriented." *Chris Shore does her homework, very impressive. I like that.* I also liked that Iran, Iraq's next door neighbor, was coming up yet again.

"So, Khalid has the local Denny's franchise?"

"It's more like a little two burner café, plus a haji shop. He sells pirated DVDs, brass lamps, candy, hookahs, a little jewelry, the usual crap GIs buy."

I was getting excited. We were on to something. This guy felt right. History, connections, and money; all the right ingredients for a who's-the-suspect pie. Having a shop catering to GIs made perfect sense. Just like the jewelry shop back at Victory.

It wasn't rocket science. The kids come into the snake's lair to buy trinkets for Suzie back home or some pirated DVD to jerk off to. The grinning cobra behind the counter couldn't be a nicer guy. He's so helpful and gives great deals because he "loves America." *Yeah, right.*

"You look so tired. You okay? Everything alright?" says the cobra. Before you know it, the kid's confirming he's tired from the all-night capture operation they did in Al-Shwarmaville. Not good.

I've seen this same ploy back home. The Wiseguys on the Westside and in Beverly Hills were famous for it. I worked one of those cases during a short stint in Internal Affairs.

Khalid was in excellent position to pump the local GIs for information while selling them all manner of crap for the girl back home.

"So, when can we go to town for a little sit down with Khalid?" I was anxious to get a move on. We were burning daylight and evil was rampant in the land.

Captain Clark glanced at Lieutenant Shore. "I guess we could throw something together this evening, about 1600. I'll get a squad together for security. Lieutenant Shore will be there to assist you."

Lieutenant Shore was gonna be there to make sure I didn't steal any crayons. That's cool. But they don't know me. Hell, if they did, Clark would come too.

I looked at my watch. It was getting close to noon and my stomach was very unhappy.

"When's chow around here?"

"The hall's open now."

CHAPTER 17

ROUGHING IT

I stumbled my way back to the transient hooches and knocked on Nancy's door.

"Security," I said with my best Iraqi accent.

"Who's there?" She didn't sound happy.

"Security, ma'am. We have report of a rapist in neighborhood. You must open door."

"Go away, I'm busy saving lives."

"Whose life you save?"

"Yours, asshole. Now go away."

I lost the confused security-guard persona and reverted to my old charming self. *I'm a chameleon.* Another of my many talents. "Major Weaver, Sir . . ." *That should really piss her off.* "It's lunch time, and I thought you might enjoy a small repast with your favorite old fart."

She cracked open the door wearing an Army T-shirt and very unsensible panties. My favorite kind.

"Screw lunch," I said, checking her out. "I need to lose weight anyway."

"Get in here before someone sees me."

I didn't need to be told twice and bounded over the threshold.

"We're gonna head out this afternoon. You want to grab me, or some chow?" I asked full of hope.

"Actually, neither. I've got stuff to do, reports to read. I have to meet with the medical team."

"Want to tag along when we go to town?" I asked, knowing what the answer would be.

"Sure, I'll be there. Give me about twenty minutes before the briefing so I can gear up."

Nancy leaned over and gave me a very nice, polite kiss. I can take a hint and said goodbye.

The camp chow hall was close to the latrine and laundry room, which could be convenient depending on the food. The camp itself, an industrial plant abandoned years ago, was a dump. Not bombed out or war-ravaged, just a dump. Perfect for an Army facility and another home run for the Directorate of Boredom and Discomfort. The dusty chow hall—and I use "hall" liberally—was a conglomeration of plywood and Saddam-era masonry. No windows or Zagat ratings apparent.

It was the maître d's day off, so I signed in, washed my hands, and grabbed a tray to get in line behind a couple of stout young troopers. One had his twenty-pound SAW "light" machine gun dangling from his shoulder. *A lot of iron to pack around if you ask me.* The mess guys dispensing the gruel were young and sweating like pigs. Their T-shirts had more sweat stain rings than California's oldest redwood. My formerly ravenous appetite was declining rapidly.

The sign over the grill proudly proclaimed award-winning hamburgers. From its appearance, I was pretty sure the meat may have come from a mammal. The other marquee item was a stack of grilled cheese sandwiches with enough grease to lube an Abrams tank. Wisely, I moved on to the salad counter.

There was your usual rabbit food, protected by sneeze glass and something that resembled potato salad with fresh insect garnish. Trays of green Jell-O with embedded fruit cocktail, and finally, stale bread and cold cuts. Flies were dutifully performing combat air patrols overhead. The mess crew were trying to shoo them away, but it was an effort reminiscent of Little Bighorn.

I loaded my plate with cold cuts, chips, and a bag of Famous Amos cookies. That hermetically sealed bag was fly-free and held a little slice of home. I remember when Amos had his cookie shop in Hollywood on Sunset Boulevard—a little A-frame building. It's still there, but alas, Amos sold the biz to Nabisco or some other mega-conglomerate. The cookies ain't the same, but they'd do.

CHAPTER 18

WAR STORIES

grabbed a water and a ginger ale, and found an empty seat at a table full of young soldiers. Two specialists and a buck sergeant. The sergeant spoke first.

He glanced at my nametape.

"Mr. Sutherland, you coming with us this afternoon?"

"I believe so. I need to see a man about a stolen camel."

They just nodded and smiled. *I can't even buy a laugh around here.*

The sergeant glanced at my holstered M-9 annoying device.

"You got anything bigger than that with you?"

"An M4 and a few mags."

"I want you to have a full load out, so we'll fix you up with a couple more. Things got hot for another patrol a few miles down the road, and I want everyone to be prepared. Also, bring your hydration system. We don't need any heat casualties."

"You got it, Sarge."

Christ, more weight to carry. I didn't need more than a couple of mags for the carbine. Two extra mags plus one in the gun was ninety rounds. More than enough. Plus, I also had my M9 noisemaker and three mags for that. That was a hell of a lot more firepower than I ever carried at LAPD.

I needed no convincing on the hydration issue. A couple of months back, I went out on an early morning dismounted patrol with some troops from another Forward Operating Base. I ignored the advice of a trooper and didn't fully hydrate and nearly went tits deep in Indian country. The rule is that you drink water until you're pissing clear every thirty minutes or so. Remember the color-coded cards in the urinals? Well, I didn't. What can I say? I'm a dumbass civilian.

The guys and I sat around the table for a while and shot the shit. They mostly wanted to know what it was like being a cop in LA. I recounted a few tales of daring do from the good ol' days. They had a few daring stories of their own. The sergeant, who had made the suggestions about my ammo loadout, recalled a few stories of tangling with the Taliban at 10,000 feet in Afghanistan.

In one instance, he and some other guys were waiting to ambush some local bad guys. They got flanked by a Taliban welcoming committee, and five guys, including the patrol leader, were wounded immediately. They called in air and Medevac. A pair of Italian fighters arrived but only dropped flares and a bottle of chianti. Not impressed, the Taliban continued the assault.

Six hours and four dead Americans later, they get off that spot. The sergeant said that he was down to his last full mag when he got out of there. That settled things for me. If the sergeant said I needed seven magazines, I'd hump seven magazines.

CHAPTER 19

NAP TIME

We had three hours to kill before the briefing, so when I was done with chow, I went back to my hooch and got my gear ready. I hadn't checked the M4 carbine before I left, so I decided to have a look. The internals were as dry as a Bedouin's fart. No lube at all. Not a drop. As for the barrel, don't even ask. It was full of dust and crap. I didn't have anything to really give it a good cleaning. Using an old sock, I wiped out most of the dust and carbon buildup. At least it was a little cleaner. Probably wouldn't need it anyway.

Just as I was putting the contraption back together, I heard a couple of guys talking in excited tones outside my door. Despite my shitty hearing, I was able to pick out the word *grenade*.

I took a stroll across the compound to the TOC and walked in. Things were more than a little tense. Lieutenant Shore, on the other hand, was the picture of calm. She issued instructions and was clearly in control.

One of the enlisted guys told me that somebody tossed a grenade at one of our vehicles a couple of kilometers outside of town. "He said everything's cool now and they are on their way back."

Everything is cool now? The bad guys just threw a grenade at your

HUMVEE, but it's cool now. Such is war and the resiliency of kids. God bless 'em.

I stood by in the TOC, listening in on the action. Phones were ringing now as the radio traffic intensified. Clark hustled in, and briefly conferred with Lieutenant Shore. Clearly satisfied, he stepped back and watched her do her thing.

I could hear chopper pilots being vectored to the location of the patrol. It was fascinating. Occasionally, I could hear the patrol respond to a query or give a status update.

I was about to leave when I heard something that perked my ears up. Some other unit was in the area and was asking for the grid coordinates of the other patrol. The soldier making the request sounded familiar. I couldn't quite place it, but I knew I'd heard that voice before. I stood there for a while listening for another transmission from the familiar voice, but nothing. Captain Clark gave me a quick nod and walked over.

"Some asshole playing with grenades. No injuries, just a little scratched paint. The patrol is about five minutes travel time back to base."

"Can we still go out and play this evening?" I asked hopefully.

"I don't see why not. This kind of crap happens all the time."

"You mean they don't love us yet?"

"Love is very complicated over here."

"Like Man Love Thursday?" I asked.

"Sort of," he chuckled.

"What time do you want to brief?" I asked.

"I want to wait for the team to get back so I can find out what happened. If there are no surprises, I'm thinking about 1700."

"Sounds good to me."

"Why don't you and Lieutenant Shore meet with me at about 1615 to go over the op?"

We shook hands and I started back to my hooch. As I walked across the compound, I saw some GIs throwing horseshoes in a pit next to a mortar emplacement. Several guys and one female soldier were smoking cigars. I felt like a smoke, so I joined them. I hadn't burned one in a couple of days, and it would give me a chance to hang with the homies.

"Mind if I join you?" I asked.

"Nah, pull up a bag and make yourself at home." I plopped down on a sandbag and fished out my travel cigar case.

"You're the retired LA cop, right?" the female soldier named Jones asked.

"Yep, retired a few months ago and came over here."

"I'm from Reseda," she replied.

I didn't offer my regrets, but I wanted to. Reseda used to be a nice place to live. Operative phrase—*used to*. I used to like the Valley until I used to be married. *I used to have a nice house there too.*

"I worked Van Nuys Division for a while."

"Jones, when did you work the street? Maybe you've met Mr. Sutherland before," one of the other soldiers joked.

"Fuck you, jackass. You couldn't buy what I've got," Jones shot back. I liked her style. She was my kind of people. *This could get entertaining.*

"I never worked vice in the Valley," I lied. Actually, I had a lot of fun working massage parlors while assigned to Valley vice. Knowing just when to lower the boom and flash the tin is tricky. In order to get the violation, "unlawful happy endings," you had to get them to engage in the act for money. Technically, you were supposed to stop it right before the magic moment, but timing could be elusive. Too soon and you might lose a solid violation. Too late, and you'll need a towel. Regrettably, mistakes can happen. Police work is fraught with all manner of peril.

"Any of you guys know this Khalid dude we are going to visit tonight?"

I never like to rely on one source of information when more are available. Maybe one of these kids knew something Lieutenant Shore didn't.

They all shook their heads with that not-me-officer look every cop knows so well.

"Any of you been to the haji shop?"

"I've bought a hookah there," a baby-faced kid named Jaramillo replied.

"Shop's next to the restaurant, right?" I asked.

"Yes, sir," he replied.

"Many of you guys go there?"

"A few. Some of the guys have eaten there. Goode got the shits, but the locals seem to like it."

Okay, now that we've settled that, I won't be having dinner there tonight.

"Can you guys buy DVDs there?" I asked innocently.

"Yeah. They're all pirated. Khalid's are pretty good. I got *Iron Man*, and *The Dark Knight* from him."

Wonder why Khalid's were better?

"Most haji DVDs are really grainy. His are clear and not jumpy."

"Why are his better?" I let that dangle for a moment.

Jones chimed in, "I hear he gets them from overseas or something. Maybe China or Iran."

"Iran is not overseas," another soldier said as he sat down across from me. His nametape read *Hernandez*.

"No, but China is," I said.

"China makes everything, man. We don't make shit," Hernandez observed.

The kid was right. We don't make much.

On that depressing note, I took a couple more drags on my stogie and called it. I had confirmed the intel. Khalid had to be connected.

I walked back over to my CHU. I closed the door and started get out of my ACUs, when I heard a light tapping on my door.

"Yes," I answered.

"Security, sir." *A female voice?*

"Don't tell me there's a rapist in the area and you want to make sure I'm okay."

"That's right, sir. Just want to make sure our civilians are safe and sound."

I opened the door and there was my Venus. She blew past me in a flash. I closed the door just in time.

Nancy threw her arms around me and began a very thorough examination of the family jewels.

"I didn't know you were a urologist!"

"I'm taking a correspondence course and had a homework assignment. Can you help me out?"

"Help is my middle name."

We got straight to business. I'm in reasonably fair shape for an old fart, but she damn near killed your humble correspondent. She must have been reading books or something. Anyway, we were done and lying on that narrow rack when she began nuzzling my ear.

"Rick."

I feigned coma.

"Rick," she prodded.

She was clearly determined to have a post-coital conversation, also known as a PCC. In my experience, PCCs rarely end well for yours truly, and dare I say most of the male heterosexual world. For me, it's akin to that other terrifying moment, when your beloved says, "Honey, I have an idea."

Foolishly throwing caution and good sense to the wind, I responded, "Yes, my caduceus wearing dove, what may I do for thee?"

"Rick, I know this is going pretty fast, but I think we should talk. About us. Where is this going?"

"You mean I'm not just a piece of meat to you?" I deadpanned.

"Funny, asshole," Nancy replied.

"Is it funny? I never knew. To tell you the truth, except for the occasional hemorrhoid flare-up, I've never really looked. But you, being the healer, I'm guessing you've looked at a lot of them."

"Yes, I've seen my share. In fact, I may be looking at my biggest yet."

"I was once told by an LAPD commander—who later made chief and shall remain nameless—that my asshole was my best side. But what did he know? He was just a cop."

"I've heard cops know a great deal about assholes."

"We see our share."

"Do you always dodge important questions with inane babble?"

"Only when it involves money, freedom, or virility."

"Now can you get serious?"

"About what?" This was getting fun.

She jumped up and pulled on a tee shirt and panties.

"Nice tan lines. Very sexy."

"This may be the last time you'll see them."

"Nah, not possible. I'm like a Lay's potato chip. You can't just eat one. I'm irresistible."

"Yes, you are like a potato chip. Salty, full of fat and cholesterol, and bad for me."

"Bad, but *very* tasty."

I could see it was time to stop toying with her and get serious—sort of.

"Well, Doc, I always thought we could just have a little fun together and see where that goes."

"That's fine, but I'm scheduled to rotate back to the States soon, and despite my best efforts to resist, you've wormed your way under my skin."

"Like one of those tape worms they pull out of some guy's nose that's three feet long and weighs ten pounds?"

"Like that, only nastier."

"That's me all over."

Obviously, she wanted more than a casual fling, and so did I. We were at a textbook JIR, "Juncture in Relationship," moment. JIRs are ticklish. Sort of like milking a black mamba. One slip, and you've got fifteen minutes to live. I was now about to milk the snake.

"Look, I've really enjoyed our time together, and I really like where we are at right now. But I guess I'm still a little gun shy after my divorce."

You have my permission to call bullshit on the "I'm just a little gun shy after the divorce" line. She knew it too. I could see it in her eyes. She knew I'd fallen for her too. The General Order No. 1 crap was a complication. If we got caught doing the nasty, I'd just get sent home without my lunch. She could get court-martialed.

Yet she clearly wanted this relationship to progress to the "next level," whatever that was.

"Where would you like to see this go?" I asked.

"Well, I'd like to see if we can't continue this back home. You won't be over here forever either."

I was groping for a safe response when the alarm went off on my Blackberry. I hated the thing, too many bells for me. Yes, I carry two phones.

"What the hell was that?" Nancy asked, clearly annoyed.

My Blackberry ringer was set for the old *Dragnet* theme. *Dump daa da Dump daa dump da daa . . .*

"That, my semi-clad vixen, was the theme from *Dragnet.* You must have lived in a cultural vacuum."

"I know what it is, dork. Remember cops run, or more correctly, occur, in my family."

"Occur" sort of sounded like diphtheria or something even more attractive, but I let it go.

"We need to gear up," she said, all business. She was pulling on her pants and blouse and caught my leering gaze.

"I'm falling for you, asshole. You better not fuck this up. I shoot back!" She winked, gave me a quick kiss, and was gone in a flash. I sat on the bed for a minute pondering my fate. Then I pulled on my clothes and grabbed my battle rattle. It was showtime.

Lieutenant Shore and Captain Clark were in the TOC. Clark was still in his PT gear. Lieutenant Shore on the other hand was seriously prepared. She had more shit hanging off her than my ex's Christmas tree. We discussed the plan and what I hoped to learn. That done, we walked outside to brief the members of the patrol that would escort me.

Lieutenant Shore briefed the patrol, then she introduced Major Weaver.

"Major Weaver is standing in for Doc, who's got the squirts again." Nice to hear I hadn't been the only one. "She's got Doc's bag, so if you get any splinters or paper cuts, the major will fix you up."

Lieutenant Shore said we'd walk in with one MRAP shadowing. I thought about asking to ride in the MRAP. Why walk when you can ride? Then I took one look at Nancy and all the crap she had on plus the medic bag and thought better of it. If Medicine Woman could hoof it in, so could I.

Lieutenant Shore continued with the briefing. "Finally, if myself or staff get hit, take care of business, then deal with us. Neutralize the threat first."

"Steve's got the long rifle, Mike and Phil have SAWs and Pete's got the 203." I searched out Pete who was armed with an M-16 rifle with an M203 40mm grenade launcher slug underneath. He was studded with fat little "golden eggs" in pouches on his body armor. That 40mm egg could scramble your ass up very nicely if you were on the receiving end. Good to have around.

After the brief was over, one of the guys, a Hispanic kid from New Mexico, led a short prayer.

"Lord protect us and keep us safe so that we may return to our families one day. Bless all our brothers and sisters in arms and keep them safe. Amen."

I wasn't much of a church guy, but I got a bit of religion not long after arriving in Iraq. I didn't go to services or anything, but I had a word or two with the Almighty daily. I needed all the help I could get.

CHAPTER 20

WALKABOUT

"**O**kay, guys, let's load up and move out." It was now 1740 hours, or 5:40 PM for you civilians. The group: Lieutenant Shore, Nancy, and your semi-humble correspondent, walked single file thorough the camp over to some red fifty-gallon oil drums. Each drum had a large rectangular hole cut into the top. The barrels were filled with sand and intended to contain an accidental discharge caused by some errant ding-dong who didn't know how to safely load his or her weapon. I was very familiar with these things from my days at LAPD. Every facility had several of them, and I knew from personal experience they worked very well. *Anyone could make a mistake.*

One by one, each soldier moved up to the barrel and chambered a live round. I stepped up and did my thing; first with my pistol, then with the M4 carbine. The looks I got from a few of the guys told me I passed muster. Medicine Woman handled her weapons like a pro. No surprise there.

We formed up in two lines, each patrol member about five meters apart. Lieutenant Shore and another kid were in front.

We started for the town center, which was about half a mile away. It was nearly dark. Soon, the Iraqi version of ghetto dogs started barking.

A few approached us as we moved down the street. The huge tan MRAP stayed about twenty-five meters behind us.

As we walked, I scanned the ground for any indicators of a buried mine or IED. Realistically, I knew this was unlikely, but after all they called it a "combat operation" *for a reason.* Every person except for Nancy and myself had probably walked this same stretch of road hundreds of times. It had become routine for them. It was not for me. All of my senses, sight, hearing, and unfortunately smell, were in a heightened state. I cradled my carbine in my arms, business end pointed down, right thumb resting on the safety.

My olfactory senses were soon caressed by the delicate aromas of burning rubber, wood, shit, garbage, and more shit. Everywhere I stepped, there was trash. Hardly a speck of earth was devoid of discarded wrappers, bottles, or cans. Somebody needed to talk to these people about their diet. Too many processed foods could kill them before they got a chance to put on a suicide vest. On second thought, maybe all this store-bought processed food was part of an overall victory strategy—assuming, of course, there was one.

As we walked, the staff sergeant lapped the column like a mother hen. He must have walked three times as far as the rest of us. I was impressed. It was hot and muggy, I was soaked, and we were just getting started. I brushed away a bowling-ball-sized bead of sweat, and I noticed that the fair Nancy was just hitting her stride. She must have been humping twenty extra pounds of gear. Far more than me, yet not so much as a single bead of sweat was visible. I hated her. She probably did Zumba, wearing her full battle rattle and maybe nothing else. *Steady lad, steady. Keep your head in the game.*

It was exhilarating and a bit scary. I also felt a tremendous sense of pride and awe. I was surrounded and protected by the finest young people America had to offer. Smart, compassionate, motivated, and fit. Generous in peace, ruthless in war. It was my high honor and privilege to be with them this night.

I heard the recorded call to prayer, the *azan,* as we entered the town. I always found it fascinating whenever I heard it. It has a mystic and haunting quality. Of course, this also had an air of bullshit about it. The timing was all wrong. There are very specific times for the call to evening prayer, called the Maghrib, and it wasn't 1805 hours. I checked before I left. The Maghrib call to prayer on this night was supposed to sound at 1901 hours local time. This counterfeit call to prayer was actually a warning. Five-0 was here.

My hand tightened on the grip of my weapon. I was ready. Well, truth be told, I was ready to shit my pants if the bullets started flying.

One of the kids in front of me slowed a bit and pulled alongside. "You good?" he whispered.

"Yep, all good," I said in my most confident big boy voice.

"We are about three hundred meters from the objective."

He glanced around and whispered, "Looks pretty quiet, but—"

His voice trailed off ominously. Well, if things did go south, I felt that these guys could take care of business. With that, he moved a few feet forward and reassumed his position in the formation.

Walking into town, they sort of reminded me of that final scene from *The Wild Bunch* where Pike and crew calmly walk back into the village to get their guy back. Of course, that movie ends in one hell of a shootout where damn near everybody gets killed.

After a few more minutes of walking, we rounded a corner and there it was—Chez Bistro De Merde. Chez Merde for short. No valet or even a lawn jockey to tie up your camel. I didn't see a Yusufiyah Department of Public Health and Sewage Production health grade rating either. My guts involuntarily rumbled. Not a good sign. Next door was a standard issue haji shop complete with funky movie posters, hookahs and other odds and ends in the front window.

I watched as the soldiers started taking up security positions at various points on both sides of the street. A couple of locals were laughing and slapping Iraqi style at a table near the front. They hardly gave the GIs a second look.

Parked in front of the place was a beat up old blue Toyota sedan. I wasn't crazy about this vehicle parked in front, and from the looks of it, neither was the staff sergeant. He assigned a couple of GIs to give it a once over. Soon, the back seats were out and on the sidewalk. Just like we used to do in the old days. The only thing that was missing was a pair of thugs in cuffs sitting on the curb. How I miss those simpler days.

After a good five minutes, the all-clear sign was given, and the rest of the patrol moved forward, taking up security positions around Chez Merde. Lieutenant Shore, a couple of enlisted guys, and the interpreter moved up next to me.

"Mr. Sutherland, we are ready to make contact. Khalid is just inside."

"Okay, let's go then." I looked around for Nancy, but she was MIA. I removed my name tape from my blouse and stuffed it in a pocket. Not having one would make me different than all the other soldiers and could put a bit of fear in Mr. Khalid. Besides, he didn't need to know who I was.

We moved forward to the front of the restaurant, thirty meters distant. Lieutenant Shore and the soldiers were up front with me, with the interpreter following closely.

The front of the restaurant—which, believe me, is being generous— had one table outside and four or five inside. The interior had a few posters taped to the walls of what I'm guessing passed for Iraqi recording artists, and what could have been a vacation or family photo that sure as hell looked like it was taken somewhere on Hollywood Boulevard. I needed a closer look, but now was not the time.

Khalid was sitting at a table with a cigarette hanging from his lips and a cup of tea on the table in front of him. He was living large. In his mid-forties and balding, he was dressed in a plain, but quality, white cotton dress shirt and black slacks. He had a fancy looking wristwatch and a gold pinky ring on his left hand. It was like Tony Soprano holding court at Satriale's Pork Store.

As I approached Khalid, I could see a female and a small boy in a back room, which my keen nose told me had to be either the kitchen or a toilet. I suspected she was the proud Mrs. Khalid and Junior was third in line to inherit Daddy's little empire. They had two other boys, supposedly at UCLA. Or maybe they were out back playing with grenades.

The interpreter approached Khalid and made the introductions in Arabic. I shook his hand and placed my right hand over my heart, bowing slightly as a sign of respect. I was told it means you have come in peace and with a pure heart, which in my case could be open to debate. I didn't expect Khalid to give us a damn thing, but it's always best to start in a respectful tone. Garden hoses and telephone books could come later.

The investigative technique I was using is called "shaking the tree." I'd typically use it when the case is going nowhere, and I wanted to artificially stimulate movement. In this case, shaking the tree was simply meeting Khalid and letting him know he was on our radar. Lieutenant Shore already had several covert cameras and other sneaky bits spread throughout the village. In fact, one of those cameras was aimed at the front door of Chez Merde.

We were also going to try and intercept calls made after we left. Our MRAP was equipped with the latest in SIGINT collection equipment. I suspected that as soon as we boogied, Khalid would get on the phone and start blabbing about his visit with the cops—I mean the Army—and we'd be listening.

Khalid invited us to sit with him, which we were going to do anyway. The interpreter launched into the standard Arabic greetings and "How ya doin'?" stuff. He explained why we were there and that we just wanted to help keep peace and make everyone love each other, *blah blah blah*. I swear, I could see Khalid laughing inside as he listened to the bullshit. He was trying to act interested, but he wasn't quite ready for an actor's studio interview with that old dude who seems terminally constipated.

I let the interpreter rattle on. Khalid responded in Arabic and smiled at me and Lieutenant Shore. It was then I noticed he had all his teeth. Khalid was obviously not your typical Yusufiyahite.

"He says he would really like to help you but does not know much," the interpreter Abdel said. *Wow never heard that one before.*

Based on what Lieutenant Shore told me, I was betting he understood more English than he wanted to admit.

I was used to the old "no speakie English game." Foreign born suspects played it all hoping that you'd get frustrated and give up. It usually worked. But not with me. It was time to shake things up.

"Khalid, by the way, can I call you that?" I held out my hand to shake his.

His face registered a little surprise at first, then he shook his head as if he didn't understand. Khalid was used to being the HMFIC around here. Locals and family probably addressed him very deferentially. But I'm not a local and didn't get that memo.

"Look man, you can play this stupid no English game all you want, I don't give a shit."

I left my hand out as Khalid continued with his blank stare.

"Look, I know you speak English, 'cause I've heard you." *Yes, I lied yet again.*

Khalid just silently looked at me, so I turned it up a notch.

"Khalid, here's what's going happen if you don't start making me happy. I'm going to lose my temper and have this nice lieutenant haul your ass back to the camp and throw you on the next chopper to Abu Ghraib. That is, of course, if you don't happen to fall out along the way. Happens all the time. You'd be surprised how many people who 'don't know anything' have fallen out of helicopters this year alone." I paused to let that sink in. Now for the *coup de grâce.*

"Oh, and then I'm gonna call my friends in US Immigration and have your sons dragged out of UCLA and hauled off." When the interpreter started to translate what I had just said, I motioned for him to stop. Abdel's expression went from confusion to anger. I glanced at Shore, expecting her to cut me off at the knees.

Instead, the lieutenant said to Abdel, "Why don't you take a break?"

Khalid looked at Lieutenant Shore, searching for some indication that I was in trouble for what I had just said. To her credit, Lieutenant Shore saw this and gave Khalid nothing. Khalid raised his hand in surrender and then took mine. He had a firm grip.

His sons were clearly a weak spot. Now to see what came next.

"Before we speak further, may I ask your name?"

"Call me Dennis," I replied.

"Dennis, why have you come here?" Khalid asked in an even tone.

"I heard you do a great *shawarma,*" I replied, not giving him an inch.

He gave me that *Okay, so you're going to be an asshole* look.

"Would you like tea?" Khalid offered.

My sphincter tightened at the thought of more tea. Its life had just stated returning to normal but, of course, I couldn't refuse Khalid's hospitality.

"Yes, that would be fine. Shukran," I said sincerely.

I was about to start with a few preliminaries when I heard Nancy's voice coming from the kitchen. She was talking with Mrs. Khalid, who, surprise, surprise, spoke a little English herself.

I couldn't pick up much of what she was saying, as my attention was focused on his lordship, but I did hear the word *fever.* Her Doctorship obviously had it under control and was doing her thing, so I got back to mine.

I knew I had to maintain Mr. K's undivided attention, or I'd lose the upper hand. I glanced around the room, looking for that photo I'd seen earlier. I excused myself from the table for a minute and walked over to it for a look. *Perfect.* It was Khalid and two young men, presumably his sons, standing in front of the ticket booth at the El Capitan Theater on Hollywood Boulevard. The image was tight so there wasn't much in the background, but the ticket booth was unmistakable, as were the address numerals displayed in front: 6838 Hollywood Boulevard. I know, I worked Hollywood Division for two sin-filled years. I walked back over and placed the picture on the table in front of him as I continued with the small talk about his family.

"How many children do you have?" I asked.

"Allah has blessed me with three sons. Ali, my oldest, Hassan, and Khalid." He smiled a little as he spoke. He was clearly very proud of his sons.

"God has been good to both of us. I have two sons. What are Ali and Hassan studying?"

"Ali is studying electrical engineering. Hassan, economics."

"You must be very proud. It is not easy to for an Iraqi to attend college in the United States."

"Yes, it was not easy, but with Allah's blessing—"

"Is Khalid in the kitchen?"

"Yes, that is my wife and our son," Khalid Senior smiled.

We talked about raising our boys and agreed that Iraq was better off now that Saddam was worm shit. The usual Iraqi small talk. My new BFF and I even exchanged recipes. He gave me one for date soufflé, and I gave him Grandma Sutherland's haggis recipe.

Khalid was relaxed and answered my questions easily, as if he was getting a little bored. His back was to the kitchen, but I could see that Nancy in full-healer mode. Khalid Junior was on a table and Nancy was palpating his abdomen. The poor little guy cried out in agony. That wasn't good.

"Khalid, is your son ill?"

Lieutenant Shore looked a bit surprised.

"Yes, Dennis, he has been sick for the last day. We were about to take him to a clinic when you came."

"Khalid, don't worry, he is in good hands. That female soldier examining him is a physician."

We made more small talk. It's considered impolite in the Arab world to get straight to business during a meeting, and if I'm anything, I'm polite. He looked vaguely familiar. It was very possible I had come across a report on him during my time on the Joint Terrorism Task Force. I'd need to reach back to them to see what details they had on Mr. K.

"Dennis, you are no soldier. Why are you here?" Khalid asked.

Dennis? Who's Dennis? *Oh, shit, that's me, I almost forgot.*

"I'm with the health inspector and so far, I'm not liking what I see. You don't have the allotted number of flies in the kitchen, and the smell of decaying meat is simply not strong enough for you to get an A-rating."

He smirked. "You are funny, but no soldier."

How can he tell? Crap, my humor had blown my cover again. I guess the Army guys had little to no sense of humor. Maybe it was from getting shot at and blown up.

"Khalid, you've got a problem, and I'm going to help you. Your friends no longer trust you. That means that one day, you and your family will get in your car. You will turn the key and, in an instant, you and your wife and son will be dead." I was winging it with this, but a guy like Khalid is always looking over his shoulder. He was probably on somebody's shitlist and he knew it.

"My family is safe. I do not need or want your help. You people invaded our country and got Saddam. That is a good thing. He killed many good Muslims and was a devil. That is over now, and it is time for you to leave."

"Leaving or staying is not my call. If it was up to me, we'd have never come to your country. Your local squabbles are your problem. But when Americans die, it's my problem."

Khalid was expressionless.

I leaned over the table and spoke very softly to him as I'd done to hundreds of guys just like him. No *CSI Miami* dramatics, no fist-pounding or chair-throwing. Just the facts.

"Khalid, it's your choice. You can continue to trust your murdering friends, or you can do the right thing for yourself and your family and help me stop this." I waited.

"If you do not help me," I went on, "I will come for you and your family. You're right, I'm not a soldier. I'm a policeman and I'm good at it. Unlike these soldiers, I have no rules." That was, of course, bullshit, but in Iraq, the police had no rules and were consequently hated and feared. Maybe knowing I was a cop would add a little stress to his day.

I glanced at the picture of him taken in Hollywood and pointed to the two young men. "Khalid, I know who you talk to. I know your role in the attacks, and I know who wants you dead. I can be your best friend or your worst nightmare."

He remained unmoved. Whatever, I was on a roll and having fun.

"Khalid, I really don't have a problem with you. You're a family guy like me. But some of your friends like to kill Americans and Iraqis a little too much. It's them I'm after."

"If you would leave, no Americans would have to die," Khalid responded.

"We've already covered that. I'm done with you."

Back in LA, threatening jail time would sometimes get a crook's attention. But in Iraq, bad guys frequently didn't make it to jail. They simply get a little tribal justice in a roadside ditch. Not that there aren't any jails or prisons in Iraq. The ones I'd seen were primitive, with more blood stains than bars. Average life expectancy in an Iraqi prison was five years or less.

I started to get up when Major Nancy Weaver disturbed my mojo.

"Lieutenant Shore, I need to talk with you and, ah . . . Dennis for a minute."

I shot her a glance. She could ruin my carefully backstopped cover.

"Sure," Shore responded.

"Excuse us for a moment." Lieutenant Shore and I got up. Shore motioned for one of the troopers to move in and watch Khalid while we huddled.

"I think the boy has appendicitis. He has a very high fever, nausea, and severe abdominal pain, lower right quadrant. I've seen this too many times in kids. He needs surgery soon, or we'll lose him."

"I could see that the poor little guy was in pain," I said.

"Have you explained this to his mother?" Lieutenant Shore asked.

"Yes, she understands. She's pretty worried, as she should be," Nancy said.

"What can we do?" I asked.

"She seems to trust me. She understands her son needs surgery. I think she gets my explanation of what's wrong."

"I'll have the interpreter give you a hand," Lieutenant Shore offered.

"Thanks, that will be good. He needs a Medevac."

My seasoned and somewhat twisted mind went into overdrive. "Hey, kids, it occurs to me that this could be an opportunity. Young Khalid is sick, we save his life. Momma will love us, and Daddy will follow. He'll roll on his homies like a big fat dog, and we'll find our bad guys."

Doc Nancy and Lieutenant Shore looked at me like I had just grown horns and a forked tail. I probably shouldn't have revealed my plan, but it could work and maybe save some young American lives. I've always followed the adage that you get more with honey than vinegar, and I could be as sweet as they come. Just like a plate of honey-soaked baklava, that's me.

"I'll order up a helo," Lieutenant Shore announced.

"And I could use your interpreter now," Nancy said as she glared at me.

"Sure, I'll send him back in," Lieutenant Shore replied and quickstepped out to the MRAP.

I looked out the front door and could see the interpreter knew what was up already. He bounded in straight back to the kitchen and got to work.

I sat back down with Khalid, who also clearly already knew what was happening. "Your doctor is good?"

I wanted to say, *"Brother, if you only knew,"* but my keen sense of decency and decorum ruled that out. "She is an excellent physician. Your son is in very good hands." I studied Khalid's face as I offered this last bit of reassurance. The indifference and arrogance were gone, just as I knew they would be. He was a father like me. His son was hurting and could die. Many Islamists are so rabid with hate they would reject any offer of assistance from an American, especially if it came from an immodest infidel woman dressed as a man.

My gut told me Khalid was a pragmatist, not an Islamist. His bottle-throwing, fist-in-the-air, "Death to America" radical days were behind him. He was now simply trying to survive and raise his family in war-torn Iraq. A place where loyalties shifted in a heartbeat, and you'd better be able to pick the winning side before they know they're winning. Mr. Khalid was a survivor. I just needed to exploit this and provide the proper motivation. But now was not the time to continue our talk about his playmates. That would come after Medicine Woman had worked her magic and Junior was out of danger.

Lieutenant Shore returned and walked past me straight to Nancy. I excused myself and joined them, just as Lieutenant Shore was delivering some bad news.

"The choppers are down. There's a sandstorm blowing in. The window for any air transport will be closed in ten minutes or less.

"I can operate back at the JSS if I have to," Nancy offered. "There's an improvised OR. I checked it out. It's not pretty, but it will do. Lieutenant, your medics can assist me. I'm sure Dennis here would also be glad to lend a hand. Especially if it helps him get what he needs."

"That drew blood."

"It should," Major Weaver replied. Lieutenant Shore's look told me she was in lock step with Nancy on this one.

Nancy was interrupted by a young trooper who announced we had company—two carloads of MPs who were part of a Mobile Training Team. They were asking for Lieutenant Shore. She excused herself and walked outside. I turned to Nancy.

"Cut me some slack, I'm trying to help the kid and do my job."

"I get that, but it wouldn't hurt to have a little compassion for these people."

"I've got compassion by the truckload. But my priority is saving our kids. I'll cut every corner and exploit every advantage to make that happen. Including the kid."

"Fuck you."

"Only if you insist."

Nancy turned and stormed off, leaving a trail of fairy dust in her wake. On some level deep inside, she knew I was right. But this was war, American kids were dying every day, and I had a job to do.

As a former partner who was a Vietnam veteran once told me, "War is hell, and combat's a motherfucker."

CHAPTER 21

THE DOCTOR IS IN

I waited a while before I joined the party out on the street. I wanted to poke around the building and keep an eye on Khalid while he sat at the table. He was smoking and constantly wiping sweat from his brow.

Nancy was preparing to move Khalid Junior. Apparently, she had convinced Mom to let her treat Junior. Mom, in turn, worked Khalid senior over, ultimately getting him to agree. Nancy retrieved her large black duffel bag from one of the MRAPS and brushed past me back into the restaurant along with four soldiers, one of them carrying a stretcher. Not a word, a look, nothing. *Guess she's still pissed.*

I watched the MP patrol dismount their vehicles. Their mission was to bring professionalism and the rule of law to the Iraqi Police, even if they didn't want it. The team comprised a second lieutenant, two noncommissioned officers, and five troopers. The lieutenant looked to be of Mid-Eastern decent, which would make sense even for the Army. I walked over to introduce myself, extending my hand.

"Rick Sutherland, overpaid civilian."

We shook. "Lieutenant Habib, 827th MPs."

"I'm retired LAPD, working a counter-IED contract with Applied Logistics."

"Yes, I know of you," Lieutenant Habib said.

"You do?"

"Yes. Major Copeland said I might run into you out here."

"Yes, well, here I am. How is the good major?"

"He was good when I last saw him."

"When was that?" I asked innocently.

"About an hour ago. He's headed this direction with his team."

That was good news. Copeland and his handpicked team would probably be useful handling Khalid. Not to mention the added firepower they could bring to bear.

"Great," I said. Just as I started to ask another question, Lieutenant Habib interrupted. "I'm sorry, Mr. Sutherland, but I've got to check on my guys. Will you excuse me?"

"Of course," I replied.

Lieutenant Habib walked over to one of his vehicles, an up-armored Humvee, and said something to a figure in the passenger seat.

Nancy called out. "I could use your help now." I turned to see her framed in Khalid's door with that look that every married man knows and fears.

"Yes, Major, how may I be of service?"

"Would you speak with Khalid? He seems to be having second thoughts about letting his son go with us."

I hustled over to Khalid. One of the soldiers I'd shared lunch with was standing with him. I gave him a nod, and he left us.

"Major Weaver said you have changed your mind."

"I want to take my son to a doctor near here," Khalid said.

"How far away?" I asked.

"About twenty kilometers."

"Do you know the doctors there?"

"No, I do not know them."

"Khalid needs surgery. Are they equipped to operate there?"

"I believe so."

I studied the man's face as we spoke. He looked tired and a little scared, like he might be just going through the motions.

"Khalid, I'm going to tell you something about Major Weaver. She is a very well-respected physician. She has helped many of our soldiers and has even treated me twice. Major Weaver has told me she needs to operate on your son in the next few hours, or he may die."

Once again, I put my right palm over my heart in the Arab way to signify I was speaking with a pure heart. "Khalid, my friend I would trust her with my own sons."

"Thank you, Dennis, but I must take him to one of our own doctors. I hope you can understand."

I thought about telling him there was a sandstorm coming, but then I had a better idea.

"I will speak with Major Weaver to see if there is something that can be done here." I knew there wasn't, but it would delay things for a while.

I walked back outside and asked the nearest soldier "Where's Khalid's ride?"

"Excuse me, sir?"

"Where's his car?"

"It's parked out back. Blue Nissan van."

I walked around back and spied a couple of troopers, one carrying a SAW machine gun standing watch nearby. I nodded at them confidently and walked over to the blue Nissan. It was covered in a thick layer of Iraqi dust and the back was full of empty juice and water bottles. It reminded me of how Charlotte's car always looked, except it was missing a yoga mat.

The two soldiers were looking for threats and paid no attention to me. I crawled under the rear of the car and pulled out my Emerson knife. The blade snapped open instantly, and I set to work. Rather than stab the tire from the outside, which would be a little obvious, I drove the blade of my knife through the inside sidewall of the left rear tire, close to the rim. The escaping air hissed and kicked up all manner of dust and crap in my face. *The things I do for my country.*

With the tire now flat, I directed my attention to the spare tire. It was mounted on a rack in the back. I removed the valve stem cap and pressed the stem releasing air from the spare. Presto-change-o, two flat tires. Well, not completely flat. I left enough air in the spare, so it was not immediately obvious until you pulled it off the rack. There would be no time to change that tire before the storm hit, and Khalid would know it.

I returned to the restaurant and approached Major Weaver.

"Any luck with Khalid?"

"Nope. I told him he was risking his son's life, but he's not listening. He insists he wants to take the boy to a clinic."

"He will now," I said.

"What'd you do?"

"Let's just say he won't be taking any road trips for a while. But he needs to discover this on his own. Let him go through the motions." Nancy looked at me like I had two heads. "Trust me," I assured her.

She shrugged. "Okay, but I'm not sure *trust* is the word I'd use with you."

"Whatever, Doc."

Nancy told Khalid and the missus that they could do what they wanted, but they were risking their son's life. Khalid did all the talking, while Mrs. Khalid stared daggers at him. She remained silent like a good Arab wife, but it was written all over her face.

Khalid said something in Arabic to her that I'm sure was "Get Junior ready and I'll warm up the Ford." I bit my lip as he went out back. *This should be fun.*

About five minutes later, he returned, dusty and red faced. He approached the little missus and said something in Arabic to his wife, no doubt. "We're fucked, have it your way." A heated exchange followed. Maybe Mrs. Khalid wasn't a good Arab wife after all.

Khalid walked over to Major Weaver, who was applying a cold compress to Junior's forehead. I moved closer to listen.

"Doctor, my car will not drive. Will you please care for my son?"

"Yes, it will be my honor. We will move him to our base immediately.

You and your wife may come along."

"I will come along. My wife will stay."

"We had better get moving," Nancy said. "The storm is coming."

I started to move away so I didn't get caught eavesdropping when, as if on cue, Lieutenant Shore approached us both. "I wanted to let you know that I've asked for several other vehicles to be sent over here from the JSS. They should be here in about ten minutes."

"Lieutenant, that sounds great, my feet were hurting a little anyway," I responded.

"I'm concerned about the time it will take for them to arrive. The boy is very ill," Nancy said.

"Can you arrange transport sooner with the MRAP and the MPs here? They could provide escort."

"We can load everybody up in the vehicles we have here and head out now if you wish."

"That would be best, Lieutenant."

"Yes, ma'am," Lieutenant Shore replied, leaving to make it happen.

I hustled outside to take a casually indifferent, yet alert pose. I was counting the seconds until she emerged. I didn't have long to wait. True to her word, she walked alongside the stretcher carrying Khalid Junior. She held an IV bag in her left hand and the young lad's hand in her right. The boy was sweating and moaning. Khalid's father was on the other side, holding the boy's hand and whispering something to him in Arabic.

As they loaded the kid in the MRAP, he looked up at me and smiled and so did Nancy. Daddy, on the other hand, did not. You must admit, two out of three ain't bad.

Lieutenant Habib and his MP unit loaded back in their vehicles, which I now noticed had a few Iraqi beauty marks on them. It looked to me like small arms and maybe some grenade fragments. The driver of one of the Humvees pulled alongside and motioned for me to get in. The left rear passenger door popped open. Well, not really popped open. The armored HUMVEE/M1151's doors don't pop anywhere, unless you're talking about the poor slob who pops out his shoulder trying to get one open.

I slid into the passenger seat. The guy that would have occupied the right rear seat was up in the small turret manning a 7.62mm machine gun. I could only see his legs as he stood in his turret position. The guy in the right front, which is traditionally where the leader sits, was on the radio talking Army gibberish about something. He had an Eastern European accent.

"Roger, we are escorting patrol back to JSS. Moving in five mikes. Will advise. Out."

The sergeant in the right front turned to me and smiled. He had on his Kevlar helmet and a pair of Oakley's, but damned if he didn't look like Khanov, the guy I surprised in the latrine the other day.

"Do I know you?" he asked.

"I don't think so."

"Yes, you knocked over bag in the shower."

"You got me there."

"Yes." He turned and faced forward.

"We will give you ride back."

"Great," I replied halfheartedly. *Maybe I should walk. Nancy says I need exercise.*

Soon, the little convoy was on the move. The driver and the dude in the right front said nothing as we slowly drove back toward the JSS. Our vehicle was leading the little convoy. I looked out the small bulletproof viewing port as we bounced along. It was dark, but a few locals were out and about. Just as we rounded a bend in the road at the edge of town, I heard three shots bounce off the armor plate on my side of the vehicle. The driver's head ducked instinctively.

Without missing a beat, the dude in the right front got on the radio and in a cool, controlled voice said, "We are taking fire from green building on left." I saw flashes coming from a window as we drove past. Our gunner opened fire with his machine gun; hot brass came tumbling down with each outgoing burst. I could see our answering fire's red tracers streak through the window and impact all around the green brick wall.

The driver started to slow, which didn't exactly thrill yours truly.

"Speed up, keep going," the dude in the right front ordered in a calm, almost deadpan voice.

Good thinking, I agreed. Whoever this Khanov was, he was one cool customer.

"Pull to corner." To my horror, the driver complied. We were going to provide covering fire for the rest of the convoy.

"Keep fire on window," I heard him tell the gunner over the vehicle's intercom.

The gunner complied with another burst of machine gun fire. I bravely looked through the viewing port and could see the other vehicles in the convoy bringing the green building under fire as they passed.

Then I saw dismounted soldiers moving on the building as our gun provided covering fire for them to maneuver. This wasn't some Hollywood bullshit scene with the hero pulling the pin of a grenade out with his teeth. This was real.

I turned and saw Nancy's MRAP carrying Khalid and the kid speed past then stop about 50 meters down the road. The MRAP's remotely controlled turret, called a CROW (Common Remotely Operated Weapon), scanned the area for more bad guys. Then the huge vehicle slowly moved on.

I looked back at the building just in time to witness the impact of a 40mm HE grenade. Thick black smoke and debris blew out the opening. That little *golden egg* blew the shit out of that room and likely smoked anyone inside.

I watched as the troopers advanced methodically, each one moving forward a few feet, taking a position of cover, while another moved past them in a leapfrog-like movement.

The troopers cautiously entered the building. I heard nothing after they went in, not a shout or a shot. After a few minutes, Lieutenant Shore emerged. She must have been with the rear element of the patrol when all the fun started.

She and another soldier ran over to our vehicle. The guy in the right front opened the door and stepped out. I could overhear their conversation.

"We have one EKIA insurgent in the building. He had an RPG and a couple of AKs. We're going to stay here and handle the SSE. Can you provide cover until we are done?"

"I'll get out and take a look," I announced.

"Fine," Sergeant Khanov replied. He didn't seem like he cared either way.

I watched as Lieutenant Habib joined their little powwow.

I fumbled with the door latch for a second until I felt it release, grabbed my M4, and stepped out onto the street and right into a pile of shit. I hoped it was canine.

"Lieutenant Shore, I'll take another 1151 and escort the MRAP back to the JSS," Lieutenant Habib offered.

"That would be great. We need to get the kid back quickly," Lieutenant Shore replied. "I'll let them know. See ya back at the fort."

Lieutenant Shore then spoke into her mic. "This is Shore, head back. The MPs will escort."

"Roger."

I walked over to Lieutenant Shore who was giving instructions to a young soldier.

"Jaramillo, grab Frankie and secure the northeast corner. Keep an eye out for more bad guys. If you see something, get me on the net. We'll try to get SSE done quickly and blow this dump." SSE stands for Sensitive Site Exploitation. It means collecting evidence and intelligence.

Iraq's own version of *ADAM-12* pulled up. Only Officers Reed and Malloy were replaced by Ali and Mohammed. Both were armed with AK-47s and both dumb-shits had their fingers on the triggers. Very professional. I greeted them with a heartfelt "Salaam," and they responded with an equally heartfelt Arabic version of "Gringo Go Home."

"Mr. Sutherland, can you find the interpreter?"

"Sure, LT." I ducked into what was left of the little green building. Upon entry, I was once again greeted with the delicate aroma of explosives, smoldering flesh, fresh blood, and, you guessed it, shit. Likely not canine. I climbed up a flight of stairs to the second floor and met a couple of soldiers and the interpreter who was over in the corner looking through some papers.

"Abdel, Lieutenant Shore needs you out front to help with some IPs."

Can I just say, we really screwed the pooch when we left the Iraqi Police in charge and dismantled the Army. In Iraq, the people respected the Army and despised the thoroughly corrupt police. Unfortunately, folks in the Bush Administration didn't get the memo. Dismantling the Army and leaving those dopes in charge was a major fuck up. Theft, bribery, torture, and murder were all part of their playbook. The things these guys could do with an electrical cord would bring more than a tear to your eyes, especially if it were being done to you.

Abdel dropped the papers and left. Being a curious sort, I naturally picked them up. They looked like identity papers, complete with a picture of the recently departed, but the national seal was wrong. Iraq's official government seal consists of an eagle proudly looking to the left with a red, white, and black shield on his breast. This guy's papers had the seal of Saudi Arabia, which has a palm tree reminiscent of Hitler's Afrika Korps, and two crossed sabers, naturally signifying peace and brotherly love. The two symbols were strangely similar in appearance.

I looked down at what was left of the newly reformed terrorist asshole. He was a military-aged male, clad in standard issue man jammies and sandals. He was probably one of those famous Saudi students you heard about all the time. This one was no doubt in Iraq to study the highly evolved Iraqi sanitation system.

In the center of the room was a large duffel bag that the soldiers were just throwing evidence into. There was no marking or individual bagging of each item. Nor were they wearing latex gloves, or even sketching a diagram and noting the location of each item found. They were just picking shit up and stuffing it in that bag. As any CSI fan will tell you, that is not how it's done.

It was a straightforward crime scene. One dead asshole armed with two AKs and an RPG, which thank God he never got to use, and a few papers. Pretty simple. I looked at the loaded RPG. *Why didn't he use it first? Odd.* Usually, they start with the big stuff to hopefully disable a vehicle or two. Then they lay down small arms fire on our kids as they dismount their vehicles. As I poked around the room, I saw a small black rubber antenna poking out of the rubble. This could be good.

"Specialist, could you come over and take a picture of this before I clear the rubble away?" I asked.

The kid moved over and looked down at the rubble, obviously not getting the possible significance of my little discovery.

"I need you to focus on that for the picture," I said, pointing at the antenna.

"There." I bent and pointed directly at the antenna.

"Sir, that looks like one of ours."

"Yes, it does."

He took a couple of photos. Then I removed the debris, revealing the cracked body of a PRC 148 tactical hand-held radio made by Thales. I don't know shit about radios other than they were the first thing to go out in any surveillance, but I did know enough to recognize this radio.

"Holy shit!" the specialist said. "What's this asshole doing with one of our secure handhelds?"

"That is the million-dollar question," I responded.

The radio was pretty busted up. It looked like it took a bullet or piece of frag in the case below the little screen and keyboard.

"Do you have any evidence bags on you?" I knew the answer to this one before the words left my mouth but hope springs eternal.

"Negative, sir."

"How about in your vehicles?"

"There's a box of ziplock plastic bags back on my vehicle."

"Great, we're gonna need them."

He left and returned in an instant. I looked around the room a little more. Nothing, just the usual empty bottles and candy wrappers, the stuff that guys consume while they're waiting to kill you.

"Specialist, you see all this trash?"

"Yes sir."

"All of this shit could have evidentiary value. We can get DNA from the empty bottles and discarded clothing, even food wrappers and empty shell casings. We can also get fingerprints. Do you know what DNA is?"

"Yeah, they can use it to identify my remains if I got blown to shit."

"Yep, that's it. But to be of any value it must be packaged properly to prevent cross-contamination. You can't just pick it up with your bare hands and stuff it into a duffel bag. You risk cross-contamination."

"You got some gloves?"

"Yes, sir."

"I'm Rick," I said as I offered him my hand.

"I'm Tommy, but they call me TJ."

"Okay, TJ, let's get this done and get the fuck outta here."

CHAPTER 22

MEANWHILE BACK
AT THE RANCH

We loaded up after the SSE was completed. The IPs took the rapidly decaying dead guy with them, which was fine. Normally, Coalition Forces take the insurgent KIAs with them for further investigation, but a new edict had recently come down giving the commander—that being the fair Lieutenant Shore—discretion to release the body to the Iraqi Army or the IPs if the situation warranted it. Apparently, in this case, the situation did. I was later told during my ride back with Lieutenant Shore that the senior IP guy was a bit of a prick and was insisting on conducting his own investigation. As if he gave a crap about a dead guy. The IP officer even threatened to have his men detain the GIs who had assaulted the house. Well, that wasn't going to happen.

The IP officer was either trying to solicit a bribe or assert his authority. Shore had dealt with him before and knew how to play him off. She shut him down on detaining our soldiers and gave him the stiff Saudi as a compromise gesture. *Smart thinking.* I really liked Lieutenant Shore. Smart, tough, did her homework and was cool under pressure. *She'd make a great cop.*

We arrived way too late for an evening snack, and I was famished.

I walked over to the TOC and asked after my favorite major and young Khalid. The duty NCO said she was still in surgery and Khalid Senior was standing by. Lieutenant Shore walked into the TOC and joined us.

"The sergeant says Major Weaver is still doing her medical thing and Daddy's with them," I reported. I then asked, "Hey LT, what's the chances of us getting some chow?"

"I could use something myself. I'll find somebody," she replied.

"Meet me at the chow hall in about thirty minutes."

"With grenades on," I responded.

I walked out of the TOC and dragged myself over to my room, threw the door open and turned on the lights.

"Scarlett, I'm back," I announced to a nearly empty room. I propped my carbine up next to the door and started stripping off my battle rattle.

Taking all that crap off reminded me of my days in uniformed patrol. At the end of a shift, especially day-watch in the summer, you could feel the trapped heat escape as you lifted the flaps of your bulletproof vest.

I pulled my body armor off and eased it down slowly to the floor. My CamelBak was dry. I unzipped my blouse. The T-shirt underneath was soaked through and smelled awful. I placed my pistol on the floor next to the bed, reached over and shut off the lights. I needed a little nap. My exhausted brain replayed the day's events as I tried to relax.

The bed felt great. I started to drift off into the comforting embrace of my beloved Jessica. I could even feel her fingers tickle my neck and shoulder as I surrendered to her feminine wiles. That was strange, her fingers were now tickling my nose, and they were hairy. We needed to speak about a depilatory. All that tickling made me sneeze.

I involuntarily opened my eyes only to stare into the two beady eyes of the father of all camel spiders in the known universe. Good thing I was dehydrated, 'cause no doubt I'd have pissed my pants. I let out a shriek that only sissies and twelve-year-old girls would be proud of and leapt out of bed. As I looked down, the monster reared back like a boar grizzly, snarling at me and bearing its fangs, which were dripping camel spider venom onto the comforter.

I quickly scanned the room for a weapon. I snatched up my Kevlar from the floor and smashed it on him with all the power I possessed. I heard a crunch like a Cheeto being stepped on. "Got ya fucker!" I yelled defiantly, like Leonidas must have after sticking yet another Persian at Thermopylae. I lifted the helmet expecting to see the lifeless form of an ex-camel spider. But nothing. I looked at the helmet in total disbelief. I scanned the bed frantically.

Then I spied him. To my horror, he was still clinging to the helmet, and was he pissed. He lunged at my fingers, no doubt hoping to sink in his fangs and exact a terrible revenge. Well, they don't call me "soul taker" for nothing. With mongoose-like reflexes, I flung my Kevlar against the wall, praying that I'd finally dispatched my seemingly immortal nemesis.

I carefully passed my flashlight over the helmet and wall. I could see a couple of hairy legs stuck to the imitation wood paneling. He was clearly wounded but might not be out of the fight. I kicked the helmet aside. As it rolled away, I saw his lifeless form. I scooped him up and tossed him out onto the dirt. I suppose he could have been a she, but with camel spiders there's a rule that guys are always attacked by male spiders. Don't blame me, I don't make the rules.

"Screw this. I ain't sleepin' here," I mumbled as I put my pistol belt back on. I grabbed all my gear and moved it next door to Nancy's room.

I was famished and needed to eat. All this warrior shit had really burned up the calories. I looked at my watch. I was fifteen minutes late, but I walked over to the chow hall anyway. I'm a civilian, they expect me to be fashionably late, and I'm not one to disappoint.

As I walked in, Lieutenant Shore was devouring what smelled like a cheeseburger. Probably not up to "In-N-Out" standards, but for Bumfuck, Iraq it would have to do. I could see the mess sergeant frying up a dozen more. I asked him for extra cheese and grabbed a Coke.

"Will you join me?" the good lieutenant asked.

"I'd be proud to."

"Thanks for helping with the SSE."

"My pleasure."

"We get anything good?"

At first, I was tempted to hold out and perhaps shade the truth a little. I couldn't help it, force of habit. In my business, you learned to keep your cards close. But she had impressed me and had handled herself beautifully with both the IPs and back at the restaurant during the little dust up.

"Yes, I think we got some good stuff. One of our radios, Saudi papers. I was surprised he had that stuff. Usually they travel pretty light."

"A radio?" Shore asked, surprised. "They usually have cellphones if anything."

"I recently read some intel saying they figured out we are pretty good at listening to cellphones," I offered.

"Do you know what kind of radio it was?"

"TJ said it looked like one the Special Operations guys use. Made by Thales."

"It won't be the first time they've gotten a hold of our stuff," Shore observed. "But SOF sensitive items like commo gear are usually pretty tightly controlled."

She was right. The Special Operations guys kept tight control of their gear. They understood the principal of Op Sec (Operational Security) very well. Hell, their lives depended on it. But even the "high speed, low drag" guys screw up sometimes.

"Sir, your burger is ready."

I got up and grabbed my burger. You know, it didn't look too bad.

I looked around the chow hall and didn't see any of the MPs who had helped earlier.

"Where did the cops go?" I inquired.

"Headed back to Victory about forty minutes ago."

"Heard anything more on the kid?"

"I talked with Clark. He said Doc Collins was all prepped when Major Weaver arrived. They took him right into surgery." Lieutenant Shore checked her watch. "They've probably been in for about an hour and a half. I'm surprised you're not in there buddying up to his dad."

"Nah, I didn't want to come on too strong with him at a time like this. When his kid gets fixed up, I'll move back in. Sometimes it's best to give it a rest and let your subject ponder life for a while. I'm betting he's thinking pretty hard right now."

The first bite of my burger was fantastic. Lieutenant Shore could see my pleasantly surprised look.

"The mess sergeant gets the meat and the buns from the exchange on Liberty. It's decent. He sets them aside for special occasions." Lieutenant Shore took a swig of diet soda. "I've always had a feeling about Khalid. Smarter than most around here. Got a little money. College. Never felt like he was hardcore."

"You're spot on. He's been to LA. He's smart enough to know the propaganda the Mullahs spew about Americans is bullshit. Hell, his two other boys are in UCLA right now swilling tequila. I don't get the feeling he's a committed jihadist. Sure, he's probably passed information to the bad guys, smuggled weapons. Stuff like that. But I just don't see him pulling the trigger on an American."

"My intel never fingered him as a bomb thrower."

I looked at my watch. Ninety minutes in surgery seemed long. The kid was small and skinny, so how hard could it be?

Hell, I could have done it with it a fifth of Jack and a pocketknife. How many movies have you seen where the hero does open heart surgery with a whiskey bottle in one hand and a bowie knife in the other?

I finished my burger while we bullshitted about the Army and cop work. I checked my watch during a lull in the conversation.

"Time to check up on the kid."

Lieutenant Shore nodded, and I left the semi-air-conditioned comfort of the chow hall and walked out into the sauna that is Iraq. I saw Major Herself walking toward the TOC from the med shed. She was dragging. Gone was the energetic quick step I had grown to hate during our little hike into the village. That seemed like a lifetime ago. She didn't see my stealthy approach.

"Good evening, Major. Or should I say, Good morning?" It was after midnight.

"Oh . . . hi. Guess I zoned out a little. Junior is doing well. Dad's been a pain in the ass, but he's calmed down now. Slipped him a Xanax."

"How'd you do that?"

"Xanax screwdriver. Three parts orange juice plus one finely ground Xanax."

"You had better not try that with me."

"What makes you think I haven't?"

"You're a cross between Doctor Crippen and," Just as I started to say Jane Seymour—the actress, not the queen—we both heard a screeching sound that I was becoming all too familiar with.

"Incoming!" she yelled at the top of her lungs.

Christ, not again, I thought as I scrambled alongside her to a concrete shelter that was about twenty meters away. We hunkered down just as the round flew overhead. I could see the glow of its rocket motor as it streaked downward. It looked like it was headed straight for the TOC building. Thank God it missed by about ten feet and landed on the opposite side. We waited for the detonation, but it never came.

"Must have been a dud," Nancy said. "I've got to get back to the med shed."

Before I could offer a protest, she was gone. Man, she has guts. I watched her streak toward the medical office running for all she was worth. *Running toward the sound of the guns.*

For a split second, I weighed my options; stay safe like the sissy boy I truly am or follow Nancy and get my ass blown off? I started to pull myself out of the shelter when another round impacted in the center of the compound. I hit the dirt and flattened out like a pancake.

This one detonated in a cloud of smoke, dust and frag. I saw chunks of plywood fly off the roof and sides of the JSS workout room. Hopefully no one was in there getting their daily dozen in. A fist-sized chunk of concrete smashed into the roof of the shelter I was cowering in. I had to find Nancy, but I wished I had my Kevlar and body armor with me.

I scrambled out and ran for the med shed. I could see that the door had been torn by flying shrapnel. Then, another round impacted the corner of the building. It turned into sticks and dust in an instant. The blast wave knocked me off my feet. I pulled myself back up and tried to blink away the tweety birds dancing and chirping before my eyes. My ears were ringing, and everything seemed to slow for a second. Another round came screeching in, but it went long and missed the compound. Haji's shooting was a bit off this time.

I freed the shed door and pushed my way inside. I had no idea where Nancy and the boy were. I couldn't see a damn thing through all the dust and smoke, so I pulled a small red LED light I carried on my dog tags.

I felt my way down the small hallway aided by the tiny red light. After a few feet, I reached a T-intersection. I could just make out two doors to my right and one to my left. The hallway was a mess. Storage lockers and cabinets that lined up on either side of the door were all down and smashed. I picked my way across the tops of the cabinets trying not to slice my hands on the glass shards blanketing the place. As I inched closer to the door on the left, I felt something snag on my right pants leg and boot. After a few tugs I freed myself only to hear a tear and feel a sting in right calf. I ignored it and continued to the door. I forced it open with one push. It swung wide to reveal a storage room full of supplies. *No little boy, no Nancy. Shit!*

I heard screaming and pounding coming from the other end of the hallway. I sped up, ignoring the glass shards, pushing past the debris. I reached the door and could hear someone tearing at a wall on the other side. I tried to push open the door with my hand. It wouldn't budge. Next, I tried my shoulder. It gave way a few inches and then stopped.

It was time for the ol' Starsky and Hutch door kick move. Usually, this doesn't work, but desperate times called for desperate measures.

I backed away as far as I could from the door and kicked out with my right foot, aiming for the doorknob. It moved about six inches. I gave it another kick and whatever was blocking it gave way. I pushed my way through just as a soldier was prying open a seam of the plywood wall. The room was full of dust and blinding smoke. I couldn't see more than a few feet in front of me.

"Doc's hit!" I heard him yell. My heart sank as I frantically struggled through the debris. As I inched closer, I could just make out the poor little guy on the table. His eyes were open. Then I saw Nancy. She had covered the boy's head and upper body with her own to shield him from the blast. I moved to her side and shone my light on her face. She glanced up at me and smiled. The right side of her face was cut in a couple of places and covered in dirt and grit.

"Are you okay?" I asked.

"I'm fine. Check the boy for me."

I did a quick scan of Khalid Junior. No obvious signs of injury. The little dude was understandably scared and confused. He managed a weak smile as I gave his shoulder a light squeeze. I smiled back and gave him a wink. Khalid responded, blinking with both eyes. *All good.*

"Your patient looks fine. No injuries. In fact, he just gave me a wink."

"Thank God. Rick, can you check on Doc Collins? I think he's been hit."

I started scanning the room for the enlisted medic known as "Doc Collins."

"Hey," I heard Nancy say. I turned back to her. "By the way," she whispered, "it's good to see you."

"It's good to see you, too." I squeezed her hand as she slowly lifted herself off Khalid Junior.

I stood just as the guys on the outside finally pulled the plywood wall away.

"Rick, I need you to move the boy to a safe place, I've got to help Doc."

"You got it."

I yelled to the soldiers making their way in. "Guys we gotta get the boy outta here. I'm going need help with the IVs."

Three soldiers moved to my side. "I'm going to cradle the boy in my arms and carry him to the CCP. You guys carry the IV bags and clear a path." CCP stands for Casualty Collection Point.

Without a word Jones, the sharp-tongued soldier from Reseda, removed the bags from their stands, while the two guys cleared debris out of my way.

"We're ready sir," Jones announced.

"Let's move."

I stroked the little guy's cheek and give him another wink. "It's going to be okay," I assured him in a language he didn't understand. Gently I picked the boy up and slowly carried him out of the building. Jones was at my side carrying the IV bags as the other two guys led me to the CCP set up near the chow hall. I laid Khalid Junior down on a cot as another soldier covered him with a blanket. He was okay.

I could hear guys yelling for help as they struggled to move Doc Collins out of the wrecked med shed. After a few moments, they emerged carrying Staff Sergeant Collins on a stretcher, with Nancy following closely. He was conscious and groaned in pain as they carried him across the yard to the CCP. Someone said, "He's hit in the lower back and legs," as they lowered his stretcher to the ground near Khalid Junior. Nancy squatted next to me and looked at the boy. "He's gonna be fine," she said. "He tolerated the procedure very well."

"He's a tough little guy," I said. "I'd have been crying for my momma. But he held it together. How's Doc Collins?" I asked.

"Frag in legs and back. May be superficial, but I need a better look. You got this for now?"

"Yep," I replied. Nancy moved to Doc Collins' side.

I heard a man wailing in Arabic. It was Khalid Senior, and it sounded like he was praising God for saving his son. Khalid dropped to his son's side, took his little hand, and gently kissed it. Then he gave me a bear hug as tears streamed down his cheeks.

"Thanks to you and your friends for saving my son. Thanks to Allah!"

More than once, I'd rushed one or both of my boys to the emergency room for injuries sustained while doing stupid kid stuff. Those memories came flooding back to me as I carried young Khalid in my arms—pretty heavy stuff. I stood up to let Khalid have this moment with his little boy. I also needed to wipe away a tear or two myself.

I looked at Nancy hard at work doing her magic. I noticed a trickle of blood running from her scalp down the side of her face. A young soldier who I'd not seen before came up carrying a medic's bag. He must have seen the blood at the same time as I did.

"I should check her out," he said to me. His nametape read *Cook*, and he had the three chevrons of an E-5, "buck" sergeant.

"Sure, Sarge," I said. *Good luck with that,* I thought.

"Excuse me, Major, but you're bleeding from a head wound."

Nancy ignored him. He tried it again. Still no response.

"Major Weaver, the sergeant urgently needs to speak with you," I chimed in. *I'm so helpful.*

I was relieved to see that we finally got Her Doctorship's attention. She turned to face the sergeant, who dutifully reported that she was bleeding from a wound in her scalp.

"Thanks, Sergeant, I'm okay." She looked at the young soldier and noted he had a black medic's bag with him.

"Yes, ma'am, thank you. If you wouldn't mind, I'd like to take a quick look."

"Sergeant, I'm fine. It's nothing," she said in a firm tone.

I could see the sergeant start to lose his determination, so I decided it was time to give him a hand.

"Major Weaver, please let the good sergeant have a look. As you know, head wounds are nothing to mess with," I said helpfully.

"Bullshit, I'm fi—"

"Major, be a nice doctor and let the sergeant do his thing."

Nancy nodded in surrender. Then glared at me. I winked at the sergeant, and he went to work. Soon, he uncovered some tiny wounds caused by frag splinters in her scalp on the right side. If you don't know, head wounds bleed one hell of a lot and can be scary to the uninitiated. I've probably seen hundreds, so I wasn't too concerned by the blood.

Sergeant Cook gently cleaned Nancy's wounds and removed a couple of splinters. He put some magic salve on the cuts and was done.

"Ma'am, I've done all I can here. Do you feel like you can stand?"

"Sure, I told you I'm fine," she replied testily.

I shot her a WTF glance. Then she said, "Sorry, Sergeant, thank you very much. Can you give me a hand with Doc Collins now?"

"Yes, ma'am."

Doc Collins was being attended to by Lieutenant Malaki, an Iraqi Army doctor, as well as another soldier. I had met this guy during a previous visit to the camp and had learned that Lieutenant Malaki liked Playboy magazines a lot. No doubt it helped him with his anatomical studies. Lieutenant Malaki was more of a physician's assistant than an MD. He spoke perfect English and laughed at all my jokes. Even the ones he didn't get.

Lieutenant Maliki recognized me.

"Mr. Rick, I heard you were here with a physician?" he asked.

"Lieutenant, that is Major Nancy Weaver, an Army physician. Maybe you could give her a hand with the boy?"

"Yes, very happy to help any way I can."

I walked over to Nancy and knelt next to her.

"I've got help for you. An IA doc."

"He's a real physician?" Nancy whispered in my ear.

"Doctor Ibrahim Maliki, lieutenant Iraqi Army Medical Corps. Speaks perfect English, graduated with honors from BU Medical School."

"Mr. Sutherland. are you lying to me?"

"I would never lie to you," I said firmly. "Relax, he's gonna take great care of the kid."

"He went to Med School in Boston?"

"The only BU I know is in Boston," I replied. I then noticed that Sergeant Cook was taking this all in with a barely suppressed grin.

"I'll stay with Lieutenant Maliki and Khalid Junior. Don't worry, you'll get a full report when you return," I offered.

Lieutenant Maliki moved beside a soldier who was tending to the boy. The soldier was dressed in his PT gear with a Kevlar and his M4 on the ground next to him. I watched Maliki check the kid's IV line, making sure the drip was at the proper flow. The boy was now sleeping peacefully. Nancy must have given him a post-op sedative just before the attack. I thought to myself that they may need one for Dad too. Khalid Senior's eyes were fixed on his son. Then he suddenly looked up at me with eyes filled with rage.

"Khalid, I'm very sorry this happened, but I am relieved to see you and your son are okay."

"If it is Allah's will, my son will live. One of your soldiers may die, because he tried to save my son. He shielded my son with his body. So did your doctor. This, I will never forget." He turned back to the sleeping boy, wiping away tears.

We were now joined by Lieutenant Shore.

"Only one wounded. We were very lucky," Lieutenant Shore said. Then she noticed Khalid and motioned for me to follow her outside. Once outside, she resumed. "The storm has passed, so I called for a medevac, but they are short on birds again," Shore said, sounding exhausted.

This short on "birds" shit was getting old.

"We've got to get the boy to a hospital," I reminded her. "Getting shot at can't be good for his convalescence."

"They were going to move air assets to our AOR, from Balad, but the sandstorm has moved north and shut things down up there. Al Asad got rocketed and is also shut down for now, so is Delta and Basra. I can't even get ISR coverage."

"Did they all get hit?"

"Yeah, looks like it. IDF and attacks all over from Balad south to Basra." Lieutenant Shore was reviewing her options. "I suppose we could throw together a CLP and get them to a hospital that way, but it would take hours to get to Victory, even in good conditions."

I translated for myself—CLP, Combat Logistics Patrol. *Why in God's name don't they just say "convoy."*

With Haji out shooting the place up, a convoy, even with air cover, sounded like a really bad idea to me. A ground convoy without air sounded even worse.

"Without birds, we may not have a choice. I wish the MPs were still here. We could use their help."

I nodded. Lieutenant Habib was a little standoffish, but there was no doubt that the extra guns and vehicles would be a huge boost.

"Okay, Lieutenant, what can I do?" I offered.

"Why don't you get your gear on and stay with the kid until we can get him and Doc Collins evac'd?"

"Sure, LT," I replied. Of course, I had no intention of putting all that crap on again, but she didn't need to hear that. However, maybe a Kevlar might be in order, just in case Haji decided to send a few more kisses in our direction.

"Rick, I'm going to continue to try and get us some birds. I'll be back." Lieutenant Shore hustled off. As soon as she was gone, I quickly stepped over to the chow hall to put the *habeus-grabbus* on an abandoned Kevlar I had spied lying on the ground by the front door. I put it on and tightened the chinstraps.

Khalid was sitting with his son as a pair of soldiers looked on. He seemed to be praying or something. I kept silent and listened.

He finished and looked at his son, brushing a few strands of hair away from the sleeping boy's face. He must have sensed my presence, for he stood up.

"I need to speak with you," he said grimly.

The soldiers looked at me as if to say, "Are you cool with this?" I gave them a nod and followed Khalid.

"Mr. Dennis, I am very tired of the killing. The young men are not. They want only blood. They say they only want to defeat the Jews and the infidels. But they do not care who is killed. They say if good Muslims are killed in an attack on the infidels it is Insha'Allah. It does not matter, for they will see God that much sooner. But, if they were bad Muslims, they deserved to die. I do not believe this." He paused to gather his thoughts. Excitement mounted as I sensed a breakthrough moment.

I was ready to promise Khalid anything—a crate of Rolexes and a lifetime supply of virgins. Whatever it took to keep American kids safe. I kept my mouth shut. Let him talk.

"I know some things that will be very important to your government.

You know this. I believe that is why you came to my home."

I stood there, stone-faced, and did not respond.

"I will tell you about some plans to attack the Americans here and in other places. I know these things. But you must do something in return."

"What is that?"

"Before I say anything, you must bring my wife here. I fear she is in great danger and will be killed." *Then why did you leave her to mind the store?* I still did not respond, but just listened.

"I also want my family moved to America and citizenship."

"Okay," I responded. "That's all possible, but we need to know more before we risk American lives to rescue your wife."

"I know, that is why I brought this with me." He held up a small canvas bag.

When we left to bring Khalid Junior here, Dad brought a small bag with him that had a few clothes and other items. The guys searched it, but I guess they missed something.

Khalid opened the small canvas bag and emptied its contents and sifted around until he found a very small pocketknife. He opened the blade, which couldn't have been more than an inch and a half long, and started to cut way at a corner of the inside lining of the bag. He reached into the hole and removed a small plastic baggie that contained a couple of printed cards, not much bigger than a business card. He handed them to me. One side looked like Arabic, and one in English.

"Interesting, but it's in Arabic."

"Not Arabic, Dennis, Farsi."

The English side of the card looked like a list of frequencies. One word jumped out at me immediately—*Thales*. Christ, I was holding a cheat sheet on how to operate a Thales radio. I'm guessing identical to the one our late Saudi student was carrying. If the card was really in Farsi and not Arabic, it meant that the Iranians had operatives using our Special Operations Radios. Still, he could have found this anywhere. I needed to probe a little deeper.

"What does this prove? This means nothing to me."

"These are the frequencies and instructions for radios used by your special soldiers."

"You could have gotten this anywhere. It proves nothing."

"You are right. These are just pieces of paper. Useless without the device that reprograms the radios."

Reprograms? "Okay, but again you have told me nothing that would make me want to risk going back."

Khalid looked me straight in the eye. "Hidden at my home I have such a device."

"Okay, tell me about it. How did you get it?"

"When my wife is safe, I will tell you everything."

"The Army will want more."

"But they must bring her. She is in great danger."

"Why is that?"

"The rockets that hit this place were meant for my son and me. You were right, I am suspected now. They will torture my wife to get at me."

"Why do they suspect you?"

"I'm here with you."

CHAPTER 23

FRIENDLY PERSUASION

I found Captain Clark in the TOC dressed for battle.

"Hey, how you doing?"

"I'm fine, but a little busy right now. What's up?"

I could sense from his tone that broaching the idea of a rescue mission back in the village was not a good idea, so I let it pass.

"Nothing much, just wanted to let you know that father and son are fine. I'm sure you heard the doc's okay too."

"Hell of a thing she did. Saved the kid's life."

"Yeah, and Khalid Senior knows it too. He's ready to talk for real. No more bullshit. I'll keep you informed."

Okay, so I lied again just a bit, but I wanted to ease him into this before I gave him the full story. Sort of like letting a horse smell the blanket before you put the saddle on.

I decided to hunt down Lieutenant Shore and run the rescue idea past her. Let her try to sell it to Clark. She can talk better Army than I can. Hell, Francis the talking mule can speak better Army than I can. Yes, I know, I just dated myself with that one.

I walked back over to where I had left Khalid. Nancy was there checking on the boy.

"He looks good. His color is good, so are the vitals. I think your son will be fine. I still need to get him to a hospital, but he is doing very well. He is very strong."

Khalid Senior smiled proudly, as any father would. He touched his right hand to his heart.

"Thank you, Major, for all you have done to save my son. You and the soldier who protected him will be blessed by Allah a thousand times."

"Thank you, sir, but it's just what I do."

"Yes, I know that, but I know you also shielded my son with your body. I and my family will never forget what you and your friends have done for us this day."

I heard his voice crack a little with those last words. He wiped his eyes and went back to his son's side.

Nancy motioned me to join her outside.

"I think he might be ready to help us now."

"Yes, I think so too." Then it occurred to me that Nancy was the best person to test my rescue idea on first. She knew the Army, what was at stake and all the players. I went for it.

"We need to talk in private," I whispered.

"We can talk in my hooch."

"Can you leave Junior and Doc?"

"Relax, detective, *Doctor Maliki* and Cook have it under control."

We walked across the compound and into her hooch. Just as I closed the door, she turned and wrapped me in her arms. We stood there for a minute just holding each other.

"The boy will live. Doc will live, too, but his leg is a mess. It was peppered with frag. Christ, I had just complimented him on his technique. He said when he got out, he was going back to school and finishing his biology degree. Fucking war." She squeezed me even tighter, then looked into my eyes.

"I think I'm falling in love with you." She wiped away a tear.

"I know, I am too . . . with you."

She looked at me kinda funny, prompting me to clarify a bit more.

"I'm falling in love with you too, Major Weaver."

We kissed and held each other some more. She'd been through a lot, and she needed to know I was there for her.

"There is something I need to talk to you about."

She looked up.

"I've been speaking with Khalid Senior, and I think he's ready to give me the keys to the kingdom, but first, we have to rescue Mrs. Khalid."

"You mean go back?"

"Yes, exactly. I think Khalid has ties to MOIS or IRGC. But after today's attack, which he believes targeted him and his son, plus how you and Doc risked your lives to protect his son, I think he's ready to come over to our side. But we need to get Momma out."

"Hmm. I see. What if it's a trap just to lure us back? Getting captured and tortured to death by IRGC is also probably not in your famed retirement plan."

"We'll be fine," I assured her.

"Who exactly is 'we'?"

"Well, I figured I would return with a few guys, get in, grab Ma, and get the fuck out. Naturally, I assumed you'd need to stay here anyway, so—" I trailed off as I realized I was digging that hole again.

"What do you want from me?" the good major said, sounding slightly pissed.

This wasn't going too well, so I switched gears a bit.

"You're Army, I'm not. I just need some insight into how to sell this rescue mission."

"It's going to be pretty tough, if not impossible. Clark has casualties he needs to protect, as well as this compound. He's not going to allow his strength to be cut even further by a rescue mission. I could see it if the MPs were still with us, or even the Iraqi Army, but who the fuck knows about them?"

Then I heard the low rumble of several engines driving onto the compound. I looked out the window and saw several Army vehicles. The door of the lead vehicle opened and out stepped Major Copeland. "Well, darling, the cavalry has arrived." Nancy looked out the window. "That was lucky."

"Yes, it is."

Nancy and I met Clark, Copeland, and Shore in the TOC.

Major Copeland smiled warmly as I walked into the room with Nancy. I grinned back. Then I realized he was looking at Nancy. "Hello, Major Weaver, I hear you got hit. How are you feeling?"

"I'm good, thanks. A couple of cuts. Nothing."

"Mr. Sutherland, it looks like you made it through fine."

I started to respond, but he turned and resumed his conversation with Captain Clark and Lieutenant Shore. *What's the deal with his Cheshire cat smile for Nancy?*

"Captain Clark, you were saying Khalid Al-Rashidi and his son were brought back to this JSS."

"Yes, sir, the boy Khalid, who we are calling Junior, needed emergency surgery. Major Weaver, perhaps you could fill Major Copeland in on the medical situation."

"I'd be happy to. Khalid Junior presented with fever, nausea, and severe abdominal pain centered in the lower right quadrant. I diagnosed acute appendicitis that required emergency surgery."

Major Copeland interrupted, turning to Captain Clark and Lieutenant Shore. "So, you brought him and his father, a known insurgent, back here?"

Nancy responded to his interruption. "Major, speaking from a medical perspective, we had no choice if we were to save the boy's life. Khalid Senior wanted to take his son to a clinic about twenty kilometers away. Based on the boy's symptoms, I didn't believe he would have survived the trip, let alone Iraqi doctors. All air had been grounded, so a Medevac was out."

"So, saving the boy's life was the priority?" Major Copeland sniped.

"Yes, of course it was."

"Sir, if I may," Lieutenant Shore interrupted. "Khalid Senior has been under constant guard since we left his restaurant." When Copeland turned his attention to Shore, the lieutenant glanced at Captain Clark as if to say, *"Sorry, boss, but I had to say something."* Major Copeland saw this and pressed even harder.

"Oh yes, Lieutenant Shore, you led the patrol to the restaurant, right?"

"Yes, sir."

"Why did you go there in the first place?"

"We went there to meet Khalid Al-Rashidi."

"For what purpose?"

"To search his residence and businesses and question him about some recent IDF attacks at Victory and other places."

"Oh, I see, but that is why I am here, Lieutenant. I'm collecting intelligence on those attacks, not you, nor you, Captain Clark. Now that we've got that straight, please continue Lieutenant."

"We searched the location and found nothing significant. However, Khalid's son was ill."

"Yes," he said impatiently. "Continue."

"We convinced him to allow us to bring his kid to the JSS which we did. His wife was left to mind the restaurant. Major Weaver treated the son while—"

"So, you diverted soldiers from other duties to provide security for a known bomber?" Now turning to Captain Clark, he said, "You're a reservist, aren't you? What do you do back home?"

"I'm a detective-II with LAPD, Van Nuys Division."

"Chasing car thieves in the Valley is a little different than commanding troops in combat, isn't it?"

"Major, I picked up a few things about combat from the Ranger Regiment, but of course, I bow to your experience, sir," Captain Clark seethed.

I could barely suppress my grin as I watched Major Copeland's face go from pink, to crimson, to *purple.*

"Thank you, Captain Clark. Perhaps later we can discuss your exploits in the Ranger Regiment, but now, I'm concerned with the security of this camp. So, Lieutenant, please continue."

"Yes, sir. We brought Khalid and his son back to the camp. We left his wife there at his request. Major Weaver treated the boy, then we got hit."

"Lieutenant Shore, you're the intelligence officer and you don't see a correlation between Khalid being here and the attack? How do we know he didn't communicate with the insurgents outside and give them targeting data?"

"He was under constant watch by my soldiers, he was thoroughly searched prior to his being transported, and—"

Okay, that was it. I'd had enough of this guy. I had thought he was okay, but clearly, my usually reliable instincts were on vacation. *Who the fuck did he think he is, George Patton?*

"Excuse me, Lieutenant, if I may?"

Lieutenant Shore nodded.

"Major, we knew Khalid didn't call in fire on this camp, because the fire was aimed at him and his son."

"How do you know that Mr. Sutherland?"

"Call me Rick."

"Sorry?"

"It's Rick, Major Copeland. Rick Sutherland."

"Yes, sorry, my hearing hasn't been too good lately."

"I've noticed. We know that because all the rounds that impacted this camp went wide of the mark except the one that hit the med shed. It was a direct hit. Khalid may be a bad guy, but he wants his son to live. That is plain enough. Which brings me to the reason why Junior and Daddy were brought back here." I was on a roll. If it got me sent back home, fuck it. I was done listening to this dipshit hammer my friends.

"Here's the deal. My investigation into the recent IDF attacks at Victory has led me to Khalid Senior. He's connected to the Shia insurgency. His brother is IRGC. He may be Iraqi by birth, but he's Iranian by heritage. He's been to America, visited LA. As a matter of fact, his sons are both attending UCLA."

I went on. "But Khalid's not too happy with the Shia insurgency and would like a change. He's tired of the killing. In his heart, he knows the ayatollahs are full of shit about America. He's seen it with his own two eyes and has tasted the good life. He knows we aren't so bad, our women are pretty our booze is good and so is the food." I made a slight show bow to Nancy and Lieutenant Shore.

"Something happened with Khalid and the bad guys. I don't know what, but now he's on their shit list. They've tried to kill him and his kid twice."

Okay, maybe I exaggerated a little. The first sniper attack on the road back to camp was pretty lame. But it could have been a message, a warning to a fellow jihadist.

I could see it wasn't the best time to broach my rescue proposal. Major Copeland was on the warpath and bringing up a rescue would be like throwing kerosene on a brush fire. But the clock was ticking, and it was time to fish or cut bait.

Major Copeland replied angrily, "Most of the local Shia here are connected one way or another."

I wanted to choke this schmuck out. I looked at Nancy. She returned my look. Her eyes said, "No, don't go there." For once, I took direction and continued.

"Yes, I know that, but I'm not out here investigating pot shots and roadside IEDs," I offered.

"Why exactly are you out here? I spoke with your boss George and he said he had no idea why you were here. Your company's contract does not cover this kind of activity. You are operating outside the scope of the SOW."

Out here a SOW is not a cloven-foot beast with tasty ribs. It's actually DoD shorthand for the Scope of Work to be performed under the contract. George's answer didn't surprise; I'd have given the same myself. George was just following long established IC (Intelligence Community) protocol. Lie, deny, confuse, and make counter charges.

Copeland, being an MP officer, could be in the position to give a negative report up his chain of command on how my employer was performing on the contract. The MPs had contract oversight. I didn't know exactly how, but I knew that an asshat like Copeland could cause trouble for me and the company.

I still had my Mikey card, but I wanted to save that one for something more serious than a major with a stick up his ass. But the strange thing was Copeland had to know why I was out there and who sent me. *Why was he playing games?*

I looked at Major Copeland, considering a slightly more satisfying response. Nancy, sensing this, pressed my right foot, causing me to wince slightly, thus saving Major Copeland from a near-death experience.

"Yes, Major, as I started to say, Khalid is connected to something a lot bigger, maybe Mahdi Army or IRGC. Or maybe both."

"IRGC," Major Copeland scoffed. "You are way out of your lane *and* your depth on that one. You have no idea what you're talking about. There is no reporting on IRGC in this area."

"That's not what I'm seeing," I replied. One of Major Copeland's minions scurried up. Major Copeland stepped away for a few moments. I looked sideways at the other three. Captain Clark rolled his eyes and gave me the official LAPD nod that means *let's just kick this guy's ass.* I nodded in agreement. Lieutenant Shore and Nancy could sense what was being communicated, but wisely maintained ignorance in case there was a court martial.

Major Copeland returned, "Captain Clark, we are going to have to leave your camp. There's been a TIC involving some guys from 3/7th. They lost a vehicle, have one wounded and need our help with the local IPs." Of course, the IPs were Major Copeland's playmates. A TIC is shorthand for Troops in Contact, i.e., combat.

"Yes, sir."

"Captain, you will need to get Mr. Sutherland back to Victory on the first available. He is way off the reservation and unless I miss my guess, he may be home sooner than he thinks. I'll be forwarding a report on this to higher."

"Major, next week, why don't you swing by my office?" I said. "I'll buy you a cup and show you the IRGC intel."

He wisely ignored my thorny olive branch, which showed he was capable of at least some higher thinking.

"Nan . . . Sorry, ahh, Major Weaver . . . gentlemen." Then he turned, smiled, and gave me the subtlest of winks. None saw it but me. I mouthed, *"Go fuck yourself,"* as he walked past.

CHAPTER 24

CONFESSIONS

I was about to ask Captain Clark for his assessment of what Copeland had said, but he beat me to it. "Fuck him. Pompous little prick." With that, I knew we were all good here. Now, we just had to convince Clark's higher ups that we needed to go play again.

Interestingly enough, Nancy gave me the most static. I met her back at a makeshift infirmary that had been set up next to the men's showers.

"So, what do you think?" I asked.

"I think you need to stop playing soldier before you get your saggy white ass shot off or wind up in prison. That's what I think."

"It's more toned since I started Pilates."

"Rick, you don't belong out here. Copeland was right. You are way out of your lane."

"Wait just a minute here. You're the one who got me involved in this little whodunit in the first place."

Whenever I argue with a woman, I always try to counter with the facts or quote their own words. It never does any good, but it makes me feel better.

"By the way, Major Dickhead called you Nancy. What's up with that?"

Nancy's face hardened to stone in a millisecond. "Not a damn thing . . . and yes, I did get you involved in this. But that was before I fell in love with you."

Okay, I'm an asshole. But that comes as no surprise to those who know me. I prefer to think of myself as more of a loveable asshole. Apparently, so did Nancy.

Guess she didn't want me to get my "saggy white ass shot off" because she loved it, and me. How can you argue with that? Wisely, I decided to disengage and retreat to the TOC. I smiled sheepishly and said, "Sorry."

As I dragged my tired body to the TOC, my thoughts were consumed by Copeland. The prick had probably hit on Nancy. I needed to get him out of my mind and concentrate on my goal of going back and grabbing Mrs. Khalid.

Back at the TOC, Captain Clark knew he had to pull off one hell of a sales pitch with his higher on this rescue operation. His higher was Headquarters Company, 3rd Brigade Combat Team, located at Camp Striker next to BIAP.

Captain Clark sent a secure email to the 3rd BCT Deputy Commander Major Menucci, advising of the situation and requesting a secure conference call. The response came thirty minutes later. We were to have a secure conference with the boss at 0500 hours. Thirty minutes to prepare our pitch. Lieutenant Colonel Clancy was an early riser.

"I will brief Clancy on our situation and the proposed op. Rick, I want you to lay out what you know about Khalid and his suspected involvement with local Shia insurgency and the IRGC. Give him specifics on what you expect Khalid to give up and what he's said already."

"Understood."

"Specifics but keep it short. Remember, *bottom line up front.*"

Ah, yes, the old Army briefing adage, BLUF. Give 'em the bottom line and then tell them why. I guess it works for them.

"Chris, give him the intel on this. Your intel backs Rick's, right?"

Shore nodded.

"Right, so make sure Clancy gets it. He can be an impatient prick and is bound to get in your grill. Don't take it personally, and don't stammer. If you sound unsure, we're fucked. Questions?" There were none. "Okay, we've got twenty minutes before the call. Get your notes together and meet me back here in fifteen."

I left the TOC and ran to go find Khalid. I needed to beef this up a bit, and Khalid was the only one who could do it.

I found him sitting by Junior, who was sleeping. I motioned for him to join me in a corner.

"Look, I'm about to try and convince our leaders that we should risk more Americans to rescue your wife. But I have nothing to give them other than your word. I need to . . . no, *you* need to give them something more, or this rescue will never happen. But do not lie. You know what will happen."

"I understand, Dennis. If you wish, I will go with you. If I am lying, you may kill me and my wife at your pleasure." *I ignored that.*

"Okay, so what do you have?"

Khalid paused for a moment. "At your base near the airport."

"Victory?"

"Yes."

CHAPTER 25

TINSEL TOWN

Armed with additional intelligence from Khalid, I went to a corner and scratched out a few notes. I didn't want to give this new information up unless pressed. Clark and Shore were already on the line with the Brigade S-2 intelligence officer and a Green Beret captain named Meyer, who was a liaison guy from 10th Special Forces Group. I sat, and they announced my presence to the group.

"Mr. Sutherland is now present."

I greeted everyone.

"Captain Clark, I just got off the phone with Major Copeland. He had some interesting things to say."

"Yes, Colonel, I'm sure he did. However, I believe we have some significant information that the major may not be fully aware of."

"Okay, Captain, let's hear it."

Captain Clark spoke for about ten minutes, making his argument and answering questions from the staff officers present. Then he looked at me; it was my turn with the lions. I took a deep breath and began.

"Gentlemen, pursuant to my responsibilities as an embedded subject matter expert with the Counter-IED cell at Victory, I've been conducting an inquiry into a recent uptick in IED strikes in this AO. Collaterally with that, I've also been looking for connections to the recent IDF attacks on Victory Base Complex and other Coalition bases in this AOR. This inquiry led me to Yusufiyah and Khalid Al-Rashidi. It is my opinion that Al-Rashidi has played a significant role in the local Shia insurgency and possesses information identifying who is behind recent attacks on VBC." I droned on for a few more minutes and then began fielding questions.

"Mr. Sutherland," Lieutenant Colonel Clancy began, "before I green light this op, I need more specifics on Al-Rashidi's information and its reliability."

I didn't want to give up the new information as it was too specifically attributable to Khalid. Besides, old cops like me never like to give up the goods until we have to. Call it paranoia or what you will, but it's how we roll.

"Sir, while in Al-Rashidi's restaurant, I discovered photos of Khalid, and others taken back in the States."

"Where in the States?" Clancy asked impatiently.

"In front of certain high-value soft targets located in Los Angeles. Based on the photographs, it was apparent that he had probably been conducting an intelligence collection op on the location." Clark and Shore both shot me simultaneous "WTF stares, which I ignored. Ol' Rick was on a roll now. "I recognized the location and the apparent collection techniques. I made some inquiries back to CONUS and confirmed my suspicions."

"Yes. Go on."

"With all due respect, I cannot go into the details of the information I learned from an FBI Joint Terrorism Task Force investigation, but I—"

Colonel Clancy interrupted me again. He and Copeland must have gone to the same finishing school. "Mr. Sutherland, I'm very familiar with Los Angeles. Can you tell me about the area he was photographed in?"

Make him work for it. "Yes, sir, it's a very significant soft target located in the area west of downtown."

"West of downtown is a big fucking area." I could see bulging veins in his neck. Would getting Clancy to stroke out be considered a friendly fire incident? Would I get full credit for the kill?

"Sir, this is an active FBI Joint Terrorism Task Force investigation. I'm not sure I can be more descriptive. I may have already said too much."

I knew that I was safe name dropping the FBI. They would never give up the gory details of an intelligence case to the US Army. Trust me, never.

"I need more," Lieutenant Colonel Clancy said. His face was getting that warm stoplight glow, and I was getting close to my first confirmed kill. Well, my first in Iraq anyway.

"Okay, sir, I understand. Sir, it's a very well-known venue located on Hollywood Boulevard."

"I know the area. Been there with the wife and kids." He interrupted again. "Motherfuckers. Okay, Sutherland, I've heard enough. Captain Clark, what do you have from your Two Shop?"

Was it possible we'd won him over this easily? Was it possible he was that stupid? Probably not.

"Lieutenant Shore." My new BFF looked at her notes and took a deep breath. It was all riding on her shoulders now.

"Sirs, local sources indicate that Khalid is a mid-level actor in the local Shia insurgency. Additionally, it is believed that he has familial ties to elements of the IRGC that are likely embedded in the area. That said, we have a high degree of confidence that Khalid has had a change of heart about working with the insurgency and is now willing to assist Coalition Forces. We believe this is a result of his young son's life being saved twice in the last twenty-four hours by US medical personnel, and his belief that he and his family have now been targeted by the insurgency."

"Lieutenant Shore, there is no reporting on IRGC in this AOR. Major Copeland said he pointed that out to you a few hours ago," Lieutenant Colonel Clancy said.

"Yes, but with all due respect, sir, my local sources indicate otherwise."

Captain Clark suddenly gave Lieutenant Shore a cutting gesture across his neck.

"Lieutenant Shore, that's enough. Thank you."

"Captain Clark, I will get back to you. Out here."

Before Clark could offer a word of protest, the screen went dark.

Lieutenant Shore sat motionless staring into space.

"I'm going to call Meyer in a few minutes to get a read on things, but I wouldn't hold your breath. Clancy's MO is to sit on the close calls until they get stale. He'll get back to us, but it will be too late."

I walked out. I thought I had Clancy convinced, but shit happens. It wasn't Shore's fault. Copeland had already poisoned the well, way before we got there. In fact, I doubt we even had a chance. The lieutenant colonel was just going through the motions. I'd seen it too many times before at LAPD.

As I crossed the compound headed toward the showers to check on the boy, I passed an Iraqi Army officer walking toward the TOC. When I arrived, Doc Nancy was sitting by the boy's side, letting him listen to her heart with her stethoscope. It was amazing how well Junior was doing. Dad was sitting on the other side watching. Nancy got up when she saw me and motioned me to a corner.

"I heard there are two helos inbound to evac us back to Victory. There's a seat with your name on it."

"Sorry, I've got vertigo, can't fly today," I replied.

"Copeland has given orders to Clark to get your ass back to Victory. If you don't fly, it will be Clark's ass as well as yours."

"Fuck Copeland. Besides, I have no ass."

"Clark does," Nancy replied.

I smiled and looked at Khalid. He looked up and I motioned for him to follow me. Khalid and I walked outside.

"We are trying to get approval, but it's not going well."

"I understand." He paused for a moment then took in a breath. "There's something else that I have not told you about that you should know." The last time an informant had said that to me, he admitted to being part of a stick-up team that had killed a clerk the week before. These kinds of announcements never go well.

CHAPTER 26

THE TURNING WORM

After that last little surprise discussion with Khalid, my mind was spinning. I was bone tired and needed to think, so I returned to my room to ponder my next move. This latest intelligence dump from Khalid was pretty hot. I normally don't work with snitches who parcel out information like Khalid was doing, but in this case, I felt the reward made it worth the aggravation.

Khalid said something big was being planned. He wasn't sure what, but it would be an event that could change everything for the US in Iraq. He said that someone on the base, possibly an American, had recently murdered an interpreter on Victory just before an IDF attack. *That had to be the guy who was murdered in his hooch, Mohammed Salim.* Khalid said moments before we arrived at his place, two guys had dropped off a package they said had a cell phone preprogrammed with contact information for other bad guys involved in this "big operation." He hid it inside the restaurant moments before we walked in. He said the two guys saw him get rolled up by us and no doubt reported back to their command. The car that was parked on the street in front of the restaurant was theirs. He also mentioned that a few weeks ago, these same guys had commandeered a shed he owned that was located near the restaurant.

At first, this all sounded a little too convenient, until he got to the part about Salim getting murdered. That was "close-hold" information, known only to a select few. But I didn't get why he had held this back. It was weird and gave me pause. But on the other hand, maybe he was like me and didn't like to give it all up too quickly.

I needed to think this one through for a minute before I approached Clark and Shore. There was a sudden pounding on my door. I opened it half expecting to see an amorous Major Weaver, only to be greeted by the freckled face of a young soldier I recognized from the TOC.

"Mr. Sutherland, Captain Clark needs you in the TOC right away!"

"On my way," I said.

As soon as I walked in, Clark and Shore motioned me over to the Two Shop.

"It doesn't look good. Clancy's first words after the brief were not positive."

"Copeland."

"Yep." Captain Clark said Meyer, the 10th Group officer, had confirmed my intel on Khalid. In fact, his SF boys had been planning an intelligence gathering mission focused on Khalid for a few weeks but had not launched due to scheduling issues.

"Meyer said if Clancy did give us a green light, he was willing to send us some guys from ODA 1027." An ODA is a Special Forces Operational Detachment "A" Team, in this case from the 10th Special Forces Group. Having these "shooters" along could be invaluable if things got hot.

"Where does that leave us?" I asked.

"Something else has come up that may change all of this." Captain Clark replied. "The IAs are going to conduct a raid on a local asshole in the same village, and we need to tag along." I shot a glance at Clark, who remained stone faced. *Coincidence? I think not.* Clark must have called in a favor or something. But as long as the rescue operation was on, I briefed Clark on the latest from Khalid. He was interested but busy with mission planning.

My gut was saying Khalid was telling the truth, but his parceling out information was a red flag. I needed a second opinion. I left the TOC to get my gear and find Nancy. She'd spent a lot of time with Khalid and her impressions would be valuable. I found her in her room repacking her gear.

"Hey, I need to run something past you."

I gave her the *Reader's Digest* version of what Khalid said.

"I think it's probably true. Whatever else he's got going on, Khalid seems to be devoted to his family. He talks about his wife to the boy all the time. I think he's pretty concerned for her safety. Why would he be so concerned if something wasn't up with the bad guys? He's a kinda big deal in town. No one would normally mess with him or his family except for the insurgents or even the IRGC. I think he's probably telling the truth."

"That's exactly what I was thinking, but I needed a fresh look," I replied.

"So, are you going to head out with us?" she asked.

"No, I've got one more adventure in me. I think I'll stay."

"It's your butt if you do."

"I guess you'll be flying out with your patient."

She moved to give me a hug just as there was an urgent pounding on the door of her CHU.

I opened it to see a young soldier ready for war.

"Choppers just landed. A guy got off and asked for Major Weaver. They flew on but will return in fifteen."

"Where's he at now?" Nancy asked.

"He's at the aid station with the boy and Khalid."

"Specialist, would you please tell him I'll be there in a minute."

"I'll tag along."

"Second thoughts about staying?"

"Nope, I'm gonna finish this."

Nancy just smiled and moved off through the morning sun with me following.

I waited until Nancy was done briefing Specialist Baker. As I overheard what she was saying, I got the impression that she wasn't going back on the chopper. She finished with young Jason and moved to check on Doc Collins.

I walked over to Jason. "Is Major Weaver flying out with you?"

"No, sir, she's staying here."

"I see."

"She said something about going back for the kid's mother."

"Yep, that's what we're going to do." I noticed Khalid Senior approaching. "Look, Jason, do me a favor, take your rank tab off your blouse."

"What, sir?"

"Just do it. I may need to reassure Khalid that you're a doctor, otherwise he might balk on letting his kid fly."

"Got it, sir."

Turned out Khalid was fine with all of it. I guess I'd really gained his trust. It was now time for me to get my gear.

"Well, have a safe trip back, Jason."

"Sir." Jason held out his hand. "I just wanted to say thanks again for your advice."

"No worries, it was nothing."

"No, sir, it was. I'll never forget what you shared with me. Watch your back out there. Get 'em off the street, sir."

"Roger that, Jason," I smiled. "Thanks." We shook hands. I turned and walked back over to the TOC for a word with Clark and Shore. *The kids' gonna make a fine peace officer.*

CHAPTER 27

BOOTS AND SADDLES

We were going to move out in a column comprised of a pair of IA Humvees and two of our vehicles. Each vehicle mounted either a .50 or a 7.65mm machinegun, except for the MRAP, which had a Mk 19 40mm grenade launcher. We would travel with a total of fifteen personnel, including IAs. I figured it should be an adequate force to deal with any issues. Captain Clark would be coming along this time, leaving Lieutenant Shore behind to mind the store.

Captain Clark conducted the pre-op briefing in the courtyard in front of the TOC.

"Okay, that's about it, except that Major Weaver will be coming along with us to provide medical."

I looked around the assembled patrol but didn't see her smiling face.

"Okay, we are moving out in five."

I walked over to my assigned vehicle just in time to see her ladyship toss her aid bag through the vehicle's side hatch.

"I thought you were going to head back with Junior."

"Nope, Specialist Baker is going to take care of that. I'm afraid you're stuck with me."

"The kid with the needles and lead foot?"

"Yes, the one whose career you almost ruined."

"Great kid. Very helpful, but will Junior be safe with him?"

"Perfectly. He's fully qualified."

"You know best, Doc." That one is absolutely guaranteed to produce at least an icy glare from any member of the fairer sex, and I wasn't disappointed.

"Not in your lane, Mr. Sutherland." Then she said, "Don't worry about me either, unless, of course, you want to." *I hate when she does that.*

"But Dad's another story," she continued. "He's riding with Clark. You might want to go with them to help keep an eye on him."

"I'd rather ride with you. You smell better."

"Dad is a bit hygiene-impaired." Man was she right on. Daddy Khalid, being a sophisticated captain of local industry, could afford the latest Iraqi version of Old Spice. But despite his daily Old Spice shower you could still get that pungent aroma of weeks' old sweat and who knows what else.

The scary part is he was one of the clean ones.

A few minutes later, we were through the gate and on our way. I was with Captain Clark and Khalid in the second vehicle. The point vehicle, also known as the IED sponge, was an IA HUMVEE occupied by an IA lieutenant and three minions. For the most part, Dad was quiet during the ride. He did ask a few questions about Specialist Baker, a.k.a. Dr. Baker. He was clearly worried that Medicine Woman wasn't escorting Junior back to Victory. I assured him that Doc Baker was a highly trained specialist and even more qualified than Herself. That last bit seemed to appeal to his innate patriarchal tendencies, and he seemed satisfied. As long as he didn't repeat the bit about Baker being a physician, we should be okay.

Our objective was, of course, Chez Merde. *Maybe I should stop calling it that.* We were playing without a safety net on this one. We had no air escort, and the op was kinda off the books. For the record, we were responding to a last-minute call for assistance from our comrades in arms, the glorious Iraqi Army. The Special Forces dudes weren't gonna be on scene until well after we got there. Clark considered holding the mission until they could join us, but you can't sit around and wait for everything to be perfect for every mission. Hell, what if Eisenhower had waited for better weather? *What if* . . . I could have gone on forever.

Captain Clark and I were sitting there—well, actually, *bouncing*—while swapping war stories from the fabled good ol' days. We were only a couple of blocks from the restaurant when the lead IA vehicle came to a screeching halt. Sudden halts in Iraq are seldom good. Ordinarily, if you're getting shot at, the logical course of action would be to apply the gas and power through, hopefully avoiding the bullets and other flying objects. However, the Iraqi Army—our friends and allies—were not known for applying logic, tactics, or even courage in such situations. This moment was no exception. IA officer in the lead vehicle got on the shared communications net and announced that his driver had stopped because he had seen what he thought was an IED poking out of the roadbed.

"Jesus Christ. Fucking idiots," Clark yelled. "Lieutenant, tell your driver to move or get run over. Where is it?" After a moment's delay, the IA lieutenant replied it was nothing and apologized for the driver, which I thought was damn nice of him.

The IA vehicle lurched and slowly picked up speed, and we arrived at Chez Merde a few minutes later. The IAs deployed as outer security, if you could call it that, and our guys posted at various corners around the building. I walked up to the entrance with Captain Clark and Major Weaver. I poked my head in and instantly got a very bad feeling. I could smell food burning back in the kitchen. The place was deserted. No Mrs. Khalid, no hungry patrons. Nothing. I moved in cautiously, carbine at the ready. I could also sense that Major Weaver was behind me as I advanced. Actually, I could smell her perfume. It was nice. We could get into a blazing gun battle in the next few seconds, but at least it would smell nice.

We moved to the kitchen, rifles at the ready. Some kind of local delicacy burned in a huge pot on the stove. We entered the residential portion of the building and cleared each room. Nada. No sign of Mom anywhere.

I heard Clark call out. "Guys, come to me." We joined Captain Clark at the double.

He was holding a pair of glasses. "Those look like Mom's," I said.

Nancy agreed. "She wore glasses while I was with her. I think she had seriously impaired vision," she offered.

This ain't good. "Where did you find them?"

"Under a table." One lens had a small crack in the corner. I scanned the room for other evidence of a struggle. Nothing. All the chairs were in their places. Nothing out of place. Just the glasses and burning gruel.

Khalid entered, escorted by a wary young GI. His face registered panic as soon as he saw the glasses.

"She must have those. She would not leave them." Frantically, he rushed around the place searching for his wife or some clue of her whereabouts. Khalid returned to our position a few moments later. "She has been taken. They have her because my son and I went with you." He was right. He and his wife would probably be fine if we hadn't shown up yesterday. But for Khalid Junior, probably not so much.

Captain Clark's radio cracked. "I'll be right there," he replied to the unseen voice. "Higher got wind of our little adventure. Wish we had ODA with us. Clancy is going to have my ass."

"Not yet," I said. "Not if we can save the day and make him look good."

"Easy for you to say, but, unless you're holding a miracle in your back pocket, I think we're pretty much screwed. He ain't gonna buy the helping our brothers in arms story."

We were pondering our options when Clark's radio crackled again; it was Clancy. From what I could hear, he wasn't happy.

BANG! I felt an angry hornet brush past my ear. But it was no hornet. It impacted the pavement three feet in front of me and skittered off in a new direction.

"SNIPER!" I yelled and fell flat on my belly. Other guys were moving to cover, or searching for the shooter. I looked at Clark and instantly knew what he was thinking. This sniper was buying us time, a commodity we desperately needed.

Clark spoke into his handset, "I'll get back to you, Colonel. We're taking sniper fire here, out."

We all got up and ducked back into the restaurant and took cover, as more incoming rounds shattered the front window. The GI manning the Mk-19 spotted the building the shots were coming from and gave Mr. Sniper a couple of rounds of 40mm. The first round hit just under an upstairs window. The second went right through the open window and detonated inside.

Now all was quiet. Nancy moved up beside me and whispered in my ear. "You need to see this; I think I know where Mom is."

I quickly followed her out the back door across a dirt lot to an outbuilding. *Khalid had mentioned a storage shed.*

"Look at this." Nancy pointed at the dirt below the door. It was blood. Fresh blood. Probably Mom's. The door itself seemed a little stouter than normal. The doorframe was metal instead of the usual semi-rotted wood, and the door was secured with two brass framed heavy-duty padlocks. Without bolt cutters, I figured breaching this door was going to be a bit of a challenge. Specialist Hernandez stood by the door.

"Specialist, I think we're gonna need to break down this door. Got any ideas?" I whispered.

"Aaagh . . ." A muffled gasp coming from behind the door. It sounded female.

Nancy looked at me and then Hernandez. "Specialist, we gotta get in there fast."

"Yes, ma'am. We've got breeching tools in the vehicle."

Without another word, he took off.

Nancy pressed against the door. "We hear you. Hang on."

I could hear labored breathing and the occasional groan.

The kid was back in a flash lugging a "hooligan tool," a small ram and bolt cutters.

"Sir, do you know how to use one of these?" he asked out of breath.

"Probably from before you were born," I replied as I reached out for ram. "You set the pick and I'll ram," he said.

"Hold on, guys," Major Weaver ordered. "We need to make sure the door isn't booby trapped. Get your light and look for wires or anything else that looks out of place."

"Yes, ma'am," replied Hernandez.

Damn good thing someone was thinking, because after about a whole two seconds of searching he whispered, "Ma'am, I think I found something." Cautiously, he pointed to the corner. There, tucked under the jamb, covered by dirt and debris, was a thin green wire. It looked a lot like Christmas light wire, which bad guys use to trigger IEDs. The light strings can act like a pressure plate switch, using the victim's own action to initiate the device.

"Fuck," announced the good major. "Do we have an EOD guy with us?"

I knew the answer to that one but deferred to the specialist.

"No, ma'am, we do not."

"She sounds bad. We've got to get her out of there," whispered Major Weaver.

"Yes, I know. I checked the perimeter and there is no other opening. I didn't check the roof," I foolishly added as a postscript.

"Can you please check for me and the specialist?"

"For you, Major, anything. Let me find a ladder or something."

It didn't take long. I grabbed a couple of crates and a wooden pallet outside and was on the roof in no time. There was nothing but a small vent hole covered by a sheet metal thing that looked a lot like an old soup can. I crept up next to it for a good peek. Nothing obviously dangerous was noted. I pulled my Leatherman tool out and using the built-in wire cutters I was able to free the can from the vent. I looked down the hole and couldn't see a damn thing. It was pitch black. I could hear a woman's labored breathing. I shone my Surefire light into the opening and could see a pair of bare legs sprawled out on the floor. The legs were bloodied and bruised, and definitely female. I couldn't see anything else.

I moved the light beam over to the area of the door and could see an object that looked suspiciously like an old-style hand grenade wedged under the door like an improvised booby trap. I could see that the safety pin was missing, so moving the door would release the firing mechanism and ignite the grenade's fuse. Three seconds later, *boom*. No more Rick. *What about the green wire Hernandez spotted? Is it connected to a second device, or just trash?*

I climbed back down and reported my observations to Major Weaver. "What does the device look like?"

"It looks like an old style frag grenade. It's wedged under the door and rigged to pop when the door is opened."

"How we gonna get in there without an EOD guy?" she said, full of desperation.

"Me," I replied.

"You?"

"I've had a few classes in this stuff," I replied.

"What classes?"

"It was online, *Popular Mechanics.*"

"I feel better now."

"Actually, I did two FBI post-blast courses and some JIEDDO counter-IED stuff in the desert at Ft Irwin. It's not EOD, but I'm willing to give it a try." JIEDDO is the Joint Improvised Explosive Device Defeat Organization, in case you were wondering.

"Well, it's your ass if it blows."

"You're quite right Major. Now, I'm going to need your body armor and a look at your aid bag."

A couple of minutes later, I was ready. I took all my gear off except for my IBA, Kevlar helmet and ballistic goggles. I also put on Specialist Hernandez's IBA minus the plates. The extra bulk and weight of those plates would be too much. From the good Major's medical bag, I took a supply of tongue depressors and a couple of forceps. My plan was to force a tongue depressor in between the fusing mechanism and the bottom of the door. I was going to try and maintain downward pressure on the fuse until we could either get rid of it, get a safety pin back in it, or smother it with the major's IBA. Yes, I know, it was a really stupid plan, but it was all we had.

"Major, it just occurred to me we might want to let Clark in on our situation."

"Good call." Nancy looked at Hernandez. "Can you ask Captain Clark to hustle over here?"

Hernandez made the request on his portable radio.

"Rick, are you sure you can do this?"

"I think I'm the most qualified to try. Besides, we don't have time to wait for help."

Captain Clark arrived with Khalid and his escort. I promptly briefed him on my plan. Captain Clark said, "Gotta say, I'm not loving it."

"That makes two of us."

Major Weaver then whispered so that Khalid could not overhear her words. "She sounds pretty bad. If we wait for EOD, she might not make it."

"Okay, got it. Time is critical and Iraqi buildings are shit. What if we avoid the door altogether and break a hole in the wall? There's probably no concrete or rebar reinforcement. Couple of hammer blows and we're in," Captain Clark suggested.

"You will not get in." I turned and looked at Khalid who was crouched behind me. "It is built very strong, to protect my family, for when Saddam comes."

"Or the Americans," I whispered. He nodded in response. "The door is very strong, and the walls go a meter into the ground. There is also a hidden room beneath the floor that my family could hide in."

"So, I guess we are back to you, Rick," Captain Clark said.

"Sirs, I've got a suggestion," Specialist Hernandez piped up.

"Go ahead, Danny."

"Sir, we've got a bomb blanket stowed in your vehicle. Once the door is opened, I could throw it over the grenade to smother it. Maybe we could put a rock or a big tire on top to hold it down until we can free the lady."

"Great idea, Danny. How did we get the blanket?" Captain Clark asked.

"It fell off an engineer vehicle a couple of weeks ago. Remember, I told you?"

"No, I don't remember. Which is probably good."

"I hate when that happens," I chimed in. "Danny, where are you from?"

"LA. El Sereno."

"A lot of stuff falls off of trucks there too?" I asked innocently.

"Sometimes, sir."

"Guys like you make America great," I offered. "Why don't you grab the blanket and I'll look for a tire or something."

"Yes, sir."

Khalid directed us to a large truck tire still mounted on its heavy steel wheel. In a couple of minutes, we were ready to go. I was relieved that I didn't have to play junior EOD man. Truth be told, I was badly hungover during most of those post-blast classes anyway.

"Okay, we are set. Sergeant Goode and I will go in. I'm going to toss an extra IBA over the lady while Goode cuts the restraints. Danny, you toss the blanket as soon as the door pops open. Rick, you follow up with the tire. And be ready to deal with any threats that might pop up. Once she is free, we'll pull her out."

"Captain," Khalid added, "there are some boxes in the back. You could hide behind those."

"Might be a better idea. That grenade has a max three second delay. There might not be any delay," I said.

"You're right. We'll just grab her and hunker down behind the boxes."

"Major Weaver, stand by with lots of Band-Aids and aspirin. This might get ugly."

"Guys," she said, "everybody check your eyes and ears." Good thing she did too because yours truly had neglected both. I pulled on my ballistic goggles and plugged my ears with the GI-issue earplugs.

With the remaining Americans and Iraqis maintaining security for us, we took our places around the door. Two soldiers were poised at the door, one with a pick, the other with the ram. I was behind Danny on the right of the door balancing the truck tire on its tread. It was a heavy sucker. Danny had the bomb blanket. Clark and Goode were stacked facing the door, but back about three feet. Nancy was hunkered down behind a low wall ready to pick up the pieces and glue them back together. I don't mind saying my asshole puckered. This was some scary shit.

Clark looked around at everyone and got thumbs up all around. "Okay, guys. Ready?"

"Three, two, one, EXECUTE, EXECUTE!"

The so-called "very strong" door popped open like it was made of balsa wood. I think everyone was shocked by how quickly it collapsed. I caught a glimpse of the grenade a moment before Danny smothered it with the bomb blanket and then rolled out of my way. I dropped the tire right over where I thought the damn thing was and rolled to the other side. Clark and Goode dashed in just as a woman screamed, and in the same instant, something loud popped like an M-80 firecracker. Shit. My mind raced. Had the bomb armed, or was that a pistol shot from inside the room? I got behind a fifty-five-gallon drum and leveled my carbine on the front door. There was sure to be a blast in any second. A second scream was followed by heavy objects crashing around.

From the inside building we heard, "Goddammit!" then a thud, then silence.

Dead silence. No shots, no bomb, no nothing.

Danny peeked around the corner toward the door. "Captain Clark, you okay?" There was nothing for a second. Then Clark yelled, "Coming out!"

Three human forms flashed past me. Clark, carrying Khalid's wife, took her behind a low wall where Nancy was waiting.

Sergeant Goode yelled, "GET DOWN! FRAG OUT!" Everybody knew what to do, even me. I dropped and made myself into as small a target as possible. We all waited there for what seemed like minutes but was likely only thirty seconds. Nothing. Just silence. Soon heads started popping up as guys started looking around wondering why there was no explosion.

Being the resident idiot civilian, I decided it was time to move. I jumped up and ran to the low wall and came up next to Nancy who was busy doing her medical thing.

I looked at her patient. Mrs. Khalid was in bad shape. Her face was a mass of bruises, both eyes were blackened and swollen shut. Although she was wrapped in a blanket, it was clear she'd been tortured. I looked over to Khalid. His eyes were fixed on his unconscious wife.

"We need to move her inside. Let's set up in the restaurant."

Captain Clark and Sergeant Goode gently lifted her onto a stretcher. Danny grabbed one end and another soldier grabbed the other. Together they carried her through the back door and into the restaurant. Khalid and his escort followed, with yours truly bringing up the rear. Just as I stepped through the door's threshold, I heard a boom come from behind me. I turned to see a cloud of dust and dirty gray smoke erupt from the front of the building.

"Holy shit," I heard Danny say.

"Holy is right. Someone was looking out for us on that one. Clark, you are one lucky son of a bitch," I said.

Captain Clark pulled a small gold cross from under his blouse and kissed it. "My wife gave me this before I deployed. Said it was blessed by the pope."

"I need one of those," I said.

"It would burn a hole in your chest," Major Weaver said. Clark chuckled.

"Rick, why don't you and Danny take a look in the building? Watch out for secondary devices or trip wires."

"Yes sir," I said, and with that, Danny and I went back to the outbuilding.

CHAPTER 28

VIEJO

The place was still choked inside with dust and debris, but we could see fairly well. With our weapons at the ready, we entered. I could see the post Mrs. Khalid had been bound to, a length of white electrical extension cord on the ground next to where she had been tethered. Lying next to the post was a small electrical transformer and two leads with alligator clips on the ends. The concrete pad surrounding the post was stained with blood and the room smelled of urine. *She must have been in there for a while.*

Danny spoke first. "Whoever did this is in serious need of an ass whipping."

"Or a bullet right between the horns," I said.

We inched forward cautiously. Danny was looking for trip wires or pressure plates. I was fairly certain there would be none, but it pays to be cautious. After a few minutes that seemed like hours, we checked every inch of the building. I was soaked to the bone and pretty fried.

There were the boxes, just as Khalid had said, stacked about three high. I scanned the floor with my weapon's light until its beam fell upon what looked like the corner of a trap door, under some small boxes of dry goods and trash.

"Do you think we should check it out ourselves or get more help?" Danny said.

"I think we'll be good. Let me move a few of these boxes and we'll get to it."

I let my carbine hang from its sling and I picked up a box. It was labeled in what looked like Chinese. It was heavy, so I set it aside and picked up the next one, exposing the trap door made of plywood with a recessed handle at one end and hinges at the other. There were no visible locks. Danny got down on his belly and using my flashlight, he carefully examined the door.

"Looks clean, no wires."

"Okay, I'll open it up. Why don't you get behind a couple of those boxes? In case we missed something," I said, praying that we hadn't. *Rick, you're in way over your head on this one,* I thought.

I liked this kid from the oldest barrio in Los Angeles. The Avenues area of northeastern Los Angeles was famous for some of the baddest Hispanic gangsters ever. A very busy place for the cops of LAPD's Northeast Division, like Sadr City was for the Army.

Danny hesitated for a minute.

"Go ahead, I'll be fine," I assured him. I watched as he moved back behind the boxes.

"If you hear a little girl screaming, that will be me, so come running."

"Don't worry, Viejo," he said, "I've got your back."

I held my light in my left hand and my pistol in the other. I pulled open the door and shone the light inside. Nothing. I slowly scanned the room.

Just more boxes and crap. "Looks all clear," I said. Danny moved to my side.

"Why don't you let me go first?" he offered. "You move slower than old people fuck."

"Be my guest."

I moved aside as he lowered himself down to the dirt floor below.

"There's a ladder down here. I'll set it up for you."

I climbed down the ladder. "Let's see what's inside," I said motioning toward some boxes.

The first few were pretty boring—books, shoes, clothes, heavy rubber gloves, industrial grade breathing masks complete with filters, yellow hazmat suits, matching boots and lead aprons, the usual mess you find in your typical hidden storage bunker in Iraq.

I took a step back. "Danny, this stuff looks like it's been used. It's probably contaminated. Why don't you head back up?"

Danny wisely mounted the ladder in record time. I, on the other hand, being a bit slow, lingered to take one or two pictures for show-and-tell later.

I shoved one of the boxes out of the way to get a quick shot of the hazmat stuff. This could have been a very bad move on my part. But we may not know for say, ten or fifteen years. But at least when I develop some rare cancer, they'll name it after me.

Anyway, the box I had shoved didn't move too well. There was something small, but very heavy inside. So naturally, I took a peek.

Inside was a metal container that looked like the extra-large can of beans you buy when you're having a cookout for a bunch of drunken cops. Except its label didn't say baked beans. The label on this can was not one you want to see too often—a red triangle with a three-bladed radioactive propeller-looking thing at the top. Below it was a skull and crossbones symbol, and a picture of some dude running away. Which is exactly what I did. After I snapped a quick pic of course.

My guess was somebody was trying to put together a radiological dispersion device, known as an RDD. It's a conventional explosive coupled with radioactive material. When the bomb detonates, it disperses radioactive material over a wide area, contaminating everything it touches. Not a good thing in a city or on a large military base like Victory. In an instant, the place could be rendered uninhabitable. Even for the Army.

Our people could better deal with the blast and contamination than the disorganized multitudes of Baghdad. If it were to go off there, Fatima bar the door.

I've been told by experts that the actual threat from an RDD is overblown, but I've also been told by other experts that you should never listen to someone who calls themselves an expert.

So now I had some pretty solid PC (cop talk for probable cause) that we had stumbled into a very large and serious plot. No doubt those party animals from IRGC were up to their five o'clock shadows in this.

Danny and I had found the fabled weapons of mass destruction, more popularly known as WMDs. Now we needed to get word up to higher, so they would have ample opportunity to respond incorrectly.

"Danny, let's back out and secure this building. I will advise Clark what we found."

"Okay, so you want to leave the Mexican kid to guard the radioactive shit while you, Viejo Gringo, return to safety to spread the good news?"

"Rank and age have their privileges. I'll be back before you have a chance to miss me."

With that, I turned and ran the sixty meters back to the restaurant, where the party was just getting underway. I found Captain Clark in his vehicle on the radio net. From the sound of it, he was getting reamed out by Lieutenant Colonel Clancy or one of his minions.

"Yes, sir. I understand. Yes, sir . . . yes, sir . . ." I signaled that I had something pretty hot to tell him. He responded with a Boston hand salute and a look that translated to, "Fuck off, you got me in this mess in the first place."

Finally, he was done. He tossed the headset indifferently onto the seat and stared off into space for a second. I let him be. The radioactive material we had just discovered wasn't going anywhere. Not with El Sereno Danny on the job.

"Mister Sutherland, so good to see you."

"It's good to be seen," I responded, trying to lift the humor level a little. It didn't work.

"That didn't go well. Good thing I still have the PD to go back to, presuming they don't send me to Leavenworth first."

"That bad?"

"Yes, insubordination, disobeying a direct order . . . blah, blah. After a few minutes, I lost count. He got wind of our little adventure and is a bit hot. I'm to RTB (Return to Base) immediately and stand by for my replacement. I've been relieved."

Time to spring the good news on him. "Fear not, my brother from another mother, by the time I'm done, they're gonna run out of medals to pin on you."

"Rick, seriously, I'm in the shit and don't have time for your retired asshole bullshit. We've been ordered back to base. Copeland is en route to take charge of Khalid and his wife."

I knew that he was past wanting to hear anymore from me, so I decided to pull out my trusty camera and show him a few pics of what I'd found. After less than five pictures, his mood softened. I had him. Now all I had to do was convince Copeland and Clancy.

"Lighten up man, this is big, and you know it. We've stumbled on the terrorist version of the mother lode."

Captain Clark turned to Sergeant Goode. "Sergeant, I'm going to check out what this civilian retread is so excited about. I'll be back in a couple."

The sergeant nodded, and together we walked back to the storage building.

"Seriously, Rick, my ass is in a sling over this shit. The Colonel wants my scalp."

He was right, and I was feeling bad about this. I'd gotten him moved up to number one on Lieutenant Colonel Clancy's shitlist, but I was sure what I was about to show him would change all of that.

CHAPTER 29

GOING KINETIC

Danny had hunkered down behind the tire we used earlier, his weapon at the ready. He got up when he spied our approach.

"Hey, Danny, is this pinche gringo making you crazy?"

"Nah, sir, he's okay . . . for an old white boy."

"Thank you, Danny, for your vote of confidence."

"Okay, so where is this shit you're so proud of?"

I pointed toward the ladder. "Follow me, my son."

Captain Clark and I were climbing out of the hole when we heard the first shots. They were close. I could hear bullets impacting on the shed's walls. Danny returned fire.

"This is getting entirely too exciting for me," I said as I crouched by the right side of the shed door. I could see Danny looking intently at a low brick wall about seventy meters to his right. Clark whispered, "Danny, what ya got?"

"I just took a few rounds from that wall. I put their heads down, but didn't hit shit."

Then there was a tremendous explosion on the street fronting Khalid's restaurant. It must have been an RPG or something, because it turned one of the IA vehicles into a blazing junk heap.

Just as suddenly, small arms fire was heard coming from the restaurant. Things had heated up, and we needed help fast. Another explosion erupted, and we saw our command vehicle, the MRAP, engulfed by flames and thick black smoke.

"Fuck, there goes our commo," Captain Clark said.

"We're fucked."

"Not necessarily. Shore was going to try and get a drone to provide over watch. The TOC could have eyes on us."

"That would be helpful," I replied.

A big chunk of masonry blew out of the wall above me, fragments bouncing off my Kevlar pot. This was getting nasty. Danny was on his second magazine already.

I turned to Clark just in time to see his face jerk violently. Then he went limp.

"Danny, Clark's been hit," I yelled, but he couldn't hear me over the sound of his own weapon. I yelled again, "Danny, Clark is hit." He turned for an instant. I motioned to the still form of his captain. He mouthed "Fuck" and motioned for me to take over returning fire. I nodded.

Danny pointed to the bad guy's position and yelled. "Put fire there!" I already knew what to do but nodded anyway.

I low crawled toward the end of the wall I was cowering behind and stopped just short of its end. I went into a prone position, lying flat on my belly. Instead of popping up and shooting over the wall like the insurgents expected, I was going to roll out from behind the wall and fire a quick pair of shots, then roll back to safety. I hoped to do this a couple of times before the opposition figured it out and adjusted their fire. The operative word was *hoped*.

I brought the butt of my carbine tightly into my shoulder, and looked into the holographic sight. I took a deep breath and rolled out. Two hajis' heads popped up like groundhogs in a farmer's field. I squeezed off three rounds at the closest one and saw his head explode in a cloud of torn flesh, blood, and brain. His rifle flew straight up in the air. I moved to the second, gave him a quick pair, and he dropped.

"Damn," I said, somewhat shocked. But there was no time for high fives as a bullet whizzed overhead. I scanned for the source; nothing. I glanced over my shoulder as I rolled back behind the wall. Danny was working on Clark. Head wounds are never pretty, but I had to put it out of my mind and concentrate on keeping us alive until help arrived.

I saw a puff of dust rise from the right rear of a nearby Toyota pickup. Instantly, a couple of rounds impacted the dirt to my right. I rolled to face this new threat and waited for my adversary to show his face. I didn't wait long. I squeezed off two quick shots, but they must have missed. *Damn!* I fired another three and he disappeared behind the car. I heard a groan come from the pickup and then saw the now former jihadi flop over dead. Then, a machine gun opened up. The impacting rounds kicked up a hail of rocks and dirt all around me. I made myself very small behind that wall. I was scared shitless and very pissed off.

I figured that the machine gun was firing from a position directly in front of me. I needed something to get their heads down for a second so I could line up and take an aimed shot. I didn't have any grenades or other such fun things. The military generally doesn't give them to civilians. I looked at Danny. I could see a grenade in a pouch attached to his web gear.

"Danny, pass me a grenade." He looked at me puzzled. "Danny, I need a grenade!"

To my everlasting surprise, he passed me an M67 frag grenade. "Here, it's a four second delay," he said.

The thing was kinda squat and round and painted OD green, but not as heavy as I expected. I looked at it, wondering for a brief second if this was a smart thing to do. I instantly dismissed this thought when I recalled that I had long ago ceased doing smart things. As far as I knew, we only had one of these, so I had to make it count. I decided to take a quick peek before I threw it just to make sure of the gun's position. I crawled to the opposite corner from the one I'd been shooting. I popped my head up and damn near got it shot off. I also think I shit my pants, but that's a story for another day.

The machine gun was set up on the hood of a wrecked car about twenty meters away. I could just make out two figures hiding behind the car. "Okay, fuckers, I've got something for you," I whispered.

I gripped the body of the grenade, holding down the metal safety handle called the "spoon." I pulled the pin out, released the spoon and counted to three. I raised up and threw it at the machine gun position and hit the deck. BOOM!

Carbine at the ready, I poked my head out and looked. Through the cloud of dust and black smoke, I could just make out the bad guys. The grenade had landed short by about a couple of meters or so. But I bet it rattled their cages. I saw one rise to start shooting again. I dropped him with a pair of shots. Then I kept shooting at the machine gun until my rifle went dry.

It took my stressed-out brain a second to recognize the problem. I dropped down and pulled a fresh magazine. The bad guy opened up again, and soon it was raining bricks. Then the firing stopped. I waited a second and rose. My adversary was clearing a jam. I popped him twice, and he dropped like a rag doll.

I glanced over at Danny who had dragged Clark back into the storage shed. Danny applied a Hemoclott bandage, which soon had the blood flow under control by causing it to clot up. A now fully conscious Clark looked over at me. He gave me a thumbs up. I reached out, grabbed his hand, and gave it a squeeze. "You had us worried, man. Danny done good," I assured him.

Captain Larry Clark, US Army Reserve, detective-II Los Angeles Police Department, Van Nuys Division, nodded in agreement and looked up at Danny. War is a crazy thing. Back home, either myself or Clark might have been chasing Danny all through the alleys and vacant lots of El Sereno. But that was LA bullshit. This was Iraq bullshit, and we were all brothers here. I guess I knew this, but I never really understood it. The brotherhood of war. It's the same for cops too.

Since I didn't have a radio, I asked Danny to get on his and check in with the rest of the patrol. He touched his mike and called out.

"Nothing, man. Give me a hand, it's on my back upper left side." Danny reached up to the radio housed in a pouch high on the left side of his back. I could see its antenna from where I was squatting. He turned, and my keen, finely tuned powers of observation immediately recognized the problem. Lead poisoning.

"Danny, it stopped a bullet for you." I pulled it out of its pouch. Dead center in the middle of the hand-held radio was a neat 7.62mm hole, no doubt made by some wayward AK round.

"That was damn lucky," I said. Danny just smiled.

It was time to have a look-see at the situation at Chez Merde and the surrounding flora and fauna. Danny was doing the Lord's work tending to Captain Clark, who although stabilized and conscious, needed a medevac. That left yours truly to do the sneak-and-peek thing. I'd burned through one and a half magazines of ammo. Danny had used two. Clark had seven fully loaded magazines, and he wasn't likely to use any of them at this point.

"Danny, why don't you top off your ammo from Clark's vest and hand me one while you're at it?"

"Good idea. Captain, do you mind if we steal a couple of your mags?"

Captain Clark nodded his approval. Danny pulled two fresh magazines from Clark's pouches and gave one to me. I placed it in my load-bearing vest and checked the mag in my weapon. It still had lots of shiny little things in it. But I wasn't sure how many, so I replaced it with a fresh one. Better safe than shot.

I was now ready, except that my mouth was drier than an Oklahoma dirt road. I pulled out the drinking tube from my CamelBak and took a few sips of warm water. The water really hadn't had a chance to breathe yet, so I guess it's not really fair to judge, but I guessed it tasted like jock strap sweat aged in plastic with a strong rubber finish. Not very tasty, but it did the job, which was, of course, to keep me vertical. "Hey, I'm going to sneak back and get help," I whispered to Danny.

I'm really not sure what I was thinking. This sneak-and-peek crap was also not in the retirement plan, but I guess someone had to do it. I checked my weapon, took another sip of Château le Swamp Ass, and said a short prayer.

Satisfied that the Almighty and maybe even Archangel Michael were now on my shoulder, I low crawled to a corner of the wall and cautiously poked my tender gourd around the corner. All looked quiet; no bobbing heads, no nothing. I scanned for a safe place to stop. The machine gun position with the two departed jihadis looked safe. Besides, I figured that if the shit started flying, I could put the machine gun to good use. It was only about twenty meters or so from my position, but I would have to cross the main thoroughfare, Saddam Hussein Boulevard. I did another quick scan. All clear. I held my rifle at low ready and ran across that street like a scalded cat.

I made it to the machine gun emplacement with all appendages still intact, sliding into a mess of congealed blood, brain matter and empty brass. Part of my right pant leg was coated with it. On the brighter side, I was glad to say it hurt them more than it hurt me. I knelt behind the car in a pile of brass and shattered car parts. *Christ, that hurt.* My very tender and, may I add, tired knees were not happy.

I looked up just in time to see a Bongo truck driving down the street hell bent for leather. I could see the passenger had a serious case of five o'clock shadow and an AK. The driver was not nearly so savory looking. I glanced at the machine gun resting on a bipod before me. It was an RPK equipped with a drum magazine that looked like it was properly seated and hopefully still loaded, but there was no way to know without removing it, which I was not about to do.

I gave the RPK's charging handle on the right side of the receiver a partial pull and thought I saw a round start to come out of the chamber. That was a good sign and told me the weapon was hot and ready for fun. I picked it up off the truck and placed it across the rapidly cooling corpse of one of the jihadis. I saw Danny raise and fire a quick burst into the truck, but it had little if any affect.

I only had a half second to line up the Bongo in my sights. I squeezed the trigger, but it didn't budge. *Shit!* They had seen me set up on them. The driver turned and was now heading straight for me. I pulled on the trigger again with all my might, still nothing. Then it hit me. *Safety lever, dipshit!*

I pressed it down and praise God, it clicked into the fire position. I took careful aim at the very ugly driver and squeezed off a burst. The windshield vaporized from the high velocity slugs and the driver's face literally exploded. He slumped over onto the passenger, just as I let loose with another burst, this time at the passenger. The Bongo crashed into the corner of a nearby building, and that was it.

The Bongo is kind of a mini-utility van with an enclosed compartment behind the passenger compartment. I prudently decided to give this cargo area a little flow-through ventilation for good measure. I fired a ten-round burst, figuring that anyone hiding back there probably caught one or two slugs for their troubles. Just as I released the trigger on the last round, the weapon's magazine went dry. I didn't know how much ammo one of those Soviet-made buzz saws carried in their drum magazine, but thank God it had been enough.

I released the RPK and looked for a fresh magazine but only saw empties. But I did see a couple of Soviet-style F1 grenades lying in the dirt and gore. I snatched one up. Ya never know when you might need another grenade—especially in Iraq.

CHAPTER 30

MEALS READY NOT TO EAT

I arrived at the restaurant out of breath. Nancy was treating a couple of wounded IA soldiers. I could see that the IA command vehicle was now a smoking hulk. The US and IA guys had set a perimeter around the restaurant with the remaining vehicles parked to provide cover. Nancy did a double take when she saw me.

"You okay?"

"Fine."

"Your legs. Blood," she said pointing to my gore covered pants.

"I'm okay, it's not mine. But Clark caught a round in the face. It looks like it clipped his jaw. He's conscious. Danny's with him." I was sure she didn't have any idea who Danny was. "He's not a medic."

"Got it." She nodded. "We've requested a medevac, but there's a delay. The airfield is getting mortared again. It sounded like we lost a bird."

"We are also going to need some gunships or fast movers to cover our exfil," I said.

"I'm sure help is inbound. Higher knows we are in a TIC," Nancy offered.

"I sure hope so. We've found something pretty big in that storage shed. They're gonna want to know about it, ASAP. By the way, can I borrow your sat phone?"

"Why?"

"I've got to call and let 'em know what we've stumbled on."

"Sure, but I'm gonna need it back."

Nancy shrugged and got back to her patients. She was a doc. Helping people was her business. Locking them bad guys up was mine, but killing them was not.

My hands were shaking. I needed to sit down for just a second. My legs felt like overcooked linguine. I was fried, pumped, and scared shitless all at the same time. Hell if I knew which order that fell into. My exhausted brain was beginning to wander. Then I was reminded that I needed to make that call to Mikey and let him know what we'd discovered. Maybe get us some help. I had to be quick; Danny and Clark were waiting.

I found a quiet corner and dialed the number for baby bro's office. A staff officer answered. He spoke so fast that I could barely discern his words. Something about "Headquarters" and "General Sutherland's office."

"Is the general in? This is his brother."

"Ah, yes, Mr. Sutherland, the general asked that I forward all calls from you to Command Sergeant Major Galloway. Stand by."

"Galloway."

"Sergeant Major, this is Rick Sutherland."

"Yes, Rick, the general said you'd call."

"Ah, yeah, in the village of Yusufiyah. We've had TIC and have several wounded. However, we've found something out here that's pretty significant. It's related to the matter Mike, sorry, I mean the general asked me to look into."

"Yes, he briefed me. What do you have out there, and do you know your map grid reference?"

"Actually, I'm calling in the clear on an unsecured sat phone. I don't know the grid, but I can get it."

"Don't worry about the phone, just tell me what you've got."

I finished the call and put the phone down. I took a deep breath and exhaled slowly, just like my yoga instructor used to tell me. Christ, was she flexible. That made me smile for a second. Then I looked at my pants leg. Back to hell now. The shit was already thick, and we weren't close to being done yet. I needed a whiskey and a smoke, STAT.

After a few seconds of staring blankly at the floor and the blood and crap on my pant legs, I stood. It was time to get back into the game. Navel contemplating time would have to wait. I saw an opened MRE on a table. MRE stands for meal ready to eat or, alternatively, meals rejected by Ethiopians. I've heard both used and found the latter to be more accurate. Not being a total hog, I only snagged the crackers. I also grabbed a bottle of water.

I scarfed the crackers and washed it down with some good ol' Oasis water in about three seconds. It was a wonder I didn't choke to death.

Sergeant Goode walked up and said, "The doc told me that Clark is hit. I'm gonna need you to help us get him back here."

"No problem. Let's do it."

He looked at my freshly decorated pant legs. "You okay?"

"Yeah, just fried."

He smiled. "Roger that. You ready?"

"Yep."

The sergeant had grabbed a pair of our guys and a couple of wide-eyed IAs. They looked how I felt. One was nervously fingering the safety lever on his AK. That was not a good sign.

At some point, I had to tell Goode about our little find. But first, we needed to get Captain Clark back here so Nancy could do that medical magic she does so well.

The trip out to the shed was uneventful. Danny had things well in hand. I was relieved to see Clark sitting up, bloody but alert. Danny had placed a large compression dressing on the wound and, of course, Clark's blood was everywhere. He was one lucky dude. Danny said he caught a fragment of the bullet, not the full slug.

Bullets often do weird shit, as any homicide detective, coroner, ER doc or Warren Commission member will tell you. The slightest obstruction can cause them to suddenly jog off in a different direction or simply self-destruct. Apparently, the latter is what happened in Clark's case. The round that had his name on it apparently smacked a wall, a brick or dog turd, and started coming apart. The copper jacket covering the bullet's lead steel core separated and that's what hit Clark. It cut his face up, but thankfully, lacking momentum, it didn't shatter his jaw. In fact, Danny found it embedded in the Kevlar padding of Clark's armored vest and cut it out. Danny gave it to Captain Clark who had the pointy memento in his hand.

"I'm taking this home and having it set in that epoxy shit they put badges in. It's going in my bar."

"Nah, ah, ah, not so fast, Red Ryder," I interrupted. "General Order 3-Oh-You-Ate-One-Too clearly says you're not supposed to take any shit home from this God-forsaken hell hole. Especially something that wounded your sorry ass. I have personal experience with this order myself."

"Fuck that bullshit, my soldier career is over anyway. The colonel is going to have my sorry black ass when we get back. No thanks to you, I might add."

"I live to serve," I replied.

"Sir, let's get you back. Mr. Sutherland, can you give me a hand?" Sergeant Goode said.

"Sergeant, you can call me Rick."

"Or asshole," Captain Clark added.

"It's my middle name," I smiled.

Just then the sergeant's radio came to life.

"Sir, they're telling me the MPs just arrived. Its Major Copeland's team."

"Fuck," I mumbled under my breath.

Apparently, Clark's hearing was unaffected because he clearly heard me. Based on the look he shot me, he was none too pleased.

"Rick, could you stay and help out with the security on this place until I can get some guys over to do an SSE?"

"Happy to help," I lied. Actually, I wanted no part of this place. Despite what you might think, I'm no gunfighter, and this combat shit got old yesterday.

One of the young troopers set up his SAW light machinegun at the corner of the wall facing our rear. He quickly made a makeshift barricade of a couple of old car tires and an old wooden crate. It wouldn't stop bullets, but it couldn't hurt. I took a position just inside the shed's door.

The other soldier found a seemingly safe spot on the roof that gave him a fairly decent view for a hundred meters in all directions. Hopefully, the three of us would not have to sit here for long now that Major Copeland and the cavalry were here. I watched the SAW gunner scan the surrounding buildings with a small pair of binoculars. He paused at the window, doorway, and rooftop. Nothing was moving. All the locals were either safely tucked away in their little hiding spots or had unassed the place altogether. I suspected the latter.

"Do you mind if I borrow those for a second?" I was curious what was going on at Chez Merde. It didn't take long to get the drift. I could see Major Copeland huffing and puffing around looking quite the leader. His faithful companion, Sergeant Khanov, aka Boris Badenov, was at his side. That dude gave me a very bad feeling. The incident in the shower, the icy looks. Not good.

I watched as Copeland walked over to his vehicle and picked up a radio handset. The SAW gunner sat up slightly as he listened intently via his radio's earpiece. Then he turned to me.

"The major wants us to return to his position."

"What about the SSE? There is some serious stuff hidden here. We need to secure it and advise higher."

"Sorry sir, we've been ordered back immediately."

I could hear the soldier on the roof starting to move. Soon, he was down from his perch and crouched behind the low wall with us.

"Guys, we can't leave this stuff here," I objected.

"We've got to head back now," replied the SAW gunner.

He was right. He had to go back. Copeland had given an order and *these* guys had to obey.

CHAPTER 31

SOWS AND ASSHATS

The three of us now picked our way back to Chez Merde. The "roof guy" was in front. I was in the middle, and the SAW dude was in the rear.

I arrived just in time to hear Clark getting reamed. Christ, the guy was wounded, and Copeland didn't give a shit. He noticed my presence and stopped.

"Ah yes, Mr. Sutherland. Nice of you to join us. What are you doing out here? Ever hear of an SOW. You are so far off the reservation with this little stunt that your company will have no choice but to send your ass back."

Ah, yes, the ole' statement of work yet again. I assumed that's what he meant by SOW, or maybe he was talking about his mother? For a fleeting moment, I considered asking for clarification. When you are dealing with a terminal case of acute assholiness, it is best to let them rattle for a while. So, I did.

"You are not supposed to be out here. This is not what we pay you to do." He looked at my blood-stained pants and the empty magazine pouch on my chest. "Did you fire your weapon?" *Is he fucking kidding? Did I fire my weapon? Do fat SOWs have gas?*

I replied stone-faced in a flat monotone, "Ah yes, major, I believe I did."

"How many times?" he shot back.

"Do you mean number of rounds or instances?"

"Is there a difference?"

"Why, Major, yes, there is," I said keeping my voice steady.

"Let's start with rounds then," Major Copeland shot back. His face reddened. I was praying for an aneurysm, as no doubt was Clark.

"I'd say between seventy-five and a hundred."

"Using this rifle? Which, by the way, I'm betting you're not authorized to carry. Break out your arming-authorization letter, I want to see it." My letter said that I was only allowed to carry the 9mm annoying device. But I had recently qualified on the M16 rifle and the M4 carbine. In fact, a new Arming Authorization was in the mill allowing me to carry all three weapons. But this was getting fun, so I kept that to myself. Proud and unrepentant prick that I am.

He knew I was fucking with him, and yet the fool continued. "Did you fire anything else?"

"You mean besides this?" I asked, touching my slung M4 carbine.

"Yes," he replied in a low menacing tone. "What else did you use?" He was getting redder. Now for the *coup de grâce*.

"I used this," touching the M4 again, "and one of those big noisy things that they shoot at us with. It has a big round thing under it and one of those leggy things to rest it on." In the corner of my eye I could see Danny and his sergeant grin and turn away.

"RPK?"

"I think so. I don't know much about guns. They scare me."

Copeland turned and walked a few steps away. Clark took the opportunity to send me an unspoken *WTF, and I love you*. I looked back. *I love you too man, but this is too much fun. What an asshat.*

Sergeant Khanov saw all this and walked over to his boss, whispered something, then returned to their vehicles.

Major Copeland walked to where I was standing and shot a dagger look at Captain Clark, who returned the look defiantly. His bullshit meter was pegged too.

"Mr. Sutherland, I know you think you're very funny, but there's nothing funny out here. People have died out here today."

"I'm pretty sure I know that." I paused for effect. "Major, I'm just a retired cop hired to help you guys do your jobs, and maybe if I'm lucky save a few lives in the process. Today got a little hot, and I had to protect myself. I don't know why this matters right now. It seems to me you are wasting valuable time. We have discovered some things out in that shed that need to be recovered and analyzed immediately. I believe it's evidence of a significant attack being planned."

Captain Clark stood and faced Copeland. "Major, he's right about the evidence. We have photos of what we found. However, I think we need to talk privately to fully brief you on this."

"I'm not interested in some bullshit you and your cop buddy concocted to save your career. You're through."

"Major Copeland, we need to take this conversation inside." I jerked my head toward the restaurant. "This is some pretty sensitive shit and should not be discussed in front of our heroically duplicitous Iraqi allies." He relented, and we moved into the restaurant.

"Look, inside that shed we found filter masks, lead aprons, biohazard suits, and cans labeled with the radioactive materials symbol. We have photos." Copeland was unmoved. I could see he wasn't hearing a word I was saying. "We need to do a quick SSE and recover that stuff. This is evidence they are building RDDs."

"What makes you so sure it's anything but a bunch of trash? What could you possibly know about RDDs?"

We all have our breaking point and I had just reached mine.

"Listen, you puffed-up douchebag. I've forgotten more about this shit than you'll ever know. RDDs are radiological dispersion devices. If they set one off, it will change everything."

He took two steps forward and was now in bad breath range. His smelt of coffee and camel ass. Okay, I'm assuming it was camel ass. He started screaming about shipping me home and charging me with UCMJ, *blah blah blah*. I wasn't listening. Two can play that game. To this day, I'm not sure why I didn't put one in his determined little glass jaw and walk away. But discretion, even for your humble correspondent, was the better part of valor. I knew if I'd decked him, he'd win and there'd be nothing anyone could do.

Finally, he was finished. "You done?" I asked. That set him off again on another rant. I dared not look at Clark while this was going on. No need to cause him more grief.

"Get your shit loaded up," he demanded. Thank God he'd finally stopped. My legendary discretion was beginning to weaken. In everyone's life, there is a moment of decision. A point where you are faced with two paths. The easy one leads to an inch and a half thick ribeye and the best French wine to wash it down with. The other is a shit sandwich and a glass of vomit. I knew what was in that shed was huge. Security of the free world stuff. Not to mention the added fun I could have shoving it up Major Douchebag's ass. One of those containers with the radioactive markings was just about the right size.

Anyone could explain away the suits and masks. But there was no getting around the radioactive material markings on those cans. I pondered the situation for a moment. I figured I would need about five minutes to run to the shed, grab a can, and get back. There was only one person here who could buy me that time—Medicine Woman.

While she didn't outrank Copeland, she could play the medical necessity card that trumped pretty much anything short of bad guys climbing over the proverbial wall. Unfortunately, we were fresh out of walls and almost out of time. I needed an audience with her now.

I found Herself in a vehicle, comforting Mrs. Khalid.

"Do you have a second?"

"I'm a little busy at the moment," she replied icily.

"Just a minute. Please." She hadn't heard me use the *P* word much. It must have gotten her attention. She gently placed her patient's hand down and motioned for the medic to take over. She exited the vehicle and we walked around the corner. In a whisper I said, "Look, we found evidence that the bad guys are making some kind of radioactive infused bomb in that shed." I covertly glanced in its direction. She nodded. "I've gotta get back out there and grab some evidence. I just need five minutes." She looked a bit bewildered.

"Why are you talking to me and not Major Copeland?" Nancy asked.

"Copeland doesn't give a shit. In fact, he's ordered us out. I need you to stall him for five minutes."

"How am I supposed to do that?"

"Whip up a little medical shit on him. Tell him you need to do a heart transplant. Something. I don't know." I could see she was not warming to my entreaties. Perhaps it was the "medical shit" reference. *Regrettable choice of words.*

"Copeland doesn't believe us. He thinks we're trying to save our asses with some made up story."

"I can't imagine you trying that," she replied.

What can I say? I guess she knows me.

I was now reduced to begging, a technique familiar to all married men. "Nancy, I know I'm right. I just need five minutes. That's all. I'll be back before you know it. Please don't make me beg."

"Are you done?"

"Yes, ma'am," I replied with sincere respect.

"Mr. Sutherland, this is the Army, not some bullshit cop show. We follow orders here and it usually works out pretty well. I suggest you get your shit and load up like Major Copeland has ordered."

Well, that was that. There was no way I could return to the shed now. We were done, and I was fresh out of ideas. I started to walk back to the restaurant hoping to get through to Copeland when Major Weaver hurried past me. That was a bit surprising. I stuck my head in only to get it chopped off.

"Get the fuck out," the major ordered in a rather unpleasant tone. The two of them were talking. Nancy was pretty animated from what I could see.

I walked back to the vehicles and tossed my daypack in. I turned just in time to catch Nancy walk past.

"Five minutes."

Son of a bitch. She'd done it! I raced after her and mumbled. "Thanks, Major."

"Don't thank me, just get it done," she shot back.

CHAPTER 32

THANKS, MR. EMERSON

My solitary and quite sneaky quick step back to the shed had been mercifully uneventful. I still carried Nancy's iridium satellite phone that I planned to use if Copeland didn't come to Jesus. She wasn't too happy when I asked for it, but it was in my pocket now, wasn't it? That had to count for something.

I climbed back down into the hole. Thankfully, the masks, suits, and the radioactive storage containers were untouched. I froze for a second as a sudden and uncharacteristic wave of good judgment swept over me. *Radioactive. Fuck me. What the hell am I doing?* Today's fun and games were probably sufficient to satisfy my scared shitless quota for the next ten years—if I lived that long.

I had to quickly select the evidence I was going to use to sell my case, first to Copeland, then higher. Obviously, the most compelling evidence would be the small radioactive containers we had found, but they were contaminated. They must have transported the stuff in some kind of shielded case. I figured I had about two more minutes on site before I had to head back.

I tore around searching through the boxes. One wooden crate with

Arabic or Farsi writing looked promising but turned out to be empty. I was about to give up and just toss a can, some gloves, and a discarded mask into a burlap sack I'd found when I spied a box shoved under some old clothes labeled *B-D*. I recognized B-D as the logo the medical supply company, Becton Dickinson. I had already suspected the radioactive material had probably come from either a hospital or university. Back in my Joint Terrorism Task Force days we were told hospitals and colleges would be the most likely sources for illicit radioactive materials. Maybe they were right.

I tore at the box. Sure enough, inside was a metal case that sort of resembled a Halliburton briefcase. It was very heavy, and my gut told me I was back on track. I popped it open. *Jackpot.* Inside were cutouts that exactly matched the external dimensions of the radioactive material containers. I slipped on the gloves, which were also unusually heavy, and placed one of the containers inside. I snapped it closed. I also grabbed the bag containing the used filter mask and a biohazard suit. It pays to be prepared.

Climbing out of the hole was not very easy. I tossed the case up, then the sack, and then pulled myself up. Just as my head cleared the top of the hole, I found myself staring down the muzzle of an M4 carbine wielded by none other than my old shower buddy, Sergeant Khanov.

"Get out slowly, or I will spray brains all over wall." I thought "spray" was an unusual and yet, very serious choice of words. Not to mention poor verb conjugation and syntax. Undoubtedly, English was his second language, so I let his poor sentence composition go for now.

I meekly complied with his orders and climbed out of the hole in as unthreatening a manner as possible. He had an Iraqi Police officer with him who had been lurking in the shadows. As I stepped out, the IP gave me a butt stroke with his AK in the small of my back, sending me face down into the dirt. It hurt like a son of a bitch. Fortunately for me, the brunt of his strike hit the ceramic plate of my vest, and I was not as injured as one might think.

Feigning injury, I moaned and drew my legs up into a fetal position. I could tell that I'd impressed my IP adversary, but I suspected Sergeant Khanov would be a different matter altogether.

My mind raced trying to come up with an exit strategy that ultimately separated one retired American cop from two terrorist assholes and left the gringo alive and armed. My holstered pistol was out of the question, but I did have one of Ernie Emerson's very sharp Commander knives concealed under my blouse. *Maybe I can stick one of them with it? But then the other one will light me up for sure.*

I looked up at my adversaries. Sergeant Khanov had the muzzle of his rifle about three inches from my forehead. I couldn't see the IP. He must have been behind me.

"Mister," Sergeant Khanov said. "I am going to cut head off, and the others' too. We will enjoy Major also. Then she will die. We will make video of you begging for Allah's mercy. Your family will be shamed by your death."

I had to assume that he meant the beloved Major Weaver versus not so beloved Major Copeland. Which, of course, begged all sorts of nagging questions about the motivations of one Major Copeland. I hoped to answer these and other questions if I survived the next few minutes. But now was not the time.

I needed to provoke them to hit me again. In the confusion, maybe I could pull my blade and stick Khanov. The IP would probably shit his pants. Then I'd cut him while he was making number two. It was another really bad plan.

In my feigned agony, I stole a quick glance trying to gauge where both my adversaries were. The IP was standing just behind me with the muzzle of his AK pointed at my back. I think I saw that the safety lever on the side of his rifle was still up which, happily, is the "safe" position. That could be a lucky break, or maybe I got it wrong and would get a few bullets in my back as a reminder to be more observant. Sergeant Khanov was standing right over me, the muzzle of his M4 was pointed right in my face. I was fairly certain that his weapon was not on "safe."

Okay, here goes. I looked up at Khanov and snarled, "You goat-fucking, backwards-ass trait—" Boom. I felt a slam to the back of my head that made me see stars. Then another impact, this time in the small of my back. I bent over in an even tighter fetal position and moved my left arm to protect my head. At the same time, I slid my right hand under my blouse and instantly felt the rough grip of the Emerson. I knew if I yanked it hard, the hook on the top of the blade would snag on my pants and the blade would pop open with a snap. Khanov would probably hear that, but with luck it might be the last thing he heard. I had no time for stealth or ninja bullshit.

I gripped the Emerson and yanked. The hook machined into the top of the blade snagged on my pants exactly as Ernie had designed it, and the blade snapped into place with a pronounced click. I looked up just time to see a flash of recognition on Khanov's face.

I brought the now fully extended blade out and drove it with all my might into what I assumed was his ball sack. In that same instant I raised my body and turned my helmeted head, which was just enough to deflect the muzzle of his weapon. Good thing I did. Khanov let out a shriek as I was giving him my own version of a Brazilian. I watched as he tried to pull the trigger on his own weapon. Nothing. It was on safe! How about that, Sergeant Khanov was practicing safe weapons handling procedures after all.

His face was contorted in pain as I pushed and twisted the blade deeper. I was trying to cut the femoral artery, or at least turn him into a gelding. The IP just stood there frozen in fear. Probably making doodoo. I continued cutting upward with my blade as I stood. My blade's upward motion was halted by what had to be his pelvic bone. I was going to try and knock Khanov back with a head butt, disarm him, then deal with the IP.

Just as my helmet and upper body was making contact with Khanov, I felt his body jerk and then suddenly go limp. I looked up just in time to catch the tail end of pink spray blast out from his head. Then in nearly the same instant, the IP dropped. A jet of arterial blood shot from his chest, just as chunks of skull, flesh and brain blew out the back of his noggin. There was no sound. No shot. Nothing. I glanced down at my blood-soaked right hand holding the Emerson. Wow that is one hot shit knife, but I knew my two adversaries had been expertly dropped by someone with a suppressed rifle.

I dropped to the ground and rolled to one side. Someone out there had excellent taste in targets and was a really good shot. Not wanting to end up as collateral damage, I needed to get out of the line of fire just in case. I hunkered down and tried to catch my breath. In that instant I felt the room start spinning. My eyes got blurry. I felt a sharp pain in my back, exactly where the late, but not lamented, IP had butt stroked me. I closed my eyes as I tried desperately to regain my composure and senses. Friendlies must be out there, given their discretion and shooting skill; I needed to hang on.

My mind raced with possibilities: Copeland would soon check on his buddies. *Shit, his buddies, Copeland . . . FUCK!* Copeland must be playing for the other team. Nancy was there with him. So was Clark. I needed to get back to them. I forced myself to stand. I grabbed a box for support. Just as I stood fully erect, the room did a 360, and I did a 180, straight down on my face. Lights out.

Soon I was joined by Gisele. But why was she calling me Skippy?

"Skippy. Skippy, you there? Skippy come to the light. Come to the light, mate."

"Skippy."

Wait a minute. Skippy? Who is calling me Skippy?

"Skippy come back to the light." *Who is that? Where am I?*

Slowly I cracked open my eyes. I saw dark shadows hovering over me. Some were close, some not. They are calling me Skippy. Only my best bud Steve and baby bro Mikey called me that. Even in my vastly reduced state, I knew that Steve, who rarely leaves his pipe and book, would not be with me in Iraq. It had to be Mikey.

"Mikey, are you there?"

"No, mate, but a friend of his sent us."

My eyes finally began to focus again. A guy in some kind of camo was about to jab a needle that had to be an inch wide and four inches long into my arm. I started to pull my arm back, but it seemed to be held in a vise. Then I heard the needle guy's radio come to life.

"Delta Two Zero, we have Skippy. He's awake."

"Copy, Delta Two Zero. Tell him bro says, 'Get back to work.'"

"Back to work!" I said.

"Well, Rick, I can see you're back now. My man is going to give you an IV to set you right. You've been out for a bit. Just relax, he's done this at least once before."

I looked at the guys kneeling around me. They were Brits, but their equipment was different. Some had M4s instead of that weird bullpup rifle the Brits carry. All their rifles had suppressors and high-speed optics. This was a dead giveaway, as the regular soldiers usually don't get such toys. But most telling, several had some serious handlebar mustaches and beards.

Were these guys SAS or some other British special ops group? Having worked around some of those high speed, low drag guys before, you can just tell. They are very fit looking, quietly confident and have the coolest gear taxpayers can buy. Fancy weapons, the latest night vision, non-regulation boots and rucksacks. . . . They call it Gucci gear. Like I said, you can always tell, but I also knew it was best not to ask them too many questions. Better to wait for them to identify themselves. But it really didn't matter who they were. They were here, and thank God and General Mikey for that.

"Rick, we need to get you rehydrated. Shouldn't take long."

"Did you guys see the stuff I found?"

"Right, one of the lads is an intelligence specialist. He took a look and uploaded some photos back to his shop." *This guy must be the boss,* I thought.

"What did he think of it?"

"I'm no expert, but my man was quite excited. I think you've stumbled onto something big."

I watched one of the Brits move cautiously to a corner of the low wall that I had used as cover earlier. The trooper raised a suppressed pistol, fired two muffled shots in quick succession, and then ducked. The shots were so quiet, I only heard the sound of the pistol's action working. Then things went really quiet, except for a few clipped words I could overhear on their radio net. The boss sneaked outside for a look. Then he poked his head back in.

"We've got company. Stay here."

My fogged brain was now coming to life. The real concern in my mind was Nancy and the others. Were they still safe? I asked, "Is the patrol still at the restaurant?"

"We've got eyes on them, but we're waiting for some help with that. Should be here soon." I guessed there were probably no more than five or six guys here with me, so that made sense. Especially if Copeland and his team was playing for the other side. This also meant that Nancy, Clark, and the others were in grave danger.

"Guys, I think there are some bad guys in our uniforms over there mixed with our people."

"Yes, we know. A few minutes ago, two US marked vehicles pulled up with at least six or eight more guys. My man says there's something not right with these new people. They met with a major, who seemed to be expecting them."

"That major is Copeland. I think he's turned," I said. "That sergeant I had to stick back in the shed was named Khanov. He was with Copeland."

"Yes, I presumed as much. Problem is they've got at least double or maybe triple our strength, and hostages too. We'll need some help. A minute ago, they sent a guy over here to have a look. My man dropped him. But more will be coming. We're going to need to move soon."

"Excuse me, Rick," the presumed leader said as he stepped away. This guy had to be an officer. But whatever he was, there was no doubt in my mind the small unit he was running was either British Special Air Service (SAS) or maybe Special Boat Service (SBS). They could also be from this new super-secret group I recently heard of called the Special Reconnaissance Regiment (SRR). The SBS is like our SEALs; as for the SRR, who knows.

The SAS is the British Army's unit that specializes in all manner of seriously badass stuff, including direct-action missions. The US Army has a similar Special Mission Unit (SMU) whose very existence is classified, so I won't go there.

CHAPTER 33

MALMEDY

The medic whispered something into his headset, then turned to me. "Rick, it's gonna get a bit hot. Get your head down and get ready. Hostiles are inbound." The air soon filled with sounds of automatic weapons fire, answered by muffled shots in disciplined pairs. There was a sudden explosion, then silence.

"Roger that," the medic said into his mike, before announcing, "clear." That was the good news, but what about Nancy and Clark and the rest of the patrol? Then the boss hustled back into the shed.

"Change in plans. Some of the vehicles have just left. Your people are with them. We are going to move to secure the restaurant. How are you feeling?"

"I'm fine. You say they left?"

"Yes." The boss glanced at the medic as he answered me.

"He's good."

"Right. Be ready to go in two minutes. Rick, you stay with me."

"Yes, sir."

"Very good."

I looked at the medic. "Can you pull that spear out of my arm?"

"Yep. Just lie still." I could see the bag still had some juice left, but for once I wasn't lying. I did feel fine. Not a bit "wobbly," as these guys would say.

I sat up slowly, still all good. Nancy would have been proud. Well, proud might be overstating it a bit. The medic handed me my carbine first and then my blood-stained knife. "You'll be wanting this, sir. Did a fine job on him. I think you made him into a bird." I smiled and replaced the blood-stained Emerson in my right pants pocket.

"How's he gonna pleasure all those virgins without his junk?" I wondered aloud.

"Where he's going, buggery's more the thing."

"One can only hope. Thanks for the cocktail."

"Pleasure, sir."

"What's your name?" I asked.

"Mick."

"What about the boss?"

"The boss is Duncan."

"You all from Hereford?" Hereford is the home of the SAS. Okay, so I was getting curious. It never hurts to ask.

"Naw, I'm from Norfolk. Duncan's from Dundee, the other boys are from all over."

"Christ. You know what I mean," I replied.

"Sorry, sir, have to get moving now."

"Right."

Mick looked at me as he hitched up his rucksack. "Yes, we are."

"I thought as much. For one thing your mustache looks like something out of an American Western."

"It's a good 'un but can't compare to Tony's."

A huge bear of a man stepped in carrying a radio in one hand and an M4 with a grenade launcher in the other. His mustache was truly a thing to behold. The narcs back home would have been green with envy. Jet black and bushy, it tapered to waxed tips on each end.

"Mick, as we move, stay behind a few meters with our Yank here, and cover our six."

Thank God the movement to Chez Merde was uneventful. As we moved, I passed the corpses of three dead insurgents, all dressed in civilian attire, weapons at their sides. The locals were either all gone or hunkered down in their homes. Mick and I arrived at the shop a minute behind the main element.

The troopers were setting up security and checking out the burnt vehicles when we walked up.

"Mick!" Duncan, the lieutenant, emerged from the shop with a grim look. "Bring your bag. Rick, come here."

As I walked past the front door of the shop, I smelled it immediately. *Fresh blood. Death.* I braced myself as I walked into the back room. There, lined up on the floor, were five US soldiers, four Iraqi soldiers, and one lifeless female form covered in a blanket. It was Khalid's wife. The men had been stripped to their underwear and their hands bound tightly behind their backs. From the looks of it, all had been shot once in the back of the head. As I moved closer, my boot crunched an empty shell casing. It looked like a 9mm. Then I looked up and recognized Sergeant Goode. One of the kids I'd smoked a cigar with the other night was next to him. It was awful.

I stuck my pen in the case mouth, examined its base. It read *LC 07* and had a circle with a small cross inside. This marking, called a headstamp, told me it was US government issue 9mm ammunition. LC was the code for the United States government arsenal at Lake City, Independence, Missouri. The circle and cross marking meant that the round had been loaded to NATO specifications. These people had each received a single round of 9mm, possibly fired by a United States government issued M9 Beretta. Copeland had one of those, so did I. But the weapon used for this must have been suppressed, otherwise we would have heard the shots. The standard M9 does not have a threaded muzzle and is therefore incapable of accepting a suppressor. However, suppressed pistols are pretty common in the Special Operations world. Copeland must have special friends with him.

Murder scenes have always affected me, especially when the victims were slaughtered like these people were. It reminded me of pictures I'd seen of the GIs murdered by German SS troopers in a snow-covered field outside Malmedy, Belgium. Helpless prisoners, just like these guys.

As I looked at the other faces, I didn't see Nancy, Clark, or Khalid. Come to think of it, I didn't see Danny either. They must have taken them hostage, which brought me relief and concern. The Brits were on the radio describing the scene in cold precise military shorthand. Duncan came up to me and put his hand on my shoulder.

"Rick, I'm sorry. Maybe if we moved sooner, we could have stopped this." I could hear the frustration and anger in his voice.

"Sir, it's not your fault. You couldn't have stopped it with your five or six guys." I still didn't know how many he had. I assumed he always had one or two guys hidden in some over-watch position. When those two Humvee loads of guys arrived, it changed the odds considerably. If Duncan had moved on them, they probably would have killed everyone. At least now there was a fighting chance we could recover the others.

"Duncan, we need to get after these guys. Do you have a UAV up? We can track them until they stop, then move in."

"Rick, your guys are following the vehicles now. They've got it. We've got to stand by and secure this location."

"They've got two American officers, a soldier, and my informant." I didn't mention I was in love with one of those officers, but I was sure he could sense the desperation in my voice.

"*Informant?* What do you mean?" Duncan asked.

"He's a local Shia guy. He owns this place. The storage shed you found me in is his also. He has ties to the Shia insurgency and the IRGC."

CHAPTER 34

WHO CARES WHO WINS?

"**S**orry mate, but I've got my orders. Standby until relieved."
This was going nowhere fast, and I was starting to freak out. I knew what those thugs were capable of. I had to maintain. *Be reasonable and rational, Rick.*

"Orders? Fuck orders!" I announced reasonably. "If I'd followed orders, we'd have never found that radioactive crap in the shed." Duncan's face was still impassive. I decided then and there to try a different approach. I played my final card—an appeal to SAS tradition and history. The ethos of the regiment.

"Who dares, wins, right?" I said rather pointedly. Those three simple words epitomize what I understood to be the very core of the Special Air Service. A smart bunch of tough-as-nails, risk-taking blokes who were willing to put their asses way out there to accomplish the mission.

What can I say? I read a lot, especially on planes. I had picked up a paperback by a guy named Chris Ryan during a layover at Heathrow. Apparently, Ryan was a former SAS trooper and a good storyteller.

"We are staying here until relieved."

When a commotion erupted on the street in front, I followed Duncan out to have a look. It was El Sereno Danny, looking haggard, but fully equipped and alive. A couple of the Brits had weapons on him as he approached.

I walked out to meet him. "It's okay, guys, he's one of us."

"Danny, what happened?"

"Fuck, man. I was over there behind that building pulling security, watching the approaches." He motioned to a two-story building across the street. "First, I saw you sneak out, then about five minutes later, that MP sergeant and an IP headed your direction. I watched them searching for you then disappear in the shed. Then I saw some 1151s heading toward us. 'Cool, help is here,' I said. I watched as the guys drove past. But something was wrong. I don't know, but fuck, man, they were too clean. Didn't look right."

"Danny, did you see Khalid, Major Weaver or Captain Clark?"

"Yeah, man, they've got 'em. Weaver and Clark were zip-tied and stripped of their gear. I didn't see Khalid."

"Did you see what happened to them?"

"No. They moved them inside a vehicle. I also saw some of the other guys move a heavy box from one of the 1151s to Copeland's vehicle. I had to duck down when some local started yelling at his kids. Everyone looked in my direction."

"Did they see you?" I asked. Duncan and big Tony had come over to join us.

"Gents," Duncan said, "we need to get off the road."

As we walked in, I spoke softly to Danny. "Before you go in, I've got to tell you something. They executed some of your guys. Laid them out on the floor and shot 'em in cold blood. I'm sorry."

Danny froze in mid-stride. He swallowed hard. "Who?" he asked.

I didn't answer. "Danny, I'm sorry, but I need you to put it out of your mind for now. We need to get these guys and get our people back, and we don't have much time."

"I hear you."

We all entered the restaurant just as one of the troopers was placing a towel over the face and upper torso of a dead GI. Danny looked down, steeled himself, and looked up. I realized I hadn't introduced Duncan and

Tony.

"Danny, this is Tony and—"

"I'm Duncan Sinclair," he said as he offered his hand.

"Danny, I'm very sorry for what happened here,"

Danny nodded.

"Danny, these guys saved my ass over at the shed. Gentlemen, this is Specialist Danny Hernandez."

"You guys must have popped Khanov. Fuck him," Danny said. "I didn't like that dude. Had a bad feeling. Really bad."

"Your gut was right. It seems he and Copeland have gone over."

Big Tony then jumped in. "Actually, Rick here did the honors on Khanov. Stuck him in the bollocks."

Danny looked a little confused. "I stuck him in the nuts, Danny."

"You go after the manhood, you get their attention," Danny said.

"Danny, tell the guys what you just told me."

Danny retold his story, and now we really had Duncan's interest. I could tell Danny was just barely holding on.

"There were four guys in each vehicle, but something wasn't right about them. The vehicle markings or something, I don't know. It just didn't look right. Anyway, they hooked up with Copeland and from what I could see, he seemed pretty happy to see them. I also noticed that when they got out, they didn't move like normal guys. They looked more like SF dudes. They were pretty ripped. They had our gear and weapons. They even had those radios all the SF guys carry. Another thing that wasn't right. They all had those high-speed NODs, not the shit ones we get." NODs are night vision optical devices.

"Thanks, Danny." I looked at Duncan and Tony. "Quds Force?"

"Sounds like it to me. Wouldn't be the first time."

Danny looked puzzled.

"Iranian Special Ops," I said.

"Shit, man. That makes total sense. I heard about those assholes."

I turned to Duncan and Tony. Time for one last bite of the apple. "Guys, I think this might change things a bit."

CHAPTER 35

PURSUIT

We were headed down the same road Copeland and his pals had used earlier. Tony was driving the vehicle I was in, and Duncan was in the right front on the radio. Bouncing around in the vehicle reminded me that I had Nancy's sat phone. I gave General "Baby Bro" Mikey's office a call. To my surprise, they put me right through to the great man himself.

"Mikey, it's Rick. I don't have much time. I'm talking in the clear on a sat phone. We are following some bad guys who may be carrying something very nasty. We have an 0-4 who's gone over to the other side. He's got some new friends that just joined him that are probably from out of town." I was speaking in half-assed code, but I'm sure Mikey was getting the message.

"Rick, I think I know who your guy is and probably his friends."

"What do you mean, you know who it is?" *Holy Whiskey Tango Foxtrot.*

Mikey, sensing that I was about to have a stroke, said, "I can't give you all the details, we just put this together a few hours ago. The Bureau and CID hit a place here and discovered some good stuff. Your guy has been playing for the other team since college. His mother had some family connections to leaders of the revolution. He's smart, managed to keep it hidden for years. Rick, where are you now, and who are you with?"

Duncan gave me a map grid reference number, which I relayed to Mikey. "I'm with some Brits."

"Are the Brits attached to some of our guys?"

I relayed that question to Duncan, to which he responded, "Affirmative," which I passed on to Mikey.

"Okay, Rick, I know who you are with now. I'll reach out to their chain and get the full story. Be careful."

"It's a little late for that bro. See ya. Out."

Duncan turned to me. "I've passed on a sit rep to our higher. Your contact should have it shortly. Who is Mikey?"

"My baby bro. He's got some juice around here."

"We've got a UAV up following the target. They are about twenty clicks ahead of us. But we're catching up. For some reason, they're not in a hurry. We have to watch for an ambush."

"Where's the other group that's supposed to be following them?"

"Hung up with an IED strike. No casualties, but they lost a vehicle. They are now about fifteen behind us."

IED strike? Christ, with all the shooting and bullshit, I forgot about IEDs. Maybe that's why Copeland was traveling so slowly.

"Are we going to get some air assets on this too?" I asked Duncan.

"A pair of Apaches are inbound. ETA six minutes."

"Great, that will even things out." Then I thought about Nancy and Clark being held hostage. "Do the Apaches know there are friendlies with the bad guys?"

"Yes, they do. I've also advised them personally."

That was a relief. The plan, if there was one, was of course to take Copeland and at least some of his playmates alive. A pair of Hellfire missiles fired by an Apache would not be helpful.

After what felt like an eternity, but was probably only few minutes, Duncan turned to me. "They've stopped. The Apaches are nearly on station and will be standing off a few clicks. We should be on them soon. The

Yanks are coming in from the west. We will wait for them before we make contact." I was starting to feel like we had this back under control. We had Army Special Mission Unit hitters, SAS and, of course, Apaches. Our odds were improving.

CHAPTER 36

TAKE-DOWN

"They're entering an abandoned factory," whispered Duncan, who was radioing regular updates back to us. "We've got eyes on them."

Straining to see ahead, the buildings were still hidden from view as I felt myself tensing up with each passing kilometer. Looking for an ambush, I scanned every bush and bit of debris as we passed. It felt like the longest excursion of my life.

On the horizon in front of us, I spotted a small glowing object streaking skyward. Another followed shortly thereafter, then two more and a burst of fire and black smoke marked the sky several kilometers north of the factory.

"Fucking hell," shouted Duncan. "They've got SAMs (Surface to Air Missiles)."

His voice was strained, but still calm. Then the radio net went nuts. One of the Apaches was hit and going down while the other was trying to provide cover.

Two more SAMs launched from the area of the factory, and I said a silent prayer for the Apache crews as I watched. When a bright fireball and huge puff of smoke now erupted from the second Apache, it seemed my prayers were in vain, and my gut tightened. I felt our odds of success slipping away.

Duncan ordered our convoy to a halt. In a muffled voice over the vehicle intercom, his voice sounded calm and in total control. "They're expecting us. We'll dismount here and approach on foot. The Yanks are only about five minutes behind us. Keep an eye out."

Ordinarily, he'd have us stay with the vehicles, but every gun was needed for this one. I checked my gear and weapons. It was all there and probably still worked. I had a nearly full load of magazines, including one of the old Soviet grenades I'd picked up earlier. I'd assumed that Danny had been given the same instructions by the crew he was with. If Copeland had Quds Force assholes with him, we were in for a serious fight. While not as good as our guys (the Americans and Brits), they were highly skilled and motivated. In short, nobody to mess with. They undoubtedly also had insurgents hiding in the area, just waiting for us to move in.

We parked under a stand of palm trees about 500 meters from the factory and waited. After a few minutes Duncan gave the word and the guys dismounted, moving silently into position. They all were pros, ready to unleash hell on the bad guys. I, on the other hand, was scared shitless, yet also strangely confident and proud to be there.

Danny and I followed Tony to a spot behind a big dusty bush. Suddenly, he turned and whispered, "Lads, stay behind me." Danny nodded like it was no big deal.

The three of us crept in single file about five meters apart, weapons at the ready. Edging closer, the twin black smoke columns marking the Apache crash sites could be seen off in the distance and I prayed that help was on the way.

Until the cavalry rode in, it was all on us. A handful of US and UK Special Operations soldiers, a tough Hispanic kid from LA, and one trembling old LAPD retread. Not much of an Army, but I still liked our odds.

We stopped about a two hundred meters short of the factory perimeter and sat, and I made out our objective through the dense brush and palms. It appeared to be a collection of metal-sided dilapidated wrecks with a large building in the center. There also were remnants of a high fence, and a pair of wrecked guard towers in opposite corners.

I glanced over at Tony, who was whispering into his throat mike, and then turned to us. "Follow me," he said, with seeming urgency.

We continued our slow approach for another minute, until Tony motioned for us to stop and take cover. Not knowing what all the hand signals meant, I followed Danny as we dropped behind a bunch of thorny bushes. Tony advanced to a burned-out vehicle, checked it out, then gave the all clear. Moving forward, we quickstepped to Tony's side as I heard a muffled pop about twenty meters to my right. Tony gestured with a pistol motion and grinned. Some jihadi sentry just got whacked.

We now were positioned only thirty meters from the fence, when Tony whispered, "The guys will be hitting it soon. I'm taking you to that stack of barrels, so stay put and cover the door in front of you."

We advanced to a stack of fifty-five-gallon drums. "Watch this corner," whispered Tony. "Here's a radio. Call out if you see something."

Danny slid the radio into a pouch and inserted the earpiece, then looked over at me. "We need to stay down and wait for—" but I didn't hear him finish the sentence. He went prone behind the left corner of the stack, and I followed on the right. I knew we had been detected and was surprised they allowed us to approach unopposed. *Where the fuck are their vehicles?*

It was a two-story building, about two-hundred feet long by a hundred feet wide. The sides were masonry and sheet metal, and I could hear the muffled sound of a gasoline engine or generator running inside.

After several minutes, four guys emerged from a small outbuilding to Danny's left, stacking in single file adjacent to the wall and to the left of our door. The lead guy examined the door, probably looking for booby traps, a tactic that had recently become all too familiar. He pushed the door, just slightly, but it failed to budge. He signaled to the number two guy, crouched down, and a guy from the stack moved up and took up position on the right of the door. I watched as he placed a fist-sized rectangular object on the door near the lock. It had to be an explosive breaching charge designed to blow the door in. It only took a few seconds for him to place on the door.

Then I heard it. A loud sharp blast near what had to be the rear of the building.

"Explosive breach," Danny whispered. The door in front of us exploded inward, and the team of operators disappeared into the smoke-filled void. Two more blasts went off from what sounded like the opposite side of the factory. Then came the thuds of suppressed weapons firing. Hopefully, it was ours.

Danny heard the same thing and glanced over at me. I shrugged and held tight. A pair of blasts, sounding like grenades, erupted inside the building. More shooting followed, as I tensed and remained in position. Single rifle shots were punctuated by answering bursts of machine gun fire.

Bullets tore through the thin sheet metal walls and whizzed above our heads, then slamming the ground in front of us. One pinged off a fifty-five-gallon barrel.

"Danny, if someone pops out that door, you should—" I never got the chance to finish.

"No worries, gringo, I got it."

I figured he'd take the lead on whatever happened next. He was the professional soldier, and I, only a marginally talented amateur. Danny undoubtedly had worked with Special Ops guys and knew their tactics.

Danny tensed, raising his rifle as he took aim at the door. "Squirters coming our way," he shouted. The door blew back open and three guys in US Army ACUs ran out. I was lined up on the door, but they sped past my line of sight. Although dressed in American uniforms, they weren't equipped like our SOF operators but looked like regular Joes.

"Freeze motherfuckers!" ordered Danny.

Shit! I couldn't see them. If I shifted positions to back up Danny, I'd lose sight of the factory door and maybe even miss more bad guys heading our way.

"Danny, I'll hold the door unless you need me." No reply.

"Get down fuckers. Get down . . . NOW!"

Then shots. Danny fired five or six rounds as fast as he could pull the trigger.

"Down now!"

More shots, but this time not from Danny's rifle.

"Fuck it," I mumbled, before crawling next to my partner as he let loose with another burst. Then I rolled out to Danny's left and took a look. Two bodies were sprawled on the ground between the door and our position. A third guy was on his knees, a trickle of blood oozing from his left thigh.

"Rick," yelled Danny. "You got a zip tie or cuffs?"

"No."

"I've got spares in the top left side pocket of my pack."

I rose and opened the pocket, and inside were three zip ties.

"Got 'em," as I handed them to Danny who slid them into the cargo pocket of his pants, never taking his weapon off the kneeling bad guy facing him. I was impressed, but he was one-hundred-percent focused on his target.

"Rick, you cover, and I'll secure them," whispered Danny.

"Okay, partner, be careful."

He snickered. "Fuck 'em."

I put my rifle's sight on the wounded guy's gourd while Danny moved around and behind him, keeping his carbine at the ready.

"You move, you die, motherfucker," Danny warned. Then he ordered the guy to lie down spread eagle, and to my amazement he complied.

Danny closed the distance and was about to cuff him, when I heard a low metallic thud. Danny spun, dropped flat on his back as the bad guy leapt to his feet and produced a concealed pistol before taking off with blinding speed. Puffs of dirt erupted around me, as I squeezed off several answering shots. With no time to aim, it was spray-and-pray time. He fired his last shot, then fell face down on top of me. Frantically, I rolled him off and put two more rounds in him before observing that his face was gone.

Next, I focused on Danny, who wasn't moving. No sound, no breathing, nothing.

"Danny, Danny," I whispered.

Something hit the barrel above my head. *Sniper!* I scrambled to the other side of the barrels as another muffled shot rang out and I hit the dirt. I turned and looked behind me. Danny was still frozen. No signs of life. If I moved to Danny's side, I'd be exposed. My mind raced, searching for options. I looked at Danny, trying to think.

"Danny!" I exclaimed, louder than a whisper. Then I saw it. On his left side, attached to a side pouch of his load-bearing vest was what had to be a smoke grenade. That could work, if he could get to it.

"Danny!" I saw movement. His left hand moved slightly.

"Danny, can you hear me?" I whispered. He signaled a thumbs up. "Do you have a smoke grenade?"

Again, a yes. I was sure the sniper was watching us both. I would need a distraction to buy time for Danny to deploy the grenade.

More shooting and shouts erupted from inside the factory. "Danny," I whispered, "can you pop the grenade when I start shooting?"

He gave me the thumbs up a third time.

Okay, so where is the fucking sniper? I hadn't heard the first shot and barely heard the second. A suppressed rifle could only mean a sniper. Not some half-assed, back-shooting jihadi with AK, but a properly equipped and trained professional marksman probably wielding a Soviet-made Dragunov sniper rifle fitted with a sound suppressor.

Okay, time to focus. "Danny, hang tight, bro," I whispered.

I crawled over to the far side of the barrels, took a deep breath, and popped my head out for a millisecond. There were no buildings where the shots had to be coming from. It had to be something else. I took a second peek. A muffled shot erupted. A bullet whizzed past, just inches from my head. *Dumb shit.* Never expose yourself in the same spot twice in a row. Even a twelve-year-old *Call of Duty* veteran knows that one.

Despite nearly having my head shot off, I spotted the sniper hide in a pile of fallen palm tree fronds about forty meters away. He had to be there. *Fuck, he better be, or I'm dead, sure as shit.*

I crawled over to the other side. I planned to pop out rifle blazing, putting as much fire as possible down on the suspected sniper hide. Simultaneously, I hoped that Danny could deploy his smoke grenade, providing me cover so I could affect a rescue. That should work no problem, right?

I ejected the used magazine from my M4 carbine and inserted a full one, setting the old one aside as it probably still had fifteen or twenty rounds on board. Waste not, want not. I pulled a second fresh magazine and set it on the ground next to me. Then I felt the F1 Soviet grenade that I had picked up a few hours ago. I pulled it out and placed it next to the mag. With all preparations made, it was time to go to work.

"Danny, get ready, I'm going hot in ten." I went into prone position and pressed the butt of the rifle tightly against my shoulder. Shifting a few more inches to be just short of the edge of the barrels, I looked through my sight and thumbed the safety to fire. My borrowed M4 did not have a full auto position, just safe and fire. This would have been a good time to have fully automatic capability, but also a good time to be sipping a Mai Tai on a beach in Maui.

I rolled out into the kill zone and started blazing. At first, I wasn't watching where my shots were impacting.

Slow down Rick, watch your shots. Inhaling deeply, I settled in and soon was able to walk my shots into the target area. I could finally see leaves and crap jump with each trigger pull.

I realized I hadn't heard the pop of the smoke grenade fuse activating, but dared not take my eyes off the target to let up firing. Whatever I was doing, it was having some effect as there had been no answering fire. Then, my weapon went dry.

Automatically, I dumped the empty magazine, grabbed a fresh one, and slammed it home to resume shooting just as I saw the first wisps of yellow smoke drift past me. Danny had done it!

For just a split second, I looked up to confirm and the spot where Danny lay was now fully enveloped in a thick yellow haze. I ceased fire, jumped up, and ran over to him. Danny was coughing from the dense smoke, and I grabbed his load-bearing vest and dragged him back to the barrels.

His eyes were open, he was coughing incessantly but no visible blood. I couldn't do anything for him now. My focus needed to be the threat that still existed out there. Dropping back into position, I rolled out to look when a cloud of dust erupted around me. *Shit!* I answered, with several shots to get his head down.

"Hey, *guero,* frag his ass." It was Danny.

"What?" I replied, popping off a couple more rounds.

"Frag the motherfucker!" His voice was pained, but surprisingly strong. I looked at the grenade beside me. He was right. I could keep shooting and run out of ammo or try the grenade. The distance had to be forty or fifty meters. My last throw was about twenty meters and ended up short.

"Go for an airburst, man." Christ, I'd be lucky to get close let alone achieve an airburst. My heart pounded as I sat up and got ready. Clasping the safety pin ring, I gave it a good yank and the pin popped out.

I took a breath, released the spoon, and heard the loud pop of the fuse igniting. One-one thousand, two-one thousand . . . I rose and threw that sucker with all my might, then dropped behind the barrels to wait. *Boom!* I chanced a peek. The grenade had detonated ten meters short. Flying shrapnel, blast and thick smoke probably put my adversary's head down, but that was it. *We're fucked.*

I turned to check on Danny, then I heard the thud of a 40mm grenade launcher being fired. I looked up just in time to see a very nice high explosive detonation, dead nuts on the sniper's hide.

A wave of relief swept over me as I looked behind me for our savior. It was one of the guys from the entry team with a high-speed grenade launcher that I'd never seen before. He ran to our position.

"How is he?" our savior asked with a pronounced Southern drawl.

"I don't know." I felt bad that I hadn't done anything for Danny yet, but there hadn't been time.

Our new BFF, who was no doubt from the Army Special Mission Unit, knelt alongside Danny for a quick assessment. "Where are you hurt?"

"My right side. Fuck, it hurts."

The operator felt around and found the entry hole in Danny's body armor. A couple of quick swipes of his knife, and he had the side panel off. My heart sank as I saw bright red blood on Danny's T-shirt. The operator opened the shirt and closely examined the wound. It was a small through and through, where the bullet had passed through the plate and Kevlar of Danny's armor and entered the skin on the upper right side missing his rib cage. Then it traveled a couple more inches under his skin before exiting.

"Dude, you are one lucky motherfucker," the operator announced. It just broke the skin. Nothing vital was hit. I'll patch this up, and you'll be good to go."

Our Southern savior then turned to me. "Can you keep eyes on the hide until I get a couple more guys to clear it?"

"Sure," I replied, and then got back into the prone and lined up on the suspected hide. It was still smoking, and there were no signs of life. I started to thank the operator for saving our asses, but he had already gone. Danny was sucking on his CamelBak hydration tube, which reminded me that I'd better hydrate soon.

I saw a small cylindrical object poke up through the smoldering fronds and debris. "Danny, I've got movement," I whispered, removing my rifle off safe.

Danny got on the portable radio he'd been given. "I've got movement at a sniper hide on the north side of the factory," he reported. Then reassured me that help was on the way.

Sure enough, not a minute or two later, our original Southern boy and two other high speed, low-drag types arrived at our position.

"What you got?" one asked.

I replied while keeping my eyes on target. "Some kind of small cylindrical device popped up from the hide. It moved a little, then went back down.

"It's a small periscope. We'll move to clear it."

"Cover our approach."

Danny moved over to the other side and took a position to back me up.

The operators crept off swiftly and silently, and I watched as they popped another 40mm HE grenade into the hide before advancing to clear it. The whole episode took less than a minute. Suddenly, the shortest of the three guys fired a burst into the hole, while his partner dropped a small grenade, which blew with a loud thud as thick smoke rose from the hole.

Soon we were joined by Duncan, Tony, Mick, and another SAS trooper whom I'd not seen. Mick got out his medic bag and redressed Danny's wound while the others joined the SMU operators. I heard orders in what sounded like Farsi being shouted into the hole.

Then Mick told us they'd found our Clark and Nancy inside alive. I told him I was going to head into the building. Mick got on his radio and warned them that I was about to enter the factory. I headed straight for what I thought were the main factory doors, and an operator posted by the door waved me on through.

"Where are the male and female prisoners?" I asked.

"Office on the left."

I moved to the office, not knowing what to expect, and when I stepped into the room I was caught by surprise. There was Major Nancy Weaver. Captain Larry Clark was sitting on the floor being tended to by a team medic, while Nancy was working on a gravely wounded male wearing ACUs while an operator stood guard. Suddenly, I wondered about the whereabouts of Copeland.

I knelt beside Clark. "Hey, man, how ya doing?"

"I'm okay. These dudes saved our ass."

"Yeah, I know the feeling. They did the same for me. I see Nancy is good."

"She's trying to save some Iranian asshole. After what they did to my people, I'd rather he bled out."

Larry Clark looked like a beaten man. He'd witnessed the execution of his soldiers and the IAs, which must have been awful. I changed the subject. We still had a job to do.

"Did you pick up anything on what they were up to?"

"No, man." Larry looked at the medic who had just finished redressing his wound. When he was done, Larry stood, and we both moved to a spot out of earshot of the wounded Iranian. Then Larry continued.

"Copeland and his buddies were pretty careful to speak only Farsi in front of us. They had a couple of large, hard-sided cases that they offloaded from Copeland's vehicle. Have no idea what was in them, but I bet I could guess."

"I bet you could. Do you have any idea where they put them?"

Captain Clark shook his head.

"You said they had two?" *Danny told me he'd only seen one.*

"Yes, I saw two." Larry's face flushed, and his eyes welled up with tears. "They murdered my guys, Rick, they fucking murdered them in cold blood. I loved them. They were the best." His voice was cracking with raw emotion, recalling the horror just witnessed that day, which undoubtedly would haunt him forever. I ached for my friend.

Larry continued. "Weaver and I were zip-tied and blindfolded. I only heard suppressed shots and thought we were next, but Copeland—"

"Larry, do you have any idea where he is?"

He shook his head. "He and some dude took Khalid and disappeared right before the assault."

"Was Khalid going along with them?"

"No, he was zip-tied. They smacked him around."

"Did they know we were out there?"

"No clue."

"Who's the SMU honcho?"

"Dude named Bray."

"We need to find Copeland and those cases," I said.

"Roger that."

I glanced over at Nancy. "Does she know anything more?"

Larry shook his head. "I doubt it. We were together the whole time."

I nodded, looking longingly at Nancy and wanting to embrace her. There would be time for that later, but for now I'd let her do her thing and I would do mine.

I needed to find the boss of the SMU guys. Time was of the essence, but we still had no details of the plot such as timing and target set.

I searched for Bray around the interior of the factory. Scattered throughout were the bodies of guys in what looked like US Army issue ACUs. I noticed that many seemed to have been shot in the face, a trademark of our Special Operations hitters.

So far, I hadn't seen any sign that our people had been injured in the assault. Considering that they had assaulted a semi-prepared position probably occupied by Iranian Special Ops guys, this was indeed a testament to their prowess.

Suddenly, I heard some loud commotion behind me. Five operators rushed in escorting what had to be the injured Apache gunship crewmembers. All four were conscious, two clearly injured but ambulatory, and one guy was on a stretcher with an IV plugged into his arm. All were taken to the makeshift aid station supervised by Nancy.

I continued moving through the building, which evidently had been some kind of facility that handled a lot of liquids. Large pipes, valves, and pumps were everywhere. I hoped it wasn't a nerve gas plant operated by the previous management. Coalition Forces found chemical-agent-filled projectiles and storage containers all over the place, several thousand at last count.

I put that thought out of my mind and moved on. Then I found him. He was talking to several guys, one of whom I recognized as our bearded savior with the grenade launcher. I know that sobriquet sounded like the name of some Catholic church in Belfast, but that's what he was. I patiently stood by while they finished their conversation.

"Excuse me, sir, I'm—"

"You're Rick, the retired cop and equal opportunity pain in the ass. Call me Pete," said Bray, offering his hand.

"You know me."

Pete Bray stood with open hand and a big grin on his hairy face. Christ, all these guys have beards. I took his hand as he shook it warmly.

"Yes, a certain Command Sergeant Major gave me a call. Said you were in the neighborhood looking for trouble. Based on what happened here, I think you found it. I just heard about how you held that sniper off while rendering aid to a wounded soldier. Well done."

"Thank you, sir."

"Pete."

"Right. I wanted to make sure you were fully up to speed on what we think is going on here."

"Duncan gave me a couple of things but go ahead."

I gave him the bottom-line-up-front version of my story, punctuated with the nagging question of where the bomb-making stuff and our not so BFF Major Copeland were.

Pete said they'd found one presumed RDD device in a back room of the main factory building, fully assembled except for the fusing.

"My EOD guy said it looks like more than one was assembled here."

"Where the fuck is the other one?"

"Good question. My guys are in there searching."

"Copeland and IRGC are at the core of this. We need to grab him fast."

"We've found a few spider holes," Bray offered.

"Spider holes. Christ!" It occurred to me that there could be a network of tunnels under my feet. Maybe they connected to the sniper's hole we'd found.

"What?" Bray asked.

"The sniper that pinned us down was shooting from a prepared hole. At one point it felt like he was in multiple holes."

"My guys cleared it."

"I'd still like to take a look. Can I borrow a couple of folks?"

"Knock yourself out."

At that moment, Tony, the SAS giant, walked by with Danny and another SAS trooper.

"Hold up."

Tony stopped and turned.

"What's up, gringo?" Danny asked.

"How do you feel?" I asked, surprised to see Danny up and about.

"Dude, I'm okay. Fucking thing hurts like a bitch, but I can still move and shoot if I have to. At least till help gets here."

"Guys, I need your help. Copeland and Khalid are missing."

"What do you need?"

"I need you to help me take a look at the hole our sniper was in."

Tony chimed in. "It's been cleared."

"I know, but I want to be sure."

"Need to let the boss know first," Tony replied.

"Sinclair knows and is good with it."

Tony eyed me suspiciously for a moment. Then he pressed the button to activate his radio headset. "Boss, you up? Rick is asking us to help clear a hole."

"Copy."

Tony smiled and turned back to us. "Lead on."

CHAPTER 37

RAT HOLE

It took only a minute or two to return to the infamous stack of barrels. From there, we moved a little more cautiously back to where the sniper hole had to be. I turned to Danny, who was walking five meters behind me. "Hey, you sure you're okay to do this?"

"Dude you're not my Jefe'. I'm cool. Besides, I'm hoping for a little pay back, *tu sabes?*"

"*Si vato.*"

All I can say is we are damn lucky to have kids like Danny out there protecting us. Damn lucky.

My heart was pounding as we closed the short distance to the hole. The former tenant was lying face down a few feet from the hole. They must have pulled him out after they cleared it. His white-man jammies were scorched and soaked in blood. He also was wearing ACU pants and GI-issue desert boots. Danny kicked the lifeless body over, exposing the face.

"Rick, I've seen this dude before. I think he was with the MPs and that asshole sergeant you shanked."

"You mean the late Sergeant Khanov," I reminded Danny.

"The one you took the bollocks off," Tony recalled, grinning.

While turning another man into a gelding was, at the time, completely necessary, it was not exactly what I would consider a shining moment in my life. I looked hard at the body. The face was blackened and bruised severely.

"I know that guy too. Danny, can you wipe some of that crap off his face?"

"Sure, boss." Danny found an old rag and cleaned the corpse's face. Then he ripped open the front of the loose white garment the corpse was wearing, exposing an ACU blouse. "His patches, nametape and rank tab have been removed," Danny observed.

"Danny, that's Lieutenant Habib. Part of Copeland's crew." Another traitor. Both he and Copeland deserved a firing squad or worse for what they'd done. Habib had cheated justice. I prayed we could grab Copeland alive.

Tony and I removed all the debris surrounding the hole. Some of the palm fronds were still smoldering. Danny stood guard while we worked. Soon, the hole was completely cleared. Tony looked down from the edge. "Just a hole, mate." I looked down; he was right. It was just a hole. About six or eight feet deep. There was a crate that must have been intended as a prop to stand on. It was wooden and about three feet square. There were also some empty water bottles, a few cigarette butts, and some candy wrappers.

I turned away in disgust. An empty hole. Then, suddenly, an image flashed. I'd seen a box like that one before. In the shed behind Khalid's place.

"Guys, I've seen a box identical to that one before. So have you, Danny."

Danny, who now looked slightly annoyed, looked over the edge. "Fuck, man, you're right."

Tony looked at both of us and I swear he had that "All you Yanks are loony" look.

"I'll have another look." With that, he dropped down into the hole, set his rifle aside and grasped the box with both hands. It wouldn't budge. "This thing's heavy." He pulled on a side and a board that had been weakened by a grenade detonation broke off in his hand. "Shit," he said under his breath. Tony pulled out a small light and shone it inside the box. "There's a fucking ladder and tunnel under the box," he whispered.

"Just like the shed," I whispered to Danny. Tony grabbed his rifle and climbed out of the hole. The dude was strong. "You guys keep an eye on this. I'm gonna get some of the lads and have a look." With that, he quickstepped back to the main factory building. No sooner had he left than none other than Major Weaver showed up. She was carrying an M4 at the ready, which was admittedly very sexy in an earthy, battlefield way.

"I'll take care of this," I whispered to Danny, who had his rifle trained on the hole.

I smiled and raised my hand as Nancy approached. I motioned for her to stop and move back toward a corner of the factory. For a woman who had just been rescued after a blazing gun battle, witnessed the murder of fellow soldiers, and had no doubt seen more than one bad guy with his brains blown out, she looked remarkably strong and composed. I'd have had a complete nervous breakdown.

She had quite a few bloodstains on her ACU pants and her T-shirt, but otherwise she looked damn good.

"Hey, it's good to see you again. I didn't want to interrupt you earlier, but you were kinda busy."

Nancy grinned. "I was busy. It's good to see you too. What's going on out here?"

I told her about looking for Copeland, Khalid, and a missing RDD. Then I told her about the tunnel entrance Danny was watching.

I could tell Nancy was holding something back. No surprise there, she'd been through hell. I couldn't imagine what thoughts and images were running through her head. But something else was eating at her. I could feel it.

"Nancy, what is it?"

She turned away for a second, then back, eyes flooded with tears. Then she took a breath to compose herself. "Rick, I'm sorry. So sorry. I should have figured it out sooner."

I clasped her hand. "Hey, it's okay, what do you mean?"

"It's Copeland. I treated him a few months ago. He seemed nice enough. We met for coffee and exchanged life stories. He said his dad was a diplomat with the State Department, his mom was from Iran. Said he spent a lot of summers abroad. Went to UCLA. Naturally, I thought nothing of it. Then he got weird on us at the JSS. He was being such an obstructionist prick. I should have known something wasn't right with him."

What Nancy had just shared with me dovetailed nicely with Baby Bro's info. Copeland probably was closer to his mom than dad. As a diplomat, Dad probably traveled a lot so naturally, Mom would have had a huge influence on him. The travel overseas was interesting, but students travel all the time.

Major Copeland was a murderous traitor. He'd fooled a lot of smart people along the way, including some intelligence guys and God knows who else. So now we add a retired LA flatfoot and an overworked physician to the list. So what?

"I didn't see him again," Nancy continued, looking straight into my eyes. "Nothing happened." Nancy wiped away a newly formed tear. "Rick, I'm so sorry for not telling you. Maybe you could have saved—" Nancy started sobbing. I held her close.

"Nance. It's okay, it's okay. Don't blame yourself. He fooled us all. Hell, he's an expert at it. Even if you'd told me, it wouldn't have changed a thing. He sucked us all in. I had no clue something was up with him other than he was a just an officious prick."

Sobbing, Nancy looked up and saw one of the SMU dudes waiting to speak with her. Instantly, she pulled it together and stepped back, wiping her tears. *She's back.* The grieving and hurt would have to wait. She had a job to do.

"Mr. Sutherland, I'm sorry. I guess I lost it."

She faced the waiting SMU guy. "I'm sorry, can you give us a minute?" The operator nodded, "Sure, no problem."

"Do you have any idea where the device might be?" she whispered.

"I'm thinking it might already be in place. These guys had been waiting for a sophisticated timer-triggering device, which they got today.

They found evidence that more than one had been assembled, but we think they only had one trigger."

"Got ya. Do you think Copeland is in that hole?"

"When the Brits get back, we'll find out."

Tony arrived with three other lads in tow.

"Major, are you okay?" Tony asked politely, though it was really code for, "Why are you standing out here when you should be safe inside?"

"Yes, thank you, I'm fine. Just checking on my guys."

"Yes, but you should get back inside, this area is still a bit hot."

"Tony," I interrupted, "I've seen her in action, she's good. I suggest we check the tunnel."

Tony grinned. He and his guys trotted over to the tunnel.

"I'd better get back to it," I said and then turned to join them, Nancy on my heels.

"Rick, just a minute. How are you doing? Are you okay? Hydrating?"

"I'm good to go. Drinking like a fish," I lied yet again. *My CamelBak had been dry for hours.*

The Brits went into the tunnel first. At first, they didn't want me tagging along, but I assured them that I could be of some value. Besides, I knew our quarry very well. It wasn't a hard sell. By now they knew I could take care of myself.

The climb down the ladder had to be a good eight or nine feet. This was not some half-assed hand-dug hole, but a sophisticated tunnel with concrete walls and shoring, even electrical lighting. Of course, the lighting didn't work. The height of the tunnel itself was only about six feet and about four to five feet wide. This forced me to bend slightly as we moved forward. The four SAS troopers and I moved forward slowly and silently. My heart vibrated with every step. The operators all had sophisticated night vision, which I didn't have, so I stayed close. After about twenty meters we came to a chamber. One of the guys popped a couple of chem-light sticks so that I could see.

The room was soon bathed in an eerie greenish glow. I took a moment to scan the room. It was a storage area. More boxes and crap strewn about.

Not to mention empty water bottles and food wrappers. I spied something familiar wadded up in a corner. I walked over and took out my light. There on the ground was an empty Oasis water bottle and shiny green plastic wrapper for the infamous US Army issue Hooah energy bar. I sampled one CRC at Fort Benning, Georgia. Tasted like shit. But maybe Major Copeland had recently snacked on one.

I picked up the wrapper with my fingertips and slid it into my cargo pants, and then the water bottle. They could have Copeland's DNA.

Tony motioned for me to hold here. One of the other guys handed me a couple more chem-lights. I gave them a thumbs up and took a position of cover behind a couple of boxes in the corner nearest the tunnel entrance. My back was to the wall, my favorite position.

From my spot, I could hold the main tunnel and a section that doglegged to the left. I knelt and tried to relax. This was some scary shit. For one thing, I don't do underground well. Caves, mines, and small tunnels are not my favorite places.

I squatted there, ears straining at every sound. My mouth was dry and the air inside was dead. I had stopped sweating a while ago.

My moment of rest was disturbed by a muffled thud, which was answered by a burst of automatic fire. My right hand tightened on my rifle's grip. My thumb moved the safety as I readied myself. Then there was a guttural yell. Someone was hit. I heard two more thuds and then silence. The Brits' weapons were all suppressed. The muffled thuds were probably theirs.

A minute later, I was greeted by the sight of Tony and two others hustling back to my position, dragging a body dressed in ACUs. I lowered my rifle.

"Copeland." The bastard lay still on the dirt floor. He looked to be hit in the upper thigh and lower abdomen, just below the lower edge of his body armor. One of the Brits was bleeding from a wound on the hand. It didn't look bad.

I moved closer. Copeland's eyes were closed, but he was breathing, his face contorted in pain.

"He was hiding in another room," Tony said. "They had tortured people in there. Even kids. There's an IA officer who was beaten half to death and another guy handcuffed to the wall. Boxes with Chinese and Arabic labels. We need to clear the other tunnel. Watch him. We'll be back."

I lowered the muzzle in Copeland's direction as I looked down on him. His eyes were squeezed shut in obvious pain. Stomach wounds are like that. He moved and fidgeted with every pain spasm. A moderate amount of blood was oozing from the gut shot, but the thigh wound seemed to hardly bleed at all. We needed to know where that fucking bomb was and there was no doubt in my mind that he knew. He had to be kept alive.

I opened my first-aid pouch and pulled out a dressing. Then I remembered my training at Fort Benning. *Always use the victim's first-aid kit, save your kit for yourself. You might need it.* I pulled open the nylon cover on Copeland's first-aid pouch and grabbed a set of gloves and battle dressing.

Copeland's eyes shot open, and he started to rise. "Not so fast, man, you're hurt pretty bad. Let me help you out," I said as I gently pressed on his shoulders and lay him back down. He grimaced in pain and closed his eyes.

"Just relax, we'll get you some help soon," I said innocently.

He gave no reply. I opened his vest and blouse and cut away the front of his T-shirt. I applied the dressing to the tiny entry wound.

"All clear," Tony announced as he and the others emerged from the tunnel. I winked at him and shot a glance at Copeland. Then I said for Copeland's benefit, "Can you get a medic down here? This officer is hurt badly."

Tony replied, "Sure, boss." Tony asked for a medic, then motioned for me to join him. Another trooper took over tending to Copeland's wounds.

Tony whispered to me, "Lots of intel. Maps, satellite images. The lot." Two other troopers helped the injured IA officer back to the room we were in. They placed him opposite Copeland. One of the troopers went to work checking him out.

"I want to keep Copeland guessing as to what we know about him. Let's be nice for now."

"We'll be good." Tony smiled. "I'll pass it on."

"You said there was another guy in there cuffed to the wall?"

Tony then described Khalid to a tee. "I'll go have a look."

"I've got a guy with him. We're waiting on some bolt cutters to free him," Tony replied.

"No worries, I probably have a key." With that, I produced a small key ring complete with a very well-worn Bianchi handcuff key. "This should do it."

Khalid was on the floor handcuffed to a large iron ring set into the concrete wall. His hands were turning blue. An SAS trooper was standing over him. I showed the Brit the key, knelt next to Khalid and smiled. "I didn't think I'd see you again, my friend." I inserted the key into the old Peerless handcuffs. It worked perfectly. American-made handcuffs, regardless of brand, are keyed alike, so this was a no-brainer.

Khalid rubbed his bruised wrists to try and get his circulation going again. The cuffs had been on pretty tight. He had dried blood on his face and on the front of his shirt. His face was bruised, and his nose looked broken. Seeing this left me with no doubt that as soon as Copeland was done with the IA officer, Khalid would have been next.

I looked around the room, which reeked of stale urine and shit. An Iraqi Army officer's uniform was piled up on the floor with women's clothes next to it. In the middle of the room, below another pair of dangling handcuffs, was a pool of rapidly congealing blood. There were also a pair of dead bad guys next to a dropped AK and an empty pistol. One was clad in ACUs, the other in civilian attire. Both had taken two shots to the chest and one to the head. *Nice shooting, especially when you're getting shot at. Remind me not to piss these SAS guys off.*

Khalid stood and faced me. He looked emotionally and physically exhausted. For once, I didn't know what to say or do. How do I tell him his wife was murdered? There's no best way to break that kind of news. But on the other hand, I still needed his help. He may have heard something or seen something that could lead us to the RDD device or worse still, *devices.*

"Khalid, are you okay?"

"Yes, Dennis, I am fine." Deep sadness was written all over his face.
I lay a hand on his shoulder. "We need to talk."

"I know, Dennis, I know." His eyes were filling with tears.

"Khalid, I'm so sorry."

"I know. You are not responsible for her death. I am."

"Your boy's safe in an American hospital. He is being well taken care
for. You have my word."

"*Alhamdullillah*. I thank you and your Doctor Weaver for saving my
son, and Doctor Baker also. May the blessings of Allah be upon you."

I nodded, biting my lip. Major Nancy Weaver, MD, would have had
my guts for garters if she knew that I'd told Khalid that Specialist Jason
Baker was a doc.

CHAPTER 38

RECKONING

An SAS trooper helped me escort Khalid out of the room to a spot near where Copeland was laying. I wasn't crazy about this, but I didn't want Khalid to be seen by anyone else yet.

I heard Tony behind me. "Rick, can you fetch the doctor? We're a bit short-handed down here."

"Okay." I knew I wouldn't have to look far.

I ran back to the entry, announced I was coming up, and scaled the ladder.

Nancy and Danny were waiting.

"We've got Copeland. He took one to the gut and one in the thigh. Khalid is also down there, and an IA officer who's been beaten very badly. They need your help." I forgot to tell her about the slightly wounded trooper, but she'd find out soon enough.

"I'll get my pack."

As Nancy trotted off, I told Danny, "They were torturing people down there. We found an IA guy beaten half to death."

"Fuckers."

"Yes. Can you stand by while I go back down and have a look? Send the doc down when she gets back."

"Sure thing, boss. I don't do underground anyway."

"That makes two of us. Are you my brother from another mother too?"

He chuckled. "No way, dude. You're too pale."

Below, I found Mick busy treating Copeland's wounds.

"Major Weaver's on her way."

"Very good," Mick replied. "The IA officer is okay. A few bruises, but he'll live. He says his wife was shot by your gut-shot major before we got here. He was trying to get intel out of the IA officer, and when the officer wouldn't talk, they dragged her in and shot her in front of him. Her body's in the grove near the tunnel entrance."

I shook my head. Copeland and his playmates were beneath contempt. They deserved no mercy. Pick their brains, then pop 'em in the face was sounding good to me.

In the room the bastards had used as a torture chamber, I found the spot where they'd shot the IA officer's wife. It was much like other homicide scenes I'd seen; a pool of blood, scattered with small chunks of what had to be brain and skull fragments. Handfuls of long black hair and a few broken teeth. Copeland or his buddies must have shot the officer's wife directly in front of him while he hung from the handcuffs. Some handwritten interrogation notes, possibly in Farsi, lay on a table. Next to it was a video camera on a tripod all set up to record the carnage. I'd seen enough, so I moved to the next room.

This one was more organized, like a war room. A second video camera on a tripod stood in one corner aimed at a black drapery hung from the ceiling and a couple of propped-up flags. One looked like a red Mahdi Army flag, the other I didn't recognize. This must have been their stage for propaganda videos.

There were also maps and charts on the walls. Some in English, some in Arabic or Farsi. I examined some satellite images of what I recognized as BIAP and Victory Base. There were also images of buildings in the Green Zone—the US Embassy, the Coalition Provisional Authority building, the Al Rasheed Hotel. Pictures of other US installations included a whole series of VBC soldier housing areas.

My blood boiled at the shots of soldier housing destroyed in the mortar attacks, no doubt directed by Copeland and his pals from this very room. There were also three computer stations and a communications desk equipped with an old US military PRC 77 radio set and a current issue SINCGARS radio set. There was even a radio charger bank full of Thales portable radios identical to the one I'd recovered during the attack on our convoy. My head was spinning. All of this crap could have facilitated insurgent attacks throughout the entire region.

It was plain as day. Copeland had to be some kind of mole working for the insurgents, the Iranians, or both. Based on what we discovered, Copeland was involved in operational planning and execution for the Shia insurgency. He was also a participant in the executions of Khalid's wife and the captured soldiers at the restaurant. Locked up in his twisted brain were the details on past operations and the RDD bomb plot we had just discovered. I spent a few more minutes looking through maps, photos and documents. Everything was in either Arabic or Farsi, or both. There were also a few US Army issue training manuals and booklets on things like IED detection and an Iraq orientation booklet issued to all soldiers serving in country.

It was quite a haul, but I could hear my old boss Jerry "No Ass" Stark whispering in my ear, *"Rick, someday all this crap will make for a great book, but what does that do for us right now?"* He was right then, and he would be right now. The bottom line here and now was that we needed to find out where that other device was, and fast. Knowing the intended target set would be a huge help, but right now I could only speculate on what that might be. The US embassy was always on the short list as was BIAP. Then it could be something else even bigger.

I walked back to Copeland, arriving just in time to greet Nancy and Duncan, the SAS officer. A couple of other guys were with them that I assumed were also SAS. Nancy, of course, headed straight to her patient's side, and the Brits adjourned to the war room. I naturally followed.

"We need to fully exploit this and the other room. Grab everything, photos, computers, the lot," said Duncan. "Mick, find out how soon the American officer can be moved. Let's get the Iraqis out of here as soon as you feel it's safe."

I left them to it and looked on as Nancy examined Copeland. The lower half of his T-shirt was soaked with blood. He was very pale and barely conscious. She and another trooper now rolled him over to have a look at his back. A bloody mess. Mick had already established an IV flowing to stabilize him.

Watching Major Copeland's fists clench in pain, I had a moment of pure inspiration. Well, maybe not pure. I watched as Nancy worked to seal the exit wound with one of those magic dressings from her bag. I leaned close and whispered, "Can he be moved yet?"

"No, not yet. I need to get him stabilized and the bleeding under control."

"When you have time, I need a minute."

"Not now."

"It's critical that I talk to you soon. Trust me."

"Okay." She frowned, impatiently.

What I had in mind would require all my considerable powers of persuasion and some good ol' fashioned luck. But first, I had to set the stage. I returned to the torture chamber to find Tony and Duncan busy searching for materials and evidence.

"Duncan," I began, "can you guys leave all this stuff in place for a minute? I want to photograph everything here and in the war room for the court martial."

"No problem." Duncan glanced at me with a very subtle look that I swore meant, *Court martial, are you fucking kidding me?* Interesting. I knew I liked this guy from the start.

Back in the war room, I photographed the pictures of Camp Victory, soldier housing, and the US Embassy. For good measure, I threw in some shots of the computers and communications gear. I was nearly ready.

When I returned to the main chamber, Nancy was tending to the Iraqi Army officer, a few feet away from where Copeland lay on the dirt floor, one arm zip-tied to a section of electrical conduit. His eyes were open, but his face was stony. Danny was now standing guard over him. He didn't look happy. I knelt beside Major Copeland.

"Hey, man, how you feeling?"

No answer.

"Major Copeland, I know you're in there. Why don't you let me help you? We both know you're in a bad spot. You're all shot up and may not live. I'm also beginning to think you might have some other more serious issues if, of course, you live." He turned his head away from me.

"Look, man, I don't care about why you did it. I'm sure you had your reasons. I just want to save lives. Help me. I think you'd agree there's been enough killing here. Help me stop it."

He just blinked. Perhaps a more direct approach might get his attention. I shook my head in mock disgust, got up and walked away. I needed to rattle his cage a little. Copeland always struck me as thinking he was the smartest guy in the room. I was sure he was still thinking that. I returned to the torture room and approached Duncan.

"Can I speak with you for a second?"

Duncan stopped what he was doing and joined me in a corner.

"I believe Major Copeland must know about these missing RDD bombs. He's up to his beady eyes in this shit. I need to rattle him a little. Can you grab some photos of our embassy?" I told him the rest of it.

Back in the main chamber, as I knelt beside Khalid, Duncan walked in excitedly as instructed, carrying photos and other "evidence."

"Rick, have a look at this."

In an Oscar-worthy performance, I stood and rushed to meet him.

"Holy shit!"

We talked in hushed tones, Duncan saying "RDD" barely loud enough for Copeland to hear. As we spoke, I kept one eye on our traitor. His head was turned away from us, but when Duncan uttered the magic word, his head moved just a hair toward us. It was as if he had keyed on "RDD," started to turn to hear more, then caught himself.

I thanked Duncan and returned to Copeland's side, knelt close to his right ear, and whispered, "Tell me about the bombs." He didn't budge for almost a minute. Neither did I.

"There is no bomb," he said in a strained voice. I noted he used the singular bomb, not *bombs*. I was on the right track.

"Didn't you get any tradecraft or deception training at IRGC U? Dude, either you got ripped off or went to sleep in class. You're the worst liar I've ever seen. Thanks to your superlative deception skills, I've now established there are *bombs* out there, and you know all about them. Why don't you help yourself and tell me about them to clear your conscience?" I was watching him for any clues that I was making progress.

Finally, he took a pained breath and spoke. "I am a major in the United States Army and you have no authority to question me. I won't answer your questions." Of course, he was right. I was way out of my lane on this one. But I was also probably the only guy within twenty miles with any serious investigative and interrogation experience, and the clock was ticking.

"Okay, suit yourself. I was only trying to save you and me some trouble. We'll figure it all out eventually, maybe even find the bombs in time. Of course, you'll be court-martialed. But because you refused to help, they'll hammer you. You'll get death by lethal injection. They say the shit burns like hell as they pump it in. Then there's that feeling of suffocation, just before the lights go out."

I stopped to let that sink in.

"Don't play cop games. I'm not some poor kid you can scare." Then he turned and looked back at the ceiling.

"Have it your way, Major." Interview over.

The injured Iraqi Army officer was about fifteen feet away on his back. The broken expression on his face said it all. Watching his wife's brains blown out in front of him and the physical beating he'd suffered were more than most could stand. And yet he was clearly a very brave man who had sacrificed much for his country. Unlike the piece of shit next to me, the Iraqi had kept the faith. I wondered if I could have been that strong. I stood but must have risen too fast, for I suddenly felt lightheaded.

Eagle-eyed Weaver saw this and shot me a concerned glance. I gave her a thumbs-up and a wink that all is well.

"Major Weaver, do you mind if I take a few photos of this officer's injuries?" I indicated the IA officer. "For the investigation."

She nodded. I took a couple of shots of his face and hands showing the marks left by the handcuffs.

"Now then, Major, do you mind if I ask him a couple of questions?"

"Go ahead."

I knelt beside him.

"Sir, may I ask you a couple of questions?"

The man simply nodded. *Good sign. Maybe I won't need a translator.*

"Sir, where are you assigned? What unit? "

"Headquarters First Special Operations Brigade." His voice was pained, but strong.

"Baghdad?"

He nodded. I met with a couple of guys from his unit not long after I arrived. They seemed pretty sharp and highly motivated. The First Brigade had a counter-terrorism and training components made up of Kurds, Sunnis and Shia's. I needed to know more about this guy. Finding out where he was born could give me some answers.

"Where are you from?"

"Erbil. Ainkawa."

Nancy tugged on my sleeve. I turned, and she whispered in my ear. "He's a Kurdish Christian."

"Chaldean," the IA officer whispered.

"Yes, sir," I said as I looked at Doctor Big Mouth. So much for whispering.

The officer took a breath. "I am Major Yousif Mansour. I am a staff officer at Army Headquarters Baghdad."

A Christian Special Operations officer from Army headquarters. *Lots of secrets in his head,* I thought. *What are they after?*

"Major, what were they questioning you about?"

"Security arrangements for your vice president and secretary of state and the British prime minister."

"Did you tell them anything?"

He remained motionless, staring up at the ceiling.

Obviously, I touched a nerve. I nixed that line of questioning and changed directions.

"Can you tell me what they were after?"

"Schedule," he replied tersely.

Shit. They're after the VP, secretary of state and the Brits. If they pulled it off, it would be a game changer.

"How much do they know?" I asked.

"Everything." He sighed. Then he said, "What time is it?"

I looked at my watch. "1830 hours."

"The Americans and British are meeting now . . . your embassy."

A hell of a target. I looked at Nancy. She got it.

I gently clasped the major's right hand. "Major, you are a very brave man. Thank you."

I had all I needed from this man. I stood. Nancy looked up at me. "Do you want to talk now?"

"Yes."

We moved to the war room. "I'm not stupid. I know what you just did, but I can't do that." This woman was scary smart. How the fuck did she figure that one out?

"What do you mean?" I replied lamely.

"You were going to ask me to help you question Copeland."

Now what? How do I answer that? Lie and deny, but she'd see through that in an instant and it would get me nowhere. Or I could simply go for it.

"I need your help. We need your help. Copeland probably knows where the RDD devices are. He's been part of the planning and maybe even placed the fucking thing himself. If it goes off, you and I know its game over. Besides killing thousands, it will contaminate the area for dozens of years. We have to stop it."

"Yes, you're quite correct." I saw Duncan standing in the room watching us. He walked over to join our discussion.

"Major, Rick's right," he said. "We have to stop them. We can't afford to wait for the expert interrogators to have a go at him. There's simply no time."

"I'm a physician, not a torturer," Nancy replied firmly. "I took an oath. We don't torture people."

"I don't want to hurt him either," I replied. "At least not permanently. Just give him a little pharmaceutical encouragement to spill his guts."

"Major Weaver, I'm an officer in the British Army. It's my sworn duty to protect members of her majesty's government, by any means necessary. If I have to let my lads take a crack at him, the results will not be pretty."

"But he's a major in the US Army," Nancy retorted.

"No, he's not," I said. "He gave that up long ago." I indicated the satellite images of the Victory Base CHUs. "You know what happened there. We both saw what he and his friends did. He's no US Army officer."

"We'll be court martialed."

"You may be, but I'll be tried in federal court. If we can save more lives like those kids they killed, it'll be worth it."

The federal court part was for dramatic effect. For the record, I had no intention of being tried by some eager assistant US attorney. I just hadn't quite figured out the exit strategy for that one yet. *One thing at a time.*

"I need to think." Nancy walked out of the room.

"Rick," Duncan said, "we have to move fast and keep this between my lads and you. Nobody else down here."

"When did you guys get so ruthless?"

A smile lurked. "Sometime before 1066, I should think. We've forgotten more about this than you people will ever know." He was right there. The Brits had been in the spying and dirty tricks business for a long time. Way before us.

"Good to know." I really liked these guys. There was no bullshit with them. Who dares, wins.

CHAPTER 39

WITCHES' BREW

'd asked Danny to go back up top to guard the hole's entrance. I could see he was in a bit of pain, but he made no complaint. Nancy, Duncan, and I were in the main room, Nancy in a corner with her medical bag cooking up something, a pinch of this, a dash of that. I didn't know what it was or would do, nor did I want to know. Tony was standing watch over Copeland. Major Mansour had been moved to the war room by Mick, who was with him. Time for round two.

Nancy whispered, "I'm going to inject this into Copeland's IV. After a minute or so, he's going to feel like his belly is on fire. Once that kicks in, he might make some noise."

"Got it," I said.

She then turned to Duncan. "You might want to send your man up after the injection."

"Very good," said Duncan. He glanced at his watch. "We have only ten minutes," he said, indicating Copeland, "before we have to pack him up."

"Once this starts to work, he's gonna be in agony. His only relief is this." Nancy held up a liquid-filled syringe. "This will sedate him and ease his pain significantly."

"How much time will we have before the pain becomes life-threatening or he loses consciousness?"

"Everybody's tolerance is different. I would say a couple of minutes. Maybe six. But no more than that. I DO NOT want to kill him."

"Duncan, do you mind if I question him?" I asked.

"You're the bloody detective."

I nodded at Nancy. It was time. I took off my body armor and ACU blouse. I wanted to look as human and unthreatening as possible. Duncan walked over to Tony and whispered something. Tony nodded and left. I whispered to Duncan, "What did ya tell him?"

"Don't let anyone come down here till I tell him to."

"Good," I replied.

Copeland had his eyes closed, maybe sleeping. Good. I wanted this to be a surprise. Duncan faced the entrance while I knelt next to Copeland. Nancy injected the cocktail straight into an IV port. We all waited. I checked my watch. Nothing. I shot Nancy a puzzled look. She mouthed, *"Be patient."*

Suddenly, Copeland's eyes shot open, and his body went stiff as if he'd just received a thousand volts. His fists clenched tightly as he gasped.

"That did it," Nancy said.

"I believe you have his attention now," Duncan said.

I whispered into Copeland's ear. "You in pain, bro?"

Copeland glared at me. "What did you do?"

"Nothing. Not a goddamn thing. You're gut shot. Very painful. My first shooting, I gave the crook a pair of .38s in the guts. Paramedics took forever. After a few minutes, he was begging for one in the head. But a high velocity rifle round in the gut like you took. Hell, I don't need to tell you. Your insides must be a mess. You're in for a rough ride brother. A very rough ride."

Copeland stiffened with another spasm of pain that must have shot through him like a lightning bolt.

Mick walked around the corner and asked, "You need any help?"

Nancy replied, "We're okay here. Just a few spasms. Medevac should be here shortly."

"You still here, Major?" I said. "How you feeling now? Like I said, gut shots are a bitch, but we can make the pain go away. Just tell me about the bomb and all will be well again."

"Fuck you," Copeland gasped as another spasm gripped him. He was writhing, hopelessly trying to find a second of relief. The spasms came on more intensely. I almost felt pity for a second, then the horrors I had seen brought me back.

This guy's a traitor and a murderer. Nothing more.

All of these shitbirds saw themselves as latter-day Saladins. Warriors for Islam. But in fact, most were cowardly back shooters who indiscriminately planted bombs to kill soldiers and innocents alike. They decried the moral sins of the West in one breath, then raped boys and girls with equal vigor. They routinely decapitated and burned people alive with no more concern than one expresses ordering lunch.

The courageous warriors of the past who fought and died in the name of Islam must have been spinning in their graves at the atrocities committed by squirming turds like this one. I let him writhe a little more before I tried again.

After a minute or two, it was time. I gripped his right hand in mine and looked straight into his tortured eyes. His pale skin was covered in sweat.

"Look, man, I can save you from all of this. Just give me what I need. Let me help you."

He mouthed, *"Fuck you,"* in between gasps. Maybe Copeland still needed to sweat a bit more. I backed off and let him suffer alone for a while longer. Getting a crook to talk is a game requiring patience, like smoking a brisket. It can't be rushed. It will be ready when it's ready. Not before.

I looked at my watch. *Time's running out.* We wouldn't be able to operate down there much longer before someone got curious. I moved beside Nancy and whispered, "Got anything else that might spice things up a bit more?"

"NO!" she replied firmly. "The pain has only just started. It will intensify dramatically before it subsides. Just be patient."

"But he's your patient," I said with near instantaneous regret. Nancy glared at me, got up and turned away.

Suddenly, Copeland's back arched dramatically as he strained to free himself from the pain and his restraint. We had to be getting close to the breaking point now. The anger and defiance in his face were gone. I gave it one last shot. I bent over and looked him in the eye.

"Ben, this is only going to get a lot worse. Let us help you." He turned his head away which was my signal to continue. I leaned over and whispered menacingly in his right ear.

"You know lots of things can happen before you get to Balad. Unfortunate things. Then there's the hospital. Lots of injured soldiers. Soldiers talk. They'll find out who you are. Who knows what could happen?"

No reaction.

"Then of course the court martial. But we've already gone over that. I'd say life's not going to be too rosy for you or your family. I know your mother's dead, but your father, the retired ambassador; how will his pals at the club feel about him after your escapades hit the front page of *The New York Times*? Should be fun." I shook my head. "Ben, I'm your only hope."

He said nothing for a moment. His eyes were closed. Then he breathed the word, "DFAC."

"Did he say DFAC?" I asked Nancy.

"One near DFAC, one at motor pool, palace."

So, there were two devices. Probably at Victory. "Ben, that's good. Very good. You're helping yourself. You're going to save lives. I just need a little more. Are they both at Victory?"

He nodded yes.

"Both?"

He nodded again.

Almost done. I could see the pain getting more intense by the second. Copeland sucked in a breath then whispered, "Conex near East Palace Bridge. Empty CHU near DFAC."

"Excellent. Thank you, Ben. You're doing great. Just tell me which

DFAC?"

"Oasis," Copeland whispered.

"Thank you, Ben." I had gotten what I needed. The look in his eyes was pure defeat. The defiance and arrogance were gone.

I stood and motioned for Nancy to do her thing. She was ready to go with the syringe. She injected its contents into the IV port. The effect was instant and really spooky. He calmed down and after a few more seconds, his eyes closed. Copeland drifted off to sleep.

"Duncan, did you get all of that?"

"Every word. I'll tell Bray."

I had done my job. I just hoped it was in time. The rest was in the hands of the military guys and the spooks. As I stood there trying to deal with all that had happened, all that I had seen and done, a wave of extreme nausea hit me. I felt lightheaded. I looked to Nancy for help. My legs turned to rubber. I wanted to puke. I tried to speak.

"Nan—" The last thing I remember was looking up at a light in the ceiling. Then it went black, and down I went.

CHAPTER 40

BALAD

I awoke on the floor in the aid station in the old factory. The whole place was spinning. I closed my eyes as another wave of nausea swept over me. I started dry heaving but had nothing in my stomach. I heard Nancy say something about giving me something for nausea. I closed my eyes.

I awoke to a most God-awful racket, like I was laying on top of an engine. A hot wind was enveloping my body. I opened my eyes. I was flat on a stretcher in a Blackhawk. An IV was in my arm. The room, or should I say the Blackhawk, wasn't spinning anymore, which was an improvement. I looked around. My head hurt like a son of a bitch.

It looked like Nancy and a medic were working on somebody lying a few feet from me. I couldn't tell who it was, but they were sure working hard. One of them had those defibrillator paddles. I said a silent prayer for whoever that poor soldier was and closed my eyes. I was very tired.

I woke as the chopper was touching down. I was feeling a little better, except for my head. I reached up and felt a bandage. My scalp was wet, but it didn't feel like sweat. I looked at my fingertips. They had faint traces of dried blood on them. *Christ, did I get shot in the head? Was there an explosion? What the hell happened?*

I watched as they unloaded the chopper. A wounded guy was helped off first, then me. Nancy was outside the chopper waiting as they loaded me into a waiting ambulance. I turned back and looked at the chopper one last time. Some other guys were unloading the GI that had been lying next to me. They weren't in a hurry. Not a good sign. I continued watching as they carried me away.

After we'd moved away from the chopper, Nancy leaned over and said into my ear, "Copeland didn't make it."

Nancy got in and sat next to me. "What happened?" I whispered.

"You collapsed and cracked your head on a concrete beam. I think it might improve your disposition."

"No, I meant Copeland. What happened?"

"He didn't make it." Her eyes betrayed nothing. I let it go.

The ride to the ER entrance took barely a minute. Nancy gripped my hand and smiled. I gave hers a squeeze.

They had me out of the ambulance and on a gurney in no time. I was wheeled into the ER right next to another waiting patient. It was my old compadre and partner, Danny. He grinned, then grabbed my hand and squeezed.

"Hey, brother, you had me worried."

"I'm okay. But how are you?"

"That round I took fucked me up more than I thought. I told the Doc I was fine, but she don't play." He shook his head and grinned. So did Nancy. "At least I'll get some good chow and nurses to tuck me in."

I looked at Nancy. "How's Clark doing?"

"They're looking at him now. He'll be fine."

Airmen pushed our gurneys to opposite sides of the receiving area. I gave Danny a wave and got a "*shaka*" and a toothy grin in return. Not long after that, the docs started their thing and I drifted off again. I didn't see Danny again.

I woke hours later. At first, I had trouble focusing my eyes. I had that disoriented feeling you get after waking from a bad dream or an even worse drunk. I was in a small hospital room and was hooked up to several monitors and had two IVs going. I guess the docs had been hard at work on my tired ass. I spied a nurse walking in the hallway outside.

"Excuse me, ma'am, where exactly am I?"

She poked her head in. "You're at the theater hospital in Balad."

"Thanks. How long was I out for?"

"About fifteen hours. You whacked your noggin' pretty hard. Concussion and a pretty fair-sized gash in your scalp. I'm told nothing vital was damaged." She gave me a devilish smile. I love nurses. They're the best. Just don't tell you know who.

"Oh, so my fame precedes me."

"Yep. You've caused quite a stir. Even rated a private room. That's big juju around here."

"How is that possible?"

"Let's start with General Sutherland and work our way up from there. Even the cops and FBI have been asking about you."

Umm, the cops and FBI asking about me was probably not a good thing. By *cops* she must have meant agents from the Army CID. As for the FBI, who knows. Hopefully they were either old friends or had a very good sense of humor. Maybe it was time to start thinking about that exit strategy.

Then my mind flashed to Nancy. *Where is she?* Shit, maybe she wasn't here because they hauled her off to the gray-bar hotel. *Do they allow conjugal visits between prisoners?* Might be a good thing to know.

"Are you okay? Your color suddenly went pale."

"Mention of cops always does that," I said.

"I thought you were a cop. Don't all you guys get along?"

"It depends. How'd you know I'm a retired cop?"

"We got the word from General Sutherland's staff."

"What word, if I may ask?"

Then a couple fresh-faced guys in sport shirts, Royal Robbins cargo pants, holstered Glocks and Oakley desert boots sauntered in. *Shit! Bureau guys.* Right on their heels strode my ole' buddy, a rather grim-faced Lieutenant Colonel Harry Arnold of the 633rd Military Police. *The cops.*

My feeble and somewhat bruised brain started working overtime. "Call if you need me," the nurse offered as she left.

I decided I'd refuse to talk and ask for a lawyer. I wondered if Nancy and Duncan did the same. I knew we had to get our shit straight first before we started talking to feds, but now the MPs too. This was not good. *How am I going to get a lawyer in fucking Iraq? Maybe the JAG office?* Mikey would know.

"Mr. Sutherland, I'm Tony Vincente, and this is my partner Hank Meadows. I believe you already know Colonel Arnold." Tony held up his Bureau credentials in the prescribed, Quantico-approved manner. *Okay, this isn't a hey buddy, how ya' doin visit.*

"Am I going to need a lawyer?"

The two agents looked at each other like I had just spoken in Mandarin and started laughing. "I'm a lawyer," Agent Tony Vincente said. "You can trust me." *Hmm . . . four words that never go well together.*

"No, you fucking idiot." Harry Arnold grinned. "But on second thought, maybe you should. By the way, asshole, where's that fucking piece of frag?"

"You can trust me is my line." I fired back, as my blood pressure returned to its normal pre-hypertensive 135/92. I got a good laugh. Okay, I'm a paranoid idiot. I just threw out a red flag before the play. Dumb. It was in my weakened state.

We all shook hands. Then Agent Meadows said, "Hey, your partner from LA, George Steeler, is out here on a TDY, asked us to come by and say hi. He said he'll come by in the next couple of days."

"That's great, I haven't seen him since I retired." Steeler and I worked on the same squad in the JTTF. A very sharp agent, he was a former staffer on the Hill. "We also wanted to come by and say thanks for what you did. Both devices were located and disarmed. We're working on Copeland and the CT, CI angle. We know you talked with him. We'd like to discuss that when you're up to it."

"No problem. But he didn't say much."

"Apparently it was enough."

"Rick, you really did us old cops proud," Arnold said.

"What about the frag?"

"Screw it, brother. I think you earned it. I hear you're headed to Germany. God help 'em. Seriously, next time you're in Denver give me a call."

"I will. Harry, take care of yourself. Stay safe."

"I will, partner."

"Anybody home?" said a familiar voice. Nancy walked in and smiled at the two agents.

"Major Weaver, Agents Vincente and Meadows from the Bureau, and my old pal Colonel Arnold of the 633rd MPs. They came by to say hi."

"And thank you," Agent Meadows offered. He looked at Vincente and said, "We'll check back with you when you're healed up."

"Sure thing, guys," I replied. "Say hi to George when you see him."

"Will do," Tony replied. "Later, Rick." All three left.

Nancy checked on the IV bags and some notes on a clipboard, doing doctor stuff. Then she turned and verified the coast was clear. She closed the door and turned to me.

"FBI? What did they want?"

"At first, I was a bit concerned, but it turned out to be mostly social."

"Mostly?"

"Mostly. Naturally they'll want to hear what Copeland had to say. But that's it."

"Oh, okay. How do you feel?"

"Better, much better. Maybe I can get out of here in a day or so."

"Maybe. Then again, maybe you have a soul, but—" She was smiling. *Okay, she still likes me.*

"Ouch, even in my weakened state. For shame, doctor. For shame."

"You've got a mild concussion and head wound, plus a nasty bacterial infection you picked up along the way. All that and dehydration is why you blacked out in the tunnel. You'll be transferred to Landstuhl tomorrow. No escaping this time."

"Maybe if I make a call—" I watched for her reaction, "I could get it stopped or at least delayed."

She shook her head. "Not this time, buster. Your sorry ass is gonna be on a bird tomorrow."

I beckoned her closer. "Did the Feebs talk to you?"

"No. But I got a call—"

There was a light rapping on my door. "Rick, you decent?" It was Mikey. His timing always sucked, even when we were kids.

"Sure, Your Supreme Magnificence, barge on in."

Nancy stopped in mid-sentence and stepped aside deferentially as my brother and Command Sergeant Major Galloway walked in. My long-suffering boss, George Armstrong, followed close behind. This was starting to feel like a party.

General Mikey came to my bed, Galloway right behind him. George on the other side. I looked at George, "That reminds me, George, I may have fired your rifle once or twice."

"So, I heard. I'll be needing a memo." Everybody got a good laugh.

"It's good to see you, big brother. The docs say you'll be okay." Mikey gave Nancy a wink. "If that's possible."

"Possible just about sums it up, sir," she said.

"God help me. Does this mean he's coming back to work?" George piped in.

Christ, I'm getting hit from all sides.

"Major Weaver says they're shipping me out tomorrow. Anything you can do about that?"

Baby Bro shook his head. "Sorry, Rick, but your GI Joe Friday days are over."

"Ah, come on, Mike, do some of that general shit again. You owe me big time."

"You're right about owing you. Christ, we all owe you. You've saved a lot of lives. If Copeland had managed to detonate even one those devices, it would've been a disaster."

"Yeah, I know, but there is still more for me to do here. I can help with the investigation. The IRGC. You're going to need me to help with Khalid, to—"

Mikey cut me off with a gesture. "Rick, your work here is done. There are going to be questions raised about why you were out there, which I'm not too worried about right now. However, if you're still here dispensing your unique charm and wit on more hapless victims, things could start unraveling."

Mike looked at Nancy now. "The simple fact is both of you need to get out of Dodge, if you get my drift?"

Who spilled the beans? Fuck, this ain't good. Nancy didn't look surprised by any of this.

He went on. "I've arranged for Major Weaver to rotate out to Germany as well. Rick, your company wants you to heal up and take a few months off on them. Royce, have you made arrangements for Major Weaver?"

"Yes, sir, I handled it personally. Major, you are due to redeploy back to the States in thirty days."

"Yes, that's correct, but—" Nancy objected.

The general shut her down. "Major, you've also done a tremendous job here, but we think it would be better if you return to the States via Germany. There will be some secure debriefs about what happened while you were held by Copeland and the Iranians."

"Yes, sir. I understand," Nancy replied respectfully.

I, on the other hand, was still not getting what baby bro was throwing down. "But what about Khalid and his family and the cell at the jewelry store?"

"Khalid and his son are fine," Mike replied.

Then Command Sergeant Major Galloway shot a very icy, *Shut the fuck up* look at me.

"Sir, if I may. Khalid and his son are in protective custody. He's being debriefed by everybody and their brothers as we speak." CSM Galloway continued. "Don't worry, Rick. When the dust has settled, Uncle Sugar will be setting him up with a new home stateside."

I got it now. It sounded like all the bases were being covered. Besides, maybe a little European R&R might be just what the doctor ordered? Especially if it was with my personal physician.

"We've got to head out for an urgent conference now." Mikey took my hand in his. "Rick, I want you to know you make me very proud to call you my big brother. Not that I wasn't always proud. I was. But what you did out there . . . how you did it and what you survived . . . it was pretty amazing. Galloway was very impressed, and he doesn't impress easily."

"Yep, I was impressed. Rick, even if you are a bit slow on the uptake, you did damn well for a smartass old cop. Hell, you did damn well for a young Ranger." Galloway reached into his pocket and then clasped my hand. I could feel something large and metallic being dropped in my palm. It was a black commemorative challenge coin bearing the unit logo for the Army's SMU, a triangle bisected by a commando dagger. He smiled and said, "This is from your friends back at the factory." He paused to let that sink in, then he continued. "And this is from your new mates from Hereford." Galloway reached into his cargo pocket and removed a tan beret bearing the Special Air Service badge. For once in my life, I was speechless and maybe just a little teary-eyed. To be honored by those guys was an amazing feeling.

"Thank you, Sergeant Major. And please thank them for me. They saved our lives. They were amazing. True professionals."

"Quiet professionals, Rick. By the way, inside the cover there is a phone number. Give it a call while you're in Europe. Duncan says they'd like to play 'Get the Yank drunk' with you. But be careful. You'll lose for sure."

With that, both Mikey and Galloway shook my hand. Then Mikey said, "Rick, I'll give you a call once you're settled in Germany. Enjoy your time there. You've earned it. Both of you have." They both turned and left, closing the door behind them. That left my boss and friend George.

"I guess I didn't stay in my lane too well?"

"No, you didn't, and thank God for it. Your investigative skills and intuition proved their worth a hundred times over. Let us know when you're all rested up. There will always be a place for you." I shook George's hand.

"Thank you, George." He nodded and left us.

It was just Nancy and me now. Our relationship had been through a great deal in a very short time. We had endured the rigors of combat together, she had endured my charm and witty disposition, and had even found the time to give me the benefit of her superb medical training. Nancy held my hand and kissed me gently. This was the first real and, dare I say it, *overt* sign of affection since Yusufiyah. Much had happened since then.

"So, I guess you're going to be seeing a little more of me before this ride is over?" Nancy offered.

"I guess," I replied, deadpan.

She pulled back slightly. "Maybe that's not a good thing."

"It might not be," I replied.

"How so?" she said, mildly annoyed with my distant attitude.

"Not if you try to check my prostate again."

Nancy smiled, leaned over, and gave me a second very warm but PG-rated kiss. Her eyes welled with tears.

"I promise," she replied, "if you promise to cut the wisecracks."

"I thought my ready wit was my greatest asset."

She gave me that *You've got to be fucking kidding* look all women master around age twelve.

"Okay, Doc. I promise." But I crossed my toes.

ACKNOWLEDGMENTS

As with so many efforts such as this book, the list of contributors is long. So many have read this manuscript and offered their thoughtful criticism as well as their expertise. To all of you, I offer my profound gratitude. Without your help, this book would not have been possible. My son Ryan who is a damn fine editor—Thank you Steve B., your expertise and comments made such a difference. Steve S., Scott W., Kathleen S., your constant encouragement pushed me through to the end. Steve and Linda T., your comments and suggestions were invaluable. My sister Sharon, Gary, Wayne, Denis, Trish, Greg, and Eddie, your criticisms and encouragement were so helpful. To my literary agent, Nancy Rosenfeld of AAA Books Unlimited, who worked tirelessly to help me get this book ready for market and put together a marketing proposal that was second to none, thank you! To "Bones" who introduced me to Nancy and got the ball rolling, you are the best, and say high to Winston.

Most of all I want to thank my best friend and partner, my wife Lisa, who encouraged me at every stage and proofed this manuscript way too many times. "Writers write."

GLOSSARY

ACU	Army Combat Uniform.
AK	Soviet designed AK-47 rifle.
AOR	Area of Responsibility.
APC	Armored Personnel Carrier.
BCT	Brigade Combat Team.
CAC	Common Access Card.
CF	Coalition Forces.
CG	Commanding General.
CENTCOM	US Central Command.
CEXC	Combined Explosive Exploitation Cell.
CHU	Containerized Housing Unit.
CI	Confidential Informant.
CID	US Army Criminal Investigation Division.
CO	Commanding Officer.
CONUS	Continental United States.
CRAM	Counter Rocket Artillery Mortar.
CSM	Command Sergeant Major.
C-4	A type of plastic high explosive.
DFAC	Dining Facility.
DOA	Dead on arrival.
DShK	A soviet designed heavy machinegun.
EKIA	Enemy Killed in Action.
EOD	Explosive Ordnance Disposal.

E-4	Specialist, US Army enlisted rank.
E-5	Sergeant.
FOB	Forward Operating Base.
FSO	Facility Security Officer.
F1	Soviet grenade.
GI	US Government issue.
GROM	Poland's elite special operations unit.
HMFIC	Head Mother Fucker in Charge.
Hooch	Military slang for hut or dwelling.
HUMINT	Human sourced intelligence.
HUMVEE	High Mobility Multipurpose Wheeled.
HCS	HUMINT Control System.
IA	Iraqi Army.
IBA	Interceptor Body Armor.
IP	Iraqi National Police Force.
ISR	Intelligence Surveillance Reconnaissance.
JAG	Judge Advocate General.
JEFF LAB	Joint Expeditionary Forensic Facilities.
JTTF	Joint Terrorism Task Force.
JWICS	Joint Worldwide Intelligence Communication System.
KIA	Killed in Action.
KBR	An American construction and procurement company.
IDF	Indirect Fire.
IED	Improvised Explosive Device.
IRGC	Iranian Revolutionary Guards Corps.
IZ	NATO country code for Iraq

MNF-I	Multi National Forces, Iraq.
MOIS	Ministry of Intelligence and Security-Iran.
MP	Military Police.
MRAP	Mine-Resistant Ambush Protected-vehicle.
MTT	US Army Mobile Training Team.
M9	US military issue 9mm pistol.
M240	A medium machinegun 7.62 MM NATO caliber.
M249	A light machinegun also known as a SAW, (Squad Automatic Weapon) 5.56 MM NATO caliber.
M4	A carbine version of the M16 A2.
M67	US fragmentation grenade.
M1151	Enhanced Armament Carrier.
NCO	Non-Commissioned Officer.
NOD	Night Observational Device.
NOFORN	No Foreign Dissemination.
Phalanx Gun	Radar controlled air defense gun.
PRC 77	A Vietnam era portable radio system.
PX	Post exchange.
QUDs Force	Iranian IRGC unit tasked with unconventional warfare.
RIP	Relief in Place.
ROE	Rules of Engagement.
RPG	Soviet rocket propelled grenade.
RPK	A Soviet light machinegun.
SAM	Surface to Air Missile.
SAS	Special Air Service.
SCIF	Sensitive Compartmented Information Facility.

SFC	Sergeant First Class.
SI	Special Intelligence.
SIGNT	Signals Intelligence.
SINCGARS	Single Channel Ground and Airborne Radio System.
SIS	Special Investigations Section-LAPD.
SMU	Special Mission Unit.
SOF	Special Operations Forces.
SOW	Statement of Work.
SSG	Staff Sergeant.
STU	Secure Telephone Unit.
TDY	Temporary Duty assignment.
TIC	Troops in Contact.
TMC	Troop Medical Clinic.
TOC	Tactical Operations Center.
TS/SCI	Top Secret/Sensitive Compartmented Information.
3rd ID	US Army's 3rd Infantry Division.
UAV	Unmanned Aerial Vehicle.
VBC	Victory Base Complex.
WIA	Wounded in Action.

CPSIA information can be obtained
at www.ICGtesting.com
Printed in the USA
LVHW110748230822
726632LV00023B/450/J

9 781646 639250